THE FOURTH STRIPE

A Novel
By
Maurice Azurdia

THE FOURTH STRIPE

Maurice Azurdia

CYBER ROSE DESIGN PAPERBACK EDITION
2017

This one is for Cheryl, who stood by me through the hurricane

ONE
PRESENT TIME - BERLIN, GERMANY

The persistent noise filtered down through the layers of sleep, annoying her with the shrill ring. As she struggled to rouse herself she realized it was the ring of the phone. Who was calling? And where was she anyway? Valerie Wall woke up from a deep sleep disoriented, with growing panic, wondering if she was late for a trip.

The small room at the Schweizerhof Inter-Continental hotel came into focus. God, where was her Visine? She remembered that she was in Berlin. And why was the phone still ringing? She never set up wake up calls, preferring the sound of her own travel alarm clock, so who was calling her? She reached over and grabbed the phone, not sure whether it was morning or the middle of the night.

"Hullo?" She half-mumbled, still not fully awake, wondering what time of day it was.

"Captain Valerie Wall?" the voice at the other end asked.

"Yes."

"Captain, I'm sorry I woke you up," the woman at the other end apologized, as if realizing from the sleepy voice that she had caught the Trans Global Airlines captain in the middle of a nap.

Sorry she woke me up? This sure as hell wasn't Crew Scheduling. Crew Sked never apologized. "It's okay–who's this?"

"This is Elaine Griffin. My sister Julie talked to you this morning at Operations and she instructed me to telephone you at the Schweizerhof but I didn't realize you'd be taking a nap. I'm terribly sorry, I can call you back later..."

Julie Griffin? And who the heck was Julie Griffin?? "Who?"

"My sister Julie, she's a TGA flight attendant–she was with you on the London flight this morning?"

Suddenly Valerie remembered. She didn't yet know what time of day it was, whether it was early in the morning or late at night, but she remembered one of her flight attendants asking her for a favor or something after a flight. What was it? Oh, yeah, the scarves.

"Sure, I remember now, the scarves. What was your sister's name you said, was it Julie?"

"Yes,"

The woman at the other end had an American twang that Valerie couldn't place, Texas or Alabama probably. "I remember now, she said something about you importing scarves from Turkey?"

"Yes, Captain. She told me that you're flying the Istanbul trip this month. Julie was going to buy me some silk scarves in Istanbul, but Crew Scheduling has rearranged her schedule for the month and they're flying her back to Kennedy in the morning so I'm left in a bind."

Valerie sat up on her hotel bed Indian-style, with her legs under her body, recalling the conversation with one of her flight attendants that morning. Now it came to her. The flight attendant had asked Valerie if she could do her a big favor and bring back some scarves on her first Istanbul trip this week. That morning at the airport Valerie had thought about it and agreed to do it, but then the flight attendant had explained the situation, saying that the scarves were actually for her sister who lived in Berlin and who relied on the sale of the scarves for extra income. Valerie had then been slightly uncomfortable with the request, but there was really no harm in buying a few scarves and bringing them to Berlin, was there? She was acquainted with the Jewish merchant in Istanbul who sold scarves to TGA crews, and the man had an excellent product which he sold at one-tenth the price of the silk scarves sold onboard First Class through the Duty Free, and the merchant had even gone to the trouble of having his designer print a white scarf with the red TGA logo, which the flight attendants simply adored.

"Julie called me at home and said that you'd be willing to buy the scarves for me in Istanbul, and that I should call you in the hotel. I'm really sorry that I woke you up, and I want you to know that I really appreciate this favor, if you think you can do it."

Valerie stood up. Her body was still tight from sleep. "Sure, as I told Julie, that should be no problem. Do you want me to just buy these silk scarves for you and you can pay me when I get back?"

"Oh, thank you, Captain, but I wouldn't want you to go through that much trouble. If it's okay with you, I'd rather put them on my credit card."

Valerie liked that idea. She really didn't use scarves much, and she certainly didn't want to be stuck with several of them if this woman stood her up after her return.

"That sounds alright to me, except, how are we going to do that?" Valerie was taking out the Istanbul flight first thing in the morning, and she certainly didn't feel like getting dressed and going out just now–God only knew what time it was–to meet this woman and get her credit card.

"I can stop by the airport on my way to work. I'll leave my Visa card at your counter at Tegel airport, and you can pick it up in the morning–if that's acceptable to you."

Valerie liked that. "Sure, that's fine. I guess the owner of the store should accept your card. What did you say your name was?" she reached for a hotel pad and her pen.

"Elaine Griffin, Captain–and yes, the merchant in Istanbul will accept my Visa. Julie and I have bought scarves this way before. She takes my card and they put all the charges on it."

Where did she get all this captain bullshit? Valerie knew the Europeans were in love with protocol, and airline pilots were treated like royalty in most European countries, but this woman was supposed to be American. Maybe she just had lived in Berlin for too long. "Please, don't call me captain, Elaine, Valerie will do."

There was a slight pause at the other end. "Okay, Valerie. Sorry, I didn't mean to make you uncomfortable, it's just that this German formality eventually sticks..."

"I understand. You're American, right?"

"Yes. I married a German national and I've been in Germany for five years."

"Is that right. Well, how do I get in touch with you when I return?"

"If you don't mind–Valerie–I can just drop by the hotel and pick up the scarves."

Valerie didn't see anything wrong with that, so she agreed.

"Valerie," the woman continued, "I have no words to tell you how much I appreciate what you're doing. I don't know if Julie told you but I sell the scarves here in Berlin and it helps us out. The Germans just adore Turkish silk."

"That's alright. Be glad to do it. By the way–how many scarves do you want and what colors?"

"I need one hundred scarves and you can just tell the merchant to make them the usual assorted colors."

After Valerie hung up she walked over to the servi-bar the hotel provided in every room, taking out a plastic bottle of orange juice. She normally avoided consuming any of the goodies stacked in the tiny fridge, absurdly expensive traps for the unwary, but at this precise moment she needed something to drink awfully bad and was pleased to have the convenience.

One hundred scarves? Oh, shit. She had not intended to bring that many scarves back. The flight attendant had said nothing about one hundred scarves! Valerie had automatically assumed they were talking four of five at the most. She rapidly reached for her flight bag, pulling out her airline's Flight Operations Policy Manual, where it was spelled out exactly how much each crewmember could import into any of the countries her airline flew in Europe.

Forty-dollars-worth of merchandise purchased outside Germany was the limit, and now she had committed herself to bringing one hundred silk scarves, worth at least a thousand dollars–damn. She thought about this; she could just ignore the request and not even pick up the woman's credit card at Operations the following day since she couldn't very well call her back now and tell her that she'd changed her mind–because she didn't even have a phone number where she could reach her. Smart, real smart on her part. Her only excuse was that she had just awoken from deep sleep and maybe she hadn't been totally conscious just yet.

She evaluated the situation, feeling uncomfortable. If the Germans caught her with one hundred illegal scarves there would be all kinds of trouble, but on the other hand they had never searched any of her bags or those of her crewmembers, so perhaps she could manage to slip by undetected. The German customs people were not picky at all.

What would the penalty be if caught? She didn't know, but suspected that the inflexible Germans would probably take a dim view of a Trans Global Airlines captain smuggling anything into their country. This Griffin woman was the sister of a TGA flight attendant who usually flew the Istanbul route, so the sister probably smuggled stuff into Germany all the time for her sister, to help her out. And obviously, she hadn't been detected doing it.

Shit. Valerie certainly didn't want to do anything illegal, but she hated screwing a fellow American abroad, especially after she'd given her word. If this Griffin woman went to the extreme of calling her in her hotel room, she must really depend on whatever additional income she could muster from the sale of the scarves, which bothered Valerie because it made her feel self-conscious about her $140,000 income. The poor woman living in Germany, probably married to a struggling German national, away from home and family...what the devil–she would do it just this *one* time. But she would make it perfectly clear to this Griffin gal when she came to pick up the scarves that this was a one-time-only favor. Since Valerie had to fly the Istanbul trip four times this month she wanted to ascertain that the woman would not bother her again. It took guts for the woman to call her in her hotel room, especially with her sister being a TGA flight attendant. Another captain might not have been so generous and might even have sent in a Debriefing Report into the company, reporting the incident, which would result in disciplinary action against Julie Griffin, the flight attendant. Maybe that's why Elaine Griffin had approached her instead of a male captain, she pondered.

Since she was already awake, she decided to get some jeans on and hit the streets for a Bratwurst and a Coke. Maybe it wasn't so bad that this Griffin woman had called her after all, otherwise she might have slept right through until tomorrow, and that would not have been good because she had to prepare her charts for the flight to Istanbul.

"DID SOMEONE LEAVE A message for me?"

The customer service agent looked up into the very attractive face of one of the captains of his airline. "Oh? Ahh, good morning *Kaptain!*" The agent appeared surprised to see her because flight crews normally didn't come up to the counter, they were usually driven directly to the operations office on the ramp downstairs.

"I'm expecting a letter or a message from a friend of mine. She was going to drop it off here at the counter sometime this morning."

The customer service agent took a few seconds while he appeared to make sure he understood what the American captain was telling him. The ticket counter agent was obviously German, one of the lucky few hired by TGA to work the counter, and he was obviously puzzled by the strange requests these Americans made. "A message?"

"Yes, a letter or a message. A friend of mine was supposed to drop it off here at our counter. It should be addressed to me; my name is Valerie Wall."

The customer service agent rapidly scanned the area behind his counter. A message, where would it be? "Just a minute, *bitte, Kaptain.*" He picked up the telephone and dialed a number, then spoke in rapid German to someone.

Valerie didn't have all that much time before her flight, and she had a lot of work to do to prepare the trip. If this guy couldn't find her the Visa card within the next two minutes, she was going to leave. In a way, this would relieve her of the responsibility of her commitment.

"Ah, *ja!*" the agent barked into the phone, hanging up. "Just one minute, please, *Kaptain.*" He went in the room behind the counter and came up with a white envelope which he handed to her.

"My other agent received this, and it is for you!"

Valerie noticed that the man looked at the name on her ID tag attached to her uniform coat, then handed her the envelope. German efficiency.

"Thank you very much," she stuffed the envelope in the inside pocket of her uniform coat and headed towards the security gates. She still had a lot of work to do before the flight, but she was relaxed because she was flying with a very good first officer who would take up the slack for her if she ran a little late.

CHARLIE SMITH WAS IN operations, looking through the paperwork the dispatcher had given him for the flight to Istanbul. The weather looked good at both ends, although it was somewhat windy down there in Turkey. He calculated the performance speeds for the Boeing 727 on which he was the First Officer or copilot– in layman's terms–and wrote down the speeds for takeoff on the form provided. These were the numbers they would use to fly the Boeing 727, and he had to make sure they were accurate. The Boeing 727 was not an airplane that was flown by the seat of the pants, as many people viewed fliers. This airplane, like most big jets, had to be flown absolutely by the numbers. This job was nothing more than applied mathematics, he thought, but even so he enjoyed it tremendously. How many people could honestly say they enjoyed what they did for a living? Just take a poll among the people driving the Santa Monica freeway at rush hour.

Charlie had never flown with a female captain before, and hadn't been sure of what to expect, but Valerie was alright and he had discovered that he enjoyed flying with her. Of course, that was not something he would openly admit to the guys over beers at the St. George's bar in Berlin. They would tease him and suggest that his real intentions for giving the dame a break were maybe to get in her pants? Was that it? No, women in the airlines were becoming a common sight these days, but this was still a men's world, and nobody wanted to be the first to treat the women as an accepted member of their exclusive circle.

Regardless of social prejudice, Charlie had no problem accepting Valerie and flying with her. She was diligent and she was good, and that's all he asked for in man or woman. Actually, he did enjoy visiting with her in the cockpit on long legs, much better that visiting with some old dog captain. Talking with a beautiful woman was always far more enjoyable than talking with some bitter old salt male captain. He was cautious not to say anything patronizing to her or to make her feel like a woman. She was there because she wanted to be a captain, and that's exactly how he dealt with her. He wondered where she'd gone this morning. She was normally very efficient, and didn't let anything get in her way when she had an airplane to fly.

Charlie collected all his paperwork, leaving a copy of the dispatch release on the counter for Valerie to sign. The captain of the flight accepted the responsibility for the flight by putting her signature on that piece of paper, indicating that she agreed with all the provisions specified in the paperwork, like the amount of fuel onboard, the number of passengers, the weight and balance of the airplane, the flight plan, etc. It was a captain's prerogative to change any of the items based on individual judgment and experience, but since the weather along the route of flight was good and the weather in Istanbul was excellent Charlie doubted whether Valerie would change anything, He grabbed his hat and marched out to the ramp, where their flight engineer was already performing the preflight inspection on their gleaming red and white airplane.

VALERIE ASKED AN AIRPORT guard to open the door into the security perimeter which allowed access to the ramp area. Security at Berlin's Tegel airport had to be seen to be believed. The Germans really took their role seriously, sealing the ramp area so airtight that no terrorist would have access to it. Unfortunately, this also meant crewmembers had to go through all the tedious time-consuming procedures to gain access to their planes. The only way to enter the ramp area from the terminal at Tegel was to have a security guard go with the crewmember to a rotating metal door of the kind seen in hotels in New York, surrounded by one-inch thick bullet-proof Plexiglas. The door was smaller than a hotel rotating door, although similar in design, and it could only be activated by the keys carried by the heavily-armed guard. Valerie stepped into the tight cubicle feeling mildly claustrophobic while waiting for the German airport guard to activate the door's electric mechanism. She disliked this system because it prevented the crews from casually strolling into the terminal building to get something to eat at one of the restaurants, but realized that the system was necessary as a deterrent to keep crazy radicals from bombing her airplane, which made her feel more secure. One of her constant worries flying in Europe was the image of that hand-grenade rolling under her wheelies out of nowhere as she walked through a terminal.

German security had increased considerably after the 1988 bombing of the Pan Am Jumbo over Lockerbie, and now the Germans even went to the extent of unloading all the bags contained in the cargo hold of their B-747s before a flight and making all the passengers descend onto the ramp to identify their luggage in person. Any unidentified bags left sitting on the ramp after this procedure were removed from the flight by a bomb squad.

It was a horrendous time-consuming procedure and Valerie could only imagine the aggravation and impatience of those passengers having to march past two thousand suitcases. On the other hand, it wasn't such a bad idea, if one considered what had happened to those poor devils over Lockerbie. She had several times tried to imagine what that disaster must have been like in the cockpit and the cabin of the Pan Am B-747. Did the crew have time to realize that a bomb had gone off? Did they pass out instantly from the sudden decompression and ram air rushing into their cockpit at over 500 miles per hour? Her mind never stayed on that subject too long–thank God–some kind of protection device the mind must have against unpleasant thoughts.

"Good morning, Captain!" the dispatcher stood and approached the counter. The dispatcher had told Valerie that he was not used to female captains, but that he found the change refreshing. Flight attendants usually ignored him–he had explained–which was not good manners when viewed from a European's viewpoint, but Valerie was always courteous and polite, which he very much appreciated.

"Good morning, Ludwig. How are things going today?"

"Very well, thank you Captain. We are all ready for you. Your first officer already went through the paperwork and he left the release for you to sign."

Valerie saw her flight number on a piece of computer paper on the counter in front of her and signed her name with the gold Cross pen Paul Morris had given her for her birthday.

"An international airline captain can't be going around signing paperwork with *Bic* pens," Paul Morris had observed when he gave her the pen. She didn't really have a problem with *Bic* pens, but she enjoyed the luxury of having a gold pen. It made her feel luxurious.

"Here you go, Ludwig. Thanks for taking such good care of us!"

"You're welcome, Captain," he pronounced it *Velkome*. "Everything look good?"

"Yes."

"Good. Flight 748 is on time today, I checked with Frankfurt, so you should be able to depart Frankfurt on time." TGA's flight 748, the morning inbound flight from Kennedy was usually late, which made her flight late. Many of her passengers for Istanbul had originated in

New York the night before, and would be arriving in Frankfurt on 748. Kennedy airport was usually a madhouse during the evening departure rush, which tended to make overseas arrivals late on a continuous basis.

"Great. Thanks, Ludwig." Valerie had flown the Istanbul flight many times as a first officer and a couple of times as a captain and was aware of the potential for delays sitting on the ground in Frankfurt. She went to a computer terminal, signed in and pulled up the Istanbul weather. Everything looked good. Next, she pulled up the aircraft maintenance records on the aircraft she would be taking to Turkey. Scanning through the mechanical history of the plane she found everything in order. Satisfied, Valerie took the envelope from her pocket, removing the Visa card the Griffin woman had left her. It was a Gold Card drawn against a German bank and the expiration date was good for another two years. She pitched the envelope, inserting the credit card in her own wallet. She wondered how much room one hundred scarves would take, and decided that she would probably have to pack them pretty tight.

"We'll see you tomorrow," she greeted, walking out to the ramp.

She entered the B-727 through the jetway stairs, encountering one of her flight attendants standing ready to greet the passengers at the cabin door. The flight attendants on her crews were polite but seldom friendly, maybe because they didn't know where her loyalties fell. Was she "one of the boys?" or was she one of them? Valerie avoided being overly friendly with the cabin attendants because she feared that fraternizing with the cabin crew would cast a negative image of her in the eyes of the other male pilots. Stereotypes were hard to die, and she didn't want to open herself up for any form of criticism.

Not that she thought little of flight attendants, she knew just how tough their job was, dealing with humanity on a constant basis, but she had put out one heck of a lot more time and effort into becoming a pilot, and she would be damned if anyone was going to belittle her efforts by associating her with the flight attendants, just because she was a woman.

Her flight engineer was already at his station, running his checks, and Charlie was on his seat on the right side of the cockpit.

"Hi, guys!" She had flown with these two men on her previous trip to London two days ago, and felt comfortable with them. They were both young enough to be members of the new generation of American men who had no problem accepting a woman as an equal, provided she could cut the mustard. She had seen her share of the other kind of American male too, the old-timers bred in the days when all women had to be *"June Cleavers,"* and she had on occasion bumped heads with a captain or two, but had always ignored their insults and gone on with the game, so to speak. Cooperate and graduate, was her motto. Most of those old-timers were captains, though, and she didn't have to fly with them again as long as she herself was flying captain on the B-727.

Charlie handed her the flight dispatch paperwork. "I checked the weather in Istanbul and it looks good. A little windy, maybe. We have an extra nine thousand pounds of fuel and will have a full boat going out of Frankfurt."

Valerie took the paperwork and studied it carefully. A good first officer was a definite asset for any captain, but she always double-checked the important stuff, the stuff that could kill you. Nine thousand pounds of extra fuel meant they could hold for approximately one hour after reaching Istanbul, if that became necessary. She always liked carrying extra fuel when flying to Turkey. One never knew what could happen in that part of the world, and the last thing she wanted was to sweat the fuel. She removed her coat and hat, hanging them against the rear bulkhead, then stored her overnight bag on one of her spare jumpseats, tying it with the seatbelt. No need to have loose projectiles in case they encountered rough air.

"Valerie, the airplane looks good, no write-ups and we have our fuel." Brad, the flight engineer was a Nervous Nelly, probably suffering from high blood pressure but otherwise he seemed efficient as hell.

"Thanks, Brad. Fuel looks good, Charlie. Sorry for the delay, I had to go upstairs and pick up something."

"No sweat." Charlie gave her the airport information for Tegel indicating which runway they would be using today and she thanked him.

Valerie strapped herself into her seat, connected her headset and began the ritual which would transform her into the human brain of seventy tons of machinery.

"Let's run the Before Engine Start checklist..."

THEY WERE AT THIRTY-three thousand feet, or Flight Level 330, over the Austrian plains.

"If you look over there," Charlie said, pointing toward the West, "You can see the Swiss Alps."

Valerie admired the view from the flight deck. It was a perfectly clear day on what was turning out to be a good flight. The one-hour leg from Berlin to Frankfurt had gone smooth, and Flight 748 from Kennedy had been on time, so the operation was running as smoothly as a Swiss watch. Or should she say as smoothly as a Casio? Now that the Swiss had lost the watch market to the Japanese, maybe some of the old sayings had to be reworded.

"Valerie, did you know that the Soviet Union was the only thing keeping all these Balkan countries from killing each other?"

Valerie did not enjoy discussing politics, but she was in a good mood. "Really? And what makes you think that, Charlie?"

"Well, historically, Czechoslovakia, Romania, Hungary and Turkey have been in constant conflict with each other dating back to the days of Dracula and the Holy Crusades, but the Soviet Union took a dim view of fighting within its realm and sent tanks in here to cool them off. These people were well aware of the cruelty of their Soviet landlords, and soon realized that if they messed with the Soviet Bear there'd be hell to pay, so they lived relatively at peace for many years."

"Until the Soviet Union followed the Dodo bird."

"Precisely. After the collapse of the Soviet Union, these good people have turned on each other again just as they had done since the days of Count Vlad Dracula. Only now there's no police force to keep them from destroying each other."

"Makes sense." Valerie did not know much about Balkan history, but she was a little uncomfortable overflying these countries on their way to Turkey. In case of an engine failure enroute she would have to make the decision to land at the nearest suitable airport, which could be in Sofia, Belgrade, or Vienna–if she was lucky. These countries just did not inspire confidence, with their scratchy radio transmissions, difficult accents and questionable spirits of cooperation. She hoped never to be in a situation where they had to divert to one of those countries.

The air traffic controller issued them instructions to change frequency, and Valerie barely understood him.

"Boy, I don't know where these guys buy their radios," Charlie remarked, "but they would do us all a favor if they sent someone over to the local Radio Shack to get a couple of decent transmitters."

"Shit flows downhill." Brad stated.

"What?"

"Shit flows downhill," he repeated. "When I flew with Dan Johnson last month we had this Istanbul flight, and he educated me to the reason why their radios and their equipment are so shitty. He said their equipment is so bad because it's all purchased third hand from the northern Europeans. The Brits use the equipment first, then they sell it to the Austrians, who in turn use it for some time then sell it to the Hungarians and so on. As the equipment ages, it flows further south, which is the reason those Turks are almost incomprehensible on the radio."

They all laughed. Valerie disliked judging people just because of their inability to purchase new radios, but what Brad said made sense. Flying big jets was difficult enough without having to add communication difficulties. She was just so spoiled by the efficiency and high quality in air traffic control back home, that it irritated her, having to deal with these Balkan controllers on such difficult terms.

There was a knock on the cockpit door and Brad reached back from his seat, unlocking the door. The door was kept locked as per FAA regulations, but the reality of it was that anyone could force their way past the fragile door, if determined enough.

One of their flight attendants entered the cockpit, shutting the door behind her. "How we doing?" She lowered her head, looking out the front of the airplane. The cockpit was much brighter than the cabin in back, so the flight attendants enjoyed coming up to catch a glimpse of the outside world.

Valerie turned in her seat to look at her, not an easy proposition being strapped as she was. "Not too bad. We should be about ten minutes ahead of schedule."

"Good! Valerie, the other gals want to know if it's alright with you if we all stop at the leather store on our way into the city from the airport."

Istanbul, famous for its leather products, had seduced many a crew into buying jackets made of fine-quality leathers. The TGA crews had a favorite store-factory where the owner gave the crewmembers reasonable prices. The procedure followed by crewmembers was already long-established; airline employees would stop at the store on one trip to be measured and order their jackets, and they would pick up the finished product on their next trip through Istanbul. Since the crews usually returned to Turkey several times in one month, it became an accepted procedure.

Valerie had no problem stopping for fifteen minutes to allow the women to pick up their jackets, and said so. She didn't ask for the opinion of her other two flight officers because she felt that she could assert her authority with such a relatively simple item, without running the risk of stepping on anyone's toes.

"Charlie, have you ever bought something in Turkey and brought it back into Germany with you?"

Charlie looked at her from behind the polarized glass of his Ray Bans. "Like what?"

"Oh, I don't know, something big, like a rug or a painting or something."

"Yeah. " He smiled, "I've bought a few things like that."

"Did you have any trouble taking them back into Germany?"

Valerie assumed Charlie would think she was probing him because she wanted to buy something big herself.

"No, I've never encountered any difficulties in Frankfurt or Berlin. Of course, the really big items I've bought I've had them shipped directly back to the States."

"Oh? What did you buy? If you don't mind my asking."

"Not at all, Valerie. I bought several Persian rugs and an armoire, which these guys shipped to my home. I also bought a couple of rolls of Turkish cotton fabric which I brought back with me on the airplane."

"A couple of rolls? Where in Heaven's name did you carry those?" Valerie figured that one hundred scarves should take up at least as much room as those fabric rolls.

"I just removed the cardboard and folded them into my overnight bag. It was tighter than sardines but it worked, and those customs boys in Frankfurt didn't even flinch when I walked right past them with my bulging suitcase which looked ready to burst."

"But what about the taxes? The FOP indicates that as crewmembers we're only allowed to bring in articles worth forty dollars."

Charlie laughed. "Hey, just get yourself a receipt for forty bucks and you're covered. Those guys down there have no problem writing you out a receipt like that. All they care about is you paying them. If the Germans give you any shit, spring the receipt on them and let them figure it out. Most of the time, I've heard they'll just let you pass if you have such a receipt." Curiosity got the best of him. "Why? What are you planning on buying?"

Valerie would have preferred not sharing her plans with her crew, but Charlie was such a nice guy that she didn't want to tell him to mind his own business. "I'm buying some silk scarves for one of our flight attendants, but I wasn't sure I wanted to do it if it meant breaking the law."

Charlie sipped his coffee, appearing to scan his flight instruments. He was flying this leg because–as was customary–Valerie had flown the first leg of the day. "Don't worry about it, Valerie. As long as you don't do anything obvious, like showing up with a ten-carat diamond tennis bracelet and a receipt saying that you paid twenty bucks for it, you should be okay. Besides, silk scarves don't really take up that much room."

"These will."

Charlie looked at her again. "Why?"

"Because I'm buying a hundred."

Charlie whistled. "A hundred scarves? Why?"

Valerie decided not to give him the whole story. She didn't want Charlie to think of her as a fool for accepting the mission, since she already felt like an idiot for accepting. "That's just how many this flight attendant needed." She gave Charlie the story about Julie Griffin–the flight attendant–and how she had gone non-routine and had to return to the States ahead of time. What she did not say was that she'd never met the sister.

"Sounds to me like she's doing some heavy-duty reselling," Charlie offered.

Valerie knew that flight attendants were famous for smuggling all kinds of goodies from the countries they visited, which they used to supplement their salaries. Hell, some of the gals even went as far as lying about the number of drinks they gave away in First Class in order to steal the booze, sell it in coach and pocket the money. Some flight attendants she knew of made several hundred dollars a trip doing just that. She felt that stealing was definitely wrong, but a little creative smuggling here and there couldn't hurt anybody. "I don't know what she does with the scarves," Valerie felt compelled to add, "but I offered to help her and I'm sure glad I asked you."

Charlie felt good. "I ever tell you what I did when the Berlin wall came down?"

Valerie said no.

"Robert Johnson, another first officer and myself found out that the West German government was giving away fifty dollars in Dutch Marks to each visitor pouring into Berlin from East Germany for their first look at Capitalism. Heck, that was a gold mine, so Johnson and I went back to the States, bought eight thousand pairs of used blue denim jeans and parked ourselves near the wall, right outside Checkpoint Charlie. Those East Germans went berserk at the chance of buying genuine 100% made-in America jeans, and bought every last one of them from us."

"No kidding. How ingenious! What did you sell them for?"

"Fifty bucks apiece."

"Charlie! You guys must've made a fortune!"

"Hundred grand apiece. We shipped all our jeans on TGA, so it saved us having to pay for freight."

"Brilliant, Sherlock."

"Thank you, thank you, Captain."

Valerie suddenly felt much better about her assignment. Maybe she had worried needlessly after all. Scarves were not illegal drugs.

"I'm sure glad my wife made it on," Brad commented. He was a newlywed and had brought his new bride along with him to Europe for the month, since the company provided him with a hotel room for the entire month, and gave him $42 per day for meals. Brad had decided to bring his new bride along on this Istanbul flight although the loads were rather heavy, disregarding advice from both Valerie and Charlie against exposing her to being left stranded in Turkey if the flight filled up. She had barely made it on in Frankfurt because the airplane was full, but at the last minute a First Class seat had remained open and the gate agent had given it to her. The woman also should not have come because earlier in the day she had suffered what looked like a fractured thumb at Tegel airport.

"How's her thumb doing?" Valerie did not agree with Brad's strategy, but refrained from giving free advice on personal matters to her crew.

"It hurts, but one of the girls gave her an ice pack and I think she'll be okay." Brad had shut the VW van door on his wife's thumb by accident, which was bad enough, but then had insisted that she should not cancel her visit to Istanbul because of it.

"Is it still bruised?"

"Yeah, it's black and blue and it hurts like hell, but I told her one look at the bazaar and all pain will disappear.

Dream on, Valerie thought. What that looked like was a fractured thumb, and Brad was being unreasonable pushing his wife to join them on this trip to Turkey, particularly with all the flights booked so heavily.

ONE HUNDRED MINUTES LATER the Turkish air traffic controller brought them in over the Black Sea, turning them south towards the Marmara Sea for an approach from the southwest.

Valerie ran the radio while Charlie flew the airplane. The winds at Ataturk airport in Istanbul were gusting to thirty knots, which was a respectable wind, but Valerie was comfortable because the B-727 could handle that much wind relatively effortlessly. She took a minute to glance out of the cockpit at the hazy sea below, feeling–as she always did–insecure in this airspace. These good Turks weren't all that efficient when it came to air traffic control, and she kept a strict visual watch on the airspace ahead and to the sides of them, lest some stray airliner pop out of nowhere and ruin their entire day. Communications were erratic at best, and she didn't really pickup every single word the controller said, but from past experience flying into Ataturk she knew more or less what to expect at each stage of the approach, so she managed.

The weather was hazy and the Sea of Marmara below looked gray, cold and uninviting. The controller gave them their final turn to intercept the ILS to runway six and Charlie turned the big jet towards ancient Constantinople.

THE ISTANBUL STATION MANAGER met the crew just outside the jetway after all the passengers had deplaned. The man was stereotype Turk, short, dark and friendly with an enormous smile. Valerie wasn't exactly sure why it was necessary for the station manager himself to meet them every time and help them breeze through customs and immigration, since this was not routine at any other country, but she suspected that perhaps there was a dark side to Turkish bureaucracy that she would rather not know. She had read the book *Midnight Express*, and it had duly impressed her. After all, why complain when it was kind of nice being treated like VIPs by the airport agencies who wasted no time getting them to their bus.

They made a short stop at the leather shop to allow the flight attendants to pick up their jackets and purses they had ordered on the previous trip, and after the brief *intermezzo* continued their bus ride into town.

Valerie had initially also been seduced by the beauty and prices of leather goods in Turkey, only to find that the workmanship that went into manufacturing their products failed to meet the same standards of fabrication of Italian leather products. Although Turkish leather was second to none in softness and quality, the durability of the stitches and the simplicity of the designs left much to be desired. She had found that same problem when buying Mexican leather products in Puerto Vallarta. Now, she had become rather picky, and refused to spend money in products that would most likely fall apart at the seams after a few months.

The drive into town depressed her, with the gloomy disrepair of the buildings in the outskirts of Istanbul and the evident lack of females in the streets. It seemed to her that all Turkish men must have dark hair, dress in white shirts with black suits and go unshaven for days. Also, they all seemed to have this depressed look...

THE ONE HOUR RIDE into town was not a favorite of the crews overnighting in Istanbul, however the Grand Bazaar and the magnificent dining in the city successfully offset this disadvantage. The Greyhound-style passenger bus regularly picked them up outside the airport and drove them downtown to the Sheraton Towers, where they would rest in luxury until their departure the following morning. The bus dropped them off at the Sheraton Towers and they checked in. Valerie was given a magnificent two-room suite which was obviously intended for entertainment, with its long conference table and the large refrigerator and bar.

She changed into a gray sweatshirt, dark blue Levis, donned a leather jacket and Reeboks and hit the streets. The scarves shop was located along the main street, about two miles from the hotel, and she headed in that direction right away because she did not want to be too far away from the hotel when darkness came. Istanbul still intimidated her at night, when practically no females were visible in the streets.

The sidewalks were crowded with people as she walked to the small silk shop, which was owned and operated by a Sephardic Jew and his two sons, and it was frequented by flight attendants of many different international airlines who spread the word about the excellent prices.

She was feeling hungry, but she would just have to settle for a hamburger from room service. Turkish food was excellent, and she relished it greatly, but it was her own personal rule never to eat by herself in Istanbul while on a layover. If she went out to dinner there it was always with a male crewmember because she was determined not to become a statistic on some crime report. One of the things her father had taught her was that one could never be too careful in big cities. Especially in big Middle Eastern cities.

Valerie found the little store famous for its magnificent silks and went it.

"Alas, good evening madam!" The old man was on her like flies on molasses.

"Hello there."

"Looking for some silk scarves?"

"As a matter of fact, yes. I need to buy a few for a friend of mine in Berlin, but first of all I need to know if you'll take a Visa card."

"Visa? Sure! Visa, Mastercard, American Express, we take them all!"

"I mean, this isn't my own Visa card. My friend in Berlin gave me her card to buy her some scarves and she said you'd accepted it in the past."

The old man gave her a puzzled look, then snapped his fingers at a servant standing nearby, "Some tea, Salim! Your friend gave you her Visa card, you say?"

"Yes, her name is Elaine Griffin. Her sister is a TGA flight attendant–Julie–and she has purchased merchandise from you before."

"Aah, yes Julie, of course. And how is she?"

Valerie felt relieved. For a moment there she had started to feel like a fool. "Julie's fine, but she had to go back to New York so she asked me to buy the scarves for her sister."

"But of course! Julie! How forgetful of me! Please forgive an old man's failing memory and accept some tea while we show you our humble merchandise and you decide what colors you wish to buy." The servant had returned with demitasse-size china cups filled with some hot fluid, resting elegantly on a silver tray covered with a starched white linen napkin.

"No, thanks, I never drink tea, but thanks anyway." She was cognizant of the dangers involved in drinking non-purified water in Istanbul, and she wasn't about to tempt fate. Cholera and typhoid were but a few of the nice intestinal diseases a person could catch from their polluted water. Water had to be boiled for over an hour to be safe, and somehow she doubted these fine gentlemen had boiled their tea water anywhere near that long.

"Some coffee, perhaps?" the old man helped himself to a cup of tea.

"No, thank you. Coffee kills me on an empty stomach."

"Very well. Are you too, a flight attendant for TGA? And how many scarves were you thinking of buying?"

That question never failed to irritate her. "No, I am not a flight attendant. I am a TGA captain and I'll need one hundred scarves, mixed colors. Elaine said that you'd give her a nice assortment of different colors."

A captain? The old man took a closer look at her, as if anything in her looks would confirm that she was indeed an airline captain and not a flight attendant.

"But of course, captain, we'll get you all set up right away." The old man went in the back calling for someone in a language Valerie did not understand but thought must be Yiddish. A handsome young man of about twenty appeared at the door and immediately went to work lowering cardboard boxes from the shelves, removing scarves from different boxes until he had a stack a foot high piled on top of the glass counter. Each scarf was individually wrapped in clear cellophane.

The old man put together a large white cardboard box and stuffed the silks in it. As a final gesture he gave Valerie a white silk scarf with her airline's logo printed on one corner. "This one is for you, captain, a gift as a symbol of gratitude for doing business with our modest shop. And if you want to buy anything for yourself, you have unlimited credit. If you wish to take some scarves with you now for your relatives or your friends, go ahead! Just pick whatever you like, you can pay me later."

Valerie thanked the old merchant, handing him the Visa card she had brought with her from Germany. "Appreciate your offer, but I'm not going to take any this time. And I'll need a receipt from you for forty dollars, if you don't mind."

The old man looked at her with knowing eyes, nodded agreement, took the card and ran a voucher, filling in the totals. "If you just sign here, you'll be on your way."

Valerie did not like that idea. "Sign there? I can't do that, that is not my card."

"It's okay, captain," the old man reassured her, "it's just so the bank sees some signature on it. Otherwise they'll refuse payment on grounds that it's not signed. Initial it if you want. Use Miss Griffin's initials if you prefer, that'll do."

Valerie didn't feel right doing it, but regardless she scribbled her name on the voucher. This was going a little too far...

"Thank you very much, captain," the old man quickly wrote out another receipt for forty dollars, handing it to her with the box of scarves and her copy of the credit card voucher. "If you ever need it, you have unlimited credit at our store," he repeated himself.

She thanked him and left the store, wondering just how she was going to compress this huge box of silk scarves to fit into her overnight suitcase.

Night had arrived in Istanbul and she was still downtown, a couple of miles from the safety of her hotel. She walked at a brisker pace than before, avoiding the eyes of oncoming men. Valerie believed that if there was no eye contact with any man, then her intentions being out late in the evening could not be misconstrued in any way which could invite aggression. She did notice that the number of females out on the streets had dwindled considerably.

Her Reebok tennis shoes had been bought as additional insurance, to allow her every advantage possible in case she had to bolt; she was still pretty quick, her legs still showing the years of track and field and basketball that she had in high school and college. Paul Morris joked that her legs were made for loving, which was probably true from his point of view, but also she had to admit that her daily jogs on layovers had helped her remain in shape, and tonight these legs were made for running, if the situation called for it.

Twenty-five minutes later she reached the lobby of the Sheraton. Turkish bodyguards armed with machine guns stood around the bar area and near the registration desk, casually trying to blend in with the furniture, evidence that perhaps not everything in the mysterious city was as peaceful as the Turkish government would like tourists to believe. She noticed several good-looking young men sitting in the lobby area having drinks. Americans, she thought, discerning a couple of baseball caps with the names of ships belonging to the U.S. Navy. The crew cuts confirmed it–these guys belonged to some warship in port for the evening, and they were asking for trouble dressing like that. Their behavior, leather jackets and baseball caps definitely gave them away as American military, which made her nervous. She could envision a couple of fanatic crazy Muslims barging in there blasting and shooting at everything in sight, particularly at those evident representatives of Decadent American Imperialism. She hurried to the elevator. It was terrible to feel like that, but someone should really brief those guys about the art of camouflage and being less conspicuous, particularly in a country like this. Good thing she wasn't a blonde or she would absolutely refuse to venture outside the hotel without the 82nd Airborne to protect her.

THE CREW MET IN the empty lobby of the hotel at 4:30 a.m. The luxurious marble floors, recently waxed by the night crews were resplendent under the chandeliers.

"Good morning, Valerie," Charlie Smith was consistently the first one down in the lobby. No matter what, it seemed to her, he could not give up the discipline picked up in the Navy to be up and ready *well* in advance of the pack.

"Hi, Charlie!" This was the bad part about this Istanbul trip. In order to make their scheduled 7:00 a.m.

takeoff, the crew had to assemble in the lobby prior to the sun even showing up, which made for a very short night.

"Any coffee?"

"Right in the back," Charlie pointed toward the back of the lobby bar, where an ambitious Turkish boy brewed coffee and tea for the crews as a courtesy of the hotel, but a very profitable courtesy at that, for whoever wanted to be up early to serve the Americans would also benefit from their generous tips.

"Thanks! I just can't function this early without a cup." She walked to the back of the bar and greeted the boy in charge of the coffee brewer. "Good morning."

"Good morning. Would you like coffee or tea?"

"Coffee, please." She reached for her wallet, eyeing the thick, rich brew pouring out of the pot. The delicious smell was enough to get her mouth watering. Turkish coffee was as close as she ever wanted to come to drinking tar, but she loved the strong taste of it, provided one didn't make the horrible mistake of getting a mouthful of grounds. She fished out a couple of dollars and placed them on a china plate the boy had set on the counter for that purpose.

"Here is coffee," the boy placed a small cappuccino-style cup on the counter next to a couple of paper-wrapped sugar cubes. "Cream?" he asked, holding out a polished metal urn.

"No, thank you, black is fine. Thanks."

"I don't know why I keep bidding these god-awful Istanbul trips," Charlie had moved closer to her, sipping from an identical cup. "I absolutely hate waking up early."

"Why do this to yourself then?"

The smile behind the mustache widened. "I love the food!"

"You're crazy, no food in the world would make me get up this early on a regular basis." Valerie observed the lobby area, making sure all her crewmembers were accounted for. Four flight attendants present, but no flight engineer yet. Charlie followed her gaze.

"I also like the Bazaar," Charlie confessed. "My wife doesn't mind me flying in Europe a couple of months a year as long as I bring her back some jewelry and some leather from Istanbul. I guess it gives her something to talk about at the PTA meetings back home. I think she also enjoys having me out of her hair a couple of months a year."

Valerie was looking forward to the next three days which she had off. She planned to do some shopping at the *Kudamn* in Berlin and relax with plenty of food and Michener's *Caribbean*, which she had just received from her book club. They had to fly two legs today, first to Frankfurt and then on to Berlin and that was it. The flight attendants had a harder day with an additional two legs, but the flight deck crew had a relatively easy day.

"Here's Brad," Charlie offered.

Always on the ball, Valerie noted. Not too much escaped First Officer Smith's attention, which was good. She prized that quality in a man flying with her. You needed that degree of sharpness in your copilots to detect the doctor flying the small private airplane headed towards you on a collision course.

The crew walked out and boarded another Greyhound-style passenger bus, big enough to seat eighty, but carrying only her crew of seven. Valerie noticed that the colors of the busses kept changing with each trip, probably to keep them inconspicuous to ward off possible curiosity from the natives. She had read that somewhere in Europe a crew bus had been attacked by terrorists who were able to identify it as such because it always followed the same exact route, and many crewmembers had died when a grenade had been thrown in it. She suspected the Turkish bus company driving them to the airport must have read the same article, because they never followed the same route twice.

Security in this part of the world was no joke, she mused. These Turks took terrorism very seriously since many innocent bystanders had already been killed at airports and on airplanes because of terrorist attacks, and she liked having as much security as possible. In any of the German cities they flew, the procedure was always the same, which reassured her and worried her at the same time. After her passengers deplaned, a dozen German military personnel would board the airplane and search everywhere for bombs. They would search seat by seat, removing each individual seat cushion, looking for a stray bag or a piece of luggage that didn't belong to anyone. They would search the toilets and the galleys and no one would be allowed on the airplane after the inspection, with the exception of the crew. She guessed the Germans must figure that no pilot or flight attendant would bring a bomb aboard if they were going on the flight. The fact that there was a need for this kind of through search worried her because it confirmed the unpleasant reality that indeed, there was something very bad to worry about.

"Valerie," Brad–her flight engineer tapped her on the shoulder. "Did they stamp your passport when we came in?"

Valerie turned in her seat to look at him. "No, they normally don't stamp our passports when we come into Istanbul. Remember? We didn't even talk to a customs man."

"Yeah, I noticed that on my other trips. Is that normal?"

"I don't know if it's normal with everybody, Brad, but that's the way they've always done it with TGA crews. Why?"

"Oh, nuthin'. I was just wondering why they didn't, that's all. They didn't stamp my passport in Germany either. The first time I went through German immigration the guy just kinda waved me through. I had to ask the

German dude to stamp my passport and he was really surprised, like I had asked for something out of the ordinary."

Valerie realized Brad was one of those individuals who were overseas for the first time and were eager to collect passport stamps to prove to the folks back home all the places they'd been to. She had done pretty much the same thing on her first tour of Europe as a TGA pilot, so she could understand her flight engineer's plight. "Well, I guess they kind of eyeball you and if you look decent enough and don't fit their profile of what a terrorist should look like then they just wave you through."

"Thanks, Valerie." He sat back in his seat, next to his wife, conversation concluded.

Valerie wondered how the poor woman was doing. A foreign country was bad enough when one had medical problems, but Turkey was definitely not the place for a woman to be, alone, with a fractured thumb. She had asked the TGA dispatcher from her hotel room all the information about the flight, and one of the items she had been given was that the flight was sold out. What this meant was that Flight Engineer Brad's wife would probably have to return by herself to the Sheraton to await the next flight departing the following day. Regretfully, the company would not foot the bill for her second night at the Sheraton, and the airline discount rate for pilots was around $180 per night, so Brad was in deep shit. She had not given Brad the bad news yet because she knew that there was always a chance somebody would cancel and that his wife would get on, but Valerie really didn't have much faith in that kind of miracles.

They arrived at the airport and the crew split up. Charlie followed Valerie to TGA's Operations, a small room deep in the center of the building, while Brad and the flight attendants headed for the gate.

"Looks like we might beat the fog today," Charlie optimistically remarked. The airport was regularly subject to early morning convection fog coming in from the Sea of Marmara, and most of the airline crews flying into Ataturk tried to beat the fog by departing as early as possible.

Valerie had not been affected by the fog yet, but had heard enough captains complain about it to know that it was a real detriment to on-time departures.

"Hope so. We only have two legs today and I hope we can make them as smooth as possible."

The pair reached Operations and reviewed the flight paperwork. Satisfied, Valerie signed the release and donned her hat. "We're out of here!"

Valerie and Charlie were intercepted by the Istanbul station manager. The man seemed upset, agitated.

"Captain? Please, is your flight engineer named Brad Thomas?"

Now what? "Yes, his name is Thomas, why?"

"Thank you. I just need identification of flight engineer because man tried to pass immigration through wrong side. He said he is your engineer and immigration police very upset."

"What? What do you mean?"

"Your flight engineer did not go through the flight crew side, he tried passing through the area reserved for passengers and this is forbidden!"

Oh, hell. That dumb shit. "You mean he tried to get his passport stamped?"

The station manager looked at her with surprise in his eyes. "You knew about this?"

"Yeah, I think he wanted to have his passport stamped with an entry stamp so he could show his parents back home in the States that he'd been to your beautiful country." Unlikely story, if one was looking for a terrorist. And it seemed that these Turks were constantly on the lookout.

"You mean your crewmember want Turkish stamp in his passport?"

"Yes, that's all he wanted. So why are the immigration police upset?"

The man's attitude mellowed out somewhat. "No problem. I take care, thank you, Captain."

Valerie and Charlie watched the man scurrying away towards the immigration booths.

"Brad wanted to have his passport stamped?" Charlie laughed.

"Looks like it. I wish he'd told me his intentions so I could have asked the station manager to do it for him. For some reason these good folks don't seem to want us included in their bureaucratic red tape."

"No, it has to do with their idea of protecting airline crews. They want to keep the bad guys from getting a hold of one of our passports I guess. They've always done it this way, and really go apeshit when someone steps outside the white line.

"They want to keep the bad guys away from our passports? And who exactly are these bad guys?"

"The immigration police themselves, probably."

They both laughed.

"Strange."

"Hey, strange country, strange customs."

They reached the gate at the same time as their engineer. He looked blushed and profoundly upset.

"Hey, Brad, what gives, man? You trying to spend some extra time here in Turkey?" Charlie stopped to let him enter the jetway first.

"Did you hear what happened to me?" He was breathing rapidly, and Valerie wondered if he had a high blood-pressure problem.

"We heard."

"Brad," Valerie was not amused by his bravado. All she needed was having to cancel the flight because her flight engineer was under arrest. Try getting another flight engineer to replace him way down here in nowhere land. "Brad, don't ever do anything creative in these countries. They have an aversion to creativity and you are just lucky the station manager was around or you might have gotten yourself in some real deep shit."

"Yeah," Charlie added, "and I can't fly copilot and engineer at the same time and I do want to get out of here today, so don't do anymore cute shit."

"Sorry, guys–sorry Valerie. I just wanted to get my passport stamped and I'm in uniform, for Chrissake. What the hell did they thing I was trying to do, smuggle something out of their precious country?"

"Don't piss them off, Brad–remember–we got three more of these trips this month." Charlie looked at the view outside the gate window and changed the conversation. "We better get in there and get to work, folks, seems to me the fog is moving in!"

The three pilots entered the cockpit and took up their stations. Once again, Valerie was secretly grateful that her airline required slacks for its female pilots. Climbing into her seat spreading her legs three feet apart to vault the radio panel between her seat and Charlie's was no ladylike feat. A skirt would definitely make her life very uncomfortable and it would add an element she wanted out of her cockpit, the element of femininity. Somehow she felt the guys would not see her or respect her as their captain if they were busy trying to get a peek at her legs while she performed undignified acrobatics in a skirt.

Of course, TGA could show some consideration and produce a separate decent uniform with slacks for its female pilots instead of having everybody use the same model. Her uniform had been designed for men, and neither the airline nor the union had yet made a move to modify it to make female pilots comfortable. American Airlines had finally designed a very elegant uniform for its female flight crew members, including a totally redesigned hat, but the only reason such an event had occurred at that carrier was that enough females had been hired as pilots to gain some clout with the union. That was not the case at TGA just yet, because the airline had resisted hiring women as long as it legally was able to do so. The old captains who flew during WWII had created all kinds of obstacles for female newhires because they wanted no part of them, but finally their old boys club had disintegrated with the mandatory age 60 retirement.

"Let's get this babe ready to fly, guys–maybe we can still beat the fog out of here!" Valerie looked outside the cockpit window at the advancing advection fog. The fog formed out over the Sea of Marmara in the mornings and it then blew inland, practically shutting down the airport which was on the coast. Looking out the window she could actually see the fog cloud moving in, just like in those vampire movies where the fog suddenly surrounds everything.

She ran through her cockpit checks, preparing the big jet for flight. They heard a Lufthansa flight call Ataturk Ground Control requesting taxi clearance, which was promptly issued. The Lufthansa flight was about ten minutes ahead of them, and was also obviously trying to sneak out ahead of the fog.

"Let's run the checklist," Valerie's tone had changed from 'Your Friendly Captain' to 'John Wayne' in *The Green Berets*.

They finished their checks and called Ataturk Clearance Delivery to get their clearance to Frankfurt.

"TGA 735, Ataturk Clearance, your clearance is on stand-by. The airport is closed due to fog."

"Oh, shit," Brad contributed.

"Clearance, TGA 735," Valerie continued, "Do you have any estimates on how long this fog lasts?"

"Affirmative, it usually lasts one or two hours."

"Oh, shit," Brad repeated.

Valerie knew her engineer had been praying they could get out quickly so Nancy, his wife, could get on the flight. If there was an empty seat or two, these may be taken up by late-comers while they sat at the gate waiting for the fog to dissipate. The prospect of sending his wife back into downtown Istanbul had Brad terribly upset. Of course, that was nothing compared to how the engineer's wife was feeling, she'd told the crew that she was terrorized at the idea of having to ride back into town by herself.

This being the first time she'd ever been out of Orange County, California, she was totally intimidated by this strange country, she was in continuous pain from her black thumb and wanted nothing more than to get back to their hotel room in Frankfurt and have a doctor look at her thumb. Not to mention that Brad was a newhire with the airline and therefore was on a very limited salary. The Sheraton rates would kill them, if she had to spend a few nights there.

"Ataturk Clearance, TGA 735, thank you. We'll call you back in a little while."

"Okay, TGA."

"A couple hours," Valerie sighed. Hurry up and wait.

"Brad, tell the flight attendants about the delay, would you?"

"Alright." Brad slid his seat back, opened the cockpit door and looked for one of the flight attendants.

"What's up?"

"Linda," Brad motioned for her to come in the cockpit. "We have a delay due to the fog."

"How long?"

"Two hours."

"Oh, shit!"

"That's what I said. Linda, how's it looking back there? Are there any seats left?"

The head flight attendant had been made aware of the dilemma facing the flight engineer's wife, and she'd been keeping track of the seats. "It's not looking too good, Brad. There was a First Class seat left until just a few minutes ago, but now a non-rev flight attendant showed up and she's jumpseating back to Frankfurt with us. I don't know if she's going to give up that First Class seat.

Flight attendants and pilots at most airlines enjoyed a benefit known amongst airline personnel as "jumpseating." Basically it meant flying free under certain conditions. Most airliners have several extra crew seats both in the passenger cabin and in the flight deck, intended for extra flight attendants or FAA inspectors checking the crews in the performance of their duties. The B-727 had two such extra seats in its cockpit, and two extra flight attendant seats in the passenger cabin. Any crew member wishing to travel free could use those seats on a seniority basis provided they were not being used, with access restricted according to profession. Pilots were restricted to the cockpit seats and flight attendants to the cabin seats. If, upon departure from the gate, there were empty First Class or Coach seats available, then the jumpseat riders were invited to help themselves to these, in order of seniority. The jumpseats were usually not very comfortable, and few crewmembers would pick them over a cabin seat, if given a choice.

This benefit was highly attractive to airline personnel for two reasons, first, it was free; passes on the airline were very cheap, ranging from $20 for a domestic round-trip within the States to $160 First Class round trip between L.A. and Rome, but that was still money out of pocket. Second, if the flight was full, pass-riders–or non-revenue passengers–were bumped and had to remain at the gate, whereas the jumpseat was off limits to passengers, which guaranteed passage.

"Linda?" Valerie had turned in her seat on the left side of the cockpit and was looking at her Flight Service Manager. "Did Brad tell you about the delay?"

"Yes."

"Do you have enough drinks onboard to serve everyone while we're sitting at the gate?"

"No, Valerie. If I do that then I won't have enough for breakfast but if you think we're going to be here for another two hours we might as well go ahead and serve them breakfast. We'll need at least an hour for that."

"They told us this fog usually lasts two hours, so go ahead and do it."

The Flight Service Manager paused for a moment, appearing uncertain about the decision. Valerie knew that flight attendants did not really like initiating the service while still on the ground, since there were too many chances for potential interruptions, but if the captain said to do it, then that was that.

"Okay."

"How's Nancy doing, Brad? Did she manage to get on?"

"Not yet. The flight's full. Linda said there was a First Class seat open but now an off-duty flight attendant has shown up."

Valerie knew some flight attendants actually traveled all the way to Istanbul on shopping trips to supplement their incomes because anything they bought in Turkey could be sold at a substantial profit back in the States. Unfortunately for Brad, it seemed that one of these enterprising gals was on this trip, and it looked as if she was going to take the last empty seat in First Class. Valerie could not go back there and ask the flight attendant to give up her First Class seat for Brad's wife because that went against jumpseat protocol. It was understood that seniority had its privileges and asking for special favors bred resentment which had no place amongst airline crews. Additionally, Valerie tried to avoid situations where her authority position would intimidate a flight attendant into doing something she would otherwise normally not do. Brad had been amply warned; if his wife was left behind in Istanbul he was fully responsible for doing it because he had been advised against bringing her along on this flight.

"Well, guy," Charlie interjected, "looks like you might be spending your first year's pay at the Sheraton Towers."

"Crap, Charlie, don't say that. Nancy will die if she has to stay here by herself."

Valerie and Charlie exchanged knowing glances. They'd been with the airlines long enough to recognize situations where you just didn't push it with passes. This had been one of them.

"Ataturk Ground, Lufthansa 411."

The attention of all three pilots turned to their headsets.

"Lufthansa 411, Ground, go ahead!"

"Lufthansa 411, *ve* are out here on our way to the runway but *ve* are unable to continue to the runway, *ze* fog is too thick."

There was a pause while the Turkish controller assimilated the statement coming out of the German crew. "Lufthansa 411, what are you requesting?"

This time it was the Germans turn to pause, probably hesitating whether they should humiliate themselves on the frequency with others listening in. "Aah, Lufthansa 411 would like some help getting back to our gate. We want a vehicle to follow back to the terminal, we cannot taxi in this fog."

Charlie laughed out loud. "Trying to sneak out ahead of the fog but it didn't work out, eh?"

"Lufthansa 411, roger. We will send a vehicle out to you at once."

"Hey Valerie, ever notice how Europeans and Latin Americans use "Roger" all the time in their radio transmissions?"

Valerie smiled at this. "Yep. Guess they've seen too many Hollywood flicks." American aircrews seldom used the term, but foreign crews and controllers seemed to love it. "I particularly love it when some clown uses it out loud in a public place so the adoring crowd will recognize him as a pilot."

Linda stuck her head in the cockpit. "You guys want breakfast now or later?"

"I'm fine right now, thanks Linda," Charlie knew the cabin crew would be busier than hell for the next hour or so just taking care of their passengers, and he didn't want to load them with additional work. Valerie and Brad agreed to wait till later to eat. Back home in the States the airline had developed a "lunch bag" crew meal for the pilots appropriately known as the *Plane Lunch Bag*, which nobody craved, but here in European flying the crews were treated to First Class meals prepared by expert chefs from all over Europe. It was one of the pleasures Valerie enjoyed about flying in Europe, airline pilots were still treated with great respect and deference. For some reason the profession had taken a hit back in the States, and people just didn't give it the same level of respect. Envy? Perhaps, Valerie analyzed, but there was indeed a marked difference in perception as to how people viewed airline pilots in Europe. Of course, it didn't help having all those low-fare airlines back home with their company motif being, *why take the bus when you can fly on us?* That had done wonders for the kind of passenger found back home.

"Valerie?"

She was brought out of her reverie by Charlie's tone.

"What?"

"Look," he said, pointing to the end of the field, suddenly visible in the dissipating fog. The thick-as-pea-soup fog was dissipating just as rapidly as it had appeared twenty minutes earlier.

"Oh, beautiful!" Valerie immediately called Clearance Delivery and asked if they had a clearance for them.

"Yes, TGA, we have your clearance if you're ready to copy."

"Yeah, we're ready to copy, but what happened to the two-hour fog?"

"Say again?"

"You said this fog usually lasted two hours"

"The fog is going away," the Turkish controller redundantly stated.

"Yeah, we can see that, but you guys said it was going to be two hours."

The Turkish controller assumed that he was being reprimanded by the American woman and became defensive. "You wish to wait two more hours?"

"Negative. We'll take our clearance now. Thank you."

They copied the routing information the controller issued over the frequency and pushed the flight attendant call button on the overhead panel.

"You'd think these dumb ragheads would know how long their fog lasts, particularly if it's a daily occurrence!" Charlie was obviously not amused with the lack of professionalism professed by the Turkish controller.

"Shit flows downhill, remember?" Brad pontificated.

"Alright guys, let's just get this show on the road and get out of here." Valerie did not condone the misinformation they had received, but she didn't want to act like an Ugly American and criticize other cultures just because of one individual fuckup.

"What's up?" The Flight Service Manager stuck her head in the door. The sudden frenzy of activity in the flight deck was a dead giveaway that they must have been given departure clearance.

"Oh, crap."

"Sorry, Linda," Valerie was all business now. "Pick up the service. The fog has dissipated and they have released us."

"Valerie," Linda did not sound happy. "We already cooked all the scrambled eggs. If we don't serve them right away they will turn green!"

"What?"

"It's something they add to these eggs. If you cook them and then allow them to get cold, they'll turn green!"

"You gotta be kidding!"

"I'm not."

"Oh, damn." Valerie hated causing trouble for the cabin crew but they had a schedule to keep, and breakfast just wasn't important enough to delay it. "Wrap it up anyway, Linda. We can't stay here any longer because they'll probably need the gate and I can't justify the delay because of breakfast service. If the eggs are going to turn green, then dim the cabin lights during the service so no one can tell."

Linda left the cockpit to execute the captain's orders, cursing out whatever had made her bid Istanbul flights. Now the flight attendant had to face 154 pissed off passengers, most of whom didn't even speak English.

"Dim the cabin lights–yeah, right."

"SO, DID YOU BUY what you were looking for in Istanbul?" They were at 35,000 feet, just to the west of Vienna.

Valerie was startled by Charlie's question. Didn't he ever forget anything? She did not want to repeat that she had been suckered into bringing one hundred scarves by a woman she didn't even know. That would do wonders for her captain's image. "Yes, I did. I got some silk scarves."

"A hundred?"

"Yep, a hundred."

Charlie turned to look at her. "Somehow I hadn't taken you for someone who'd go out of her way to help a flight attendant you don't even know."

Valerie gave him a look that could bore through steel.

"I think we better change the topic. Have you heard anything else about that Boeing 737 that went down in the States?"

He was referring to a new Boeing 737-300 jetliner that had crashed unexplainably in clear weather on approach into Miami the previous month, killing all aboard.

"No, I haven't seen much about that since I've been in Germany. Have you?"

"It appears that some kind of bomb did it. They found traces of Cemtex, a Czech-made high explosive, in the remains of the cockpit instruments. Probably smuggled into one of the pilot's suitcases by your local friendly Middle Easterner."

"A bomb? No!" Valerie was aghast. An aircraft bombing in the United States. That was pushing it too far. Those rabid dogs who had no regard whatsoever for human lives should be made to pay for something like this. The World Trade Center bombing should have stirred a much bigger reaction from the government. The Oklahoma bombing still had to be resolved. Many were the nights she had laid awake thinking what she would do if someone bombed her airplane. She conjured terrifying images of the entire cockpit separating from the fuselage due to the blast, leaving her a couple of minutes in which to contemplate her own death.

"Yeah, they had that on *CNN International* this morning. They haven't been able to find any of the characteristic fingerprints from any of the countries that support terrorists though, but if they do, there will be some ass-kicking happening around these parts." Charlie had flown an A-6 Intruder against Khadafi years before when the United States Navy had bombed Libya in 1986, and had expressed to Valerie his feelings that the present Administration back home was not showing a tough enough attitude to the world. If one is to be respected, then one must be strong, not just nice, was his opinion.

"That makes me sick."

"It makes me wanna puke. With all the security bullshit we have back home and something like this happens. But you know, after all, our security surveillance in the States was never meant to deter terrorists, it was meant to deter hijackers. Big difference. What they have here in Europe is more along the lines of what we should have in place back home."

"I hate to see the whole world becoming a hostage to terror like this," Valerie knew Charlie was right though, but the idea of armed military guarding airports just depressed her.

"That's one of the two ways to try and prevent this. The other is to come over here and bomb these good people into oblivion."

"There are a lot of people over here that are innocent bystanders and have nothing to do with terrorism, Charlie. Just because greed or fanaticism drives some crazy nuts to extremes doesn't mean we should punish the whole lot."

"Tell that to the relatives and families of the dead on that Boeing crash in Miami, Valerie. You know, that explosive Cemtex, is the same one they suspect was used to down the Pan Am flight in 1988. Experts calculated that all it took to bring down the 450-ton airliner were ten to fourteen ounces of Cemtex. And get this–I just read that there are one hundred tons of this Cemtex shit *unaccounted* for in the world. One hundred tons, Valerie! God knows whose hands it's in."

"I just don't agree with using the same tactics of terror that these ignorant individuals prefer. By doing that, we become no better than they are." She decided to hang it up. She was never going to see eye-to-eye with war hawk Republicans like Charlie, and it was her own personal dogma that one should avoid discussing politics and religion in the cockpit because those controversial topics could easily erode good working relationships which were essential for the safe operation of a flight.

"Hey Brad, how's Nancy doing back there?" Valerie yelled at her flight engineer. The cockpit was a noisy place, with air rushing past at over five hundred miles per hour.

"Haven't gone back there to see her, but Linda said she's doing alright."

Linda, the Flight Service Manager, had finally convinced the jumpseating flight attendant to give up her First Class seat in order for Brad's wife to make it on the flight, which was no easy thing to ask because jumpseats were notoriously uncomfortable, particularly on a three and-a-half hour flight. Brad had been ecstatic with gratitude, and had gone back to personally thank the off duty flight attendant himself.

"You lucked out, Brad." Valerie reminded him.

"Yes, I did. Guess Nancy is not gonna want to see another foreign city for a while. She'll probably just stay in the hotel and rest all next week."

"See another city?" Charlie Smith laughed. "You'll be lucky if you ever get any bridal favors again, Brad."

Valerie thought about her boyfriend Paul Morris. She had sent him a ticket on British Airways to join her for a week together in Germany, and he would be arriving ten days from now. She wanted to take the train down to Zurich and maybe all the way to Rome with him. That was going to be one terrific week.

All of a sudden it came to her.

She would not have to pass through customs! After they landed in Frankfurt, she would ride a TGA van to the operations office directly from the jetway where she would park the airplane. She would get her paperwork at Frankfurt operations and then she and Charlie would be driven back to the airplane via the ramp. She would not have to pass through Frankfurt customs at all.

And in Berlin, she would be picked up downstairs on the ramp by another van, which would drive her and the other two pilots directly to their hotel, without ever checking through customs nor immigration.

She was so relieved she felt lightheaded. Why had she not realized this before? The only explanation she could think of was that she must have been so damned worried about smuggling that her brain must have shut off.

FIVE HOURS LATER VALERY sat in the lobby of the Schweizerhof hotel. The woman Elaine should arrive in ten minutes, if she was on time. Valerie hoped the woman would be on time so she could finish this entire uncomfortable affair. She should have turned down that crazy request from the beginning.

Was she crazy? Jeopardizing her career with TGA by smuggling? She must've been out of her mind to go along with this stupid idea. If a flight attendant wanted to risk her job and her career by doing illegal smuggling that was her choice, and Valerie felt that flight attendants didn't have that much to lose either, when compared to her own earning potential over her entire career. She grew increasingly angrier at these two women who had placed her in this uncomfortable situation.

"Valerie?"

She looked up at a very attractive woman in her forties, elegantly dressed in an expensive maroon cashmere suit.

"Elaine?" Valerie extended her hand, standing.

"Yes! Hello, Valerie, how nice to meet you!"

Valerie noticed the woman had quickly detected the package resting on the couch next to her.

"Julie has told us *soo* much about you! I mean, me and my husband. I hope we have not inconvenienced you too much with our inconsiderate requests."

Inconsiderate requests? You can say that again, sister. "No big deal, Elaine. I have your package right here."

Elaine Griffin was tall and her dark blond hair looked silky and thick. "Valerie, would you mind terribly joining me for a cup of coffee in the bar here?" She appeared to notice the captain's hesitation, "it'll only be for five minutes. My husband's circling the block in our car and I have to meet him in a few minutes."

Valerie did not really feel like wasting any more time, but the woman seemed really very nice and she did have beautiful manners and if her husband was actually circling the block in his car then this shouldn't take too long. "Sure, I'll join you."

They found a table removed from the bar and sat down. Valerie noticed the woman was as tall as she but only with the aid of her high heels–Bally shoes, Valerie observed.

Valerie paused until the waiter took their order then handed Elaine the package with the Visa card laying on top. "There you go. One hundred scarves hand-delivered. They charged them to your Visa and the receipt is inside. I had to sign the receipt or the owner wouldn't let me take them so I hope that doesn't cause you trouble."

"Oh, no–not at all. Julie does that all the time. But isn't that old fellow a riot? He's always trying to distract me with cups of coffee or tea in order to sell me what nobody else wants to buy. Crafty old devil, isn't he?"

"He was alright. Tell me, how do you like living in Berlin full time?"

Elaine removed a gold cigarette case and a Dunhill lighter from her purse. Both looked expensive. "Mind if I smoke?"

Valerie shook her head. "Go ahead."

"Thanks. Smoking is still very much socially acceptable in Germany, unlike the ridiculous stance taken by all the Bible-bangers in the States. Everyone picks on you if you smoke back there, yet none of those Hamelin rats ever bother to see that drunk drivers kill thousands more than cigarettes ever will, yet no one has started a full-scale war against drunken drivers. Julie just told me that now even popcorn is regulated so now a person can't even go to the movies and enjoy good popcorn cooked with coconut oil. No–it has to be cooked in tasteless, harmless canola oil. Don't you wonder what's next?"

Valerie smiled. That much was true. Some group or other had announced "scientific data" about coconut oil being the culprit for everything from puberty to AIDS and the movie industry had reacted in panic, changing forever the taste of popcorn by cooking it with canola oil.

"They did the same thing with Coke," Valerie agreed. "Coke here in Europe tastes like it used to when I was a kid 'cause they make it with sugar, not those horrendous corn-sweeteners they use back home. I avoid Coke anymore because of the bitter aftertaste it leaves in your mouth."

"Precisely my point, Valerie," Elaine agreed, exhaling a cloud of white smoke away from where Valerie was sitting.

Good manners.

"The point is, Valerie, everyone is out to make a quick buck. Those Coke bottlers realized they could buy fructose and sucrose a lot cheaper than sugar, which would enhance their profits, so they gradually changed over to half fructose, half sugar, eventually going to all fructose. Never mind the fact that those products taste terrible. Since the American people said nothing, Coke popped open the champagne and celebrated the additional profits. Had all soda manufacturers changed over all at one time, public outrage would have prevented the change, but they were smart–and devious."

What the woman said made sense. Those jerks! Feeling manipulated by big business always irritated her.

The waiter brought two espressos and Elaine insisted on paying. "It's the least I can do, after what you've done for us! And by the way, I'm awful sorry–I didn't mean to sidestep your question. I really do like living in Berlin. It's such a wonderful, sophisticated city."

Elaine gulped her coffee in two swigs and offered her hand to Valerie. "I gotta run. Thank you again so very much for all your trouble. You've no idea how much this helps me. A woman has to get resourceful around these parts to make some extra money."

Valerie accepted the handshake, startled by the how fast Elaine had finished her coffee. "Glad to have helped you, Elaine."

"How dumb! Here I am, leaving without giving you what I brought you!" Elaine reached in her purse and pulled out an expensive-looking jewelry box covered in Navy blue velvet. "This is a little something my husband and I want you to have for all your trouble getting these scarves to us." She handed the box to Valerie.

Valerie was taken by surprise. She accepted the box–it was heavy–and opened it to find a shiny new Rolex watch glistening in the reflection of the overhead lights. It was stainless steel, but it was a Rolex. *A little something?*

"I can't accept this..."

"Nonsense! You helped me out Valerie, and I want you to have it."

"But it's a Rolex! Is it real?" Valerie was familiar with the fake twenty dollar Rolexes and Piagets inundating New York City streets.

"Of course it's real! I used to work for Rolex and got dozens of them as bonuses instead of commissions. Don't get too flustered, that's their economy model."

Valerie was confused. Should she accept it? She loved Rolex watches, had always wanted one and she knew that sooner or later she would gift herself with one, but she just couldn't convince herself to fork over five of six thousand dollars for a mere watch, when she could buy the best darn Casio in the world for under fifty bucks. "I don't know, Elaine...you didn't buy this you say?"

"Of course not, silly! What do you think I am, rich? If I had money to buy those I wouldn't be bugging you to bring me scarves from Istanbul now, would I?"

"Well, but couldn't you just sell it and make some money on it?"

"Naw, they made me sign an agreement when I worked as a saleswoman for Rolex that I would not–under any circumstances–sell any of the products they issued me instead of commissions. And these watches all have serial numbers on them, so if I sold them I would get nailed when someone sent one in for repairs. Besides, there are lots of these around in the black market so they're not so easy to sell even if I wanted to do it."

It made sense. Valerie allowed herself to become excited. "Well, if you really think so..."

"I insist! I will be very offended if you don't accept it."

Valerie smiled. "I have no intention of offending you, Elaine, but this seems excessive. If there's anything else I can do for you, let me know. I'll be flying the Istanbul trip three more times this month." The minute the words were out of her mouth she cursed herself for saying them. What was she, nuts? The last thing she wanted was to get involved with anymore damn scarves!

"Thank you, Valerie," Elaine glanced at her own watch, a *gold* Rolex. "Oh, gosh, Karl must be going crazy outside looking for me. I have to go. Thanks again, Valerie!" She reached out, giving Valerie a hug and a peck on the cheek. "Good-bye!"

Valerie found herself alone with a cup of coffee and what must be a five thousand-dollar watch. Incredible! She had not expected remuneration for her good deed. The woman had needed a favor and Valerie had been able to provide it, but now she was sitting here with a fantastic bonus! She gently took it out of its case, slipping it on her wrist. It felt heavy, which meant it was expensive. No, this was no New York city imitation, this was the real thing. The seconds hand smoothly glided across the face of the watch, unlike the New York cheapos which spastically jerked a millimeter at a time. She admired the watch on her wrist and wondered where she should go for dinner to celebrate.

THE NEXT THREE DAYS were the kind that made airline pilots' lives so totally different from those of other human beings. Valerie didn't have to fly, so she indulged in a daily routine of morning jogs down to the beautiful *Tiergarten* park in downtown Berlin, late brunches at a restaurant near the hotel and delicious dinners of Bratwurst and beer at any of several favorite restaurants also near the hotel. She avoided the usual crew spots because she was really into Michener's *Caribbean* and didn't feel like socializing with men who would invariably attempt to get in her pants. In a way, she savored her self-induced solitude like one would enjoy a delicious meal.

On her last day before having to fly again she decided that she'd had enough solitude and dropped in at the St. George's bar, the airline crews' home away from home. Most international airline crews flying in and out of Berlin used the bar for their watering hole due to its quiet elegance and excellent location near the Kaiser Wilhelm Memorial Church on *Tauentzienstrasse*. This location was five minutes walking distance from the two best hotels in Berlin, where most international airline crews spent their layovers.

Valerie walked in and immediately spotted several pilots and flight attendants from both Trans Global and other airlines. It was not difficult, discerning the relaxing crewmembers, for they were the ones dressed in colorful sweaters, tennis shoes and leather jackets. Berliners dressed very conservatively and elegant, unlike most of the pilots she knew who dressed terribly on layovers, and she wondered why they weren't able to improve their appearance since they all enjoyed generous salaries. Their wives obviously were unable to influence these men or improve on their choice of garments, almost surely because airline pilots were generally strong-minded individuals, leaders accustomed to issuing orders, not receiving them. She smiled, realizing fashion was one area where these flyboys definitely needed additional help.

"Hey, Valerie!" A big man reached over, placing his arm around her shoulders.

"Adam!? What are you doing here?"

Adam Dee, the boisterous Irishman from her newhire class was standing there hugging her in a bar in Berlin!

"Same thing as you, sugar! I'm here to fly Seven-Twos for the glory of TGA and the health of my bank account! And what's a nice captain like you doing in a place like this?" The big man thundered.

"I came to grab a *Berlinerkindle* beer before retiring for the night. When did you get in?" Valerie was immensely pleased to run into Adam. She had heard through the grapevine that he and his wife Louise had just bought a new home in Long Island.

"Three days ago. I didn't have to be here at the beginning of the month like you did, 'cause I bid a line that goes into next month. How about you, sugar, whatyaflying?"

Valerie grabbed his shirt and yanked it out of his pants. "Don't call me sugar!"

Adam laughed, backing away from her. "Whatever you say, captain!"

She had been unable to stop Adam from calling her sugar, even after all these years, "I'm flying the Istanbul and London flights, Adam. What are you flying?"

"I'm doing Hamburg and Stuttgart. Boring as hell, but Louise is coming to meet me in a couple of days and she's going to spend two weeks over here with me. We're going to rent a car and drive to Paris."

"No shit–I mean, great! I heard you guys got into a new home, is that so?"

Adam laughed, "you bet that's so! We bought ourselves a real monument to aviation near Oyster Bay. I couldn't wait to make captain's pay so I could dump it all into a house! Louise has been going berserk with the move and all the decorating and furnishing. You know how that goes. That's why I bid Berlin for the month, to get her away from it for a while."

Valerie knew the routine, as soon as copilots upgraded to captain status and began making big bucks they either bought a big home, a big boat or a new wife. Thank God Adam had decided to stay married to Louise and buy a big house. Over the years Valerie had found that most of the captains she flew with were divorced, and she could see why. Egocentrism did not make for good marriages. Invariably, she had come to notice, the nicest captains to fly with, the ones the entire crew adored, were the ones who had been married to the same woman for a long time.

"Buy me a beer?"

"You bet, Valerie! Follow me." Adam's six foot-four frame parted the crowd like Moses did with the Red Sea.

She followed him to a corner of the bar, once again admiring the beer contraption installed behind the bartender. The draft beer was poured out of some contraption that looked like a still, but what made it unusual was that the entire ten-foot long coil where the beer circulated was frozen over with a one-inch thick layer of glaze ice. How the Germans did this was beyond her, yet she loved the ice-cold taste of the beer that came out of the spigots.

"What the heck are you doing in Berlin, Valerie? What about Paul Morris?" Adam ordered two beers from the German bartender. It would take a good five minutes to get them because the house tradition was to serve beer with as little head as possible, and it took several fillings while the bartender waited for the foam to settle.

"Paul's coming to meet me here in Berlin in a week. Maybe the four of us can get together for dinner one night."

"That, sugar, will be a real treat! So what are you waiting for? You ever going to marry that poor guy? How long have you dated anyway–twenty years?"

"No, not twenty years, just fourteen."

"Just fourteen! Jesus! How can he stand it? Aren't you ever going to get married?"

"I already am married, Dee. To Trans Global."

"Bullshit." Dee roared, "an airplane can't keep you warm at night."

"So, you couldn't wait to spend your raise, eh?" she decided to change the subject. Her relationship with Paul Morris had stagnated since she joined the airlines thirteen years earlier, and although she did love him and greatly enjoyed being with him, the thought of marriage was not attractive. She loved her life flying, and she was intelligent enough to know that marriage could very possibly change it. Paul Morris also loved his work as a computer systems engineer, and never pressured her into marriage, so she was content just to let the *status quo* reign.

"Hey, sorry I asked about Paul Morris. I guess you're doing what you like. And what do you mean, I couldn't wait to spend my raise? You mean the house?"

"Yeah I mean the friggin' house. What did you do, Adam, buy an old mansion in Long Island?"

"Yeah, kinda. Louise always wanted a big house and I liked the idea of having lots of room. I'm a big guy and all those tall ceilings sure make it comfortable for me. Figured after all those years of kissing captain's asses I owed it to myself."

Valerie giggled. Adam had a way with words that never ceased to entertain her.

"You know, Valerie, I'm really enjoying being a captain. Since there's only room for one asshole in the cockpit, I'm sure glad I'm it!"

Valerie laughed, remembering their first week of ground school when they had just been hired by

MidAmerica, before it merged with Trans Global. The word *asshole* would never have crossed their lips back then, when captains were gods in their eyes.

"What about you, Valerie–are you enjoying that fourth stripe?" Adam's eyes focused intensely into hers.

"Absolutely."

"They treating you right?"

"You mean, am I getting the respect I deserve in spite of being a woman?"

Adam laughed out loud. "Always direct, aren't you? Yes–maybe that's what I meant."

"I have no complaints." She did have a few, like the fact that several first officers had called in sick right immediately after seeing who they were flying with. Not everyone at Trans Global Airlines had accepted the controversial concept of women captains just yet, but she was not going to rag on Adam. She simply accepted the fact that there bigots in all places of employment and went on with her life.

"Valerie?"

"What?"

Adam's tone became conspirational, "anybody gives you any crap, I want to know about it."

She loved this big guy, "thanks, Adam, but I can take care of myself."

"I'm sure you can. Just the same, sugar, you got me if you need me."

"Don't call me sugar! You know Adam, maybe you are indeed the only asshole in your cockpit!"

Their beers came and they sat back to enjoy them. Valerie glanced at Adam, pensively. Thanks for the offer, Adam, but when I needed you to defend me from the jerks of the aviation world you weren't there for me, 'cause I hadn't met you yet.

THE FOURTH STRIPE

Maurice Azurdia

TWO
THIRTEEN YEARS AGO
SUN VALLEY, IDAHO, UNITED STATES

Valerie felt the blood rushing to her ears, felt her body receiving an immediate emergency shot of adrenaline, accelerating her heartbeat, dilating her pupils and intensifying her senses. Instinctively and without thinking, she stood up from the breakfast table, grabbing a hold of the edge, flipping the table with all its contents on Jack's lap.

"What the fuck!?" Jack sprung back out of his chair, anger rising in him, confused by this totally unexpected reaction to his words.

Scrambled eggs with tomato and green pepper sloshed down the front of his cashmere trousers, following the tracks left by the spilled orange juice.

"Fuck you, Jack!" Valerie cried, turning to march out the door, while all eyes in the restaurant turned, trying to match the profanity to the person uttering it.

Public marital spats–and everyone assumed that this most certainly was one–were not the accepted behavior at any of Sun Valley's restaurants. The population of that mountain refuge for the rich and famous in Idaho did not look fondly on people who made public spectacles of themselves. That watering hole of the well-to-do disliked vulgarity in any form.

The vulgar young woman had actually tipped the table over, spilling the entire breakfast collection on the tall, distinguished-looking gentleman; speculation as to why she did it would surely make the rounds of the town by that afternoon, but since none of the patrons knew the couple or had any inkling as to what the fight was about, it would just spawn all kinds of wild hypothesis, none of which would be accurate nor close to the truth. A very attractive brunette in her mid-twenties had argued with an older man over breakfast–that was all anybody really knew.

Anything to break the boredom of programmed entertainment which is so dear to the wealthy.

The man was left clumsily trying to return the table to its upright position, while the woman stormed out the door. She was young and very attractive–not an unusual combination in Sun Valley–and he seemed a couple of decades older, and quite wealthy, if one judged from the elegant "casual" clothes he wore.

Valerie walked out into the fresh spring morning air, very agitated and ready to kill the sonofabitch. How dare he? How dare he blackmail her? She momentarily paused, wondering what next, remembering then that she had driven them to the restaurant in the company's Jeep. Good! The crew's brown Jeep Cherokee was parked right where they'd left it, so she jumped in, starting the engine, congratulating herself on her decision to drive that morning. Had Jack driven them there, he would have kept the keys and she would have had to walk back to the condo, which would have meant another confrontation with the jerk. This way, she would drive herself to the condo, pick up her things and head out to Hailey, to catch a ride home.

For nearly twelve months she had put up with his advances and sexual innuendoes which had just about driven her out of her mind. For twelve long months she had dodged his moves, politely brushing off his advances, reminding him that theirs was supposed to be merely a *professional* relationship, but now he had gone too far.

Valerie had wanted to fly a corporate jet more than anything else in the world, in order to gain experience to make her attractive to the airlines, but the price tag had just become too high to continue. Sexual harassment was real and alive and living in Sun Valley.

She had known that Jack was attracted to her since last year, when he'd first offered her the job over dozens of men who had more extensive qualifications and flight experience than she did. Knowing this, she had been very clear right from the start: no hanky-panky. Of course, Jack had instantly agreed to her demands for a professional relationship, feigning surprise at her insinuations that he might be hiring her as his copilot on the Sabreliner just because he was attracted to her. That thought, he had assured her, had never crossed his mind. He was a professional pilot, he had explained to her at the time, and he ran his flight department accordingly. Well, maybe the thought of getting in her pants had never crossed his mind, but it had certainly crossed other parts of his anatomy!

She had even introduced her new employer Jack Cranston to Paul Morris, her boyfriend, and that had apparently cleared the air and set the ground rules–so to speak, far as she was concerned. She had wanted to make sure that Jack understood that she was not available for anything else except performing the duties of a copilot, and the deal seemed to have worked for a while, but lately he had grown insufferable with his persistence.

What the man wanted was clear to her, her captain and employer wanted to have sex with her as part of her on-the-job duties, and he could just as well go to hell and grow moss.

Valerie drove herself to the condo the company provided for the flight crew at the base of Bald Mountain, the primary ski resort in Sun Valley. The dwelling was small but luxurious, as was everything else that surrounded the Oster family, for whom until ten minutes ago, she had worked for. She felt a momentary pang of regret. The Osters had been good to her, and now she was walking out on them without notice, leaving them stranded in Idaho until Jack could procure another pilot to replace her.

She wondered whether she should stop at the Oster's home and tell them what had happened, but thought better of it. It would not do any good to create a scene at the Osters because she would not get the upper hand. Mr. Oster, her boss, was a regular *Don Juan* and Jack his *confidant*, which would not benefit her in the least. Mr. Oster liked to give the impression that he was a family man, a respected member of his community, but he also had the bad habit of screwing around on his wife, which Valerie found despicable because she liked Mrs. Oster very much.

Jack and Valerie had flown their employer on several occasions to rendezvous with different lovers with whom he "met" all over the country, and Jack had made it quite clear to Valerie that the crew were not to stick their noses in the Boss' business, particularly in this kind of business. Nevertheless, she still liked Mrs. Oster, and felt like a double-crossing-dog for doing this to her. Valerie knew that if she went to their house and made a scene over what Jack had said to her, that Mrs. Oster would side with her, but that would not necessarily carry much weight with Mr. Oster, who considered Jack "one of the boys."

Dirty rotten life, she thought, when women have to put up with this kind of bullshit just because the "boys" have the wallets. She parked at the condo and collected all her belongings in under ten minutes, returning to the Jeep Wagoneer and heading out of town to Hailey, where the airport was.

She began to calm down, allowing her mind to analyze the situation without the unsettling influence of a heavy dose of adrenaline. That Jack was a jerk. She had tried to ignore all his advances and his indirect requests for access to her body, sometimes putting up with a moody captain for several days, obviously moody due to her continued rejections. Valerie had not felt comfortable sleeping in the same condo with him for the last few trips. The condo only had one bedroom, which he had courteously allowed her to use since their first trip to Sun Valley, but she had kept her door locked, uncomfortably aware that he was a big man who enjoyed his drinks when off duty, and who would not have stressed himself too much to negotiate entry into her bedroom, had he so wished.

His continuous suggestions that they would make a terrific couple, of how nice it would be for a married couple to be captain and copilot, combined with his continuous put-downs of her boyfriend Paul Morris had finally driven her to consider quitting the job. Quitting the job flying corporate pilot for the Osters was not an attractive option, because she had just started sending out employment applications to all the major airlines in hopes of attaining her life-long desire of becoming an airline pilot, but Jack had really become one big pain in the ass. Her polite refusals had failed to make a dent in his armor, and he made it so that she no longer looked forward to her flights with the man. It used to be that she would get goose pumps of excitement at the mere thought of flying as a copilot in a multimillion-dollar jet plane, but lately the novelty had worn off and Jack's presence had bruised her nerves to the point where she actually dreaded going to work.

At breakfast that morning he had been brutally aggressive, insolent and demanding, and she had decided to call it quits and shoved breakfast in his face.

"What looks good?" Jack had asked her twenty minutes earlier, while scanning the breakfast menu.

"I don't know yet," Valerie had been starved since she'd had to wait until nearly eleven a.m. to go have breakfast because they only had the one vehicle and Jack slept late and took nearly two hours to get showered and shaved. She would much have preferred to go have breakfast by herself with her latest paperback novel, but unfortunately, there was no place to eat anywhere within walking distance of their condo, and anyway, Jack would have kittens if she drove herself to breakfast without him early in the morning before he got up. He would take this as a personal insult, assuming that she did not want to have breakfast with him. His argument was invariably that they were a "crew," and therefore they should eat together, but what he really wanted was the company of an attractive woman whom he could control.

So she was stuck having breakfast with this man every morning, which she had come to loathe.

"I think I'll have the four-egg omelet with everything in it," he had chirped, "and a side of hash browns and some orange juice."

Valerie had ignored him and wondered if he thought he was addressing his wife, or that she gave a shit what his breakfast menu was going to be. One thing she had noticed with Jack was that he had an enormous appetite, and that he made no qualms about it.

Real attractive.

She ordered Belgian Waffles with strawberries and a glass of milk and braced herself for her co-worker's monologue on World War II or Winston Churchill, or the best restaurants in Newport Beach. Jack, having received his education in England, considered himself an authority on history and an expert on just about everything else, and it drove her nuts, but it was part of the price she had to pay if she wanted to accumulate jet time. In a way–she thought–it was probably also good practice for when she flew for the airlines. She'd heard that some airline captains were spoiled, egocentric prima-donnas who relished telling their feats and accomplishments to their captive copilot audiences.

"Why don't you like me?" he had asked point-blank. Right to the point, bypassing all his usual morning civility.

"Like you? Of course I like you, Jack," she initially side-stepped the issue, hopefully making him change the topic. She just didn't want to believe their day would start off like this.

"No, you don't." He had looked at some spot behind her, intentionally avoiding her gaze.

"Why do you say I don't like you?" she'd known then that it was going to be a long breakfast, and wished she were somewhere else.

"Because you don't. Because you never let me be nice to you. You never want to go dancing with me or anything." His speech was rapid, obviously nervous.

"Jack," Valerie had tried making her tone of voice as light and joyful as possible, like a mother reminding a child that there is no school today because it's Sunday. "I've told you that I don't really like to dance, and you accepted that."

He looked uncomfortable. "Yes, that's right–you told me that, but I see that you didn't have a problem dancing with Rick last night." Rick Hayden, a friend of hers now flying copilot for another corporate jet, had asked her to dance the night before at The Lodge, and she had accepted. Rick had been on an overnight in Sun Valley and she had been delighted to see a familiar face other than Jack's for a change. Rick was just a good friend whom she had known for years, and found nothing wrong in dancing with the man. She had actually enjoyed the opportunity to drift away from Jack for a while, since she had to accompany her boss everywhere during the evenings. It was that, or staying at the condo with him trying to get in her pants, so she had gone with him to the Lodge. Jack would not go out anywhere at night without Valerie, and asking him to go hit the bars alone was a waste of time. If she expressed her desire to remain in the apartment because she wanted to read or be alone for a while, he would not leave, but would drive her nuts pacing the small living room while surfing through all the TV channels with the remote control.

"Jack, I explained to you last night that Rick is just a good friend who I hadn't seen for a while and I couldn't very well turn him away. "

"And I'm not a good friend?"

"Of course you are! But it's different." Valerie had sighed with relief. She had spotted their waitress headed for their table.

"What do you mean? How is it different?" The presence of the waitress standing next to him startled him, and he quickly reached for his menu.

"Good morning!" the waitress offered, eyeballing the couple, giving the impression that she was instantly evaluating their tipping potential.

Twenty percenters, she would probably guess. Not millionaires, but pretty loaded.

Jack's tone of voice and personality underwent a chameleonic transformation on the spot, becoming friendly and jovial with the server. He ordered them breakfast and smiled at the waitress a couple of times too many, checking out her body as he ordered.

This didn't escape Valerie's attention, and she found it very rude and impolite to both her and the waitress. She had eventually come to realize that this was his routine behavior. Just one more thing she did not like about the man.

"So? Where were we?" he stared right at Valerie.

"You asked me how is it different that I danced with Rick but I don't dance with you," she explained, "Jack, you and I spend a lot of time together, and we are not out on vacation, we are on the job. I just don't think it's a good idea for us to be fraternizing to the point of going out dancing and all."

Jack's frown returned. "And why not?"

"Because we work together," she added, slightly exasperated. "Haven't you ever heard that you don't mess around where you work?" She was really getting fed up with his line of questioning.

"But we're not common people," he blurted, "we are highly paid corporate pilots. We don't go by the rules of the little people. "

This favorite line of his, borrowed from Leona Helmsley really irritated her. Where did he get off with this elitist attitude of his? And just what made him think that she shared his view? "Jack, call it what you may, I still believe that it isn't right for us to go dancing. And besides, you know I'm engaged to Paul Morris and it just wouldn't be right."

"I don't know why you turn me down over some nine-to-five computer whiz kid who doesn't know a wing from a suppository."

Valerie's heart missed a couple of firings. A nine-to-five computer whiz kid? Paul Morris? She inhaled deeply in an effort to retain control. "Paul Morris is a computer systems engineer, not a computer whiz kid, Jack, and he is the man I chose to be engaged to, and I really don't want to discuss it with you."

"Oh, yes you do!" his voice increased several decibels. "You do, Valerie, because you wanted to fly jets, remember? and I gave you the opportunity you wanted, and now this is how you pay me back? Wake up! What do you think this is all about?"

Valerie was becoming furious but had to wait to reply because the waitress brought them their plates and drinks. Speed in service was one of the attractions of that place for breakfast because they had most of the food prepared ahead of time. "I don't know what this is all about, Jack, but I thought we had agreed that ours was strictly a professional relationship."

"Professional? Don't make laugh, Valerie. What kind of resume do you have? You couldn't compete against ninety-nine percent of the resumes I receive on a daily basis. *Professional* relationship? Valerie, I don't know where your head is, but I am through playing games with you. You are a beautiful woman who I'm sure can be very enjoyable, but as a pilot you were worthless to me. You had no flight experience and no idea how to fly jets and yet I took you under my wing and gave you first-class training equivalent to that found at British Airways. I prepared you for a juicy airline position and now you have the audacity to turn me down like some miserly line boy." He paused to catch his breath, then continued in a calm voice. "I can offer you a wonderful permanent job as a corporate pilot flying with me, and I'll even talk to Wolf Oster about a salary increase, but your attitude is just going to have to change, or this isn't going to work."

Valerie couldn't believe her ears.

Jack took a swig of his orange juice. His mouth was dry from talking too fast and also from nerves. Orange juice dripped down the side of his mouth. He had finally launched his ultimatum, and now he would conclude. "You either become my girlfriend or you're out of a job, Valerie, and if that happens I can assure you that you'll never again fly a corporate jet in this country, and that your name will be mud in the aviation world."

At that point her fuse had melted and she jumped up and flipped the table.

VALERIE APPROACHED THE TOWN of Hailey and reduced her speed to fifteen MPH. This was a ridiculous speed, but the town of Hailey had put together as much money as they could and purchased two new police cruisers with the latest most-expensive state of the art laser radars available. Then they posted fifteen MPH signs along the two-mile stretch of highway across their town, in hopes of supplementing the community taxes with speeding tickets written to unwary rich people on their way to Sun Valley.

Business had been booming.

Valerie reached the airport parking lot and drove into Sun Valley Aviation, the Fixed Base Operator that took care of the business jets overnighting in Hailey. She had calmed down and decided to leave the Jeep Wagoneer there for the Osters to pick up at their convenience, then hitch a ride to the other side of the airport to purchase a ticket home on America West. She gathered her belongings and decided to leave a note at the counter for the Osters. She took out her pen and wrote a short note on a piece of local stationary:

Dear Mr. And Mrs. Oster:

I must leave Sun Valley because Jack gave me a choice of either sleeping with him or getting fired, and I opted to leave. Beware that he is a sexual deviate so that you don't lose any other female pilots...

Valerie paused, read what she had already written, crumpled it into a ball and tossed it into a garbage can. It may not be a good idea to piss off the Osters since she might be looking for a reference from them in the not too distant future in her search for another job. Instead she wrote:

Dear Mr. And Mrs. Oster:

Due to circumstances beyond my control, I am unable to continue in your employment and I must return to Los Angeles immediately. Please accept my gratitude for all your consideration and my apologies for this sudden departure. Jack will be able to explain it all in detail.

Yours truly,
Valerie Wall

And let Jack explain himself out of that one.

She stuffed the note in an envelope, licked it shut, addressed it to the Osters and gave it to the customer service gal at the desk who assured Valerie that the Osters would get the message the minute they came through the terminal.

Valerie decided that her final note was a good idea. Jack would be dying, wondering what kind of scandal awaited him, and would be relieved to know that she had not ratted on him. He would also have to do a quick two-step to explain Valerie's sudden departure, but that did not worry her. Mrs. Oster would probably suspect the real reason behind Valerie's departure, but there would be no showdown with Jack and no storm. She got a ride on a tow truck to the other side of the small runway and bought a ticket on America West to Los Angeles via Phoenix with her Visa card. It still amazed her to see those huge Boeing 737s of America West using the same runway she used with the Sabreliner, and she wondered how it would feel to fly such an enormous beast into such a short runway.

Ever since she was a little girl she had been attracted to airplanes. Her father's travels as a member of the diplomatic corps had exposed her early to the pleasures of flying long-distances on shinning silver airplanes that smelled new. In those days, people took flying seriously because it was so expensive, and air travelers dressed up in their best clothes whenever they boarded one of those shiny silver Constellations or DC-7s or B-707s. Her father's position as ambassador to Italy and then to Panama had provided her family with untold travel experience, crossing the Atlantic many times to rejoin family for Christmases and summer vacations. Those had been happy times, during which she had felt safe in the comfort of her parents' home. The residual effect it had left on Valerie was to make her fall in love with airplanes, with flying and with the people associated with flying.

She sat in the small terminal room, waiting for the incoming America West flight. She had about an hour to kill before the flight arrived and she wondered what the chances were of Jack showing up there. Naw, he would not think to look for her at the airport, and even if he did he would not be able to get his hands on another vehicle so quickly. He would probably think that she was still in Ketchum, brooding somewhere but ultimately returning to him because she wanted to fly jets so bad.

Dream on, buster.

She was out of there–permanently. No job was worth putting up with the kind of bullshit she had put up with for twelve months. Now, she finally admitted to herself what she had known all along, that Jack couldn't score with a woman if he walked into a woman's jail with a handful of pardons, and that he used his position as chief pilot for the Osters as a tool to get laid. Down deep inside she had suspected this all along, but her desire to fly the powerful Sabreliner had overcome the tiny alarm bell going off in the deep recesses of her mind. Now there was no way to ignore it. The nerve of the bastard, blackmailing her with sex! Sleep with him? Not on your life, buster! If the man had an asshole transplant, it wouldn't take, because the new asshole would reject him. He was a well-educated man, obviously well-traveled and very wealthy, but he was not her type to begin with, and now that his true personality had come shining through she found him repulsive.

Valerie sighed. Now she was unemployed, with her several dozen employment applications out with the airlines. Just beautiful. She had planned her strategy so well to reach for her airline dream and now she was left hanging in the breeze. Oh, the airlines would just love to hear how she walked out of her job due to sexual harassment. No matter who was at fault, it would instantly eliminate any opportunity for employment with any carrier she told the story to. Even though Jack was the provocateur, the airlines' hiring personnel would brand her a troublemaker, controversial, unable to get along with the program, and it would be a cold day in hell before they ever called her in for an interview.

If she didn't use her job flying for the Osters as a reference, then this would not happen, but then how could she justify the hours in the business jet that she had acquired over the past year? She couldn't very well expect any kind of reference letter from Jack now, so how was she going to verify her jet time? She thought about this while her ride to L.A. showed up. She needed her jet experience on her resume, or no airline would touch her.

Jack was independently wealthy, his fortune coming from a meat-packing plant in Ireland–the largest one, as he was so fond of pointing out–but despite all his wealth he had been unable to pursue his life's dream of becoming an airline pilot because he had been one of the unfortunate ones who was ready for the airlines at a time when the airlines weren't ready for him because they simply weren't hiring.

Airlines, as Valerie had found, hired in cycles. In twenty-year cycles to be exact, and it was all a matter of luck and timing. Those individuals fortunate enough to find themselves between twenty-three to thirty years of age with enough flight experience at the beginning of each hiring cycle would be hired and have a beautiful career, rapidly rising to the most desirable high-paying pilot positions with their respective airlines. The hiring cycle usually lasted about four to five years, during which time the airlines hired like mad, trying to prepare replacements for all the pilots hired twenty years earlier who must then retire at sixty. As soon as the hiring cycle ended, the airlines would then trickle-hire a few individuals per year over the next fifteen years, giving themselves the luxury of hand-picking candidates and selecting only those who closely resembled Greek gods. It was a well-known fact that anyone not hiring on with an airline early in the hiring cycle, would end up flying Eskimos in Alaska or drugs from South America for the rest of their flying careers.

Valerie knew Jack loved his job with the Osters. He was the Chief Pilot and captain of their personal jet, and he was not treated as hired help, but rather as a member of the team of businessmen who followed Mr. Oster around the world. Valerie knew that Jack would not do anything to openly jeopardize his position with the Osters, which would keep him from ever telling his employers the real reason behind Valerie's untimely departure.

She had put the ball on his court with that last line on her note to the Osters. He would have to fabricate an acceptable reason for her departure, and she was sure he would think of something adequate.

Feeling depressed, she went to a payphone next to a coffee-vending machine and dialed her home number in Los Angeles. Maybe Paul Morris had left her a message at home. It would cheer her up to hear his voice, and God knew she needed all the cheering she could get just then.

She punched in her personal identification number so her answering machine would spit out her messages and listened to her dentist's secretary confirming an appointment a week from now, her mom calling her from Santa Barbara wanting to know if Valerie will ever be home to get one of her calls and Jolene Smith with MidAmerica Air Lines in St. Louis calling to invite her for an interview.

Her heart missed a beat.

She rapidly punched a number, not wanting to believe what she'd just heard; the number would replay the last message, and she listened, paralyzed, to the words from the personnel woman from MidAmerica Air Lines inviting her for a pilot interview!

A pilot interview! She could hardly believe the words coming out of her answering machine. When everything seems to fall apart, God or destiny shine another bright light at the end of that dark tunnel! She played back the same message a dozen times just to be sure she had heard right. Finally, satisfied that she had indeed heard from one of her first-choice airlines, she hung up and stood there, euphoric.

Few times in her life had she felt like this. When she was selected as a starter in the volleyball team back in eighth grade, when her dad had given her the down payment for her first car, when her acceptance letter had arrived from Drake University. She was feeling a near-sensual excitement. Suddenly, nothing mattered except her interview with the airline. Her mood instantaneously lightened up and she felt in great spirits.

She had sent applications to all the major airlines–of course–but she had a few favorites which she had been secretly been rooting for and hoping to hear from them. MidAmerica was at the top of that list for several reasons.

Most major airlines like United and American had adopted a horrible new tactic to reduce labor costs on their premises; these new tactics were known as the B-Scale. What this B-Scale meant was that new pilots hiring on with those major airlines would have to look forward to a 50% reduction in salary over their entire airline careers. The management at these airlines had approached their pilots with requests for pay cuts, and the pilots had fought back ferociously, refusing to take any drastic reductions in salaries, leaving management no other choice than to carve their savings off the backs of the future newhires. These airlines were very much aware that they would have to hire thousands of pilots over the next five years and had therefore reduced their pay scales to half of what they had been, for all future newhires. Valerie was well aware of this, and did not like it one bit, but there was not much she could do about it because the majority of the unionized pilots at each airline had actually approved the B-Scale for their new pilots.

The only alternative left was to shoot for one of the airlines that still paid high salaries to their newhires, like Delta and MidAmerica. Logically, since everyone else was also aware of this, those airlines were bombarded with applications from all over the country, making it extremely competitive.

The second reason why Valerie wanted to get hired with someone like MidAmerica was that they flew DC-9s, which meant she would start off immediately flying as a First Officer instead of ending up as a Flight Engineer at one of the other major airlines. Most major airlines still flew airplanes that required a third crewmember, the flight engineer, and she dreaded this non-flying position, where she could be stuck for several years without flying. The reason she dreaded this position was because she did not have much jet flying experience to begin with, and she feared that her limited skills would disappear if she was a flight engineer for too long. She wanted to start flying the big jets right off the bat, while her skills were still hot, and not have to wait too long, which would certainly lead to a disaster if she failed her initial flight training because of being rusty.

For all these reasons she had hoped to get a shot at MidAmerica, and now she was being presented with the opportunity for an interview! The news boosted her spirits and she decided to call the Osters and say good-bye, dialing their number. She heard it ring four times and then their answering machine picked up. When the thing beeped Valerie spoke calmly, "Mrs. Oster, this is Valerie. I'm calling you from the airport at Hailey because I have to return to Los Angeles right away. I have been called in for an interview with one of the airlines and Jack has agreed to let me go. He will find a replacement copilot for your flight back." The Osters were fully aware of her intentions to get on with one of the airlines, they had been enthusiastic for her when she told them that she had sent out resumes, and Mrs. Oster had called her aside one night and expressed her pride in Valerie's accomplishments. They knew Jack was not prone to fly with the same copilot for too long, and felt that they had already got their money's worth having had her for almost a year. Jack was going to be real surprised when the Osters mentioned her interview with MidAmerica, and even more so when he found out that it was true.

Next week she would call Mrs. Oster and request a letter of recommendation, and Valerie would also give Mrs. Oster's name to future employers who wanted to run a background check, bypassing Jack. She felt much better.

The America West B-737 came screaming down the short runway with the reversers at maximum thrust, the pilots straining to stop the big jet before reaching the fence at the end of the field. Valerie gawked in admiration at those magnificent men in their flying machines, as she was fond of thinking, and fervently wished she was one of them.

THREE
PRESENT TIME - BERLIN, GERMANY

"Do you think the TGA captain, Valerie, suspects anything?"

"No, she was just happy as a jaybird to get her Rolex. I think she'll work good for us."

Elaine Griffin lit a Dunhill cigarette. "I think she might've been a little concerned at first when I called her in her room to ask her for the favor, but once she saw how easy it was to bring those scarves back from Istanbul, and then after receiving her Rolex, she's sold."

"When's her next flight?" The man named Karl was in his early thirties, dark, slim and tall, very elegantly dressed in a Prince of Wales suit adorned with a Paisley tie. They had a tray with *paté* and Swiss cheese on the coffee table between them.

Elaine studied her laptop computer screen. "Thursday, she flies again on Thursday, three days from now. Our contact in New York faxed me her monthly flight schedule this morning."

"Excellent. You think she'll go along with the program then?"

"Don't quote me, but I'd say so, yes." Elaine typed some commands on the keyboard and sat back to watch the powerful utility encrypting the file named:

valerie.tga

"This DES Norton Utilities encoding program is really magnificent. Having the U.S. Government's standard for encryption is very handy for us. Very nice of Uncle Sam to make this program available to us commoners." Elaine Griffin had never attended any university, nor had any formal training in computers, but she was a reasonably intelligent woman, and had taught herself about software and hardware, avidly reading every book she could get her hands on about computers. She had realized that computers meant information, which in turn meant power. She kept a meticulous diary of her daily activities and of everything connected with her work. Of course, this was her own secret, one which she did not confide to anyone. In her line of work keeping a diary might be viewed as hazardous to one's health.

"Yes, those utilities are extremely useful," Karl agreed. The Organization had set up a magnificent communications network using notebook computers equipped with modems and encoding software. It endowed its members with the ability to communicate from anywhere in the world in a matter of seconds. The Director was updated by the field operatives twice a day under normal routine operations, more often if necessary due to non-routine operations. All modem transmissions were sent to Mexico City numbers which changed every few days. Nobody knew where the Director was, but Karl suspected that Mexico City was probably not a good guess. He suspected the only reason the Organization used Latin countries as receivers for data and modem transmissions was because of their lack of communications technology. Sending the same transmissions to the United States directly or one of the other First World countries would be suicidal because they had the advanced communications technology to intercept and decipher just about anything the Organization transmitted.

Elaine Griffin knew exactly where her communications went. They went to Mexico City, and from there they continued on to St. Louis, Missouri, where Esteban Escobar, the Director, would read them at his mahogany desk in his beautiful, elegant study. The communications did not flow directly from Mexico City to St. Louis, but they followed an untraceable path along the cyberspace of the Internet. Mexico made a good relay station. Elaine had been fortunate enough to spend one night with Escobar, which she had noted in her diary. Her one-night stand had given her rapid advancement within the Organization, but this was not common knowledge, certainly not to be shared with her dear Karl.

"Are you sending the afternoon update?" Karl had told her that he was very happy to be working with her because he detested computers and had no intention of learning their ridiculous intricacies in order to send the reports. The Organization paid them handsomely and expected all of its operatives to be computer literate but Karl had been able to bypass this requirement by working exclusively with Elaine.

"Yes, I'm just about done. The Director will approve of our new choice of recruit."

"What does that make it out of here, seven?" Karl poured himself a glass of cold Chablis, observing Elaine at work in the elegant hotel suite. They used different suites for their home plate, and he had to say he approved of her latest choice. The *Steigenberger* was probably the most exclusive hotel in downtown Berlin, and they would use it as their base for the next few months.

"Yes, Valerie is our seventh recruit out of Berlin. Not bad, eh? Our sales commissions should start becoming rather plump."

Karl nodded, sipping on his Chablis.

Elaine used the computer trackball mouse to set up the data transmission and initiated the transfer with a click of the button.

She observed, fascinated, as the tiny laptop computer fired out a small electronic bleep across cyberspace, crossing the Atlantic Ocean and the Gulf of Mexico in a few nanoseconds, carrying with it the latest update for the Director of the Organization.

"All done!" she disconnected the phone jack from the adapter they had to use in European countries to access the phone lines and proceeded to wipe out of her company notebook computer any trace of the files she had manipulated that morning. She wiped out the files from the directories any one could have access to in her laptop, but kept copies of everything in a secret hidden encrypted section of her hard disk. This secret section was where she kept her diary. The Norton Utilities also provided a handy method for doing that so that not even the world's best computer hacker could retrieve the information after she was through dealing with it. Just additional insurance in case her laptop ever fell into the wrong hands. The wonderful world of the Internet had its definite advantages.

This was her own personal insurance policy, since she kept a world of information which nobody knew still existed, with records of everything she could get her hands on.

Elaine was not a stupid woman, and was fully aware that in order to survive in a ruthless world, one had to erect certain defenses against the possibility of betrayal by even one's own friends.

FOUR
PRESENT TIME - BERLIN, GERMANY

Valerie walked over to the small lounge reserved by the hotel for airline personnel and poured herself a cup of hot coffee. She was the first one down in the lobby this morning and she was feeling particularly good. It was awful nice on the hotel's part to provide airline crews with hot beverages and croissants prior to morning departures because the hotel restaurant didn't open until later in the morning. How typical German, she considered, being so efficient.

Last night she had stayed out longer that she had intended, but Adam Dee had entertained her with his humorous stories about his adventures as a line captain. She'd only had one beer because she religiously respected the Federal Aviation Regulations mandating eight hours between bottle and throttle. Her company had more stringent rules, demanding that crewmembers abstain from consuming alcoholic beverages twenty-four hours before flight, but she personally disagreed with it. When the rules became unreasonable, then people violated them, and she really considered that twenty-four hours was asking too much.

She drank her coffee, admiring the new Rolex on her wrist. It sure looked elegant against her dark navy blue uniform coat and four gold stripes on her sleeve. Life was full of little surprises.

"Good morning, Captain." She turned to find two members of her cabin crew arriving for their morning shot of caffeine. They both appeared in their fifties, and it made Valerie extremely uncomfortable, having these respectable women who could be her mother referring to her with such protocol. "Good morning, ladies! Coffee's hot and you can call me Valerie." She offered her hand.

"Well then, good morning, Valerie!" one of the gals responded, visually relieved at being rid of the formalities. She told Valerie that she had not yet flown with a female captain in her thirty-two years with this airline, and had no idea what to expect. "Thank God they have the coffee here, I don't think I could make it to the airport without it."

Cabin crews changed every trip, which made for a continuous exercise remembering names and faces. Some of the flight attendants would start a two-week trip in New York working the Atlantic crossing, then spending twelve days flying around Europe before working their way back to either New York or L.A. on their flight home.

The airline had to have at least one German-speaking flight attendant on each flight to comply with German air regulations, so some of the flight attendants flying the German bases were either German-born or first-generation Americans of German heritage.

Charlie Smith and Brad Thomas appeared in the room.

Valerie checked the time on her new Rolex and decided it was time to head out. The airline van must be right outside the hotel waiting for them. She walked out to the lobby.

"Valerie! How wonderful that you're still here!"

Elaine Griffin was standing in front of her.

"Elaine? What are you doing here?" Valerie didn't have to ask, she had a very strong suspicion that this had something to do with more scarves and with her stupidity opening her mouth to Elaine Griffin offering more help if she needed it. She silently cursed her own mouth.

"Valerie," Elaine touched the back of her hand to her forehead, theatrically, "I am so sorry to bother you, but something terrible has happened."

"What?"

"The scarves you brought me. They are all too small. The man in Istanbul made a terrible mistake and he sent me smaller scarves than the one meter square ones I was expecting!"

Oh, shit.

"I really hate asking you this, but could I absolutely abuse you and *beg* you to get the other ones for me? I would never just show up here like this if it wasn't so important, but I have a customer already waiting, and he needs the larger ones."

Valerie was annoyed. Nobody had said anything about sizes. "Sure, Elaine, I guess I can do that for you."

"Thank you _soo_ much, Valerie! Here is the Visa card you used last time. I am so embarrassed..."

Valerie could feel the eyes of her crew on her. "No problem. Just call me tomorrow afternoon and I'll have them here."

"Valerie, you're an absolute angel, Julie was right!"

"Where are the other scarves so I can take those back?"

"No, don't worry about those Valerie, I can sell those here so I'll keep them, it's just that I already had an order waiting for those larger ones."

"No problem Elaine. Call me tomorrow. I gotta run, the crew van's waiting for us."

"Yes, please don't let me hold you up. Sorry to bother you with this, Valerie. Thank you very much, I'll see you tomorrow!"

Valerie joined the others in the van, wondering what they might be speculating about the exchange in the lobby. She was really pissed about the entire situation. This meant she would have to visit the scarves shop again tonight and sweat through the entire episode again.

Somehow her new Rolex was beginning to irritate her. Not a good way to start the morning. How was it that situations like this landed on her lap?

AT 33,000 FEET OVER the Carpathians her temper mellowed out a little.

"Valerie," Charlie asked, "Brad here is suggesting we try out something new for dinner tonight and I told him I'd run it past you, see what you think."

"And what would that be?"

"Tell her what you told me, Brad."

Valerie turned in her seat to look at her flight engineer.

"One of the other engineers told me about this fantastic ship that takes you to the other side of the Bosporus strait to this real nice restaurant on the water's edge for dinner. The food is said to be excellent and there's an open bar on the ship. All our flight attendants want to try it out, so I thought maybe we could all go as a crew."

Valerie had other things in mind for her Istanbul visit. "And how much does all this cost?" She had a self-imposed budget of twenty dollars for layovers, and she liked to stick to it.

"This buddy of mine said it should be about twenty-five dollars a head."

Valerie thought about this. She really didn't want to join the crew in this excursion, but she didn't want to be the party pooper either and twenty-five bucks wasn't bad. "And everyone is going?"

"Yes, all the girls said they want to go. Charlie here said he's game, so all that's left is you."

She accepted the invitation, provided they didn't go right away because she had some purchases she had to take care of first. She found it preposterous, Brad calling the flight attendants "girls," when each and every one of them could easily be his mother, but she realized it was common terminology in the airlines.

"Swell!" Brad blurted out. His wife had stayed behind in the hotel bed with a cast on her hand. Turned out she had a compound fracture of the thumb and she didn't want to hear another word–ever–about joining Brad on another one of his stupid trips.

VALERIE RETURNED FROM THE scarf shop to find her crew waiting for her in the lobby of the Sheraton. She rushed upstairs to drop off the package in her room and joined the cheerful group climbing into two taxis.

The drive through Istanbul at night was terrifying, just like she had anticipated. The taxi drivers raced each other down extremely narrow streets bordering deep ravines all the way down to the main street edging the Bosporus. They must be blood relations of Italian cabbies, Valerie observed, gritting her teeth.

They were dropped off by the water in front of a small restaurant-bar. The two taxis departed at once, leaving the seven Americans standing on the promenade, feeling very conspicuous in the night. Brad seemed as lost as any of them. He approached a couple of old fishermen standing nearby and tried talking to them but the poor bastards couldn't understand a word he said and just kept shaking their heads.

"If you all wait here, I'll go find us the ship!" Brad offered. There were no large ships of any kind in sight anywhere on the docks to either side of where they had been dropped off, only trawlers and fishing boats, and Valerie began to question the wisdom of her decision to join the expedition. Brad split, leaving them there, with none of them speaking a word of Turkish.

The other side of the Bosporus appeared very far away in the distance. Lights could be seen flickering across the water in the dark. Standing there in the open with four other women and Charlie she felt exposed.

She suggested they forget the whole idea and hit the *Haci Baba* instead, a good restaurant with good food.

There were no takers. Apparently, the spirit of adventure was clouding their brains.

"Let's go in that restaurant while Thomas finds this ship of his, then." She crossed the street followed by her four flight attendants and her first officer. "I'm gonna kill Brad," she whispered to Charlie Smith. She normally refrained from joining group dining because she disliked staying out late and not getting enough sleep. If she didn't join the crew then she was the elitist bitch, but if she joined in and then had an accident or an incident for lack of sleep, they would be the first to hang her because she should have known better than to stay out late, being the captain. That fourth stripe came with a lot of strings attached.

The group entered the small neighborhood restaurant which was still empty because Turkish diners did not consider having dinner before nine p.m. The entire front of the restaurant was open to the waterfront, so she felt comfortable that Thomas would see them if he ever returned with news of the ship.

The waiter came to their table but was unable to take their orders because he spoke nothing but Turkish, and none of them knew a word of it. After much gesticulating, a cook was brought from the kitchen who understood some Italian. One of the flight attendants spoke some Italian because she had flown the Rome trips for years, so she did the honors and ordered wine for everybody. Valerie began to relax, wondering if they could still make dinner at the *Haci Baba*, her favorite restaurant in Istanbul. It was about a mile from the hotel, and it served exquisite Turkish food and spirits at a decent price. She liked the place because it was not a tourist trap. The locals frequented it and it had great atmosphere. The waiters there would automatically bring a bottle of red wine to one's table and then the customers would walk back to the kitchen to point out to their waiters what they fancied for dinner after which the waiter would bring the appointed dishes to each table.

Her hopes vanished when Brad showed up less than two minutes later, excited as all hell, calling for them to join him because the boat was coming. They didn't even have the time to finish their expensive drinks.

The *boat*? What happened to the ship?

They hurriedly dropped several bills on the wooden table to pay for their wine and followed Brad Thomas to the edge of the water. To her horror, they saw that the boat Brad had commissioned to take them across the Bosporus was no *Love Boat*, it was a 25-footer with a cabin, the kind harbor pilots use to go out to ships, and it was rolling in the waves like a sonofabitch. Valerie questioned his sanity and reminded him that he was still on probation with TGA, and that killing an entire crew would not look good at the hearing. Charlie asked her to leave the boy alone, playing Protective Mamma.

The crew boarded the boat and three Turkish sailors welcomed them onboard and directed them into a small cabin which reeked of diesel fumes. The diesel engine was loud enough to inhibit any conversation unless it was of the kind that has to be screamed into the other person's ear, and as soon as everyone was seated the captain gunned the engine and they set off towards the opposite side of the strait, rolling like a drunken sailor.

Charlie and a couple of the flight attendants questioned Thomas about the 'open bar' he had mentioned and the engineer went out to convey the request to the Turks. One of the sailors came into the cabin with a half-full bottle of some clear liquor, which he then proceeded to distribute among the airline crew in paper cups.

Valerie declined the drink thinking that she would have to be out of her mind to pour that shit into her stomach while rocking and rolling on the waves. The bottle didn't even have a label! The rest of the crew drank the clear stuff and tried to look cheerful in their 'ship.'

Valerie was pissed and wished she had remained in her room at the Sheraton. She had wanted no part of this and now she knew she should have listened to her inner voice, who like it or not, was ultimately usually right. Twenty-five minutes later they reached the other side of the strait, docking at a small private concrete dock next to what looked like a classy restaurant, with low ambience lighting and white linen, visible through the windows facing the Bosporus.

The crew disembarked on wobbly legs, unsteady from the ship's rolling and the liquor. Valerie eyed the place, becoming further irritated with Thomas. This place was not going to cost her twenty bucks, two hundred maybe, but not twenty. As they paraded into the restaurant she took in the great luxury, the crystal glasses, the neatly arranged tables, the tuxedoed waiters, the flowers at each table. She had been screwed. Or was going to be.

The restaurant had no other patrons yet because it was still early. Seven p.m. was not a civilized time for dinner in Europe and apparently it wasn't in Istanbul either. Valerie felt very much out of place in her jeans and sweatshirt.

The Turkish waiters happily welcomed the Americans not unlike a hungry wolf pack sizing up nice plump sheep being offered to be devoured. After all, weren't these rich Americans? Rich, *dumb* Americans?

Valerie sat down knowing this dinner was going to cost her a small fortune. The leather-bound two-foot long menus were a dead giveaway. She opened her menu, reading it Russian style, from right to left, from the prices to the items, searching for the least expensive entree she could find.

Shrimp on rice–twenty-five dollars. Yes, that would do. Everything else was forty and fifty bucks a shot. Valerie watched in horror as Charlie ordered wine bottles for the entire crew, but was relieved when he stated that the wine would be his treat tonight.

How magnanimous of him. The wine steward left and the waiter recited some unintelligible items that were on special, but none of the crew took him up on the specials. They proceeded to order various dishes, and Valerie thought her crew was really not being cautious with their orders. They all ordered high-priced items, which left her wondering how she was going to split the bill so that each person paid for what they had ordered, and not just make it an even split as was usually the custom when entire crews dined out together. More often than not she would pick up the entire check for her crew at restaurants as an act of friendship and because she knew her salary far outweighed those of the others, but this was not going to be one of those nights.

The Turks very solicitously offered the crew soups and salads, which the fools readily accepted, thinking perhaps that they were back home at the local *Red Lobster* and that the entree included a soup and salad. Valerie had been in Europe long enough to know better, to know that for every piece of bread they were served they would have to pay exorbitant prices.

"What do you say, ladies, should we try the salted fish?" Charlie appeared to be enjoying himself enormously.

The salted fish had been recommended by the waiter, which probably meant it was expensive as hell.

One of the flight attendants named Judy accepted to share the fish with Charlie because it was a huge amount, according to the waiter, that could feed two people.

Valerie did not think it was such a good idea, but refrained from giving the happy members of her crew any advice. They appeared very cheerful and she was not going to bring their spirits down when they already suspected she didn't really want to be there.

The waiters came with four bottles of some unpronounceable wine and presented Charlie Smith with the cork, awaiting his verdict. Charlie smelled it "Excellent!" he exclaimed, signaling for the waiter to pour some into his glass. He tasted it like a legitimate *connoisseur* and gave his approval, which started the waiters serving everybody.

Valerie was tired from the long day, not really looking forward to a three a.m. wake up call and wondering at what time she would be able to get to bed with this crazy bunch.

Thirty minutes later the food came and a few other Turkish customers materialized. They were all wearing coats and ties and the women wore dinner dresses, which only served to confirm Valerie's fears that she and her crew were grossly underdressed for this place, but she suspected the Turks would make them pay *dearly* for their insolent breach of etiquette.

The food was very good, she had to admit, observing the ceremonial serving of the salted fish. Two waiters brought a small cart next to their table, added some liquor to the fish in the pan and lit it, allowing it to glow in blue and yellow flames for ten seconds after which they produced a hammer and a chisel.

"Hey, Charlie," Valerie joked, "I hope you have good teeth."

Charlie poured himself some more red wine. "Naw, the fish'll be soft inside the shell. That white stuff you see all around is the salt they cooked it in. It's about an inch thick and they need the hammer and the chisel to break it up, but the fish inside will be nice and tender."

They observed the waiter as he skillfully delivered a couple of well-placed blows to the salt shell, cracking it. A real elegant show. The white fish inside smelled wonderful, and Valerie decided to relax a little and enjoy her dinner, since she was stuck there anyway.

"Waiter! Two more!" Charlie ordered more wine, which made Valerie wonder how much this was going to cost him, and also, she didn't really like this much wine with dinner. She didn't want her crew thinking that she was lax or irresponsible, allowing her crew to drink so much the night before a trip. Charlie liked his wine, that was obvious, and it confirmed rumors she'd heard around the airline that Charlie was once canned for liking his wine a little too much, which cost him a tour of the airline's rehab program.

The flight attendants and Charlie showered their engineer with all kinds of compliments on his stupendous idea to cross the Bosporus and dine here. Thomas ate it all up, loving it. It had been a close call when he was unable to find the ship, but it had all worked out for the best and his crew was happy.

After dinner came the multiple exotic deserts and the *Amarettos* and the cappuccinos. By the time the crew finished dinner, the dining room was brimming with local upper-class clientele. Valerie enjoyed dressing up and going out to dinner to an expensive place, but being here wearing jeans and sweats was not her idea of blending in.

The dreaded moment came when the head waiter presented Charlie with the bill. Valerie was slighted irritated by this male trait of automatically assuming that the man at the table was in charge, but she forgot her aggressiveness when she saw Charlie's face. She fought back laughter.

"Oh, shit!" he blurted out, sobering right then and there.

"What's the damage?" she figured maybe sixty bucks apiece.

Charlie whistled, swallowing hard. *"Fifteen hundred and sixty-one dollars!"*

Valerie felt faint. She knew it! "What!?"

Charlie was studying the bill, shaking his head. "One thousand of it is for the wine alone," he added in a voice bordering on hysteria. He looked as if he was ready to cry.

Valerie wanted to burst out laughing but contained herself, realizing her share of the remaining five hundred and sixty-one dollars would amount to eighty bucks, plus tip! She had known all alone she should have scalped Thomas but now she was sure. She should grab the salted fish knife, rip out his scalp and attach it to her flight bag. As she had forecast, they split the bill into seven equal shares, making her regret not having ordered soup, salad, desert and liquors like the rest of the crew. They paid and marched out to the waiting boat, which made Valerie remember that they still had that bill to deal with.

The ride back to the Istanbul side was quiet and solemn. The flight attendants and the engineer were shocked at having paid eighty dollars apiece for a dinner, and Charlie appeared to be shell-shocked from the wine bill. He was going to have to get pretty creative with his wife to explain that credit card voucher when the American Express bill came. A bill that size was enough to placate the party spirit out of any group.

Valerie promised herself she would never again go out with a crew anywhere if she couldn't bail out by just catching a taxi. The boat crew dropped them off near where they had originally boarded and added to the collective shock by charging them each fifty dollars apiece for the ride. Valerie was no longer pissed, now she wanted to laugh at some of the faces on her crew. The twenty-five-dollar dinner had resulted in about a hundred and forty bucks each, which was a real blow to the flight attendants and the newhire flight engineer.

FIVE
PRESENT TIME - BERLIN, GERMANY

"Hi, Elaine. Here's the box with the larger scarves, as promised, *and* here's your Visa card." Valerie was not amused at having fallen victim to the same request twice.

Elaine Griffin smiled what must be her most gracious grin. "Valerie, Karl and I have absolutely no words to express our gratitude to you. You came through for us twice, and I'm forever indebted to you." She reached for the package and the credit card.

Valerie was amused by the flowery language. Who did Elaine think she was impressing, her? "Happy to be of help, however, I want you to know that I can't do this anymore, Elaine, my conscience is starting to bug me."

Elaine held her forearm, squeezing her lightly, "I understand, and for this very reason I'm all the more grateful for the favor."

Valerie stood up, indicating to the Griffin woman that the conversation was over. They had once again met in the lobby of the hotel and now it was time to end it. "Well, Elaine, I have to meet someone for dinner so I guess this is good-bye."

Griffin stood. "Valerie, you're not married, are you?"

Now what? "No, why?"

"But you do have a boyfriend?"

"Yes." What was it any of her business?

"Good!" Griffin opened the enormous purse she was carrying, reaching deep inside it for something. "This," she offered, "is for your boyfriend then." She handed Valerie an expensive looking jewelry case.

"Oh, no! That's not necessary, Elaine. I can't accept it."

"Don't be silly! Remember? I told you I got lots of these."

Valerie opened the case and there was a man's Rolex staring back at her, brand-new. "No, I really can't do this. Please take it back."

"Listen here, Valerie," Elaine lowered her voice. "Take it, you'll be doing me a favor. I shouldn't tell you this and get you involved in my personal life, but if you don't take it my husband will most likely trade it for booze, like he has done in the past."

Valerie was surprised to hear this since Griffin didn't seem like the kind of woman who would be living with an alcoholic. She appeared too educated and well-dressed for that. "You're not shitting me, are you?"

Griffin looked absolutely depressed. "I wish I was."

"Okay, I'll take it then, but no more after this."

The smile was back. "You won't regret it! Thanks again for all your help, Valerie. I better let you go or you'll be late for your friend. I consider myself lucky to have made your acquaintance, captain!"

Valerie took the hand being offered but kept her distance to avoid being kissed like she had before. "It was my pleasure, Elaine. Good luck here in Berlin."

"Thank you a million! TGA sure is lucky to have you working for them."

Valerie left the woman standing there and headed for the elevators. She had to use the bathroom before heading out to dinner, and she didn't want to use the bathroom in the lobby or she'd never rid herself of this woman. In the elevator she opened the jewelry box again, admiring the watch. Paul Morris was going to absolutely die when she popped this on him! She still had to decide whether to tell him the whole story behind how she obtained it, but she had time to think about that.

Valerie unlocked her room and went to the bathroom, beginning to feel relaxed for the first time in days. She had finally told that Griffin woman that it was over, that she would not be available for any more favors, which made her feel liberated. The two watches had been an incredible bonus equivalent to the salary she made in one month, and she still could not believe this.

On her way out of her bathroom she noticed something on the carpet by the foot of the bed. Picking it up she realized it was one of the scarves she had brought from Istanbul, still wrapped in its cellophane envelope.

Oh, crap! She picked it up, rapidly exiting the room, running to the elevators.

Once down in the lobby she searched for Elaine Griffin but the woman was gone. Gone without one of her one hundred scarves! *Dammit*! This was turning into the never-ending-story. Now Valerie would have to contact Griffin to give her this scarf, and she had no way of doing this, since they never exchanged telephone numbers. Wait! She could just take the scarf with her back to New York at the end of the month and drop it in Julie's mailbox at the hangar. Yes, that seemed the best course of action, provided good old Elaine didn't show up here first, looking for her damn scarf.

Beautiful, just beautiful. She returned to her room to pick up her sweater and dropped the packaged scarf on the dresser. It hit the wood hard and the cellophane split open revealing two small white envelopes within.

Valerie walked over to the scarf, ripping open the cellophane wrapping. A total of four white paper envelopes dropped out from the scarf, each the size of restaurant sugar packs. They resembled the kind of small white envelopes found in expensive electronic equipment boxes to prevent humidity.

What the fuck...

She quickly reached for one, ripping it open, feeling the plastic inside giving. A very fine white powder spread across her dresser.

Oh, shit! Valerie was no police officer, but it didn't take a fucking genius to see what was going on there. She brought the envelope to her nose, smelling it, then dabbed her index finger in the stuff, tasting it. She really didn't have a clue what she was looking for, but had seen enough cop movies to know that if the stuff was bitter then it must be coke, or something equally bad.

The stuff was very bitter.

Her heart was accelerating to emergency speed, sweat beads beginning to form on her forehead. Oh, shit, *oh, shit!* This could not be true–but it was! She had been screwed! She yanked the receiver from the cradle and dialed Charlie Smith's room. Please, be in your room!

"Hullo?"

"Charlie? Valerie here! Can you come down to my room? I need to talk to you right away!"

"Valerie? What's the matter, you alright?"

"Just come on down, Charlie. I need to talk to you right now!" Her tone of voice left no doubt that she was in trouble.

"Be right there" he said, hanging up.

Valerie stared incredulous at the white powder covering her dresser top and sticking to her fingers. That fucking bitch! She had been set up! The entire episode had been a setup! She stared at her Rolex and furiously snatched it from her wrist, throwing it on the bed. Damn! How could she have been so stupid? What in God's name had she been thinking? Free Rolexes? Yeah, right!

There was a loud knock on her door. "Valerie? Open up, it's me, Charlie!"

She unlocked the door and he walked in, surveying the room, searching for a possible assailant. Satisfied that she was alone he asked her what gives.

"You're not gonna believe what has just happened to me."

"Try me."

She told him the whole story.

"Sonofabitch!"

"That's what I said!"

Charlie sat on her dresser, staring at the white powder and at the two Rolex pieces. "Valerie, this is some serious shit."

"Tell me something I don't know, Charlie. What do you think we should do, call the cops right away?"

"The German police? Not on your life!" her use of the "we" had not escaped him. "No, Valerie, they would never believe that you had nothing to do with this. You brought in the scarves illegally, remember? and they'll take you right into one of their jails. TGA will fire your ass the minute they get word that you've been arrested for drug trafficking and it'll be up to you to prove your innocence every step of the way. No way, that is not a wise choice."

Valerie had already ran all that past her mind, but felt better hearing Charlie say it.

"So what do you suggest?"

"My first instinct is to run, go back to the States as soon as you can, tonight. Call in sick or tell them your grandma died or make up some other excuse but get the hell out of here. For some reason which we still ignore these people singled you out from among all the captains in Berlin to carry their mail, and I think that is very bad news."

"I agree with you about getting out of here asap, Charlie, but what if they smell a rat and try to stop me? The minute Elaine counts the scarves she'll realize I have one left and she'll come after me. If they somehow find out that I escaped they may think I'm going to rat on them and they'll come after me."

"Shit, you're right. Okay, let's analyze this. These sweethearts are obviously smuggling this shit, whatever it is, from Istanbul to God knows where, and they are using airline pilots and flight attendants to unwillingly carry the stuff into Germany."

"Charlie, you're assuming that pilots and flight attendants are carrying the stuff unwillingly. What about the Rolexes? Don't you think that perhaps they were paving the way for the future? Maybe more gifts? Maybe cash?"

Charlie looked at her. "A real drug-trafficking cartel within the airlines? A real scary proposition. Valerie, whatever they're doing, you want no part of it. Unfortunately, you don't speak German and the Berlin police would love nothing more than to get a real live American airline captain in their web. You cannot, under any circumstances, permit this. This is something that needs to be taken care of with Americans. Somehow we have to get in touch with American authorities and recruit their help."

"Here in Berlin? C'mon, Charlie, get real!"

"No, not here in Berlin. Tell you what. I'll get you some more hotel stationary and I want you to jot down everything that has happened since this Julie broad brought this up to you at operations. I want you to take your time and write down every single detail you can think of. Skip nothing and include everything you remember, and tomorrow morning I'll jump-seat to New York on American out of Frankfurt and go talk to the FBI, the CIA or whomever takes responsibility for this sort of operation."

"I think the D.E.A. is probably who we want."

"I'll try them too. I think maybe this is a better idea than you bolting out of here, which like you say may piss off your new friends. How many more Istanbul flights do you have this month?"

"One."

"Forget it. Call in sick, but under no circumstances take that flight. That would be an excellent opportunity to get rid of you by tipping off German customs. They will probably contact you again and ask you to bring back some more scarves, but don't turn them down, say yes initially but then develop some menstrual cramps or something and ditch the flight."

"Okay, makes sense, but you're forgetting that we have this one scarf here with its white snow and that they are going to come looking for it a lot sooner than next week when I have the Istanbul trip."

Charlie thought about this. "Well, there's always the possibility that the guy in Istanbul shorted you one scarf, but you're right. They will probably contact you soon. The only thing I can think of that you should do is play along with them, don't let them feel that you're pissed or ready to bail out."

"What do you think we should do after you talk to our guys?"

"I'll jump-seat back here as soon as possible, day after tomorrow if I can. Hopefully, I'll bring instructions and allies back with me."

"Okay, I can do that. If they contact me before you get back, I'll play along."

"Dammit, Valerie, how did we get into this shit?"

She loved him for using the "we." Charlie was definitely the kind of ally one would want when the shit hit the fan. "It was definitely my fault. Big fuck up, but now I have to do something."

"Valerie, grab some of your stuff and move to my room. Stay there until I get back. Nobody will find you that way. Stay indoors as much as possible and if you leave the room, try to keep where there's other people. This could be a small operation but somehow these two expensive watches tell me otherwise."

Valerie felt the bile rise in her throat. She had done everything so well to become an airline pilot, and now these bastards were jeopardizing everything she had worked all her life for. "I'll do all that, Charlie. Don't expose yourself on my account but hurry back!"

Charlie stood. "I'm going to my room to bring you all the hotel stationary I have. After you document your story we'll move you into my room."

"Do you think they'll be watching me?"

"Hard to tell, Valerie, but it's better to play it safe and assume so. Anytime drugs are involved it's better to think the worst and prepare for it. Have you told anyone else about this? Paul Morris maybe?"

"No. You're the only one."

"I suggest you keep it this way."

Valerie thought about this. Paul Morris could not really help her at this moment from the States, and she shouldn't use the phone for long distance calls because they could be tapping it. Later she could go out and find a long-distance telephone booth and call him collect. No way Elaine and whoever she was working for could tap into every public phone in Berlin. Phone tapping? God, was she getting paranoid or what?

"Charlie, I believe these guys have access to our crew scheduling computer system."

"What makes you think that's the case?" "Because yesterday Elaine Griffin showed up here right before we were picked up to go to the airport, remember? I asked her how she knew I'd be taking the Istanbul flight and she said that she'd just ventured a wild guess and come by the hotel hoping to find me here."

"She didn't call you first?"

"No, she just appeared here as we were boarding the van."

"No shit. She knew you were taking out the Istanbul flight then. Maybe her sister Julie gave her a printout of your monthly schedule."

Valerie assumed that Charlie had reverted to his Navy training, do not underestimate your enemy. "Yeah, that is a strong possibility. But Charlie, if I hide in your room then they won't be able to contact me to get this scarf."

Charlie considered what she was saying and had to agree that it made sense. "You're right. Stay here in this room just in case they try to make contact with you, then, if they do, move over to my room. I'll leave you my key before I go tomorrow. Don't go anywhere with this woman and stay away from sidewalks. It's all too easy to pull a woman into a parked car or a van."

"Oh, crap! Thanks. Charlie."

"Valerie, we have to keep you in one piece until I can talk to some Americans about this. I really wish we could trust the Germans but neither one of us speaks German and besides, what if these sweethearts smuggling drugs have contacts within the local police? No, we're much better off dealing with our own people."

The telephone rang.

"Jesus!" Charlie jumped.

Valerie looked at him questioningly.

"Answer it, Valerie. Keep cool."

She reached for the handset. "Hello?"

"Valerie?" It was Elaine Griffin's voice.

"Speaking, who is this?"

"Valerie, this is Elaine Griffin. I am downstairs in the lobby. After I left here I realized you'd only given me ninety-nine scarves so I came back to see if by any chance you happened to have the missing one."

"Ah, yes, I do have the missing one, Elaine. Hang on and I'll bring it down."

"Valerie, you're such an angel!"

She hung up, feeling shaken and on the verge of tears, cursing herself for her uncontrollable honesty. She should've told Elaine that she didn't have any of her damn scarves. "She's downstairs, Charlie. She counted the scarves and found she was one short."

"Didn't waste any time, did she? Good! Now, go down there and give her the scarf, this way you can go right into my room after she leaves."

"I don't know if I can do this..."

"Valerie, don't be stupid. You've got to play the game with these people or they will most certainly hurt you!"

She took a deep breath. "I can't pretend as if I know nothing since I opened that package. She will know I'm on to her the minute she sees I opened the cellophane wrap. Goddammit, I should've played dumb and told her I had no more scarves!"

"Okay, then it's up to you to make the first move. Tell her you're on to her and that you want to continue doing what she wants but that you want a cut.

"WHAT DO YOU MEAN?"

"Pretend you want to be recruited."

"No fucking way!"

Charlie stood, walking over to the window. "Valerie, if these people are what I think they are, they're not playing games. You just saw how fast they noticed the missing scarf. Bullshit them and they'll see right through it and do anything they can to protect themselves. Besides, they've already recruited you whether you like it or not. You carried this shit across the border twice already."

"You don't really think she'll believe me that I want to become a drug dealer do you? Why the hell would I want to become a drug dealer when I make a perfectly good living as an airline pilot? She'll never buy it."

"Not a drug dealer, just a mule. And she will believe you if you increase your price considerably since the only thing these people understand is greed."

She thought about this. She did not want to have anything more to do with the entire situation, and her first instinct was to pack up and return to the States, but he was right, that would be stupid. Valerie picked up the scarf from the dresser. "Should I take the open bag as well?"

"Yes, give it to her and point out that you don't want her goods, just her money. Drug dealers get very touchy when someone steals their goods."

"How would you know that?"

"I watch TV, now get moving, she's waiting for you."

Valerie collected all the pieces of cellophane, the drug envelopes and the scarf and left the room. This was a very dangerous game of cat and mouse she was going to be playing, and she did not like it one bit.

Elaine Griffin waved at her from her comfortable couch in the hotel lobby. "Valerie! Over here!"

Valerie walked over to the woman and ignored the outstretched hand being offered. "I believe I have something that belongs to you," she stated.

Griffin's face clouded over, puzzled by Valerie's words and her refusal to shake hands.

"You found the scarf?"

"Yeah, I found your scarf. I also found the goodies inside the scarf."

Elaine Griffin's face remained impassive. A true poker player. "Oh?"

"Don't play games with me anymore, Elaine. I know exactly what you're doing and the kind of business you're in."

"Is that so?"

"Yes."

"And what do you intend to do about it?" Griffin visually estimated the distance between herself and the front door of the hotel, calculating how long it would take her to cover it, then reached in her purse, "mind if I smoke?" her hand closed around a small semi-automatic Colt pistol she carried in her purse, loaded with explosive ammunition. One bullet could blow up a person's head like a watermelon being hit with a baseball bat swung by Babe Ruth.

"Please, don't. Smoke irritates me. What I intend to do about it, Elaine, is to get my fair share in this deal!"

Elaine Griffin took in the answer, exhaled and released her grip on the semi-automatic. "Your fair share? Well, in that case, dear, may I suggest we go in the bar and have a drink?"

"I'd love to, Elaine, and *you* are buying. I've already made you enough money this week."

They sat at a table removed from the other customers, ordered *schnapps* and Valerie laid the scarf with its ripped cellophane on the table in front of Elaine. "The goods are inside. I opened one but didn't help myself to any of it. I'm not interested in that shit, but I'm sure as hell interested in getting paid for my services."

Griffin studied the TGA captain. She appeared to be an intelligent woman, and it was obvious she didn't speak German, which reassured her that no deal had been made with the German police. No way the TGA captain could have set up a trap in cooperation with the *Politzei* without a decent command of their language. "You didn't like the watches?"

"Yeah, I liked the watches, but they should've been the solid-gold models, not the cheap-shit metal ones."

"Would you have believed my saleswoman story if I'd given you gold watches?"

Valerie hesitated, "No."

"There you go then."

"Screw the watches and the saleswoman story. I don't want goddamn watches Elaine, I want hard cash. I will help you out and work with you and whatever organization you're with, but I want money, not trinkets."

Griffin sipped on her schnapps. This woman seemed to have good business sense, which was a must in any operative. Perhaps they could use her indeed. "And what kind of money were you thinking of?"

Valerie didn't have a fucking clue. What was the going rate for a gram of cocaine or heroine? She didn't have the slightest idea. What was the price for a decent Mercedes Benz?

"Fifty thousand dollars per carry," she blurted out, praying that she hadn't blown it.

Elaine didn't answer her right away, but removed her lighter and cigarette case from her purse, lighting one. "Since it appears that we may be working together you might as well get used to me. I smoke."

Valerie nodded acceptance. *One for you, Elaine.*

"Fifty thousand dollars, eh?"

"Yes, and not a cent less. I make over a hundred thou a year without getting involved with your kind of activities, and if I'm going to put my neck out on the line it's going to cost you."

"Fifty thousand is a lot of money, Valerie," she inhaled and sipped her schnapps, "but I guess it's not totally unreasonable. Of course you understand that it's not up to me to decide. I have to carry your offer to those in charge of making the big decisions. I'm just a small pawn here, you do understand that?"

"Elaine, I don't care who you have to talk to or whether you're somebody's girlfriend or somebody's mother. You pay me fifty thousand dollars in advance for every operation in which you use my services and I will give you your money's worth. I can fly back and forth between any of the world's continents, which should definitely be an asset to you in this kind of business."

Griffin liked her aggressiveness. The Organization would have to follow the usual procedures with her before entrusting her with either knowledge or responsibility, but she might make a good recruit after all. "Yes, you're correct, we can use people like you in our line of work, and I'm certainly glad that you decided to talk to me about it. You do realize that there is a certain element of risk involved?"

"What kind of fool do you think I am, Elaine? I fly jets for a living, I know what risk is. And how come you bring it up now, after you exposed me twice already to German customs?"

"Before, you were expendable."

Valerie didn't like the sound of that. "And now?"

Griffin smiled at her, "now you are a potential asset, Valerie and therefore no longer expendable."

"Wonderful! I'll drink to that!"

HER KNEES WERE WEAK just like after sex as she rode the elevator back up to her room. Like it or not, she was in it up to her ears now. There was not much chance now of calling on the German police for help and expecting them to believe her story. She was making the situation more complicated by the minute but she realized it was probably the only way out without ending up in a river with cement shoes. Would Elaine do that to her? Probably. Drugs meant big money, and whenever big money was involved people became rather extreme.

She had put on a performance worthy of an Academy Award, and hoped Elaine had swallowed it. Fifty thousand dollars per carry! She felt like some cheap actress mouthing off lines from some low-budget Hollywood gangster flick. Maybe she would get back in her room, pack her things and get the hell out of here tonight.

"So you think she bought your story?" Charlie had been watching over her the entire time she had been talking business with the Griffin bitch. He had blended into the background of businessmen and tourists but keeping an eye out for possible trouble. He had joined her in the elevator at the end of the meeting, pretending he didn't know her until the elevator doors closed.

"I don't know, Charlie. She might have believed me and then again who knows?" She recounted the events to her first officer and they went in her room to gather her things.

"I don't like these assholes using TGA crews for their dirty business, Valerie. I'm going to find someone who can help us shitcan these people. If you hadn't discovered the drugs you might have been disposed of when you became no longer useful. I don't mean they would kill you, but they could very easily have tipped off the customs people and you would've been caught with God-knows-what in your flight bag."

"Tell me one good reason why I shouldn't just pack up and get the hell out of here tonight, Charlie."

"Not a good idea, Valerie. If you disappear now they will come after you, I can assure you that. Let's get your gear and move you over to my room. Don't worry, I'll sleep on the floor tonight and leave first thing in the morning."

"Don't you think we should try talking to our embassy people here?"

"Valerie, I don't know much about consular authority, but I've seen enough movies about our foreign service and its inefficient bureaucrats to know better than to depend on them. No, I think we're better off going with plan number one. I'll be in New York by mid-afternoon tomorrow and I'll get help from people who know what they're doing."

Valerie snickered. "So I guess I have been officially recruited?"

"First-round draft pick babe, I'm afraid."

"Oh, shit."

The two aviators moved some of her things from Valerie's room. No need to give away their game to the enemy by totally vacating her own room. If these folks were as good as Charlie suspected they were and if they had access to as much money as he suspected they had, then it would be a breeze to hire a room maid to check up on Valerie.

"Charlie, I have to call Paul Morris and let him know what's going on."

Charlie hesitated. "Why?"

She became slightly irritated, "because he's planning on coming out here and because I want him to know what's going on."

"Okay, okay. I was just being cautious, that's all. I would suggest you don't call him from the hotel. Go out and use a payphone in the street. And make sure he doesn't spill the beans to anyone before I have a chance to talk to the Feds in New York."

"He won't tell anybody."

"You told me he works for Honeywell in Phoenix?"

"Yes."

"Be careful what you say over the open line, Valerie. I don't know much about European communications but I know our army monitors the American airwaves very closely. Remember years ago that Delta L-1011 over the north Atlantic that fucked up and went off course because the Delta boys were newcomers to the Atlantic routes and they almost collided with a Continental Boeing 747?"

"No, I don't remember."

"Sure you do. The Delta crew called the Continental pilots on their radio and tried talking them into covering up the near-miss which the Continental crew refused to do, and the whole episode was picked up by one of our AWACS planes so the Air Force came forth and offered their tapes when it came time to hang the Delta crew."

"Okay, I recall that incident. You're correct. I'll be extremely careful when I talk with Paul."

"Did you have anything to eat yet? I've to be up early to catch my ride to New York so it'd be better to wrap it up for the night."

"No. I was going to meet Adam Dee for some German food but now I don't feel like it and I want to go outside and call Paul."

"I'll come with you. Forget Dee, he'll find someone else to eat with him. We'll get you a Bratwurst at one of the *imbiss* nearby." The *imbiss* was the German version of the hot dog cart vendor.

Forget Dee? She didn't like just standing her friend up like that. She'd been friends with Adam Dee for as long as she'd been with TGA.

"I'll leave Adam Dee a note with the front desk." God, maybe she should have dinner with Adam and get his help. They'd known each other for so long...she could still remember the day they met thirteen years before, it seemed like yesterday.

THE FOURTH STRIPE   Maurice Azurdia

SIX

THIRTEEN YEARS AGO - VALENCIA, CALIFORNIA,
UNITED STATES

Valerie called the MidAmerica personnel gal first thing
Monday morning and was given all the necessary
directions to fly to St. Louis via Salt Lake City the
following day, courtesy of MidAmerica Air Lines.

She stayed up late that night, deciding which suit to
wear to the interview, finally settling on her dark gray
flannel suit with the white cotton blouse. She had to
appear professional and elegant yet conservative. This
was a man's world she was entering, and she was smart
enough to realize that femininity could be her worst
enemy if not handled properly. Anything too feminine and
they would brand her a flirt, anything too stark and they
would label her a dike. Better to spend some time
deciding what to wear but get it right the first time, she
thought. Not that there was a second chance to make a
first impression either.

Valerie was twenty-five, single and living in a small
apartment in Valencia, California, just north of the San
Fernando Valley, where she had been for the last two
years. Flying with Jack had been an extraordinary
opportunity because it looked good on the resume and
the man did teach her how to work as a crewmember and
how to handle jets, if one ignored his other less positive
qualities. She finalized her suitcase preparations and
went in her small kitchen to pour herself a glass of cold
milk. Cracking a smile, she remembered the first time she
ever flew the Sabreliner with Jack. The biggest airplane
she had flown up to that point had been a Cessna 402, a

small twin-engine job with eight seats, so she had been electrified, sitting there next to Jack during their first take off from Van Nuys. The powerful business jet had accelerated faster than she could imagine possible and she had been way behind the airplane mentally, but nonetheless it had been exhilarating to the extreme and she had absolutely loved every minute of it.

She had been home twenty-four hours and still had not heard from Jack or the Osters, so she wondered how she stood with them. Tomorrow she would be embarking into a new stage of her life, interviewing with the airlines, and she hoped things worked out right. She knew that sooner or later she'd have to search for another corporate job, but hoped that the airlines would hire her first.

The following morning, she walked up to the Delta counter at Los Angeles International Airport, LAX.

"Good morning! And where are we traveling to today?" the chirpy airline customer service agent asked her.

"Good morning. I, ah–I'm traveling to St. Louis for an interview with MidAmerica Air Lines, and I was told that you folks would have a telex or a fax from MidAmerica issuing me a pass." Oh, shit. She should have asked the MidAmerica personnel woman to overnight the pass to her instead of having to go through this. What if someone fucked up and there was no pass? Aside from not making it to St. Louis, it would be very embarrassing.

"May I see some identification, please?"

She fumbled in her travel bag for her wallet, pulling out her driver's license and a Visa card and handing them to the man.

"Just a minute, please," he turned and disappeared through the doorway behind the counter.

Great, just great. Now he would come out with his supervisor and they would ask her what the hell she was talking about, that this was Delta Air Lines, not MidAmerica and everyone else around the counter would feast on her humiliation.

The agent returned with a brown piece of paper, obviously torn from a telex machine. "We have your pass authorization, Miss Wall. If you just give me a minute, I'll print out a ticket for you."

She felt her knees grow weak with relief and gratitude. Maybe she should just try to relax and everything would fall into place. She must not allow her excitement to obfuscate her thought process. MidAmerica did not fly into Los Angeles, so they had arranged for an interline pass to get her to St. Louis with Delta. Of course the pass was there; these were airline professionals, they would not fuck up on something like this.

The printer behind the counter buzzed and printed furiously. The agent grabbed her ticket and handed it to her. "If you just sign there I'll have you on your way, Miss."

She took the pen and initialed the ticket.

"Thank you," the agent smiled at her, placed the ticket inside a jacket and handed it to her. "That way to the boarding gates, Miss, gate thirty-seven and it should be leaving on time."

"Thank you, thanks a lot." She wanted to appear soave and sophisticated to the agent but she doubted she was doing such a good job. Valerie reached the gate and the flight was already boarding, so she went straight to the flight attendant standing by the jetway door and handed her the jacket with the ticket in it.

"Good morning," the woman offered, taking a look at her ticket. "You can go right in. First door on your left."

First door? Valerie double-checked her ticket. It was a First Class ticket! The first door to her left took her directly into the plush First Class cabin. Another flight attendant standing just inside the aircraft door welcomed her and asked to see her ticket.

"You have seat one-A, right over here."

Valerie glanced at the flight attendant and wondered if Delta had some kind of factory where they turned out similar-looking women to fill their flight attendant positions. Both women she had talked to so far had been beautiful, with seemingly perfect makeup and spotless uniforms. This particular flight attendant seemed to have a never-ending smile frozen across her face. Come on, sister, knock off the charm, I'm one of yours, for Chrissake!

"Good luck!" the flight attendant smiled at her again and went back to stand by the door.

Good luck? That was nice of her! But how in the devil did she know that Valerie was going on an interview? She pulled out her ticket and studied it to see if her status was indicated anywhere, but failed to see anything obvious. Must be some kind of airline code, she reflected. Well, it was nice of her to say that. She felt good with the camaraderie the flight attendant had shown her. It wasn't anything big, but it had made her feel good.

Bring a book to read, the MidAmerica personnel woman had suggested on the phone, because there will be a lot of waiting, and Valerie had brought her latest novel, but she found herself unable to read even the first page. Her mind just could not concentrate on reading when she was on her way to what might be her future. A future she had visualized many times, but only in her dreams.

She had called Paul Morris the minute she returned home from Sun Valley, but had been unable to talk with him because he had gone sailing to Catalina Island for the week-end with another buddy of his.

Her future husband, Paul Morris and his friend Rick had purchased a sailboat together and whenever she was away on a long trip Paul Morris would go out and play with it. Since she wasn't expected back for another week, he had taken off. She had left a message on his machine anyway, just in case he called in to check for messages from Catalina. She wanted to share with him what had happened in Sun Valley with Jack and the excitement of her first interview with the airlines. She knew that one had to interview with several carriers before landing a job, but there was always the hope that the first one would be it.

Her mother had been thrilled by the news of her interview, but Valerie had intentionally avoided telling her about the incident in Sun Valley. Her mother had always disapproved of her chosen path in life, and Valerie knew that telling her mother about the Jacks of the world was an invitation for I-told-you-so. Her dad had been proud of her desire to fly and given her his complete financial and moral support, without which she could have never made it, but her mom's opinion was that women should play certain designated roles in life, and that of a female pilot was not one of them. Her heart grew sad thinking of her dad, and she silently said, see, Dad, I told you I would do it. Here I am, going for my first airline interview!

Her dad had left them five years earlier, succumbing to a fatal heart attack which had taken him at fifty-one.

She once again ran through the mental checklist she had prepared, making sure that she brought along her logbook, licenses and miscellaneous required paperwork.

FIVE HOURS LATER SHE was at Lambert Field in St. Louis, checking the courtesy phones for hotels in the vicinity of the airport. MidAmerica Air Lines had picked up the tab for her First Class ticket, but she had to pay for her own hotel and meals while she was there. She regretfully bypassed the Hilton and the Sheraton, looking for something more affordable, and picked up the line to the local Econolodge. With a name like that, it couldn't be that expensive, she mused.

The hotel van picked her up in front of the main gate and drove her to a decent hotel about a mile from the airport. She checked in and found herself in a clean room with two double beds, a TV with pay-per-view cardboard signs on it and a little, clean bathroom. Now she had to hurry up and wait, which was always the bad part. She unpacked, wondering where she could go to get a hamburger before turning in. She intended to get as much rest as possible.

SHE CALLED FOR A taxi at seven-thirty the following morning and the Yellow Cab was at the door of the hotel ten minutes later. Valerie slid into the back seat, wondering what item she might have left behind. Of course, if she had left anything important behind, now it was too late, so she decided to relax and enjoy the ride.

"What's there to do here in St. Louis?" she might as well make conversation with the African-American cab driver.

"Yo first time here, Ma'am?"

"Yes, and I'm surprised how green everything is. It looks more like the Amazon rain forest than the Midwest."

The black cabbie smiled and looked at her in his rear-view mirror. "Ma'am, if you ain't got nuthin' to do, St. Louis is the place to do it at!"

Valerie laughed and made some more small talk until the driver stopped in front of a three-story concrete building next to the control tower. "This is it!" he barked.

"This is the MidAmerica flight operations building?" she had expected something bigger.

"Yes, Ma'am. This is it. I've brought several of you pilots here over here this past week. I'm sure, this is it." Then he added. "You are a pilot, ain't you Ma'am?"

Valerie proudly replied that yes, she was a pilot, paid him and left the taxi. So the cab driver had brought several other pilots before her, uhm? Not good. She would've liked to have been the first one called in, but of course that was not realistic. MidAmerica had probably already called in for interviews all the top guns, the number one draft picks, the ex-military jocks. No use getting depressed.

She walked in.

As it turned out there wasn't much time to read her paperback. She spent the first hour filling out paperwork and the next hour undergoing a preliminary medical examination with a company nurse. She was weighed, measured, shoved into a sound-proof booth to test her hearing and asked to give a urine sample. She was the only female candidate she could detect around, although she was not really sure who was a candidate because there were so many people coming and going all the time. Finally, she was ushered to the office of the Chief Pilot, where she joined six other individuals, probably pilots, sitting in the waiting room.

All men.

She sat at one end of the room, discreetly checking out the competition. From what she could estimate, their ages ranged from their mid-twenties to over forty, and they all *looked* the part. Almost to a man they were wearing navy blue suits, white shirts and very short haircuts. Valerie felt self-conscious sitting there with this group. They were probably all F-16 pilots and resented her presence in their world, but if that was the case, then tough luck, guys. She was just as smart as any of them, no, actually smarter, because she was in there interviewing along with them, and she had the odds stacked against her because she was a woman.

"Good morning, gentlemen!" The voice of a man who must be the chief pilot brought her back in a snap.

"And lady," the man added once he saw her sitting at the end of the row. He looked in his fifties, slightly overweight in a gray two-piece suit. They all stood.

"My name is Robert Eakle and I am the Chief Pilot for MidAmerica Air Lines." He paused to look at the candidates. "I want to welcome every one of you here and give you a little bit of information. You are all highly-qualified individuals with Airline Transport Pilot licenses and averaging three thousand hours of flight experience, and you have all been hand-picked by our hiring captains for this interview. As you know, we're a small airline, we operate fifty DC-9s and we're very careful about expanding. We will be adding five new aircraft to the fleet and that is the reason why you're all here. We'll need to hire ninety new first officers by the end of the year and you are among the first to be interviewed."

Valerie was absorbing every word, not wanting to miss anything.

"The sequence of these interviews is not relevant as to who gets hired because we will look at all the candidates before we make the decision to hire. We'll be interviewing close to eight hundred candidates for classes starting towards the end of this year."

Valerie's heart sank. Eight hundred candidates? For ninety positions? That meant that only one in nine would get a job offer! And not until the end of the year!? She felt angry and disappointed at the same time. The odds were ridiculous, and they had brought her all the way to St. Louis for a job that might not even be there for another six months!

"We pay $900 a month your first year with the company and $4,000 a month starting your second year. If you are with us for five years and become disabled, you will retire with fifty percent of your highest W-2. It takes about twelve years to make captain with this airline. Today you will each have the opportunity to interview with me and later with another one of our line captains. Those of you who are selected will then be flown in for an intensive medical exam, which if you pass, we will then offer you a class date as DC-9 first officers. I wish each and every one of you the best of luck and let's get started."

The pilot at the opposite end from Valerie stood up, shook hands with the chief pilot and followed him into his office, shutting the door behind them.

Valerie's spirits sagged. Eight hundred applicants. And all with high qualifications. And now she was stuck having to wait for her turn with the chief pilot after all the other candidates had gone in because of her sitting position. Oh, shit.

"So I guess we're among the chosen few, eh?" The candidate sitting next to her offered. He looked like an ad for a Navy recruiting poster, tall, lean and dark, and with a boyish smile that was supposed to melt women foolish enough to fall for it.

"I guess."

"The name's Adam Dee." He offered his hand, which she took reluctantly. She was definitely not in the mood to make casual conversation.

"Hi, Adam. I'm Valerie. Valerie Wall."

"What're you flying now?" He questioned, "if you don't mind my asking that is."

She did mind, but then he could be a stool pigeon, placed there by the personnel office to do some additional, discrete screening. She must appear friendly.

"I fly a Sabreliner," she said curtly.

"A Sabreliner? Wow! Jet time! I wish I had some of that."

Her curiosity got the best of her. "Why? What are you flying?"

"I just got out of the Navy. P-3 Orions."

Oh, yeah. P-3s, antisubmarine patrol aircraft, and that's all? Figures. P-3 Orions, the military version of the Lockheed Electra. Antisubmarine patrols probably, and the dumb sonofagun wanted jet time! She felt like a schoolgirl next to Adam Dee. How could her few hours flying copilot to Jack compare to the experience this guy had? This guy had probably flown all over the world, landing in places she couldn't even pronounce!

One hour later she was sitting across the desk from Captain Robert Eakle.

"I see that you went to Drake," he had a friendly, warm smile.

"Yes, aerospace engineering." She didn't really think she had too much of a chance to get hired with such odds, but she liked the captain and decided to be polite.

"My wife is from Iowa," Eakle continued, smiling, "from the Quad Cities area."

No shit. "Really? Are you from Iowa?" she asked.

"No, Springfield, Missouri. What about you, you from Iowa?"

"No, but my dad was from Middlebury, Indiana. I live in Los Angeles now, but I'm kind of from all over."

"Army brat?"

"No, my father was with the diplomatic corps." No need to expand on that one; if she told him that her dad had been an ambassador he might assume she was just another spoiled rich girl who didn't really need this job.

"Diplomatic corps. Eh? Well, you must have gotten a good Midwestern education at Drake. My wife would really like you. She works with several of the universities raising funds for our special program that we have here at MidAmerica. We fly terminally-ill children to Disneyland with their parents."

Valerie's impression of Robert Eakle and of MidAmerica Air Lines gained a couple of points. "You guys do that?"

"You bet. We try to give kids the dreams they might not be able to pursue otherwise. My wife is on the executive committee that organizes the entire program."

That got him going and before he realized he had exceeded the designated time slot he had set aside for Miss Wall. "I didn't mean to go on like this about our program. Sorry about that."

"That's okay, I find what you are doing absolutely extraordinary." How did she go from interviewee to counselor, she didn't know, but she had enjoyed the talk.

"Anyway, as I mentioned to you all out there, we're fixing to add some new aircraft to the fleet, and we'll select our newhires after all the interviewing has been completed." He paused to look at her with a fatherly shadow across his eyes. "Valerie, my advice to you is this: accept the first offer that comes your way from any airline. Don't sit there waiting for your favorite. In this industry luck counts as much as preparation and experience, so don't turn your back on any offers."

Valerie was slightly annoyed. They had flown her all the way to St. Louis to tell her this. She already knew this, and now she had given up almost all hope of ever flying for MidAmerica. She wasn't dense, what he was basically telling her was: don't wait for us to call you.

"Thank you for the advice, Captain Eakle, but I really like MidAmerica and I want to live here in the Midwest, so I'll wait. I'm in no hurry, I've got a good job." She couldn't believe she was actually saying this. What it got down to was that she realized they were not going to give her much of an opportunity to work there, so she really didn't care what happened at this point. Might as well leave on a good note, though.

The chief pilot stood up, extending his hand. "Good luck!"

She thanked him and was directed to another office, where she was met by a tall, blonde man in his mid-fifties.

"Captain Don Ostmann. Come in!" He invited her to take a seat across from him and explained to her that he would ask her a few questions that were asked of all the applicants. He was very pleasant and courteous, and Valerie liked him right away.

"Did Robert treat you right?"

"Yes, he was very nice."

"Good, he's got a reputation for toughness, but he's all heart. I read your application, and you seem to be pretty experienced. Tell me, what can you offer

MidAmerica that makes you better qualified than the other applicants we have interviewed?"

She hated this aspect of the interview. "Captain Ostmann," she managed to produce a smile, "since I don't know the qualifications of the other applicants you have interviewed, I can hardly compare myself to them without sounding presumptuous. What I can tell you is why I feel I would make you a good first officer. I have been flying a Sabreliner for the past twelve months, which, as you know, is a twin engine jet operated by two pilots, which is a very similar operation to yours. From what I understand, the handling characteristics of the Sabreliner are somewhat similar to those of the DC-9s, which would probably make my transition to your fleet relatively painless." She paused for air. "Other than that, I can assure you that given the opportunity, I would give my best to this airline." That sure must be the corniest speech Captain Ostmann had heard all day, but she didn't really care.

She saw him write down her answers for the next fifteen minutes, then he shook her hand, gifted her with another big smile and she was done.

The taxi ride back to the hotel and the van ride to the airport did not even register in her memory. She found herself back at her apartment in Valencia, fumbling in her purse for her keys, exhausted both mentally and physically. She had allowed herself to get high on the possibility of getting her first job offer, and had not counted on the reality of airline hiring. The odds were ridiculous–eight hundred interviewees! What kind of odds were those? That was a joke.

She greeted her cat Mustang and removed her traveling clothes, pouring herself a Coke. Tomorrow will be another day, as Scarlet used to say. She would tackle reality in the morning; for now, all she wanted was to get some sleep. Maybe she had made a mistake wanting to become an airline pilot. How could she hope to compete with guys like that Adam Dee, with antisubmarine experience? They would probably laugh at her.

One thing she did not want to do except as a last resort was to fly for the commuters. She had enough friends flying commuter aircraft to know that it was not a desirable job at all. The pay stunk, they flew your ass off and safety was not paramount because of low cash flows. No, she really didn't cherish the thought of flying for one, but she suspected that perhaps that might be the way to get some quasi-airline flying experience and lots of flight time. She would think about this in the morning.

THE FOURTH STRIPE

Maurice Azurdia

SEVEN
PRESENT TIME - BERLIN, GERMANY

"AT&T International?"

Valerie cheered up hearing the voice of the American operator. It was like a part of home. She placed a call to Paul's work number in Phoenix giving her credit card number to the operator from one of the yellow public telephone booths across from the church. It was almost nine in the evening in Berlin, so it would be nearly noon in Arizona. She prayed she would catch him before he left on his lunch break. He carried a cellular telephone with call forwarding when he was not at his desk but he would be eating with other engineers and she wanted to catch him by himself.

"Honeywell, good afternoon. How may I direct your call?"

"Extension 236, please."

"Just a moment."

She heard the telephone switching.

"Paul Morris."

"Paul! Hi, darling, it's Valerie."

His tone became relaxed. "Valerie! Hi, honey, everything alright?" Valerie seldom called him at work, especially from overseas.

"Not quite," she didn't want to alarm him by not giving him enough information about what was going on but on the other hand Charlie thought she had to be careful about saying too much over an open line. God, she was beginning to think like a damn spook! Charlie was getting carried away by all this craziness. Nobody was going to give a crap about what she said over a public phone.

"Are you alright?" His tone was one of concern.

"Yes, I am–for now anyway. Something has come up, Paul, and we need to cancel your trip out here..."

She proceeded telling him the entire story from start to end, omitting names.

Paul Morris was silent for a moment after she finished. The ever-calculating engineer. "I'm coming over on the first flight I can catch."

"Paul, I don't know that this is such a good idea. I may have to get out of here in a hurry and I wouldn't want you on your way here then."

"What about this guy Charlie, do you trust him?"

"Of course! He's my first officer."

"That's not what I mean, Valerie. How do you know he is not working for the same people who set you up?"

"No way. He is ex-Navy, one hundred percent straight-arrow all-American. He has a family and kids and I don't think he would get involved in something like this. Trust me on this, Paul Morris. I am a good judge of character and I can assure you Charlie's clean." *How the hell could she be so sure?*

"Okay, but I'm still coming over. Do me a favor, don't tell Charlie I'm on my way over. I'll come in and stay at an airport hotel. What is the name of the airport you're flying out of?"

"Tegel."

"I'll find a room nearby Tegel and call your hotel when I get in."

"Paul? I'm staying in Charlie's room while he goes to New York. It's room 387. Don't ask for me when you call, just tell them to connect you." She didn't want Paul involved in this whole mess, but it sure made her feel good having a collaborator other than Charlie.

"I don't know if I'll be able to catch any of the transpolar flights from Los Angeles yet today, but I'll be on my way as soon as I hang up with you. Charlie's right, don't go anywhere except where there's people and don't fly that Istanbul trip. That city is too dangerous and I have a feeling human life is not worth much down there."

"Don't worry, I'll stay put."

"Good, and remember, no one knows I'm coming. Keep it absolutely secret."

"I will Darling, but do you really think you should do this? What about your job?"

Paul Morris was rapidly locking away all his personal belongings on his desk, shutting down his desktop and laptop computers and stuffing his briefcase. "Don't worry about it, far as they're concerned I have suddenly developed Montezuma's revenge from some hot Mexican food I ate for lunch and have to go home."

"Paul?"

"What?"

"I love you."

"I love you too, Valerie. Keep a low profile till I get there."

She hung up, worried about the new turn of events. She felt like a rat double-crossing Charlie like this but after all, he was running off to New York tomorrow and leaving her alone here. And what if he didn't come back because the Feds detained him, or some other reason? Then she would really be left out to hang. Maybe it wasn't such a bad idea for Paul Morris to come out.

"What'd he say?" Charlie had been standing outside the phone booth protectively.

"He's concerned and wants us to keep him updated of everything that's going on. Now let's go get something to eat before I pass out from a combination of stress and starvation."

CHARLIE GOT UP AT six, quietly went in the bathroom and showered. He debated whether he should wear his uniform going to New York but decided against it. If this drug cartel was watching the hotel, then they would certainly puzzle over a single pilot going to the airport for no apparent reason. No, he would wear his "wet suit" and blend in with other passengers. Airline pilots referred to civilian clothes as their "wet suit" because in it they were allowed to consume liquor when traveling, whereas this was forbidden in uniform.

He found Valerie awake, staring at him.

"Hurry up and get back, Charlie. I don't want to play this game any longer than I have to."

"I'll make it as fast as I can."

He left the hotel wondering what he was getting himself into. The taxi dropped him off in front of the departing passenger area at Tegel and he went straight to the American Airlines' ticket counter.

"Hi! I'm a TGA pilot and I'd like to jumpseat to Frankfurt on the next flight." He laid his airline ID on top of the counter in front of a relatively good-looking customer service rep.

"Good morning!" she eyed his ID, reaching for a form behind the counter. "If you just fill in this form, I'll notify load control and then you can take it directly to the gate and ask the captain yourself."

Charlie filled the jumpseat form, thanking the agent then headed for the gate area.

At the gate he approached the flight attendant guarding the jetway and asked her to please take his jumpseat request and his ID down the jetway to the crew preparing the airplane for flight.

"Be glad to," the woman responded, disappearing down the jetway.

How come we don't have good-looking gals like these working for us? Charlie thought. He looked out the window at the Boeing 727 sitting on the ramp like a giant prehistoric beast being readied for flight. He had planned on doing some shopping in Berlin today, but now he was going to spend the next twelve hours sitting in airplanes flying back to the Big Apple. What a place to live that was. He had moved west to Albuquerque years ago when his wife finally couldn't stand New York any longer and he used to laugh at her and tell her that Manhattan couldn't be such a bad place to live, after all, the thirty million rats inhabiting the city couldn't all be wrong! Fact was, he really enjoyed Manhattan, but had agreed to the move west because the standard of living for the kids was really much better in New Mexico. Ah, but how he missed his long walks from Times Square up to Central Park, his pizza by the slice and, yes, even the piles of shit people left in front of their buildings during garbage strikes. What the heck!

"Here you go!" The flight attendant had returned and was holding his ID and a copy of the jumpseat pass. "The captain said to go ahead and go down now."

"Thanks..." he read her nametag, "...Lynn, I really appreciate this."

"You're welcome captain."

Charlie strolled down the jetway, feeling more at home. He entered the cockpit, greeting the crew. "Morning, fellas. Mind if I hitch a ride with you all?"

The captain of the American flight was in his late fifties, white haired and patriarchal. "Dave Flett!" he uttered, offering a strong, firm handshake. "Glad to have you with us, Charlie. You can put your bag in here and grab a First Class seat as soon as our ladies shut the door."

Charlie thanked him and sat on one of the jumpseats.

"Going home?"

"Naw, just New York for some business."

"New York you say? Going out of Frankfurt?"

"Yes. I'll try to jump on you guys, if I can."

"Mike!" the senior captain addressed his flight engineer, "when we get in range call Frankfurt Ops and give them this good fella's name so they can give him one of the jumpseats on our flight 680 to New York."

"You bet, Dave." The flight engineer copied down Charlie's name on his clipboard.

Charlie thanked the crew for their hospitality and when the flight was ready to depart the gate he was invited to a First Class seat by the head flight attendant. He willingly left the cockpit and settled down to enjoy a delicious breakfast served to him on real china. Definitely one of the better perks of his profession. He removed a copy of *U.S. News and World Report* from his overnight bag and resigned himself to the first of many magazines which would keep him busy over the next twelve hours.

EIGHT
PRESENT TIME - NEW YORK CITY
UNITED STATES

Charlie Smith opened the door and invited the two agents to step in. The room at the JFK Holiday-Inn was not a standard for luxury by any means, but it did have a small table with chairs, which the three men took over.

"Captain Smith," the tall agent began, "if you don't have any objections we'd like to record this interview." He placed a small cassette recorder on the table.

"I have no objection." Charlie did not correct the agent when he addressed him as captain. If the guy was not smart enough to see that he only had three stripes on the sleeves of his coat, then let him bask in his ignorance.

"Thank you. Now, if you could real quick repeat what you already told us over the phone it would get us going in the right direction."

Charlie felt impatience with these men, wanting to get on with the football game, but if they wanted it all again from the top then he would repeat the entire episode with Valerie Wall.

"Drinks?" he gestured to several cans of Coke he had bought at the vending machine prior to the agents' arrival.

"No, thanks."

"Very well, then, as I explained to you on the phone..."

Forty minutes later the tall agent, the one who had introduced himself as "Gus" stood up, lit up a cigarette and stared at his partner long and hard.

"Well?" Charlie questioned, "What do you think? Does this smell of organized crime or what?" He popped the tab off a Coke can, drinking it without ice.

"Yes, it certainly does."

"So? What do you suggest we do? Captain Wall will be waiting for me tomorrow morning and I want to show up with something more than just my dick in my hand."

The agent put out his cigarette and stared at him. "Captain, from what you've told us we have reason to believe that you and Captain Wall have stumbled onto a very dangerous group of people."

Charlie knew his instincts had not betrayed him.

"This bunch that you've described to us, do you know if they use computers? Like the kind businessmen carry on airplanes on business trips?"

"You mean laptops?"

"Yeah, laptops, notebook computers, whatever they call them," his tone of voice left no doubt that he considered those items mere yuppie toys.

"I don't know, as I said, I only saw this Griffin woman for a few seconds and she was carrying a big purse but whether she had a laptop in it, who knows. Why?"

The agent glanced at his partner.

"Captain, it appears that this woman might belong to a group that we've been trying to detect for some time now, a group known only as The Organization. Have you heard this term used before?"

"Shit, no, except maybe in the movie *The Firm* with Tom Cruise..."

No smile crossed agent Gus' face. "So you've not ever heard Captain Wall or anyone else mention it?"

"I said no. What is this Organization anyway, some kind of drug cartel? Are the Colombians involved?"

"Captain Smith, are you familiar with the crash of a Boeing 737-300 on approach into Miami airport earlier this year?"

Charlie wondered where this dipshit was leading. "Yes, I mean, I've read what's come out in the papers, why? Is that crash somehow related to this?"

Agent Gus lit up another cigarette. "What we're going to tell you is strictly off the record, you understand this?"

Yeah, and I was born at night but not last night, Gus. Charlie did not enjoy being patronized, and that was exactly what dipshit here was doing. Why in Heaven's name would any agent of the DEA confide in an individual whom he'd just met less than an hour ago? And this guy was dumb enough to actually believe that he would buy it? This guy wasn't trusting him with confidential information. If Charlie was going to receive some information from these grunts, it sure as hell was not confidential. "Go on."

"We found traces of plastic explosive embedded in some of the flight instruments that the NTSB was able to recover from the Everglades."

"No shit." CNN International had already informed half the world of this *confidential* fact.

"And, a total of sixteen airline personnel have died under similarly questionable circumstances globally over the past fourteen months. Nine flight attendants and seven pilots, not counting the Miami crash."

"What?"

"Crewmembers from different airlines have died in different countries, under very similar circumstances, and we've reason to believe that these alleged murders are somewhat related to the people you and Captain Wall stumbled upon in Berlin."

"Who did this?"

"We don't know exactly, but a pattern is beginning to emerge, one which might help us detect this Organization and fight it."

"The people in this Organization, they operate like the ones who contacted Val—Captain Wall?"

The agent put out his second cigarette in the glass ashtray on the table after a couple of puffs. "Trying to quit. Have been trying for fifteen years."

Charlie felt his adrenaline running. A bomb in an airplane and crewmembers being murdered. That meant these people had access to explosives and people who knew how to use them, as well as hired thugs. Sure, with that kind of money...

"Yes, we have reason to believe this to be correct. Two flight attendants for a Far East airline were found with their throats cut open in a Frankfurt crew hotel. Another one was found in her hotel room in London, had been suffocated with her own pillow. One other, a Lufthansa gal was shot in the face in a very peaceful restaurant in Paris, two Iberia flight attendants were found dead in their hotel rooms on layovers in New York City and in Chicago, and so on. That in itself may not seem peculiar, after all women do make juicy targets when traveling alone, but what all those women had in common, however, was that they all had in their possession one of those laptops that you mentioned. Now, those little computers are not cheap, are they?"

"No, I don't think they are. A couple of grand apiece maybe, I don't know."

"Precisely. Now, why would each of these victims happen to have such an expensive toy in their rooms? Correct me if I'm wrong, Captain Smith, but it is my understanding that flight attendant's pay is no match for pilots' pay, is it?"

"No, it is not."

"What would you say the average flight attendant makes a month? Fifteen hundred?"

"Maybe a couple of thousand if they've been around for a while."

"So how could all these gals afford to buy such expensive corporate toys? Furthermore, we found that each single one of them had the same make and model.

Can you explain to me for what possible reason would a flight attendant carry a heavy piece of hardware like that around the world? Does your airline require its cabin personnel to acquire such tools?"

"Hell no. Most flight attendants that I can think of would have no use for a computer other than eventual word processing, but I sure don't think any gal would haul the damn thing around on trips. They certainly don't need it to do their jobs inflight."

"Can you think of any reason why your flight attendants would need to carry with them powerful computers equipped with modems for data transmission?"

"No. I can't think of any reason why any gal would do something like that."

"We checked the hotel records where these women had slept going back several months and found a rather interesting item. Most of these women had logged long distance calls to Mexico City. Now, we are well aware of the reputation of Latin Lovers, but it seems a little coincidental that all of these women would have Mexican lovers, friends or relatives, wouldn't you say?"

"Not likely."

"Right, we thought so too. The Mexican authorities, however, have been most cooperative in answering our requests for information on the numbers these women called. They promptly reported to us that every single one of the numbers has been disconnected or is no longer in use, and conveniently, no trace of previous owners was ever forwarded to us."

"So everyone is getting a piece of the cake."

"We don't accuse anybody of anything until we have solid evidence, you understand, but so far we have come out empty-handed in our search for leads. And all of the victims had been flying international routes at one time or another in the recent past."

"What about all those computers? Weren't you able to recover some of the data stored in them?"

"Unfortunately, no. We've only studied two of them, the ones recovered in this country, and were unable to find anything useful to us. The entire hard disks had been thoroughly cleaned up before we arrived. Sadly, our overseas colleagues have run into similar luck, so we have nothing concrete to go on. Ah, yes, our investigation of the Miami crash revealed that the copilot on that flight had recently acquired a laptop computer of similar brand. His wife indicated to us that he'd stayed up several nights learning how to use it."

"Damn!" Charlie had never condoned drugs nor people who used drugs but had not been overly concerned about the so-called drug problem in this country because he assumed others were doing their job fighting the bad guys, but this hit a little too close to home. "What are these guys, Colombian?"

Agent Gus sighed. "It's so hard educating people when Hollywood produces such incredible misinformation. Captain, we have drugs coming into this country from many places other than South America. For some reason the Colombians seem to get all the free publicity, but no, the Organization does not seem to operate out of Colombia. They may have Colombians working with them, but they are too well educated and highly technical to be common South American thugs."

"How do you know that?" Charlie had heard that there had been instances where airline pilots "imported" illegal drugs in order to supplement the alimony they were paying to several wives, but he never suspected the existence of a very organized network within the airlines. But after all, why not? Airline personnel were not an uneducated group as a whole, so they would make an attractive bunch to employ.

"Because it is our experience that organizational ability is not one of the prevalent characteristics of Latin cultures, and neither is mastery of high tech. They like to buy high-tech toys, but generally speaking they don't know how to use them to their full capacity, and they certainly do a poor job of maintenance. They just do not have the highly trained personnel it takes to support high tech on a large scale."

"I see. We're going off in a different direction here. What do you propose we do about the situation that has developed in Berlin?"

Agent Gus sat down, removed a cigarette from its pack, changed his mind and put it back. "May I have one of those Cokes?"

Charlie handed it to him, pushing the ice bucket and a plastic glass wrapped in cellophane closer to him.

"We need your friend Captain Wall to get us some information."

Charlie stared at the Fed. "What kind of information?"

"If she can hang in there long enough she may be able to provide us with a lead from which to nail these bastards."

Charlie leaned forward. "Explain to me what you mean by 'hang in there'."

Agent Gus gulped down half his drink. "What you both did was very brave and incredibly convenient for us. By not escaping the situation and playing along with it, your Captain Wall has placed herself in a very valuable position for us. If she can gain the trust of her contact Griffin, then maybe she'll be able to get her hands on some name or phone number we can follow up here in the States."

"You mean you want her to be a mole for you?" Charlie was not amused.

"Well, Captain, I wouldn't necessarily call her a mole. That's what they call it in the movies. Let's just say she can help us tremendously by playing along with these people for a little while with the intent of obtaining some information of value to the United States government."

"You guys are nuts. First of all, Valerie–that is Captain Wall–would never go along with this. She is an airline pilot, not a spy. Second, even if she did decide to cooperate with your ridiculous plan, those bastards would kill her no matter where she went."

"We are prepared to offer her means of protection," the other agent finally spoke. He had introduced himself as "Tom," had a hard-as-iron handshake and smelled of cheap aftershave.

Charlie laughed. "You don't mean the, whaddaya call it, the witness protection program, do you?"

"Yes, that's what I mean. We're prepared to offer Captain Wall our protection if she helps us out."

Charlie Smith laughed out loud. "You guys are really wild. I don't know what kind of people you're used to dealing with, gentlemen, but Captain Wall is an international airline captain making about twelve grand a month, and frankly I sincerely doubt that she would want to drop her airline career to become a Jack-In-The-Box manager in shittown Montana just for the privilege of providing you guys with some information."

The agents looked at each other. They had come to the Holiday-Inn because this Smith man had absolutely refused to drop by the station on grounds of wanting to remain anonymous, and now they felt slightly uncomfortable because they were not accustomed to dealing with customers who had a brain. Or who made twelve grand a month either. "Captain, it doesn't appear as if your friend has much of a choice at this point. You're right about one thing, though, these people will most likely kill Captain Wall when she meets the criteria which led them to eliminate the other airline personnel we've told you about. We are the only friends she has."

Charlie laughed at the stereotype speech. "Excuse me, gents, but you're not listening to me. You're not dealing with your common Brooklyn hood here who will view a couple of thousand bucks a month as manna from heaven. If captain Wall is going to jeopardize her airline career for you guys, you're going to have to come up with something a hell of a lot more enticing than your current protection program. Otherwise my advice to her will be to run. Get back to the United States and take her chances. And I believe she'll do that regardless of my advice, once she hears what you guys are selling."

"Captain Smith, if you do that, you could be signing her death certificate."

"Very dramatic, but is it really founded?"

"What would you consider appropriate for us to offer in exchange for a little cooperation then?" Agent Gus gave up on the Coke and lit up another cigarette.

"I don't know exactly because I can't speak for her, but off-hand I'd say another position similar to what she has right now would be the absolute minimum requirement."

"You mean another captain's position with another airline?"

"Yes, something along those lines. Another airline with another identity." Charlie was shooting from the hip. He had no idea what Valerie would think of flying for another airline under another name, but he had to raise the ante with these guys.

"That might be workable but it would not be up to me to make a decision like that, I'd have to run it past the head of the department. It would also depend on the value of the information she was able to provide."

Charlie got up, grabbed the telephone from between the beds and deposited it in front of the agent. "There's the phone. Give the head of your department a call and run it past him."

Agent Gus' grimace was definitely an indication that he was beginning to dislike this asshole. "Just because you're an airline captain and make four times the salary of a working person, don't think this makes you all that smart. This is a dangerous game you're playing, captain.

Besides, I cannot do this over the phone, you understand that. I will run it past my boss the minute we get back in the office."

"Fair enough." Charlie didn't like the tone of voice the agent used, but he assumed all these clowns had to come across intimidating as hell to get what they wanted. Charlie was wearing his airline uniform because he was aware of the fact that the dark navy blue emanated authority, which was convenient since he was outnumbered two to one. "I intend to catch the six-thirty flight back to Frankfurt tonight. You guys come up with a feasible game plan and bring it to me here before five and we'll play ball with you. Otherwise, Captain Wall and myself will be leaving Berlin permanently within twenty-four hours."

"That would be a mistake, captain. These people would come after her."

"Then it's up to you to help us out, isn't it? But you must realize that being rescued by the Titanic is not really a desirable option, so you go talk to your chief and tell him to come up with a more attractive offer before he goes asking for help from people who have a lot to lose." He stood up, indicating the end of the interview.

The agents stood and retrieved their tape recorder.

"We'll be in touch before five."

"Thank you for your help, guys. And thanks for coming all the way out here."

Agent Gus shook hands with the pilot, leaving the room. The two agents rode the elevator down to the lobby in silence. Once outside the building, agent Gus spit, disgusted. "Don't you wonder where the airlines go to get guys like these? The man is evidently intelligent, but he doesn't have the horse sense of a 42nd street hooker. He's probably never seen a cadaver before in his life, and thinks the underworld has ethics. Too bad."

CHARLIE SMITH LOOKED AT the clock one last time.

Time to go. He grabbed his overnight bag and his hat. The call hadn't come, so he would have to come up with an alternate plan. First thing, though, was to get Valerie out of Germany.

The phone rang.

"Captain Smith? Gus Olafson here."

"Hello, Gus! Glad to hear from you. I thought you'd changed your mind and was about to leave the room. Did you people come up with a fair game plan for us?"

"I ran your request past the boss, captain, and he considers it a reasonable request which he feels can be worked out. Are you still leaving at six?"

"Yes. Six-thirty flight to Frankfurt."

"Write down these numbers I'm going to give you."

Charlie had been ready for him. "Go ahead."

Agent Gus gave him three numbers to call from Europe. One was his direct line.

"That a cellular phone?" Charlie inquired.

"A what?"

"That number you just gave me where I can reach you, is that a cellular phone?" Charlie was not too thrilled about having this particular agent as his liaison, but good help was hard to find.

"No, but you can reach me here at any time. What we want you and Captain Wall to do is memorize these numbers then get rid of them. We need two daily reports from either one of you, one in the morning and one in the evening. If you fail to contact us for any reason, we will notify the German authorities about the situation and they will then move in. If you need immediate help turn to the German police and have them contact me at this number. Do not try to explain the situation to them, just instruct them to give you protection and have them call me immediately.

Tell Captain Wall to be observant but not write anything down. Tell her to avoid flying to Istanbul anymore this month. If they wanted to terminate her employment, that'd probably be the most logical place they would use."

Terminate her employment? Charlie just loved these euphemisms used by the feds.

"My boss wants you on this assignment only until the end of the month, and we'll provide you and Captain Wall with the request you formulated, provided she is able to supply us with some useful items."

"Us? Wait a minute, old boy, you are mistaken. I'm not asking you for anything for myself. I'm not involved with these German assholes who set up Valerie. I am helping her out and that's why I flew out here to talk with you gentlemen, but I'm not interested in any of the protection you have to offer because I do not intend to get caught up in this mess except as an advisor."

"I understand, Captain Smith, however, you are already involved by being here talking to me, and although you're not obliged to accept my help, we just want you to know that it's available for you too, should you need it."

"Well, thank you, but no thanks. I will relay your message to Captain Wall, and will assist her in any way I can, but don't count on me being one of your recruits. And also, that's not the way things are going to work. You're not going to condition her security to the quality of the information she is able to provide you. What do you think she is, stupid? That's no deal then. Whether Captain Wall or myself are able to provide you with any information is inconsequential. You give us what we asked for unconditionally or we're not playing with you. The risk itself is worth what we asked for."

Agent Gus paused. "Hang on just a minute."

Charlie heard him talking to someone else in the background.

"Okay, you win. We'll provide what you asked for regardless of the information received."

Charlie wondered if he could trust these guys, then mentally scolded himself. For crying out loud, relax, Charlie! These are Americans, it was your decision to come here instead of going to the Germans, remember?

"Sounds good then. And you have all this on record so in case we get framed you can come out and clear our good family name?"

"Yes, it's all on record, Captain."

"Gus?"

"Yes?"

"Gus, I'm not a captain. I am a First Officer, what you laymen would call a copilot, so stop calling me captain, would you?"

There was a momentary pause as agent Gus absorbed the news. "So what do I call you then?"

"Try Charlie."

"Okay, Charlie."

"When do you want me to call your number the first time?"

"You'll be arriving in Berlin tomorrow around noon, right?"

"Correct."

"Then we'll expect your first call tomorrow evening, Berlin time."

"Looks like we have a deal." He hung up.

THE FOURTH STRIPE

Maurice Azurdia

NINE
PRESENT TIME - BERLIN, GERMANY

Valerie woke up in panic. Someone had been luring her into a dark basement room hidden below an ancient stone tower located somewhere in Eastern Europe. This dark room hosted an unspeakable evil, an ancient vampire or other ghoulish product of her imagination, one that had evaded destruction at the hands of humans by sailing through time hidden in this tower, until enough time had passed to erase him from the memories of the descendants of those men who hunted him in the past. This was not a new dream for her, having recurred many times since she was a teenager, but she kept it buried in the deeper chambers of her subconscious mind.

She sat up, soaked with perspiration from the terrifying nightmare. She hated the dream, yet it haunted her throughout her life. The only possible explanation she could find for this recurrence was the tremendous stress she was feeling. Valerie had completed a report on vampirism while in high school, and it had sparked an insatiable curiosity in her. Was there any substance to these legends? And if so, what was true and what was mythology? One thing she'd read during her research that had especially frightened her, had been that the true power of a vampire rests in the fact that nobody believes in its existence. Nice, real nice. And she had flown over Castle Dracula on her way to Istanbul. Great.

She got up, going to the bathroom. After being awake for a few minutes her mind rapidly erased the unpleasant memory of her nightmare and adjusted to the reality of her hotel room in Berlin. Or Charlie's hotel room in

Berlin, which was the case. He would be returning today, and she felt immensely relieved. She had not slept well due to her preoccupation with the ridiculous situation she was in. She had been kicking around options in her mind but none seemed plausible. Charlie was right, talking to the Germans was out of the question. Her airline had a very high reputation to protect, and the mere whisper that she had anything to do with drugs or smuggling would be enough to get her fired. She remembered a situation a few years back when a first officer had killed a man in self-defense, and on that particular occasion, TGA had fired the pilot on the spot after hearing that the first officer had been arrested on charges of manslaughter. Eventually, a jury had found the pilot innocent and TGA had to rehire him with back pay and an apology, but that was not something she had any intention of enduring.

Her position in life had cost her untold amounts of suffering and effort, putting up with assholes like Jack Cranston, scraping to pay for her college and flight training, putting out the superhuman effort required to qualify as an airline captain...no way she was going to throw it all away by being impetuous.

Fact was, she had brought drugs into Germany on her flight, and they could hang her for it no matter what the attenuating circumstances. She hoped Charlie had instructions to head home and forget the entire episode. Yes, that would be just fine with her. She analyzed how the change in schedule would affect her pay for the month and decided that she wouldn't take too much of a hit. The perdiem mainly. Pilots received forty-two dollars a day for food and incidental expenses, or around $1,200 a month, which she'd forfeit if she left now.

That suited her just fine. The notion that she had actually brought cocaine or something equally illegal into Germany in her overnight bag absolutely revolted her. The fact that she had been tricked into doing it pissed her off, and the fact that she had fallen for it made her see red.

She had spent most of yesterday in Charlie's room, reading, not wanting to expose herself by going where there were people. This hotel must have four hundred rooms, and she felt safe being in her first officer's room instead of her own. They could hardly search all the rooms looking for her. She had avoided checking for messages at the desk, just in case Elaine had left her one, and had avoided using room service at all. Instead, she had walked three blocks to the *Wertheimer* department store and bought bread, wine, cold cuts and fruit in the basement deli. They all had small refrigerators in their rooms and she used Charlie's to avoid going out. She was unable to concentrate on her book *Caribbean* so she spent most of the day relaxing in bed watching TV in German.

There was a knock on the door.

Oh, crap! She jumped out of bed, looking through the peep hole. Charlie was standing in front of the door.

"Charlie!" she let him in, resisting an urge to throw her arms around his neck in relief and hugging him.

He dropped his overnight bag on the floor and removed his uniform coat. "Got anything cold to drink?"

"Yes, in your fridge. You want some wine?"

Charlie removed his tie. "No, thanks, Valerie. Not now, anything non-alcoholic will do."

"Coke?"

"Sure. Well, I talked to the feds."

"And? What did they say? Do we bail out of here? Are they going to tell the Germans? I am *so* happy you're back!"

"No, we don't get out of here, Valerie, at least not just yet." He popped the tab off.

What? She scanned his face looking for some optimism, but couldn't find any.

"They were very happy we came to them, and they made us a proposition."

"A proposition? What kind of proposition? Didn't you tell them we want to get the hell away from this place?"

"I did, but unfortunately there's a heck of a lot more to our buddy Elaine than we thought." He brought her up to speed on the information the federal agents gave him about the Miami crash, the dead crew members, and the deal they proposed.

"They're out of their goddamn minds! I'm not gonna continue with this charade! Are they insane? If these people are that dangerous then we oughta get lost right now. I don't want to change my identity, there's no way in hell those guys can get us hired on at another airline. You know that as well as I do, Charlie. Those idiots don't have a clue what the devil they're talking about. Every airline in the United States has a seniority list, same as us. What're they gonna to do, hire us as captains and put us ahead of thousands of pilots so we can keep our relative seniority that we have with our own company? Fat fucking chance, Charlie."

"Why do you say that?" Charlie had changed into a red T-shirt.

"Oh, c'mon, Charlie! Would you just sit there and do nothing if our company all of a sudden shoved two new captains in front of you? Two guys you've never even heard of who haven't even been on the seniority list until ten minutes ago?"

He could see her point. Airline pilots lived, worked, vacationed, breathed and died by their airline's seniority list. No way they could expect a lateral transfer.

"They could probably get us hired at the bottom of the seniority list at one of the airlines," Valerie continued, "but there's no way under this blue sky that I would accept that."

"Yeah, I see what you mean. I have to call those guys in an hour so I'll bring that up. Maybe if we can get it in writing."

"Charlie, I don't care what some two-bit federal agent in New York gives me in writing or not in writing. I just don't trust those guys because it's evident they have no idea what they're promising. Think of our airline. If a federal agency approached Leo over at pilot hiring or the Vice president of flight operations with such a request, it would generate heart attacks among the ranks. The union would have to be notified, too many people would have to be brought into the loop in order to make it work, and you can imagine what that would do to security. Right! We're trying to change identities and become Mr. And Mrs. Inconspicuous so the bad guys don't get us, never mind the fact that it'll take an act of Congress to get us hired as captains?"

Charlie had to admit that he hadn't thought along those lines. A Navy man, he had jumped straight from organized military into organized airlines, and had blind fate in what his superiors said. He believed in the integrity of the system. It had never occurred to him that the feds would lie. "You think that sonofabitch lied to me?"

Valerie shook her head. She couldn't believe Charlie was that naive. "Of course he lied to you. Maybe not intentionally, maybe this guy's boss instructed him to do it to recruit us and he would check on our request later, but Charlie, I really don't believe any of these government agencies have the power to transform us into United captains just because we requested it. Think about it. How long did it take this agent to get back to you after your meeting?"

"About three hours."

"There's no way the feds could have consulted with the airlines about something of this magnitude in that short a time. He bullshitted you."

Charlie saw the logic in her words. "Shit, Valerie, I think you may be right."

"And you know what it means? It means after we're no longer useful they will say, sorry, chaps, but we are unable to fulfill your request, however we are generous people so we can still offer you the witness protection program. Take it or leave it."

"Jack In-The-Box managers in Montana."

"Precisely."

"Fuck me!"

"Yeah, Charlie, that is exactly what they would like to do to you–to us."

She paced the small room, adding the latest developments to the equation. "This is becoming very complicated."

"I say we both call in sick and go home." Charlie did not like the feeling of insecurity Valerie was generating in him. If they both left Germany and went home perhaps they had a chance of putting all this behind them."

"Charlie, you just told me what the feds think these people have done. If it's true and these bastards really bombed that airplane going into Miami then they won't think twice about coming after us, or after me, since they don't know about you."

"Just let them try!"

"Charlie, don't be foolish, you can't fight this war by yourself."

"I've enough weapons at home to give them a run for their money if they dare show their faces."

"Right, a duel at the OK corral in Albuquerque. And what would you gain? If you knock some off they would only send some more thugs to get you. But wait a minute, Charlie! We're talking nonsense here anyway. You're not even involved here. Yes, you can call in sick and get out of here. I'm the only one directly involved, remember? Elaine Griffin doesn't even know you exist!"

Charlie had become so involved with the events that he had obviously completely overlooked that fact. Valerie was telling the truth, Charlie could just blend into the woodwork and nothing would happen to him.

"Bullshit, Valerie, we're both in on this. Where you go, I go."

She fought back tears. This man was how her father had told her a man should be. Her eyes got watery and she laid her hand on his. "Thanks."

Charlie gave her hand a squeeze and stood up. "We have to be very careful about our moves. You have not heard from our friends since yesterday?"

"No, but they may have tried to call me or left me a message in my room, I don't know since I haven't been there since you left."

"Call downstairs see if you got any messages."

Valerie grabbed the phone and dialed the front desk.

She had one message to call Mrs. Elaine Griffin at this phone number.

"I guess they must really like you, eh?" Charlie leaned on the window, staring out at the traffic in the street below. "I don't like the way things are smelling. I went through considerable effort flying to New York to be lied to by the feds, yet that's exactly the way it's looking. I guess you're right. It would be next to impossible for a federal agency to make us pilots at another airline because of the obstacle presented by the seniority list, but then again, the U.S. government has many resources, don't they?"

"They do have the resources, but why would they want to use them with us? Charlie, I don't know what to do. Should I call Elaine? Should we stay in the game? I really feel this isn't right."

"Take it easy, we have to think about this. I agree with you, I don't think the feds are being straight with us, but we can probably work something out with them. In the meantime, I think I'd like to catch the fuckers who bombed that Boeing 737 in Miami. If we stay in the game for a little while longer we may be able to come up with something to help the feds nab those responsible for it."

"You think Elaine and her husband are related to the sick fuckers who bombed that flight?" Valerie's anger at anyone who would kill innocent people ignited.

"According to the feds these people here may be working for the same organization, yes."

"That makes me sick, Charlie." The thought of having helped mass murderers made her blood boil.

"Me too, Valerie, me too. Here's what I suggest. Call this bitch and see what she wants. If she wants you to fly anything else in from Istanbul say yes, but you'll call in sick for the flight. Otherwise, let's hear what she has to say. Now we have to start keeping a very accurate record of everything that goes on so we can use it as evidence later."

Valerie evaluated her first officer's suggestion. What he said made sense. "Okay, I'll call her." Valerie sat on the bed and dialed the local number the clerk had given her. It had a room number with it, so it must be a hotel."

"*Gutten Tag, Steigenberger* Hotel."

"Good afternoon, I need room 236, please."

"*Ah, ja,* just minute, please."

She heard it ring.

"*Ja?*" It was her.

"Elaine? Valerie Wall here."

"Valerie? Hi, Valerie, how you doing? Did you get my message?"

"Yes, that's why I'm calling you. What's up?"

"Valerie, I was wondering if perhaps you could join me for dinner tonight. I apologize for not giving you more notice but I couldn't reach your earlier. I know this absolutely darling restaurant just a few blocks from your hotel, the *Dortmunder* Cafe, excellent German food. You do like German food?"

"Yes, German food's fine. What time?"

"Would sevenish be too early for you? I can come by and pick you up if you want."

"Aah, no, thanks, Elaine," Valerie laughed. "I think I can find it if you just tell me where it is. The Dortmunder you said?"

"Yes, one block north of the *Kuddamn,* past the Kaiser Wilhelm church."

Elaine had probably not missed the significance of Valerie's laughter, indicating that Valerie didn't trust her. Too bad. "That's fine. I'll see you there at seven. It'll be just you and me, right?"

"Yes, Valerie, just the two of us."

"Good. I'll see you there." She hung up before Griffin could add anything more.

Valerie stared at Charlie. "I have a date tonight with Elaine to eat dinner at a German restaurant, the *Dortmunder.*"

"I know the place," Charlie reflected, "it's a good restaurant not far from here with plenty of people. Not a bad place to meet her."

"She offered to give me a ride there."

"Not a chance. Don't get into any vehicle with her. We cannot trust that woman and you have to insist on staying in public places."

"Do you think I should get a mini tape recorder and carry it on me when I meet her?"

"No, Valerie, that's not a good idea. If these guys are professionals and they realize you're taping them they're bound to get real nasty. Let's not give them any motive whatsoever to doubt that you're anything other than a greedy airline captain with no other purpose than to make lots of extra bucks."

"Okay. You said the feds think the bomb on the Miami flight, if indeed it was a bomb, probably went off in the cockpit?"

"Yes, that's what the agent said. They said the FBI found traces of explosives on the remains of the flight instruments."

"That means one of the pilots must have carried the bomb onboard unknowingly."

"Yes, I believe they're thinking along those lines."

Valerie stood up. "I think we better operate under the premises that these people could do the same thing to us. We better examine our flight bags and overnight bags very carefully every time we get on the airplane."

"Oh shit, you're right!"

"And Charlie, we cannot be seen in public together, or coming out of this room. I don't want them to associate you with me. As long as you are clean you can act as my back up."

"I'll be your shadow, captain. Don't you worry, I won't let you out of my sight. These bastards won't touch one hair on your head without having me come down on top of them like a Texas brick shithouse!"

She touched his forearm. "Thanks, Charlie." Somehow she was having dinner with a woman who could be an international drug trafficker and a terrorist, and she wondered how life had become so complicated. She should have stayed in the States flying boring Wichita layovers instead of coming to Europe.

VALERIE LEFT THE HOTEL at quarter to seven, feeling like *Inspector Clouseau*, a little ridiculous, walking to the *Dortmunder* restaurant. They agreed that Charlie would follow her a few hundred feet behind. She was dying to turn and ascertain that he was there, but knew that if she was being watched doing so could possibly give them away so she continued down the path to her meeting. The *Dortmunder* restaurant was a Bavarian-style building in the center of Berlin with beautiful wooden floors and Southern German decoration. It had wooden booths and flowered cotton curtains hanging in front of the windows. She walked in and searched for Elaine Griffin, hungry now from the delicious aroma of cooking sausages that was reaching her nose. Once again, she noticed how there wasn't a glass of water in sight at any table, only beer. These Germans had the right idea.

"Valerie!" Elaine Griffin waved at her from a wooden booth.

Valerie waved back and wondered how Charlie was going to manage to hide in this restaurant. How was he going to remain in the background when the place was mostly empty? She sat across from Griffin, who removed a black leather glove to shake hands.

"Valerie, I'm so glad you made it."

"My pleasure, Elaine."

"The food here is splendid," Elaine promised, "beer and bratwurst and sauerkraut and we'll be in heaven."

"Why did you want to meet?"

Elaine Griffin smiled a charming smile "let's eat first, then we'll talk business, okay?"

"Okay."

They ordered the house specialty and the waitress brought them two ice-cold beers.

"How long have you been an airline captain, Valerie?"

"Three years."

"How long you been flying?"

What was this, a third degree? "If you mean for the airlines, about thirteen years. Why?"

Elaine Griffin lit up a Dunhill cigarette. "Nothing, just curious. I'd never before met an airline pilot, much less a woman airline pilot, and I'm curious about it, that's all."

"I am the fifth woman to make captain at TGA, out of thirty-five hundred pilots," she stated, not wanting to miss the opportunity to show off to this woman.

"That is remarkable."

"Thank you."

"But isn't it hard? I mean, do the men obey you?"

"Obey me? You mean the crew?"

"Yeah, the crew. Aren't they mostly men?"

"Yes, I fly mostly with male crewmembers but I have no problems with them. I'm not their master Elaine, they don't have to obey me, we work as a team and I'm the team leader, that's all."

"But it is a man's world, isn't it?"

"Not anymore, it isn't. It used to be, but not anymore." Valerie wished they'd get over the small talk and get down to business.

"Do you get hassled?"

"Hassled, in what way?"

"I mean do they sexually harass you?" Griffin was looking around the restaurant.

Valerie hoped she would not spot Charlie, then remembered that this woman could not possibly make Charlie because she had never seen him before. "Sometimes. But I let them know that it is not a good idea and they back off."

"Is it hard? The flying and all that?"

Valerie realized perhaps Griffin was genuinely interested in what being an airline pilot was like for a woman, and decided to give her a break. "No, actually it's the most fun I've ever had. It was a lot of work getting here, more than you could ever imagine, and I had to fly with some real assholes while I was a copilot, but it was definitely worth the effort." Yeah, and what an effort that had been, just trying to get hired.

TEN
THIRTEEN YEARS AGO - VALENCIA, CALIFORNIA, UNITED STATES

The following day Valerie found herself with renewed optimism and decided that she had done the right thing walking out on Jack. She was not making any money with him anyway, since he only paid her $100 per day for those days they were away from California, and she averaged just eight days a month. No, the reason she had put up with him for nearly a year was because of the opportunity to fly a jet and for resume impact. Now she was ready to move on and fly passengers. She made herself some *huevos rancheros,* showered and began making calls to secure a new job.

A call came in while she was holding for a chief pilot with a small commuter up in San Luis Obispo. The call-waiting clicked. "Hello?"

"Hi, darling!"

"Paul Morris! You got my message?"

"Yes. I've been in meetings all morning but wanted to hear your voice before the morning was over. How'd it go at MidAmerica, did you get the job?"

Paul Morris really didn't have a clue what it took to get on with the airlines, bless his heart. "No, I didn't get the job, honey. They interviewed me along with 800 others and they will select eighty candidates by the end of the year."

"You're kidding."

"No, I wish I was, Paul. I guess I'm going to look for another job somewhere else. I already started calling commuters to see where I can land job that will get me some turbine experience."

"But I thought that's what you were doing with Jack."

"Yeah, but I guess the airlines want more hours than I'm getting with Jack. I don't know anymore, Paul, I'm just going to look for a job where I can make some money and get more hours."

"I don't like hearing you this depressed. Hang in there, I'm sure you'll get called, if not with MidAmerica then with someone else. Just hang in there, you've come this far you can't give up now."

"I'm not giving up, I'm just becoming more realistic. I'm trying to compete against guys who flew jet fighters in the military, how much of a chance do you think that gives me?"

"Valerie, you knew it was a tough call when you decided to become an airline pilot and I have absolute faith in your ability to achieve your goal, just keep at it. Are you free for dinner tonight?"

"You bet."

"How about Carlos & Charlie's up on Sunset?"

"That sounds great, honey." She could use some distraction.

"Pick you up at seven."

"I'll be ready. I love you."

"Me too. See you at seven." He hung up.

Valerie smiled. Whenever there was someone within hearing distance of Paul Morris he would not say *I love you* to her because it embarrassed him. He was so much like a little boy.

She redialed the chief pilot she had been trying to reach when Paul's call came through. She finally succeeded in talking to the man.

"Why would you want to leave a job flying a Sabreliner to come fly a commuter?" The man was not going out of his way to be friendly.

"I want to get some experience flying for the airlines, and you are an airline, aren't you?"

"Yes, of course we are. Are you aware of how much we pay?"

Yes, Mister, I am aware that you pay shit money, but it doesn't matter, I need the experience. "Yes, I am familiar with your pay scales."

"And you think you can live on that? We pay starting first officers nine hundred a month."

"Yeah, I think I can survive on that."

There was a pause while the chief pilot analyzed the situation. "Lady, I'm bombarded with literally hundreds of resumes every day, and normally I wouldn't give the time a day to a pilot candidate calling me to set up an interview, since I prefer to do it by mail, but you seem enthusiastic enough and willing to do the job and I've got a quota to fill for those jerks with the Affirmative Action group so I've made up my mind. Can you be here Saturday for a Metroliner class?"

Valerie felt a surge of enthusiasm. Metroliners? "Definitely. Where and what time?"

"At the airport office here. Eight o'clock. You have to bring enough money to survive for a week. There's a local motel a couple of miles from the airport and a cafeteria on the field."

"You don't provide the hotel?"

"No. You're not being hired, mind you. Job offers will be made to some of the people who attend the training class, but until then you don't work for us so we don't cover any of your expenses."

"That's fine. Saturday at eight. I'll be there. Thank you very much."

She hung up, feeling some excitement. The Metroliner was a medium-sized turboprop complex enough to warrant taking a week long ground school, and it was a much larger airplane than the Sabreliner she had been flying with Jack. She might just enjoy this after all. The fact that the chief pilot saw her merely as a statistic with the Affirmative Action folks bothered her, but what the heck. She was growing immune to these assholes.

Her phone rang, startling her out of her reverie.

"Hello?"

"Miss Valerie Wall?"

"Speaking."

"Miss Wall, this is Dave Lannen, with Vacation Airlines in Honolulu, Hawaii. We received your resume and would like to offer you an interview if you're still interested in flying for us."

When it rained it poured. "Dave Lannen?" She pulled a chair.

"Yes, Ma'am, I'm the chief pilot here. Can you come out for an interview and to take a look at our operation?"

"Yes, of course," Vacation Airways? She couldn't recall exactly who they were but obviously she must have sent them a resume when she mass-mailed to all the airlines. "Can you get me a pass to come out there?"

"Afraid not, Ma'am. You'll have to come out on your own. But we can offer you around four thousand a month if you decide to work for us."

Four thousand a month? Wow! She had no idea they were talking that much money. "I will come out there tomorrow. Where are you located?" For four thousand a month she would buy her own ticket on United.

"We're on the south end of the field. Just grab a cab and tell him to drive you to Vacation Airways. Everybody here knows where we are. If you fly out tomorrow, I'll see you day after tomorrow at eight a.m."

"Okay, that sounds great. I'll see you day after tomorrow then, thank you very much for calling me."

"You're welcome. I'll see you when you get here."

Valerie felt a surge of excitement. Ten minutes on the phone and she had two possibilities lined up already. Hot dog! She got on the phone and reserved a seat on a United flight to Honolulu the following morning. On this short notice she did not have much hope of finding a good fare, and she was right, she got scalped.

The flight over the Pacific Ocean was not as smooth as she would have liked. The flight attendants on the United Boeing 747 seemed awful short-staffed and it took her forever to get a Coke.

"They sure make us feel like a bunch of cows inside a trailer, don't they?" The man sitting next to her commented, smiling a captivating smile. He seemed in his mid-forties, and she decided that he was right.

"Yes, I really don't like traveling on these 747s for that very reason. Too many people and not enough flight attendants. And just imagine, they are talking about building airplanes twice as big."

"The name is Eddie." He extended his hand to her.

"Valerie Wall, Eddie. Hi!"

"You going to Hawaii on business or pleasure?"

"Business. I have a job interview."

"You don't say. What do you do?"

"I'm a pilot," she offered. It always amused to see the reaction her words provoked in male listeners. Most men held the profession of pilot as a male bastion and resented females intruding on it.

"A pilot, uh? Great. Who you interviewing with, Hawaiian?"

"No, Vacation Airlines. A small sight-seeing company south of the field." After the call from Dave Lannen she had rushed to her computer to look up just who Vacation Airlines was. She had been slightly disappointed to find that they flew ancient twin-engine Beechcraft 18s, but the idea of making four thousand a month was enough to have her come out and take a look.

"I'm a firefighter myself," Eddie offered, "on the Big Island."

Valerie questioned him about living in the islands and Eddie was very pleasant. He told her about the delicious seafood available in Hawaii, the incredible vegetation and the unequaled skin diving. She began to feel the vibrations she usually only felt while on vacation.

"Well, Valerie, if you do end up settling down in the islands come by and visit me sometime. I'll take you up to the most impressive volcano you've ever seen."

She liked Eddie and took down his info so she could reach him again if she ended up staying.

The flight landed in Honolulu and she was delighted by the heat and the humidity. Honolulu International Airport smelled of flowers and pineapple and she loved it. Valerie caught a cab to a small motel near the airport and checked into a miniature room that faced a small inner patio full of orchids and hibiscus.

Ever since living in Panama as a little girl with her parents she adored the tropics, and the idea of living in such a paradise really appealed to her.

She had dinner by herself at a small roadside cafeteria near the hotel and went to bed early. In the morning she took a cab to Vacation Airways and the chief pilot had been right, the cabbie knew instantly where she wanted to go.

The drive around the airport perimeter gave her a magnificent view of Waikiki and the surrounding mountains, their tops hidden in low clouds.

The cab dropped her off in front of a huge hangar next to a house trailer. She walked in and asked an Asian secretary for the Chief Pilot. The place seemed deserted, save for two Beech 18s sitting out on the ramp by themselves.

"Miss Wall?" She turned to face a tall man of around forty with straw-blonde hair and penetrating blue eyes. He reminded her of McCloud, the TV cowboy played by Dennis Weaver.

"I'm Dave Lannen. Welcome to Honolulu!" he shook her hand, squeezing a little too hard. "I'm sure glad to see you made it here."

She took in his blue jeans and cowboy boots and wondered what she was getting into.

The man gave her a tour of the hangar, the two classrooms he had designated for ground school instruction and then took her out to climb on one of the two airplanes parked on the ramp. "These two here airplanes are down for maintenance, but that's okay 'cause Kim Tuen, the owner, likes to keep a couple of extra airplanes around just in case one breaks down. She hates to cancel tours." He guffawed in a way that Valerie found annoying.

"Kim Tuen?"

"Yes, the owner of the airline is Chinese," he pointed at the house trailer parked alongside the parking lot. "She lives in that trailer and runs a very tight ship here."

Valerie found that interesting. The owner liked to stay right on top of the operation, which was good. They sat in the cockpit of one of the airplanes and she was surprised to find very few flight and navigation instruments aboard. She questioned the chief pilot about it.

"That's 'cause these here airplanes ain't equipped for instrument flight," the chief pilot offered. "The weather here's mostly VFR anyway, so we don't need to put thousands of dollars into equipment that we'd seldom use."

Valerie was not convinced. No instruments? What kind of Mickey Mouse operation was this? Granted the weather must be good the majority of the time, but what if they found themselves in a situation where they couldn't land because of lack of instruments, then what? She was somewhat familiar with the reputation Asians had for running a tight ship, as this guy said, but skimping on instrumentation was pushing it.

She refrained from making any remarks, but instead asked the chief pilot what kind of flying she would be doing.

"You'll be taking out tours every day, six days a week. We've five different tours we offer our passengers, and they're all grandiose, absolutely world-class. On most of them you'll get plenty of free time to play golf or go lay on the beach because your passengers will be given tours of the islands on busses, and you don't have to ride along with them."

She liked that part of it.

"We'll pay you two thousand dollars a month and you'll make at least another two thousand in tips."

What!?

"You get paid only if you complete your flight for each day. If you have a mechanical and have to return to Honolulu, you don't get paid."

"Wait a minute. You told me on the phone that you paid four thousand dollars a month, and now you're telling me it's two thousand plus tips?"

Dave Lannen stiffened. "Well, yeah. The way the system works is kinda like a fixed salary plus commission, only you get tips. And you can make a lot more than two thousand dollars a month in tips. I just said two 'cause I didn't want you to get greedy and all that, but I've managed to earn up to five grand a month in tips alone!"

Valerie was furious. Tips? Five thousand a month in tips? This sonofabitch had made her spend six hundred bucks to fly out to Hawaii and now he was telling her that the actual salary was two thousand dollars? He was nothing but a fraud. Her father had repeatedly warned her that when something sounded too good to be true it probably was and she had made the mistake of ignoring his valuable advice.

No wonder he had stiffened up. For the chief pilot this must be the most difficult moment with most new recruits, but the bastard sounded just like an experienced used car salesman turned pilot, and he must think she was hooked, since she'd flown in all the way from the mainland. Once his victims flew all the way out to Hawaii, Chief Pilot Lannen must figure he had them sold on the whole idea.

They were distracted by the loud roar of two engines entering the ramp area. One of Vacation Airline's airplanes taxied in and shut down, parking next to where they were.

"Here's George!" the chief pilot yelled, visually relieved at the timely intrusion. He exited from the Beech 18 and walked over to help the passengers deplane.

Valerie was mad. She should've known enough when this guy talked to her on the phone. His poor command of the English language should have been a dead giveaway right there. What the hell did a hick like this know about making money anyway? She watched eleven tourists exit the airplane in colorful Hawaiian shirts and walked over to where the chief pilot was talking with the pilot.

"Miss Wall, this here is George Baxter! George, meet our newest pilot, Miss Valerie Wall!"

Valerie was very annoyed but managed to smile and shake hands with George Baxter, He was in his mid-thirties, dark and with a friendly smile.

"Hi, Valerie."

"George, Valerie here's going to need a place to stay and some transportation back into town. Would you mind fixing her up? Giving her a ride maybe?"

George looked at Valerie as if wondering whether she wanted his help or if bigmouth Lannen was just trying to shove him down her throat. "Be glad to give you a ride wherever you want to go."

"Good then!" Lannen added, "come by my office before you go to pick up your script and the airplane manuals. Welcome to Vacation Airlines, Miss Wall. We'll start training first thing in the morning, and you can go ahead and start memorizing your script." He walked away on bow legs, his cowboy snakeskins clopping on the concrete.

"Are you the one who was flying the Sabreliner in California?" George Baxter was built like Clint Eastwood and she liked him, sensing honesty and frankness.

"Yes. How'd you know?"

"Lannen there told us about you at the morning briefing, that he had a jet pilot coming out to fly with us."

"How do you like this place?"

"It sucks. But I have nowhere else to go for now. I was flying DC-8s interislands for Pacific, but they went bankrupt last year and I couldn't find another job so here I am. This place belongs to a Chinese woman who runs it like a slave ship. She has contacts with other Chinese businessmen who own travel agencies here in Hawaii and they kind of scratch each other's back if you know what I mean. She is one cheap bitch, and you don't want to work for her."

Valerie was shocked to hear this confession from a man she had just met.

"I lost an engine on takeoff here one day last summer, with a full load of passengers. One of the pistons on the left engine decided to depart the engine after takeoff so I had to forget about the tour and wrap my ass around this field as fast as I could. When I lined up with the runway for landing the gear refused to come down. I wasn't about to belly flop it with the wings full of fuel so I did something then that's never been done before in a Beech 18, far as I know, I went around and climbed back up on one engine while I solved the gear problem. Sweated blood for half an hour but the gear finally came down, and when I finally landed safely the Chinese bitch told me that she wouldn't pay me for the day because I had not completed my tour. I saved the asses of everyone on that airplane, including my own, and she didn't pay me because I didn't complete my tour."

Valerie was dumbfounded.

"Did Lannen tell you how you're going to be making thousands and thousands of dollars in tips?"
"Yes."

"Hate to tell you, but I've been working here over a year and haven't made two hundred dollars in tips yet– total."

Valerie became angrier.

"Oh, I've tried everything Lannen says to do, like telling the passengers on the PA that we only make money if they tip us, and all that, but it just doesn't seem to work for me. A couple of the other guys here have made some money in tips, but nothing like Lannen would like to have you believe. Besides, I'm not a hustler, I don't like having to bug people for money."

"What is that script he was talking about that he wanted me to memorize?" Valerie decided to catch the first flight back to California tonight.

"Oh, that. Lannen wrote it himself. It's a bunch of bullshit on Hawaiian history he wants you to give the passengers right after you takeoff from here to keep them entertained while you fly them to the first island on the tour. You know, about the shark god who brought the natives to these islands, that kind of crap, except he made up most of it."

"George, I really appreciate you telling me this. Why are you staying here?"

"I'm waiting for Pacific Airlines to restart operations again. I know the owner, he's been trying to obtain financing and the minute he does I'll fly for them again."

"Why didn't you try your luck with Hawaiian or Aloha?" They walked towards the large hangar.

"I did, but Aloha is not hiring and the chief pilot at Hawaiian and I don't see eye to eye."

"What do you mean?"

"He doesn't like me and will never give me a job. But what about you? Why don't you go to Hawaiian and talk to them?"

Valerie had sent Hawaiian a resume but so far had heard nothing from them. She told George this.

"That's because that's not the way they do business here, Valerie. What you have to do is walk in there in person, see the chief pilot and tell him you want to work for them."

"Just like that?"

"Yes."

"George, that's not the way to do it with the big airlines. I wouldn't even get past the guard at the gate."

"Not here, Valerie. Here it's different, they are informal and they'll talk to you if you just show up. Why don't you go talk to the chief pilot at Hawaiian? His name is Howard Machado and he'll see you."

"Machado? Is he Spanish?"

"No, Portuguese. He's over on the other side of the airport by the terminal. Just go over there and tell him what happened, that Vacation Airways is not for you and that you'd like to fly for them. He'll see you."

It sounded unlikely because Valerie knew the big airlines did everything through the mail when it came to hiring, but what did she have to lose? She had already come all the way out here.

"Alright, I'll talk to him. Just do me a favor and don't tell this guy Lannen that I'm not staying here."

George laughed. "Don't worry. Far as he's concerned you're flying with him early tomorrow morning to start your training!"

Valerie thanked George and followed him into one of the classrooms to pick up her script and her airplane manuals. The chief pilot was on the phone and he winked at her and gave her the thumbs-up.

She smiled back.

Fuck you, Mister.

George drove an old Datsun with rusty edges, and she felt bad for him. He was obviously a decent man and deserved better than this. He drove her to the airport, to the offices of Hawaiian Air.

"You gonna stay the night, or are you going to catch a flight back to the mainland tonight?"

Valerie told him she intended to head back tonight.

"I thought maybe, if you wanted to get a good taste in your mouth about Hawaii, that maybe you'd want to stay the night and go with me to my aunt's house for dinner. She and my uncle have lived here many years since he retired from the Navy, and they have a real nice place up in the hills overlooking the ocean."

Valerie considered his offer, she could sense that he was not trying to hit on her, and he was a decent man. She did want to go home with a nice memory of Hawaii and perhaps that would be a good way to do it. After all, she'd already paid for the airfare.

"I mean," George continued, "I don't want you to feel uncomfortable or anything. If you want to join me I guarantee you'll enjoy a good meal, but don't feel like you have to."

"Naw, I'm not uncomfortable. Matter of fact, it sounds like a great idea. I'll come."

George Baxter looked at her to ascertain that she was not kidding, then smiled.

He drove her to the building where Hawaiian Air had its offices. "Can you get to your hotel from here? I gotta run some errands and then I can pick you up about three."

She thought she could catch a cab to her hotel with no problem. "Sure, that's fine. That sounds good. George. I'll see you this afternoon."

"Bye Valerie, good luck with Machado and remember not to mention my name or yours will be mud."

She waved him good-bye and entered the building wondering what he could have done to piss off the chief pilot. There was no security guard at the door, which she found refreshing. No receptionist either. Now what? She walked down a corridor and found a desk with a middle-aged woman.

"Good morning–."

"Good morning, dear. How may I help you?"

"Aah I'm looking for Captain Howard Machado's office. The chief pilot?"

"Right over there," she pointed to the room across from where she was sitting. "But he's not there."

"When could I find him?"

She stood up, moving away from her desk "I'll find him for you."

Valerie couldn't believe her ears. People didn't just drop in on chief pilots of major airlines and talked to them! These people were just incredibly friendly!

A short stocky man with dark hair and a friendly face appeared down the hallway walking directly towards her.

"Captain Machado?"

"That's me. And you want a job?"

Valerie was stunned by his directness. "Yeah, I mean, yes, if you have one."

"Come into my office." He sat behind his desk and reached for a stack of resumes two feet high. He had a screaming red Hawaiian flower shirt on, and looked like Peter Falk in *Columbo*. "You sent me a resume?"

"Yes, about three months ago, Captain, but I never received a response."

The Portuguese laughed. "We don't respond to people from the mainland. Have found too many of them come out here, cost us a bundle to train and then discover they can't take island life and split. How about you, what brings you here?"

She considered giving him a story about her dad being from the islands, being a native Hawaiian and how she could live here all her life but decided against it. She told him the truth.

"And you think you could live here?" He was searching the resumes for hers, found it and placed it in front of him. "Sabreliners, uhm?"

"Yes, I've been flying a Sabreliner for a year, and I can assure you that if you give me an opportunity to fly for you I will not let you down."

Machado looked at her. "You seem pretty straightforward, you're dressed with nice clothes and your haircut is not too extravagant. You also have Sabreliner experience and seem physically fit."

He paused. "I can offer you captain on the Dash seven, copilot on the DC-9 inter-island or flight engineer on the DC-8 flying all over the Pacific."

The butterflies in her stomach fluttered in panic. She just could not believe her ears. "What do you mean?"

"Just what I said. I think you're qualified so I'm offering you a choice of flying the Dash Seven as captain, the DC-9 as first officer or our DC-8s as a flight engineer. Your choice."

She felt euphoric, wanting to jump up and kiss this man. He was so casually offering him what she had struggled all her life to attain, and he had taken her by such complete surprise that she didn't know what to say. He was actually offering her three wonderful choices that most pilots in the United States would die for!

"The company psychiatrist is in Los Angeles right now so you'll have to wait a week or so before we can give you a class date, but it shouldn't be any longer than that."

She could not believe what was going on. She hadn't even filled up an application, for crying out loud! "I'll take it! I mean, I accept!"

"Which one?"

"The DC-9. I'd love to fly that." She wanted Paul Morris to move to Honolulu with her and he wouldn't be thrilled to have her flying DC-8s all over the South Pacific on ten day trips. No, the DC-9 was definitely the perfect choice. Interisland hopping and home every night.

Machado wrote something on her resume, placing it on a stack that was separated from the rest. "Then the DC-9 it'll be. You staying in Honolulu or are you planning on going back to the mainland?"

"I'll do whatever you want. No, I mean, I'll stay here if it's just a week."

"Why don't you go home and get your stuff ready?" Machado could see that she was so excited she could hardly talk and decided to help her out. "Just go home and call me next week. I'll have a class date for you then."

"Thank you. I will. When will the class be?"

"You'll just have to take the psycho tests and then you're in. Two, three weeks max. I've got an entire class selected here just waiting for the tests."

She thanked him profusely feeling totally inadequate, but what could she say to a man who was making her most coveted dream a reality? He stood up to shake hands and walked her to the door.

Valerie caught a cab to her hotel and called Paul Morris on his cellular as soon as she entered her room.

"We are sorry, but the mobile customer you are trying to reach is not in range at this time..."

Oh, damn. She had wanted to share this with Paul Morris and he either didn't have his cellular on or he was out somewhere where she couldn't reach him. This was the most excited she had ever been in her life, and wanted to share the moment with someone who could understand just what it meant. Her mom would be thrilled, but Valerie would wait to tell her in person.

She dialed George Baxter's number.

"Hullo?"

"George? It's Valerie."

"Valerie? Hi! Did you see Machado?"

"Yes! And guess what? He offered me a job!" She felt bad the moment it came out of her lips. George had been denied the same blessing, and now she was flaunting it.

"No, shit! That is fantastic! What'd he offer you?"

She told him about the conversation with the chief pilot and George told her to get ready because he was leaving right then to pick her up because they had to celebrate this event."

Valerie hung up, feeling elated and sad at the same time. Her dream was materializing, yet for some reason George's hadn't. She would have to ask him what happened between him and Machado, perhaps after she joined the company she could help him. George was a real sport, not only pointing her in the right direction but rejoicing for her. She suddenly felt a tremendous surge of affection for this man who had just changed her life.

"SO YOU TOLD THAT jerk Dave Lannen that I've been hired by Hawaiian?" They were in George's Datsun crossing Waikiki enroute to his relatives' place.

"Yes, I told him that you thought he was a crook and a fraud and that you were going to turn him in to the FAA and the FBI for fraud and intentional misrepresentation. He just about choked on that one. He became furious and ordered me to recover his aircraft manuals and the script back from you and bring them to work tomorrow morning."

"But I didn't say any of that!"

"Of course you didn't, but I've been dying to say that to him for months, however, if I said that to him he would fire me. If you said it, he can't fire me."

Valerie chuckled. "Maybe I shouldn't be so hard on Lannen, George, after all if he hadn't lured me here I would have never met you and I wouldn't have a job with Hawaiian."

"No, Valerie, the man is dishonest just like the Chinese woman. They are not good people and they deserve all the grief they can get."

Valerie felt admiration for this strange man. All she had been able to get out of him was that he had flown out of Spokane, Washington before coming to Hawaii, and nothing else. He was not unfriendly, just not open to talking about his past.

"You see that cross up there?" He pointed at a huge cross planted between two hills west of Pearl Harbor.

Valerie saw the cross. "I see it, what is it?"

"That cross marks the site where the Japanese Zeros first flew into the Harbor on the day of the attack."

"No shit."

"Nope, no shit, cross marks the spot."

They arrived at his uncle's house high in the hills behind Waikiki and she loved it. The architecture was tropical with a large porch and incredible vegetation. George introduced her to his uncle Sam, a carbon copy of John Wayne but with a mischievous sense of humor, and to his aunt Lisette, who reminded Valerie of Jessica in *Murder She Wrote*. They had drinks outside, enjoying the delightful ocean breeze and his relatives made her feel very comfortable. Neither one asked her if she was dating George and since he didn't volunteer any information about their relationship, she took it upon herself to bring them up to speed on how they had met. They were thrilled for her about her job offer with Hawaiian and toasted to it.

George had beautiful manners and he was very considerate to her, which filled her heart with gratitude. If it hadn't been for him she would have been in a real jam. The liquor and the deliciously sensuous smell of flowers in the air began to have an effect on her. She could not believe that she was holding an airline job in her hands and that she was celebrating it in some strangers' home in Hawaii.

"Valerie was flying corporate jets in the mainland," George explained to his relatives. "She's very well qualified." He was relaxing on a hammock hanging between the building and a palm tree.

Aunt Lisette was duly impressed by this, and remarked how proud Valerie's dad must be of her.

"I'm sure he is, wherever he is," Valerie answered, her eyes growing moist.

Uncle Sam shot a glance at his wife that could have perforated steel.

"Her dad died five years ago," George put in, matter-of-factly.

"Oh, Valerie, I'm sorry...I didn't know–."

"Don't fret," Valerie managed a half smile. "You had no way of knowing. He died five years ago and he was a wonderful man and I'm sure he's looking at me this very moment and he is proud of me."

"Valerie, have you ever seen a tarantula?" George asked her.

"A tarantula? No, why?"

"Cause there's one passing right under your chair as we speak."

Valerie was out of her chair in an instant, looking back underneath it. There was nothing there. "Where's the tarantula?"

George walked back towards the bar. "In your imagination."

"You little shit!" She ran over to him, punching him in the arm. That broke the ice and everyone laughed. He held her away with one hand, accidentally touching her breast. They stared into each other's eyes.

"You were getting too serious, woman. It's bad for the party."

Valerie held his hand, liking the warmth emanating from him. "Don't you ever do that to me again."

"Okay, captain. Now, if you're through threatening me, I think it's getting a little past bedtime for me."

"You mean you wanna go?"

"No, I mean it's getting a little past bedtime."

"Alright, we'll go." She had truly enjoyed the evening with these wonderful people and regretted seeing it end, but George was right. It was time to go.

They bid their good-byes and headed back into town in the old Datsun.

"Where are you taking me?" Valerie asked him. He had not said too much since they left the house.

"He turned to look at her, "to your hotel. Isn't that where you want to go?"

"No."

George looked at her again, surprised. "No? Where did you want to go then?"

"To your place, George Baxter."

SHE SLEPT ALL THE way to Los Angeles. Staying up all night with George had exhausted her, and the excitement of flying for Hawaiian had mentally drained her. She was very surprised about what had happened between her and George, and her conscience bothered her but what was done was done and there was no use rehashing it.

She hadn't experienced a one-night-stand since her college days, and was astonished that she had ended up spending the night with George, but she knew that's all it was, a one-night-stand, and that it would not affect her relationship with Paul Morris because she would never see George again. Or would she? If they moved to Honolulu, then she was bound to run into him eventually. She had also promised herself that she would try helping him out with Hawaiian. These were things she still had to sort out in her mind but which could wait for a more appropriate moment. For now, she had a million details floating in her mind. She had to make arrangements for her car to be shipped to Hawaii because buying one there was too expensive, she had to pack, talk to Paul Morris about their future. They had decided that after they got married she would commute to Los Angeles so that he could continue working for Honeywell, but now things had changed. She didn't want to spend her life commuting between Los Angeles and Hawaii in order to go to work and she absolutely adored Hawaii so they would have to move there and find a job for Paul Morris. That was going to be a tough one.

She arrived in Los Angeles and went directly to a payphone.

"Paul Morris speaking."

"Hi, Honey–it's me!"

"Valerie! Where are you?"

"I'm back in L.A. Just got in. And guess what?"

"What? You got the job with Vacation?"

"Nope!"

"You didn't get it? Darn it, Valerie, I'm very disappointed for you. You haven't been having much luck lately, and I wish I could help you in some way, but I really don't know how. The world of aviation is totally foreign to me."

"No, I didn't get the Vacation job, that sucked and I'll tell you about it later, but guess what–I got hired by Hawaiian Air as copilot on the DC-9!"

Paul Morris whistled. "That is fantastic, Valerie! No kidding?"

"No kidding, darling. You are talking to a regular airline first officer."

"That is wonderful! Tell me, what happened? When do you start? And how did that happen? I didn't know you had lined up an interview with them."

"How about you buy me dinner at the 94th Aero Squadron in Van Nuys and I'll tell you all about it?"

"You're on. How are you getting home?"

"I took the Flyaway bus from Van Nuys, left my car at the parking lot up there. I'll be there in one hour."

"I'll pick you up at home."

VALERIE GOT HOME AFTER nine, exhausted. Dinner with Paul Morris had been a real treat, and she had delighted him with her adventures in Hawaii but she'd omitted the part where she spent the night with George Baxter, and her conscience really bugged her, but there was nothing she could do about it now and that was that. She had fallen prey to a lethal combination of tropics, the fulfillment of a life-long dream, some liquor and a good looking, gentle guy, and she would just have to live with it, but there was no need to hurt Paul Morris by telling him since she didn't intend to ruin that relationship. She had not raised the issue of her commuting to Hawaii, which she really didn't want to do, but decided to wait until a more appropriate moment to spring it on him. She fed her cat and listened to the messages on her answering machine.

"Honey, this is Mom, give me a ring when you get in, I want to know if you're coming to Santa Barbara this week-end...Hi! this is Gina with Care Vets, just want to remind you that your cat Mustang is due for her shots...Valerie, this is Diane Brooks with MidAmerica Airlines, today is Friday night at six and we'd like you come to St. Louis for a medical. Please give me a call as soon as you get this message. My home number is 314-928-7654 and I'll be in all week-end. Look forward to hearing from you, bye!"

Valerie jumped over to push the REPEAT button on the machine. MidAmerica Airlines!? But didn't they say it would be at least till the end of the year before they hired anybody? She listened to the message several times, not believing what she was hearing. What was it Captain Eackle had said that if a candidate got called in for a medical it was because she had been selected? She looked at the time. Nine-thirty, it would be ten-thirty in Missouri.

She dialed the number.

"Hello?"

"Diane Brooks?"

"Speaking."

"Diane, hi, this is Valerie Wall, I'm calling you from Los Angeles, I just got back from Hawaii and got your message on my answering machine."

"Valerie, yes! Hi, thanks for returning my call. The reason I called you is because we'd like you to come in for a medical."

Valerie wanted confirmation that if she passed the medical they would offer her a job. "How's the hiring looking?"

"It's looking good, we'd have a class date for you on the fifteenth of next month. This may not give you enough time to give your employer two-weeks' notice. Will that be a problem?"

Valerie was in shock. A problem? "No, that will definitely not be a problem, Diane. When do you want me to come out?"

"Can you come tomorrow?"

"Sure." She would come right now if Diane said so.

"Great. I'll fax the pass authorization to Delta right away and it'll be there in the morning when you go to the airport. Take a taxi to the training center building and I'll meet you there to give you directions on how to get to the clinic downtown."

"Fantastic. I'll be there around three-thirty–if Delta is on time, that is."

"They will be. See tomorrow, then."

Valerie hung up, reaching for a beer. She needed one– no! She shouldn't have one if she was taking a physical exam tomorrow. She put the beer back in the fridge and poured herself a V-8 juice instead.

A class date on the fifteenth!? She was being considered for a class date on the fifteenth? She let out a scream of joy. Whatever they had told them in St. Louis didn't mean anything now. They must have decided to move up their airplane acquisitions or something.

Two job offers! She could not believe it. What was she going to do? She ran in her bedroom, bringing out to the kitchen table all the information she had on MidAmerica Airlines and Hawaiian Air. She was going to analyze both opportunities with a magnifying glass because once she accepted one, that would be it–she would be married to that airline for life.

Hawaiian paid $24,000 during the first year, against MidAmerica $11,400, but after that first year MidAmerica jumped to $50,000, while Hawaiian stayed at a modest $36,000. Honolulu was not a cheap place to live when compared to St. Louis, which was no small consideration.

Valerie wrote down the pros and cons of each airline, studying all the information she had until late into the night. By the time she had reached a decision it was two a.m.

She would go to work for MidAmerica if they offered her a job, and since she had no reason why she should fail the medical, she knew she would have the offer.

MidAmerica was twice the size of Hawaiian, and the salary structure was definitely more convenient. Also, she could move to St. Louis by land, rent a Ryder truck and have Paul Morris help her, whereas she would have to pay a small fortune to ship her things and her car to Hawaii. Another factor was that MidAmerica flew coast-to-coast, which would provide for interesting flying whereas Hawaiian only flew between the islands, which could get very boring after a few years.

She picked up the phone and called Paul Morris to tell him.

ELEVEN
PRESENT TIME - BERLIN, GERMANY

"Do they pay you the same as the men?"

Valerie was momentarily outraged by her question, but saw that Elaine Griffin didn't intend any offense. "Yes, I get paid the same as any man. We have a union here that guarantees that. This isn't the corporate world of rats where everyone's salary is a state secret so the women can get screwed. Here all captains get paid the same for similar equipment."

"Equipment?

"Airplane types."

"Oh."

"You're right, Elaine, this job historically was a good ole boy's club, but now enough women have become airline pilots so the guys are beginning to accept the concept without too much bitching. It was difficult for me to fly with some of the old bigots who had a problem just because I was a woman, particularly because I was more efficient than most of them, but as long as I did the job they couldn't touch me professionally. See, this profession has a tremendous advantage in that it has a union to defend you from injustice. It's all very clear-cut as far as promotions and pay raises and vacations. It's all done by seniority and thank God politics don't really play a part. As you know, politics are the shield men use in the corporate world to hold the glass ceiling over women."

"I see." Elaine admired any woman strong enough to get ahead, and she particularly envied Valerie Wall her position of prestige in what she considered a man's world.

Their food came and Valerie had to admit it was delicious. The *Dortmunder* Cafe was a wonderful Bavarian oasis in the heart of Berlin. She wondered if Charlie was also having dinner in the back. She would've liked to have seen him but doing so would give him away without doubt.

"I transmitted your request to the proper people," Elaine Griffin started, "and they accepted your terms, however they expect some additional work for fifty thousand dollars per carry."

Valerie nearly choked on a mouthful of potatoes. Fifty grand a carry and they accepted? She swallowed before replying. "What kind of additional work would that be?"

"They want you to do some recruiting."

"Recruiting?"

"Yes, nothing big, you understand, but since you have access to other pilots they feel that you could do us a world of good by bringing in other captains into the business."

Oh, fuck. "You mean you expect me to convince other TGA pilots to smuggle dru...*scarves*?"

Griffin smiled. "I wouldn't put it quite that way, but if you want to be blunt about it, yes, that's more or less what's expected of you. Not just TGA pilots, any airline will do."

"Your boss is nuts. What if I recruit the wrong guy and he sings his heart out to the FBI?"

"First of all, the FBI has no jurisdiction in Germany, Valerie, second, we trust in your ability to read personalities and make an offer only to those pilots whom you absolutely trust."

"Well, what if you're wrong and I read incorrectly?"

"That would be most inconvenient."

"Yeah, it would, wouldn't it? Forget it, Elaine. I made a deal to work with you without putting my head on the chopping block and what you're asking me to do is totally out of the question."

"Valerie, if you don't accept our terms, then we can't work together."

'Well, that's too fucking bad."

"Valerie, be sensible, you don't have to recruit the entire damned airline. A volunteer here and there'll do. You can take your time, all we ask is that you try. Besides, it would make you look real good with the home office if they saw you trying, wouldn't it? I mean, think about it, you're a rookie and in a way you do have to prove yourself."

The home office? It sounded almost comical. These crooks really considered themselves a real corporation, didn't they? She rapidly considered this. If she refused to work on their terms she may meet with an unfortunate accident, on the other hand, she could say yes for the time being and buy some time in which to get lost. This deal with the Feds would not last too long anyway so she could probably afford to gamble a little.

"Alright, I'll tell you what Elaine. You tell your home office that I'll play ball with you and that I'll try to get us some more contacts among the pilots, but I am not giving you any guarantees that I'll succeed *and* I want one hundred thousand dollars for each individual I recruit, payable at the time I give you their name for initial contact."

Elaine Griffin chuckled. "I was right about you, Valerie. You're one ambitious bitch. I'll pass on your request to my boss, but I can't promise you anything. They may go with your terms and then again, they may not."

Valerie drank some beer to hide her smile. Asking for additional remuneration must have further convinced Elaine Griffin that she was legit. This much ambition could not be faked. "Fair enough. I'm not stupid, Elaine. I know too much to be turned loose now, but I'm worth nothing to you guys dead, so be a good girl and convince the brass to give me what I ask for and then everyone will profit. Remember, I have friends at every major airline in the United States, and I can set up a network for you guys that will make your head spin."

Valerie felt Elaine Griffin staring intensely at her across the table. Valerie suspected Elaine Griffin must be momentarily wondering if perhaps she may not be underestimating this TGA captain, her new recruit.

"I'll pass on your message and we'll go from there. Valerie, are you computer literate?"

Valerie' heart jumped. "I can use computers, if that's what you mean."

"Have you ever used a laptop?"

Valerie took a deep breath. Wasn't that what Charlie had said was the common denominator for all the airline personnel that had been murdered? "No, I've never used a laptop but I assume it must be the same as a regular computer, no?"

"Pretty much, except you can take it with you." She reached for her huge handbag laying on the bench next to her and pulled out a brand new Toshiba Satellite notebook computer, setting in on the table between them. "This here is one of the Seven Wonders of the World."

Valerie speculated that if Charlie was watching he would know that they'd hit pay dirt. That's if he didn't suffer a coronary from watching this first.

"Computers are doing to mankind this century what the steam engine did to us the last century, they are dramatically changing the world. This model has enough storage space to hold several Encyclopedia Britannicas in it, or about 200,000 pages of typewritten material. It can send and receive data anywhere in the world from any telephone line via modem and fax, and it can perform in one minute more computations than 15,000 engineers could accomplish working full-time for one year."

Valerie knew enough about computers to suspect that this particular model sold for nearly four thousand dollars.

"This is a gift for you," Elaine Griffin pause momentarily to evaluate the effect her words were having on the pilot. "We want you to have it because it's not prudent for us to keep meeting in person unless we absolutely have to, and this computer provides us with all the communications we need."

"You mean you want us to communicate through the telephone using this computer? What about privacy?"

"You don't have to be worried about that, Valerie. It comes with a very powerful encrypting program so that everything we send to each other will be nothing but garbage to anybody clever enough to intercept it.

"No shit." Valerie saw that Elaine appeared more relaxed. The woman must feel that the meeting was working out very nice, according to plan.

"No shit, Valerie." She pulled out several manuals out of her purse, depositing them next to the computer. "I don't expect you to read all these, but it'd be nice if you could kinda look through these manuals to start getting some idea as to how the system operates. Are you familiar with *WINDOWS 95*?"

"Yes, I've used *WINDOWS 95.*" She had it installed in the new Pentium desktop computer she'd bought the week before her trip to Germany. She still had no idea how to use the new operating system, but it wouldn't hurt to stretch the truth just this one time. What was a little white lie compared to the shit these people were pulling?

"Excellent, because everything we do is through that environment. What we'll do then is communicate through the telephone using the number in the inside of the first manual there. Read as much of this stuff as you can and send me a test fax tomorrow at the number provided. If you run into any problems call me at the same number you reached me today."

"Wait a minute, I never said anything about becoming a computer engineer..."

"Don't tell me this is going to cost us more money, Valerie, because I don't think they'll go for it."

"It's not money, Elaine, it's time. When the hell do you think I'm going to have time to learn all this? I have to fly airplanes for a living, remember?"

"Oh, yes, I remember." She reached into her bag and pulled out a thick brown manila envelope. "This is for the first carry you did for me, the one with the small scarves. Saturday I'll issue you the one for the second carry after you send me the test fax."

Valerie reached for the envelope, it felt heavy. Opening it she glanced inside at the bundles of bills packed together. She pulled one packet out. One hundred dollar bills, $10,000 per pack, as advertised on the pink paper strip holding the bills together.

Elaine was smiling at her. Elaine must think she knew what made this pilot tick, and now Valerie would surely purr like a pussycat.

"I guess I'll make time to go over these manuals."

"Good. Now be a good sport and order us some apple strudel!"

"SO YOU'RE NOW AN official part of the network?" Charlie Smith touched the Toshiba laptop that Valerie had installed on the desk in his room. Charlie was not familiar with personal computers and they intimidated him, but he'd never admit that to anyone, much less Valerie. He was highly proficient with the computers they used for navigation, and those at the crew rooms, where they signed in for trips, but other than that, he was completely ignorant.

"I guess she must really like me. We're going to communicate via the modem from now on, which is incredible, isn't it? High tech crime."

"When she pulled out this laptop out of her purse I knew the bitch was one of 'em!" Charlie had followed Valerie into the *Dortmunder* restaurant and had sat at another booth facing the two women but at a considerable distance so they wouldn't notice him. "You know, most people never became involved in anything dangerous in their lives, particularly people of our comfortable socio-economic status, yet now we're playing cat and mouse with mass murderers and drug lords."

"Yeah, I guess this confirms what that Fed told you, no?"

"Absolutely. They're going to have an orgasm when I tell them about this in the morning. Whatever group is responsible for aircraft bombing and multiple assassinations has made contact with you and they want you to become an account executive for them."

"This is beautiful, Charlie, at first it was just drug smuggling, now it's murder and espionage. We're really getting deep in this shit, you know?"

"I know, Val, but now I realize we made the right decision staying here instead of trying to run. These jokers seem very well organized and I think we better do everything we can to help the feds even if it's just for our own protection."

Valerie sat in front of the computer, hitting the switch to boot it up. "Guess I better hit the books and learn how to use this baby if I'm going to be sending a fax to Elaine in the morning."

"You know how to use one of those?" Charlie popped open a bottle of Heineken.

"Pretty much. Paul Morris has taught me a lot about computers, and they're all pretty much alike. I just have to see what programs they have in this one and learn the communications package. I intentionally didn't let Elaine know that I'm pretty comfortable with computers. The less information she has about me, the better."

"Piece of cake," Charlie was relieved that she sounded so self-confident.

"Charlie? When you talk to the feds in the morning, don't say a word about the fifty thousand Elaine just gave us."

Charlie swallowed some beer. "Now, that sounds strange. Why not?"

"I don't know, but I think I'd rather keep that money around here just in case we have to bail out in a hurry. With fifty grand we can buy our way out of a lot of sticky situations, and if you tell the feds about it they're going to harass us into establishing a courier to send them the money and I don't really want to get involved with any additional bullshit at this time. When Elaine gives us the additional fifty thousand tomorrow I want to keep that too. Look at it as insurance. At this point, we don't know what can happen."

He reflected on this. "Well, you're not the kind of person who would all of a sudden get greedy, and what you say does make sense. If we have to get out in a hurry, we could even rent a personal jet with that kind of dough. Sounds good to me. Where do you want to keep this cash?" he had been very surprised to see the contents of the envelope when Valerie had handed it to him.

"I don't know, haven't thought about that one yet."

"How about we get a couple of money belts and keep the cash on ourselves at all times? Keeping it in the rooms is out of the question, these chambermaids know all the good hiding places, and I sure as hell don't want to leave it at the front desk."

"No, of course not. Your idea is good. How about you go out shopping for money belts while I study this computer?" She had to master the use of the communications program, and she was not going to succeed with Charlie distracting her.

"I'll go for that. Don't open the door to anyone. Three knocks and you'll know it's me."

She smiled at his amateur attempt at underworld behavior. "Okay, Charlie. Also, do me a favor, buy some diskettes for this computer. I think you can probably pick up about ten boxes of formatted diskettes at that computer store next to the plaza."

"Formatted diskettes? What size?"

"Three and a half inches, I want to back up everything in here just in case we might need it later."

"Will do." Charlie dropped the money envelope on the table and left.

Valerie called the front desk asking for messages. There was one from Paul Morris, he had left a number in Berlin. She hurriedly dialed it.

The hotel operator at that number connected her to the room of one Paul Morris. He answered it after the first ring, evidence that he had been sitting by the phone.

"Paul? Honey, it's me."

"Valerie! Boy, am I glad to hear from you. How are you? Everything alright?"

She brought him up to speed on the latest development, omitting mentioning about the cash. No need to mention that over open telephone lines.

"And Charlie went to get you the diskettes?"

"Yes, he should be back within a half hour."

"Get a taxi and come over. Leave him a message that you had to go buy some supplies."

"Uhm, no Paul, that's not a good idea. He may thing that I've been kidnapped and do something stupid. Remember, I'm supposed to be learning how to use this computer. I think we should tell him that you're here."

"No. Don't do that, but I think you're right, it's better if he finds you there when he returns. Tell him that you've decided to go back to your own room and I'll come over and meet you later tonight, after everybody's sleeping." Paul Morris was feeling like a zombie after flying the all-nighter from Los Angeles to Paris and then catching a Lufthansa flight to Frankfurt and a Pan Am to Berlin. And now he was obviously anxious to get his hands on Valerie's new laptop computer because as a computer engineer he could find out one heck of a lot more than she could. He could look for hidden files which may give them some insight into this organization.

They agreed to meet in her room at two a.m.

PAUL MORRIS UNDRESSED AND climbed into bed, setting the alarm for one a.m. He had no idea what Valerie had stumbled upon but he was going to help her get out of it. He'd been at a loss about how to help her but now that computers were involved he felt a little more like a participant. He didn't like the fact that she had not gone to the German authorities immediately, but understood her reasoning. These Germans were efficient as hell but one had to speak their language in order to get a point across, or they could easily intimidate the hot cakes out of anyone. He didn't trust anyone when it came to drugs because he'd read plenty and seen enough movies to know that it was an extremely hazardous business. Valerie' copilot might be straight and then again he might not, so he decided to stay on the sidelines and not inform him of his presence in Berlin. What he really wanted to do was extricate Valerie from this mess and take her home, but his ordered mind realized and accepted the trap she'd walked into and maybe it was better to just play along a little longer.

His intuition was correct, but he would not know it until later.

VALERY GLANCED THROUGH THE peephole at Paul Morris standing in front of the door looking like a goldfish in the wide-angle lens.

"Paul!" she let him in, throwing her arms around his neck, kissing him. God, it was so good having someone she could trust no matter what.

They sat on the bed and she retold everything that had happened since she'd first been approached by Elaine's' sister about the Istanbul scarves.

Paul Morris listened to her without interrupting until she was finished.

"I see. This is worse than I'd thought. Nice of the feds back in New York to recruit you while they're thousands of miles away, unable to provide help if you needed it. What I think we ought to do is first of all take a look at this computer of yours." He opened the notebook computer, booting it up. "Did you figure out how to send the fax to this woman?"

"Yes, that wasn't too difficult. I looked through the directories and it appears pretty standard. I'm sure you'll be able to learn a lot more than I can from it, but it doesn't seem to have anything important in it."

Paul Morris began to sort through the files in Valerie's laptop, looking for something custom-made, something hidden. "These people give the impression of being professionals, and if this is the case then there'll be nothing useful in this computer, but one never knows. They may've overlooked something. This Charlie guy, how well do you know him?"

Valerie could understand Paul's distrust because he didn't know Charlie, but it was unjustified. "I've been flying with him all month, Paul. I think he's alright. Think about it, would he have gone to the feds if he wasn't?"

"How are you so sure that he went to the feds? Because he told you?"

Valerie didn't like the implications.

"Has he been buying any expensive items that you know of?"

Valerie brushed her hair from her eyes. "No, Paul, he hasn't bought any Ferraris or Rolls Royces lately, and I believe him. Besides, why would they ask me to bring the scarves from Istanbul if he was already one of them? I mean, he's flying to Istanbul just as often as I am."

"To recruit you. Look, I'm not saying Charlie is one of them, I'm just trying to develop a plan of action here."

"Good, then let's base it on the assumption that Charlie did go to the feds and that he is straight."

"We're gonna have to confirm that. You said he calls the feds twice a day?"

"Yes."

"Good, then what you need to do is make the next few calls yourself. Make sure you get the agent's name and I'll call him on the outside to verify that he exists."

Valerie reflected on this and decided that Charlie should go along with such a request, if he was legit. "Okay, I don't like it but I guess it's a good idea. What next?"

Paul Morris was still typing and musing through the laptop. "Then we must set up an escape route just in case the shit hits the fan."

"You mean from Berlin?" Valerie had not given this option much thought except for keeping the fifty thousand that Elaine had given her, which irritated her. As a trained airline captain she should consider every option available to her and she should always keep an open door. Staying ahead was the name of the game.

"Yes, in case something happens and we get wind that these people are on to you, we'd have to get out of here in a hurry, and I want us to have an escape route available so we don't have to think about it when we need it."

"You mean *if* we need it."

"When or if we need it, Valerie."

"I've already thought about the possibility of having to leave Berlin in a hurry, Darling," she reached in her purse, removing the brown manila envelope with the fifty thousand dollars inside. She dropped it on the bed next to him. "Charlie thinks we could even charter a corporate jet with this money and fly out of here."

Paul Morris stopped playing with the computer, removing the cash from the envelope. He whistled. "This is fifty thousand?"

"Yep. And tomorrow I get another fifty."

"Holly crap, Valerie, these people are for real."

She laughed, nervously. "Yeah, and I've been dealing with them for a week now. "

Paul Morris spread the cash on the bed, ripping some of the paper seals holding the bills together. "This is almost what I make in one year, Valerie."

"I know, Darling. These guys mean business, I'll tell you."

"I don't think Charlie's idea of chartering a jet is bad but don't do it until we can check out his story with the feds in New York. If that one checks out then I'll shop around and find us an airplane that is always available in case we need to get lost in a hurry."

She agreed.

"They obviously want you to become extensively involved with this business, or they would've never given you the phone numbers and the computer. Has this Elaine mentioned anything to you about who's behind all this or what nationality they are?"

"Not a word. She did tell me they use a relay system to communicate with each other, but I don't know what she meant by that."

"Is she Latin looking?

"No, she's blonde, German looking. No accent. You think the South Americans are behind all this?"

"I don't know, Valerie. Everybody blames drugs on the Colombians, but why the hell would they bring drugs out of Turkey when they have an unlimited supply in South America?"

"I don't know. Diversification?"

Paul Morris laughed, "Valerie, who knows, but in the meantime they have managed to get you involved, and I don't like it."

"I like it even less than you, Paul. So you think I should send this fax to Elaine in the morning?"

Paul Morris was back at the computer, searching. "Yes, most definitely. I think you are in too deep to pull out now without unpleasant repercussions, so we're gonna have to play their game for a while."

"I don't have to fly until day after tomorrow and Charlie said that I shouldn't take the Istanbul trip any more no matter what. If they don't want me to smuggle then they could have me killed there."

"I agree. Stay away from that place. Is that where you're going on your next trip? Can you call in sick?"

"No, the next trip doesn't go to Istanbul, we go to London and Frankfurt. The one after that goes to Turkey."

"Okay, that gives us enough time to develop a game plan here. I see they're using a utilities program called Norton Utilities. I guess they must use the encryption utility, it's very powerful and virtually indecipherable."

"Can you decipher it?"

Paul Morris looked at his girlfriend, smiling, "No. Nobody can break this code, but I may be able to get the password for it." He had written a small but powerful program that would run until it decoded encrypted password files, and had brought it along.

"But I don't see anything out of the ordinary in this computer. It's either because it's brand-new and they haven't loaded it yet or they are very careful people and don't take any chances. They have no proprietary programs, no hidden files, nothing."

"Paul Morris, you know I could lose my job over this." Her tone of voice was not as strong as usual.

"I'm aware what your career means to you, Val. It makes me furious that these bastards are jeopardizing something that you sweated blood to obtain. We'll make sure every move we take is fully documented so that if it ever gets down to it with TGA you can prove that you had nothing to do with this Organization voluntarily."

"Paul, we're playing a dangerous game here. If these bastards are the same who bombed the Miami Boeing they will certainly not have any trouble knocking me off if that's what they want. All they have to do is look at my monthly schedule in the company's computer and then they can intercept me during a layover in any city in the world."

"Valerie, after we're through with these assholes they'll be too busy with their own problems to ever come after you."

She loved him for the encouragement but somehow his bravado didn't impress her. Big organizations like these could not be destroyed by outsiders so easily. "What do you think we should do next then?"

Paul Morris shut down the computer, disappointed at not finding anything useful in it. "Talk to Charlie tomorrow about calling the feds yourself. Tell him that you want to establish personal contact just in case something were to happen to him so you're not left pissing in the wind."

"Okay, He'll buy that, then what?"

"Call the feds yourself and get a name for me. Send the fax to your friend Elaine and then sit and wait because the ball is in their court. I don't know what they'll ask you to next do but whatever it is, it won't take too long I don't think."

"How do we communicate?" Valerie was glad to have her ally in town. Now she had some power.

"Call me here at anytime if you need me. I'll check for messages every hour if I go out. If you see something you don't like, no matter how small or inconsequential, catch a cab and come over here at once. Here's the room key, keep it and I'll get another one and notify the front desk that my wife will be coming to join me. Check for messages as often as you can but try not to do it when you're with Charlie or he'll get suspicious. If I leave you a message saying that your mom will be in town tomorrow,

get the hell out of the hotel at once without even going to
your room because that means the shit's hit the fan.
Catch a cab and come here directly."

"I'll remember that." Valerie liked the quick, organized
mind of a computer systems engineer. "Keep the cash
here. Just in case Charlie is not straight, I'd hate to lose
our nest egg." Now Paul Morris had influenced her into
distrusting Charlie! She laughed, wondering what she
could be doing at this precise moment if Elaine Griffin
had never come into her life.

They made love and Paul Morris left the room a little
before five a.m. Valerie slept till ten, showered and called
Charlie.

"Meet me for breakfast in the lobby in twenty
minutes."

Charlie agreed and they met in the elegant lobby.
Although they should avoid being seen together too
much, he was still her assigned First Officer for the
month, so having breakfast together once or twice should
not attract undue attention.

"What time do you have to call New York?" Valerie
was not going to waste any time. Charlie was clean and
she knew it, but she still had to get confirmation. Paul
Morris was right, they were now playing for keeps, and
she had to confirm every detail, since her life could very
well be at stake.

He looked at his watch. "In about thirty minutes."

"Let me make the call, Charlie."

"Sure," a look of puzzlement crossed his features.

"It's just that something occurred to me. What if you
get in a situation where I can't reach you and I need to
call for help? I need to know who to contact in New York."

"Makes sense. Let's take a walk until it's time to call
and then we'll eat breakfast."

"PAUL, HI HONEY, it's me."

"Valerie. Where are you?"

" I'm calling you from a payphone"

"Did you find out anything?"

"Do you have a pen?" Valerie looked around her, searching for any suspicious-looking individuals who might be watching her. Everything seemed normal.

"Shoot."

"The agent's name in New York is Gus Olaffson. He's with the DEA or Customs, I'm not sure which, but he has a direct line." She gave him the telephone number. "He was very nice and assured me that they'll be very grateful for any information we can give them. He seemed very happy to hear that I was given a computer because it confirms that we're on to something here. I questioned him on the kind of payback Charlie and I wanted from him and he assured me that he was making arrangements for us to get what we asked."

"Which was?"

"I told you, to switch to another airline if this thing explodes."

"What else did he say?"

"He thought it was a good idea for me to contact him in addition to Charlie. He asked me to make copies of absolutely everything that's in the computer right now and anything that is loaded onto it. He said that he's working with the Interpol to provide us with local contacts here in Berlin and that he should have it set up within twenty-four hours."

"Good. Valerie, don't call me from payphones out in the street anymore. Try to find a payphone in a hotel or a bathroom or someplace where you can't be seen using the phone just in case you're under surveillance. It'd be hard to explain why you're making calls from the streets of Berlin when technically you don't know anybody here."

"Okay." That got her paranoia back and she scanned the area around her. German pedestrians crowded the sidewalk this sunny day, but it would be very difficult for her to tell if someone was intentionally watching her.

"Paul, I have to return to my room to send the fax to Elaine. I'll call you when I find a discrete telephone."

"Okay, honey. Be careful and don't let Charlie know I'm here until I can double check this information you've given me. I love you."

"I love you too, Paul Morris. Bye." She headed back to the hotel, nervous at the thought of someone following her. In the hotel she went to the front desk.

"Hi, my name is Captain Wall, I'm with TGA, room 206. Are there any messages for me?"

The counter clerk greeted her and produced a brown-wrapped small box, the size of a VHS videocassette.

Kapitän Valerie Wall
Trans Global Airlines
Schweizerhof Hotel
Berlin

It didn't have a return address, but she knew who it was from. No stamps, so it had been hand-delivered. She thanked the clerk, taking the elevator up to her room. In her room she removed the Swiss Army knife from her flight bag, cutting into the cardboard box. Inside, she found another brown manila envelope with another stack of hundred dollar bills, and nothing else–no note.

Her second fifty thousand.

She took the money out of the envelope, ripping the paper seals, spreading it on her bed. She had never held that much cash in her hands before, and it irritated her that so many honest people went their entire lives without seeing this much cash together and those bastard drug dealers could spring twice this amount with no difficulty whatsoever.

She set up the computer for the fax transmission. She carefully loaded the Norton Utilities and encrypted the letter she had typed to Elaine, then connected the computer to the telephone line and sent the fax. She had been instructed to wait for a reply so she sat on her bed studying the cash laying on it. It was easy to see how this much money could tempt someone not in her position in life. Hell, it was tempting even for her. Only a fool would ignore the buying power of fifty thousand dollars. She would have to give this money to Charlie to keep in his money belt. He'd bought two money belts yesterday and had given her one, and he believed that she carried the other fifty thousand on her.

Her computer screen droned "receiving" and she sat up, paying attention. The communications software in her laptop received a file through the modem and saved it in her directory. Valerie went back to the Norton Utilities and de-crypted the incoming file, then she loaded the word processor and looked at it.

Good Job, Valerie.

Your fax came in and everything worked fine. Your second mortgage payment was left at your hotel desk this morning. Hope it is to your liking. We have a first assignment for you.

You are to pick up a package from your airline counter tomorrow morning and take it with you to London. There, you will go eat lunch at your usual airport restaurant where they serve the excellent buffet and you will leave the package on your chair after you finish eating. Someone will pick it up from there. You are not to open it or allow anyone near it for obvious reasons. The package should fit inside your flight bag comfortably.

Upon your return from London call this number from your hotel in Frankfurt and report to us the successful completion of your assignment via email in the same manner as you have just done, but using electronic mail instead of faxing. After you memorize these instructions, use the Norton Wipeout Utility to completely erase this file from your hard disk.

Glad to have you aboard, captain!

E.G.

Valerie's pulse accelerated. Her first assignment! Oh, shit. A package to London. What would it be? Drugs? What if it was a bomb? She had to tell Charlie and Paul Morris. She waited for a couple of minutes to ascertain nothing else was coming over the modem, made a copy of the file and stuck the disk in her flight bag. She would start leaving her flight bag in Operations so nobody could access it. How the hell did Elaine know that she had a trip to London? And how did she know where the crews went to eat during the five hour layovers at Heathrow?

She left her room after grabbing the laptop and the cash, rapidly walking to Charlie's room.

"Valerie? Come in!" Charlie was in his shorts and a University of Miami T-shirt.

"It's happening. They left this for us this morning and now they've just given me my first assignment!" she handed him the envelope with the money. "Look at this."

Charlie read the message on the screen and paled. "Fuck. They want you to take this package tomorrow."

"What if it's a bomb, Charlie? Or what if it isn't and it's drugs and the Brits find them on me?"

"Calm down. Let's think about this for a second. Why would they want to give you a bomb when they just paid you a hundred grand and gave you this computer? It doesn't make sense. Valerie. If they wanted you dead they could have hired someone to do it before giving you the cash."

"Yeah, but are we willing to bet our lives on this?"

Charlie looked at her. "No, we cannot bet our lives on it."

"And what if it's cocaine or some other shit like it? If the Brits find it on me, I'm dead."

"Wait a minute, when we fly to London we go out from the airplane on the crew bus, remember? The customs inspectors who come out to the bus never look at our flight bags cause they know we're only gonna be there five hours. They know we don't overnight in London on this flight. I don't think they'll even notice you have your flight bag with you. I've taken all kinds of stuff with me through Her Majesty's customs and they've never had a clue."

"Maybe, but it's too risky. Let's call Gus in New York and tell him what's going on."

"Okay. You stay here and I'll go call him. Let me look at that message again, though." Charlie reread the fax and left.

Valerie picked up the phone the minute he was out the door and called Paul Morris. His phone rang but there was no answer so she left a message to meet in his room at nine tonight.

She had not liked this one bit before, and now she was very concerned. Taking a package like that across international borders was no small thing. If it was drugs, she hated doing it because someone at the other end was going to suffer with them. If it was a bomb, she'd be damned if she was going to jeopardize her passengers by carrying it with her. No, unless she could absolutely determine what was in the package she was not going to take it to London and damned the consequences. That fourth stripe on the sleeves of her uniform coat carried with it the responsibility of the lives of her passengers, and she was not about to play games with them. What she would do is open the package and see what was in it. If it was a bomb and it exploded on her then too bad, but she owed it to the people who placed their lives in her hands to keep them safe, even if it meant taking the chance of blowing up. What she would do is go to an isolated area of the ramp and open the box. She would tell Elaine the truth that she had agreed to working for them, but that the deal did not include her passengers, so she had to know what she was transporting.

Another idea occurred to her. Maybe she could milk this situation for all she could.

CHARLIE RETURNED IN FIFTEEN minutes.

"Okay, we have a plan of action."

"Did you reach Gus?"

"Yes, he's making arrangements–as we speak–to have your package examined by a bomb specialist in the morning. They will take the package and make sure there are no explosives in it. He's sending a confidential circular to the Paris headquarters of Interpol so they can coordinate with the Germans."

"How the hell are they going to do that?"

"He said Interpol will make arrangements. They have some kind of explosives detector that can scan through suitcases and they'll look at our package before we take it in the morning."

"How are we going to know that this has happened?? Gus could just be telling you that they're going to scan the package and we have no guarantee that they actually will."

"I don't think they'd risk blowing up an airplane full of passengers. I told Gus we're documenting everything that's going on and that another pilot has copies of everything. No, I believe him."

"So now the Germans know what's going on?" Valerie was still not sold on the idea of taking this package.

"I suppose, what the higgins is Interpol anyway, do you know?"

"All I know is what I've read. It's an international criminal police organization with over 120 member countries. They're involved mainly with international crime and they share information among themselves in order to fight people like Elaine Griffin and her type of organization. I think like you said, the headquarters are in Paris and they can coordinate police action all over the world." Valerie reached in Charlie's small fridge. "Do you have beer?"

"Top shelf there. Valerie, if you don't feel confident that the bomb squad can check out the box then let's not take the package."

"And blow my cover?"

"Better to blow your cover than the airplane."

"I think I'll just open it up."

"That would be crazy." Charlie grabbed another beer.

"No, I don't think so. Elaine Griffin doesn't know that a bomb squad is going to check the package for us so I'll just tell her that I wasn't about to take a risk like that with my passengers and I decided to open up the box and check for myself. There won't be any danger 'cause the bomb squad will have checked the package for me beforehand, but Griffin won't know this."

"They specifically asked you not to open the package. That may piss them off real bad."

"If that's the case, then too bad. We'll have to deal with it then. I'm not taking any packages unless I can open them and see what's inside. Remember the Miami crew? It's too late for them but not for us."

"Alright, let's do it your way. The package will be checked by a bomb squad, so if it doesn't explode and you're able to pick it up from our counter, then it should be safe. You have your money belt on?"

"Yes," she didn't like lying to Charlie, but Paul Morris had still not cleared him, so she had to be cautious.

"Then I guess I better strap my belt on and put these in it, eh?" He went in the bathroom with the manila envelope and a brand-new money belt he had bought identical to the one he thought Valerie was wearing.

"Charlie, I got an idea."

"What idea?" he yelled from the bathroom.

"You know how I told them that I would recruit others into this business? Well, I found my first recruit."

"Who?"

"You."

Charlie came out of the bathroom with a look of disbelief. "You're joking."

"No, I'm not. They want me to recruit volunteers and I told them I'll do it for a hundred grand a pop. If you become the first volunteer it'll achieve several objectives; first, it'll show them that I'm on the ball doing my job, second, it'll provide us with an additional one hundred Gs to have as a backup, and third it'll give you an alibi for being with me in case we get spotted together too much."

"I don't know that I like your idea, captain."

"Why not? You afraid to get involved?"

"You know me better than that, Valerie. If I drop my cover who will protect you? We gotta have a backup they don't know about, someone who can move undetected because they ignore his existence."

"You really think they ignore your existence?"

"Yeah, why?"

"Charlie, these people are very resourceful and I don't doubt that this very minute they know I'm in your room, talking to you."

"I doubt that."

Valerie drank from her beer. "I still think you should be my first draft pick. It'll help me score brownie points and establish credibility with Elaine."

"Did she agree to pay you the hundred thousand dollars for each recruit?"

"No, not yet, but I'm sure she will the minute I tell her I have our first candidate."

"I don't like having to deal with the Griffin bitch directly, but I can see that you have a point. That, and I like the idea of adding another hundred thou to the padding around my waist. Maybe after all the shit blows off we can keep the money, since no one knows about it and the bad guys won't be around to tell, eh? Okay, Valerie, if you can talk to superbitch there and get a firm yes about the money, I'll go along with it."

Valerie smiled. Her ideas had a way of getting her in trouble and she hoped this one wouldn't backfire. She would have to wait until their return from London to question Elaine about her headhunter fee. "Good! Now, about this sting operation with the bomb squad. Did Gus tell you if the German police are going to be talking to us?"

"No, he told me this is maximum security and he'll insist with the Germans that no contact is to be made with us in case we are being watched."

"Makes sense, what else did he say? Did you ask him about the modified version of the witness protection plan that we need?"

"Yes, and he said to trust him on that one. They're talking to several of the major airlines back home to see which one is willing to play ball with us."

"Call me skeptical, but I still don't see how he'll be able to pull that one off. And I want a written guarantee with a bunch of signatures on it just in case Gus baby decides to back out on us at the last minute."

"I'll tell him that tonight."

"Tell him we want his offer in writing and with the signatures of the president of the airline and that of the head of DEA."

"I don't know if he'll be able to do that for us, but I'll ask him."

"He better, or he isn't getting diddlysquat from me."

"I'll relay the message, *mademoiselle*. I'm sure glad I'm doing business on the same side of the fence as you! Cheers."

Valerie returned to her room concerned about the way things were developing. Interpol now! Too many people were getting involved in this party, and she was worried that with so many leaks Elaine would realize that she was being double-crossed and start shooting. Too many cooks spoil the stew.

SHE DRESSED AS ELEGANT as possible and took a cab to the St. George's bar. She knew the bar had an exit in the back leading to the interior of the Europa Center, a small shopping mall, and she intended to use it to lose any potential follower. The doorman at the hotel called her a cab and she climbed in, giving the driver the name of the bar which was less than two blocks away.

She entered the St. George's and immediately made her way through the crowded bar to the back exit. Anyone following her would have to use the same door or they would lose her. She exited through the back, then paused, pretending to be fixing her stocking while within sight of the back door, waiting for something to happen. Nothing did.

Ten minutes later she was on another cab headed for the hotel where Paul Morris was.

TWELVE
PRESENT TIME - MEXICO CITY, MEXICO

José Carbajal sat on the floor in the empty expensive apartment in the *Colonia del Valle* neighborhood in Mexico City, glancing at his costly *Piagét* watch.

Ten minutes till transmission.

Under other circumstances, Carbajal could not ever have afforded such an expensive watch because he'd barely completed the fifth grade at the public school in the horrible neighborhood where he grew up in the outskirts of the world's most populated city, and he would normally be unable to secure employment anywhere except perhaps unloading fruit and vegetable trucks at the *La Merced* market, but luck had favored him.

Ever since José Carbajal had been a small boy he'd been fascinated by how things worked, and had spent long hours taking apart and putting back together any piece of machinery that came across his hands. He became very skilled at these tasks. This ability had brought him to the attention of Mauricio Bolaños, the most powerful drug lord in his neighborhood, who had taken him on as his driver, liking the fact that this Carbajal fellow could fix any mechanical problem that may arise with the car on their long trips to small villages where the drug lord secured the drugs he sold. Auto repair shops were quite scarce in rural Mexico, and Bolaños did not like having to depend on strangers whenever he was in need of auto repairs on the road. In his line of work, strangers were always potential enemies.

José Carbajal, at twenty-two, had attained the status of *hombre de confianza*, man of trust, because he'd shot a man in a bar once because the insolent scumbag had the audacity to raise his voice to his boss, Mr. Bolaños. Carbajal's violent reaction in the defense of his boss had touched a rare note of appreciation in the cold heart of Mauricio Bolaños. Loyalty was a very scarce commodity in his line of business, and Bolaños was intelligent enough to prize loyalty when he recognized it, so he'd given his chauffeur a significant pay increase.

Carbajal used his money to buy expensive electronics which he found positively fascinating. One of his recent acquisitions, a *Compaq* laptop computer, had immediately attracted the attention of his boss, who questioned him at length about his knowledge of modems, faxes and communication programs. Carbajal had been playing with computers for three years and felt relatively comfortable with them, and told his boss as much.

"Would you be interested in putting your skill to work for me? It'll make you ten times what you make now as a chauffeur." Bolaños had been experiencing difficulties finding men of trust who were also technically skilled, and his role as operator and supplier for the Organization had been growing increasingly difficult lately.

"Of course, Boss. With a lot of pleasure. Just tell me what you need me to do and I'll do it."

Bolaños told him, and now, two years later, Carbajal, illiterate and uneducated, owned a fully-paid $600,000 house in the exclusive section of *Pedregal*, drove a new Lincoln Continental Towncar and had enough pussy to make him the envy of every man he knew. And all he had to do was relay communications through the Internet between different countries twice a day.

He was delighted with his position in life. His friends envied him, his enemies feared him and he had a great job with no danger whatsoever. He was uneducated, but not stupid. Carbajal knew that drugs were dangerous shit and that a lot of people ended up dead in this business, but his job as technical communications expert precluded him from getting involved in the hazardous duty of field hands.

Still, his mother did not believe him. The old woman was convinced that her son must be dealing, but in her eyes that was all right too. Let 'em all think what they wanted, Carbajal mused–long as the money kept coming he'd continue changing apartments and relaying messages. He had no idea what countries these messages were flowing in from, but had kept backup copies of every single message he had ever received. Carbajal knew the messages were encrypted because he had tried reading them with his DOS editor in his own computer back home, and found nothing but cryptic garbage, but he still kept the backup diskettes just in case someday he was able to break the code. He had no intentions of blackmailing his boss or using the information for any other purpose, he was just technically curious about what they contained and about the challenge inherent in deciphering them. Every week the telephone company would come to the apartment and change the phone line, providing him with a totally new telephone number. Obtaining a new telephone line in Mexico City was tantamount to landing a man on the moon, so Carbajal suspected his boss must be paying a fortune to someone in the telephone company to provide such good service.

He normally operated out of each apartment for one or two months and then moved on to a new one, enjoying the change. He would have preferred furnished apartments, but his boss obviously had reasons of his own for operating only from empty locations. Sitting on the hardwood floor, he heard the phone ring and the modem picked up the call.

José Carbajal became all business. He monitored the reception of the message on the active-matrix screen of the color laptop computer he had been provided for this assignment, making sure the entire message was received and saved into a file in the hard disk.

When reception was completed he removed a small diskette from his pocket, inserting it in the disk drive in front of the laptop. The daily number to call on this relay was stored in the diskette, and he loaded it onto the communications software in his computer. The number was in the United States, just like they always were, and he wondered where in North America he was relaying to. He would have to obtain one of those programs which gave one all the area codes in that country, just out of curiosity. Carbajal had never visited the powerful nation to the north, although he had cousins who'd gone over there illegally to work in the fields, returning with small sums of money as the meager fruit of very hard labor. He was mildly curious about that country, particularly because he did want to visit Disneyland, which he had heard about all his life. He would take his mother there with him when he went.

He disconnected the laptop computer, gathered his coat and left the apartment, driving his cream Lincoln to another empty apartment in the exclusive Polanco neighborhood. Once there, Carbajal unlocked the apartment and connected the modem to the phone lines, turning on the computer and preparing to transmit.

Carbajal typed a few commands into his laptop and sat back to observe his computer dial the Internet bulletin board address and establish contact with a computer at the other end. The host was contacted and communication established, and the software began transmitting the file it had just received from another computer somewhere else in the world.

In six seconds the file labeled

valerie.tga

crossed the two thousand miles separating José Carbajal from a small computer server service in North Hollywood, California, transferring itself into another hard drive inside of another computer. The receiving computer flashed confirmation that the file had been received and signed off, disconnecting from the telephone lines.

The file was then posted in a news bulletin board catering to Internet surfers interested in "French Poetry." The file had been encrypted with the Norton Utilities, and it would be nothing but garbage to anyone who downloaded it, unless they had the necessary password to decode it. The Organization believed that curious netsurfers would delete the file if they accidentally downloaded it and were unable to open it. It was their belief that no person interested in French poetry would also possess the skills required to decode a Norton file.

Each different transmission was posted on different news bulletin boards on the Internet, all across the world, and only the intended recipient of each message would be able to retrieve it and decode it. Even if the record of the call made in Berlin to the number in Mexico City was tracked down by the Interpol, there would be no way to find out where the file went from there.

Foolproof system.

José Carbajal smiled, terminating his task by making a copy of the file he had just sent and then wiping the original from his hard disk with a utility that made recovery impossible. He stored his laptop in the expensive leather case he had been provided and left the apartment, looking forward to a succulent lunch of shrimp and oysters at the *Playa Bruja* restaurant on Insurgentes Avenue.

THE FOURTH STRIPE   Maurice Azurdia

THIRTEEN
PRESENT TIME - ST. LOUIS, MISSOURI
UNITED STATES

Alfredo Hidalgo poured himself a generous glass of Chivas Regal, climbing on a barstool. "You must admit our system's working like a fine-tuned piano," he bragged.

Esteban Escobar smiled at his old friend, puffing on a long Havanero, an aromatic Cuban cigar. "Alfredo, I always knew you were a genius, and this proves it. Business has flourished over the past two years and it's all thanks to you."

"Oh, no, that's not true Esteban, you're the true genius behind this Organization, and you know it." Flowery speech was highly valued amongst Latin Americans, and both men were experts at it, although they knew better than to believe each other's compliments. They did not believe the compliments, but they still liked hearing them.

"Now, now, Alfredo, take some credit where credit is due. You're the brainchild behind this operation. It would've never occurred to me to do what you did, as it hadn't occurred to any of the other guys in Medellin or Bogotá."

"True," Hidalgo admitted, modestly, "I'll take credit for the technical side of it, and you're right, Esteban, none of those guys did what you did but that's because they're all too traditional, you know, too tied to the home turf and not willing to try any new things."

"What you're saying is that they don't have any balls, and I agree with you. Most of those guys are intimidated by the Americans, whether they like to admit it or not, that's irrelevant. You and I know the type. They can flaunt all the bodyguards they want and fly up here in Gulfstream Vs and shop till they drop, but down deep they're still very much provincial at heart and consequently very intimidated by this society."

Alfredo Hidalgo couldn't agree more with his daughter's godfather. Hidalgo was an extremely ambitious man and had seen technology as the most powerful weapon available to man today. If they could harness it, he had believed, the cocaine business would flourish. They could no longer afford to operate like a small corner store in Nicaragua, where all the money went into a tin can and nobody kept track of it. The producers he represented were moving circa seven billion dollars a year, he had told Esteban in Bogotá, and it was high time they operated like a Fortune 500 corporation, using high-tech to keep track of the inventory, sales and marketing. The money they had been losing between the cracks had been more than most Central American nations produced in a year, and that had to stop right now. The almighty Microsoft Corporation was pushing nearly four billion a year in sales, and Escobar would bet that they were run extremely efficiently, so he should be able to do even better with almost twice their sales, and oh, yeah, the added benefit of not having to pay taxes.

The process of "incorporating" their operation to the standards of large American firms had to be directed from the United States, not from the jungles or cities of Colombia, but none of the drug lords had any intention whatsoever of living away from their hometowns. These were powerful men who everybody knew, feared and respected in their home turf, but all their money could not buy them the social position they enjoyed in their own hometowns in another country, much less in the United States. This was the main obstacle preventing any of the big ones from living in North America. Hidalgo strongly felt that only by living in America was it possible to stay on top of the latest technology which would allow them to be successful at their business. Not to mention that in the United States they had their biggest market.

Esteban Escobar had been one of these reluctant Colombians, but he at least had been willing to listen to Alfredo Hidalgo about what he'd proposed. The two men had met at a reception given by the Guatemalan embassy in Mexico City twenty years earlier, and they had instantly liked each other.

Escobar had been in the banana export business back then, and he'd been invited to that particular reception because he had been trying to export Guatemala bananas to Miami.

Over the years, Alfredo Hidalgo had provided passports and other counterfeit documents to his South American friend, who eventually had become the godfather at the baptism of Hidalgo's oldest daughter. The business had eventually gone from bananas to pure cocaine.

ESCOBAR WAS OF THE opinion that, with money, one could provide a good life for one's family anywhere, and after carefully analyzing the plan Alfredo had proposed to him, he had decided to give it a try. The idea had merit, and Escobar, who had attended Harvard as an undergrad, appreciated the concept of efficient management. He was no stranger to computers either, unlike most of his contemporaries in the business, he routinely made use of computers at home. Wonderful relatively new inventions with incredible uses.

The business model Alfredo Hidalgo had advocated seemed relatively simple to establish, and was meant to provide accurate up-to-date information on the status of the Organization at any point in time. It was a relatively simple application of high-technology.

At the time Alfredo Hidalgo presented the plan, Esteban Escobar, like all his contemporaries, had lived outside of the city of Medellin in a luscious mansion. The plan presented to him by his old friend would force him to move to the United States, but since the plan of operations had appeared quite feasible, he had decided to give it a try.

He moved his family to Creve Cour, a plush neighborhood in St. Louis, Missouri and developed a very powerful organization dependent on high technology, pouring millions of dollars into training and equipment. He used all the help he could muster from the drug distributors Colombia had all over the United States to provide him with trustworthy operatives. Nobody in America or Colombia had knowledge as to Esteban Escobar's whereabouts because he needed to remain in the secure shelter of anonymity. He ran the Organization through another one of his favorite wonders, the Internet.

Escobar ran an organization with 25,000 "employees" from his studio overlooking the Missouri river, and he was able to escape detection because he used the Internet as his shield. By going through several computers in different countries he was able to completely cover his tracks. Communicating through bulletin boards, modems and laptop computers was definitely the way of the future. Criminals always were on the cutting edge of technology, and Escobar was going to be no less.

The network Alfredo Hidalgo had established in thirty-one countries was impregnable and the only cloud in the horizon was that the Americans were catching on and desperately trying to find ways to police the Cyberspace provided by the Internet. Nonetheless, the task was of such magnitude that Escobar was confident it would be years before he had to abandon his use of the Internet, but at that time he was sure Hidalgo would have come up with another technological toy to make up for it, like satellite link-ups or something.

Esteban Escobar was in his late forties, the oldest son of a Medellin doctor who had never been able to make any money in the quasi-socialistic medical environment of Colombia, but who had learned to recognize the value of education, sending all his boys abroad to get college degrees, financing their educations with the coffee plantation his wife had inherited. Escobar too, had discovered the value of education, and upon his arrival in Missouri with Hidalgo had enrolled in every computer course he could take in order to become proficient in his new endeavor.

He managed the sales and marketing, and import operations of cocaine for several very powerful men in South America, and these men were delighted to get written monthly reports on their assets, just like the ones they received from their Diners Club or American Express cards. Escobar performed an outstanding job for them, in addition to managing his own affairs, and most drug lords were ecstatic to have the privilege of working with Escobar. The man was honest with them, and although the Colombian producers didn't know how to spell the word 'honesty,' they highly valued honesty in others.

"How many employees do we have now with the airlines?" Escobar enjoyed referring to his associates as employees. It reinforced the concept of a Fortune 500 company he had come to covet. It was too bad that his corporation would never appear in the annual listings of the most successful companies in America. Or maybe he could legalize all his operations within a few years and become legit?

"Ah, about fifty airline captains and at the last count I think we had seven hundred and thirty or so between flight attendants and miscellaneous others." Alfredo Hidalgo was a senior captain with Mexicana Airways International, and had produced the brilliant idea of using airline personnel for mules and associates instead of the lower class operatives they had historically used. Airline personnel were better educated, had contacts with other professionals who understood the value of being discrete, traveled all over and were able to get cheap fares to move about, keeping suspicion to a minimum. Nobody noticed when a pilot or a flight attendant wasn't home for weeks at a time because that was the usual conduct expected of them, which suited the Organization.

The cost of using airline personnel was higher than that involved in using peons, but the payoff was substantial. They had been able to move stuff faster from several other countries instead of having to concentrate on Colombian production only, which was getting difficult to handle in the first place because of all the unfavorable publicity. That Noriega individual had not done anybody in the business any favors by attracting so much attention to the business. The U.S. Marines, sweet mother of Jesus! What else could the man have done worse than have the Marines over for lunch?

"As a matter of fact, I just got confirmation that we've recruited our first female airline captain," Alfredo offered.

"A broad? Which airline?"

"TGA. I just got confirmation from Elaine Griffin in Berlin. This particular captain will be very useful 'cause she told Elaine that she has many contacts and she's willing to recruit for us if we pay her the right amount."

"What's the right amount?" Esteban Escobar trusted Hidalgo with his life, and if Hidalgo assured him that this broad was good for the Organization, Escobar believed him.

"Hundred thousand for each new recruit. She's the one who wanted fifty thousand per carry, remember?"

"Greedy bitch," Esteban Escobar laughed. He liked greedy bitches 'cause for the right amount they could be made to do anything.

"That, she is, Esteban, and she can be very useful if she can get us a few more employees."

"Can we trust her?"

"We've got Elaine Griffin working on that now. She'll be tailed and we're taking the usual precautions, we'll get a complete dossier on her. She tries anything funny, we'll wipe her out along with her parents, kids, relatives, friends, pet cat and fish, just so there's no mistake."

Esteban Escobar assented. He liked the way Hidalgo operated, just like he was on the flight deck of his airliner, covering every angle–a true professional.

"Did you tell her that she has to make her body available to the Organization as part of her job description?" Escobar joked.

"Of course, not. Her body will be available only to me, Esteban."

"Bullshit. Since when did you stop sharing women with your friend and blood-brother?"

"Okay, you can have her. But if she refuses to blow you, don't come running to me to take care of her for you."

"Just like that asshole with that airline down in Florida, eh?"

"Yes, just like him." The men had received a fax from an operative down in Miami notifying them that a new recruit, a pilot, had requested a very large sum of money in order to keep from going to the police with copies of several confidential data transmissions he was supposed to have destroyed. Hidalgo had a very poor sense of humor, and hadn't laughed, instead, he had faxed the Miami director a request for information on this enterprising young man.

A demolition expert in Fort Huachuca, Arizona had gladly contributed an explosive device the size of a paperback novel, with no questions asked, in exchange for some college money for his kids, and another highly motivated friend of the Organization had inserted the high-explosive device in the pilot's flight bag at operations in Atlanta prior to departure. The barometric detonator in the C-4 had been set to explode when the cabin pressure reached 2000 feet above sea level on the descent, which had occurred seven miles from the airport. The blast had removed the cockpit from the rest of the airplane, killing all aboard. Esteban Escobar believed in drastic action. Cut somebody's head off for borrowing your pen and nobody in his right mind will ever think of stealing it. Scruples were for priests, not men.

"The system is working better than you had forecast, Alfredo," Escobar reached for a remote control, activating the CD player in his cavernous living room. Chopin Nocturne Op.9 piped throughout the sixteen hidden speakers. He was a man of taste, and had nothing but contempt for his countrymen who had access to enormous sums of money but who still could listen to nothing other than marimbas, mariachis and cheap Mexican music. If the Almighty in His wisdom gave certain men the privilege of having access to obscene sums of money, then Escobar was sure God also expected such men to better themselves and their offspring through education. His daughter was taking piano lessons and learning about philosophy, and his son had to read all the Greek classics. If they did not improve themselves in spite of having all that money, then they would be no better than those damned Arabs riding camels in the desert. Those people had all the oil in the world but even so they could not come out of their ignorance. Stupid Bedouins.

Escobar felt that education was primary in his decision to move to America to run his business. He smiled, satisfied. It was very nice of the Americans to provide him access to their high-technology in order to improve his position in life. Who would suspect that one of the largest operations in the history of illegal drugs had its headquarters in St. Louis, Missouri? High technology had made this possible.

"We've managed to buy into several legal businesses which are providing us with clean cash and means to launder the money we're bringing in with cocaine. You know as well as I do that someday this business will end. They will either legalize it or they'll gather enough evidence to track us down, but before that happens we're going to own so much industry that we'll be able to shut down the drug side of our operation and live like kings on the legit income from our businesses."

"The secret is to know when to pull out," Alfredo Hidalgo added.

That had also been a part of the plan. Nothing good lasted forever, and they knew that, therefore they had to look at the cocaine trade as the means to finance legitimate business which, if properly run, would eventually allow them to retire without fear. The other Colombian kingpins had laughed at the plan because they were obviously not businessmen in the real sense of the word. They could run a drug production and smuggling operation successfully only because there was so much damn money involved that they could forge ahead regardless of how much fell between the cracks. Put any of those men in charge of a corporation with a narrow profit margin and the bottom line was they would go bankrupt because hardly any had formal training in business, which was essential to any properly run organization.

"That is indeed the secret, my friend, knowing when to pull out. Just like with women, eh?" Escobar chuckled at his humor. He and Hidalgo had already invested millions of dollars in varied business enterprises.

"And you're staying away from brokers, right?"

"You better believe it I am." Esteban Escobar was aware that Hidalgo did not understand high finances enough to feel comfortable investing the Organization's money in stock speculation. Instead, they had bought hundreds of fast food franchises, small banks, gas stations, movie theaters, hospitals and schools, owning them entirely so that any profits depended merely on how well they were run and not on the whims of Wall Street, which were beyond the grasp of most men. And their business were run very efficiently because the Organization believed in hiring top-salaried executives with lots of schooling and experience to run each enterprise, which was already beginning to pay off in the form of consistent profits.

"ESTEBAN, WE NEED TO discuss the change of cities for the communications relay."

"Why? Mexico City not good enough anymore?"

"No, it's still good, but that's precisely the point, Esteban. We have to stay ahead of the game there, and the Americans have been asking questions about some of the phone numbers we've used in the past."

"Asking questions? Where?"

"In Mexico City. One of our contacts in the judicial police down there sent word that American law enforcement agencies are showing increasing interest in the names of people who have owned certain phone numbers which we've used in the past. Somehow they must've managed to intercept some of our incoming transmissions or they got the phone numbers through a traitor, or something, but I don't like the fact that they are snooping around in Mexico."

"That's a big city, and it's corrupt as hell, Alfredo. We can stay there awhile longer and just change phone numbers more frequently."

"I don't think that's a good idea, Esteban. Once the stakes get too big you never know when some guy may decide to double-dip and sell us out to the Americans."

"You're really worried about that?"

"Naw, I'm not worried, let's just say I am concerned, I think it's time to switch. And if I discover we have a traitor selling us out I'll personally cut his balls off."

Escobar got up, pouring himself a shot of Tequila. He liked diversity in flavors. "What other city do you have in mind?"

Alfredo relaxed, knowing that he had sold his friend on the idea. "Rio de Janeiro. Big, beautiful and every bit as corrupt as Mexico City."

"Okay, when do you want to switch over?"

"It'll take me a couple of months to get everything into place. We should stick to big cities where we have friends, and Rio is one of those."

"Hell, Alfredo, we keep going like this, we'll be transmitting out of Hong Kong."

"No, Hong Kong no, it's too corrupt."

Esteban Escobar roared with laughter. His voluminous belly bouncing up and down as he laughed. "Too corrupt? That's like saying too rich. That's impossible, my friend."

"No, the problem there is that everyone is so totally gone that you can't trust anybody no matter what you pay them. We can't operate like that. You can see that in the products coming in from Asia. The quality is just not there. American corporations setting up plants in China and Thailand and Korea are having one hell of a time squeezing their Asian partners into producing quality items because those people try to get away with murder. They will initially produce the good quality they committed to, but as soon as you turn your back–wham! Down comes the karate chop and they screw up the quality so they can increase their profits."

"I know, Alfredo. My old man told me never to go into business with a Chinese because they would screw me, and I haven't forgotten his words."

"Well, anyway, I'll get to work on the changeover. After Rio I think we can use Buenos Aires and then we'll see.

I'm organizing some of our own companies to have computer servers to use with Internet."

"Sounds good, Alfredo. Now, why don't we get the ladies and go treat ourselves to an excellent German meal at a restaurant I know."

"You have good German restaurants in St. Louis?"

"There's one good one that I know of." Escobar had initially considered St. Louis very provincial, and at first had been rather uncertain about having selected it for his headquarters, but now he appreciated the brilliant move. The last thing that a fish discovers is water, and the last thing the DEA would discover was Esteban Escobar lodged in Heartland USA. Esteban's cover as a South American banker justified his sumptuous lifestyle and also his constant business trips. Furthermore, Middle America was not as inquisitive as people were in larger cities, which suited Esteban Escobar just fine. The less questions asked, the better. He had conveniently deposited considerable sums of money in a couple of local banks, buying his way into the local high-society. Everyone loved money, and people in St. Louis were no different. Normally intimidated by foreigners, the St. Louis country club crowd had eagerly accepted Esteban Escobar because of his beautiful manners and well-established personal fortune. The fact that he was of white Spanish extraction made it all that much easier to be accepted. After all, this was an educated man of fine tastes who in no way resembled the stereotype of the banana republic greaseball, nor the Los Angeles-type Hispanic, or did he?

"German food sounds great. Just one other thing I wanted to cover with you. We're having real good results with our parachuting operation and I'd like your authorization to expand the operation to the Southwestern states of Arizona and New Mexico." Alfredo had devised an idea for delivering cocaine to the United States which was working like a well-lubricated engine.

Most of the South Americans used conventional methods to smuggle cocaine, Hispanics acting as mules, light airplanes, boats, etc., but these were are well-known to the DEA and Customs and were not foolproof, with interceptions costing millions of dollars.

Hidalgo had come up with very simple yet extremely effective alternate method. It consisted of parachuting boxes from airplanes, carrying the drug on tightly-sealed containers equipped with radio locating devices. A nice size corporate turboprop would file a night flight plan from say Mexico City to Miami, all very nice and legal, except that hundreds of boxes would leave the airplane over the west coast of Florida, parachuting down to waiting teams who would then retrieve the product and forward it to its destination in different cities. The process was foolproof because parachutes did not paint on radar. This little operation had been going on for a year and not one single drop had been intercepted.

"The western states? That sounds like a marvelous idea, my friend. I was waiting for you to suggest this in view of the unparalleled success you appear to be having with this operation." Esteban Escobar poured himself a glass of draft beer from the expensive tap system he had installed in his personal bar. He was fond of liquor, like most of his countrymen. "I can't believe nobody had ever thought of doing this before. The technique is still ours, no?"

"Yes, it's still ours. We've managed to keep it a secret so far, but sooner or later it'll get out and some of our competition will imitate us. When too many people start doing it, somebody is bound to get caught and the feds will catch on, but I still don't think there's too much they can do about it even if they know what we're doing. I mean, what're they gonna do, prohibit parachute sales? Gimme a break, we can buy parachutes anywhere else in the world, and if it comes to that, why, we can even set up a parachute manufacturing plant in the Far East and make our own."

"Another one of your brilliant masterpieces, Alfredo. By the way, I had Ginny make that transfer for you this morning." Between the two men they held over sixty bank accounts in thirty-one countries.

"How much was this one, Esteban?"

"Three point seven million dollars."

Hidalgo carefully jotted down the amount in his Daytimer. "Thank you very much. I'll drink to your health and that of your children, Esteban."

Escobar laughed, raising his glass to return the toast. The wire transfer had been part of the daily profit credited to each man's account from the money invested in legitimate business. Clean money, the kind they could use anywhere in the world without fear.

"*Salud, amigo!*" Escobar added salt to his beer and drank. An old habit he'd picked up while traveling through Guatemala.

FOURTEEN
PRESENT TIME - BERLIN, GERMANY

Paul Morris called the AT&T international operator and asked her to provide him with the general information number for JFK international airport. He got the number and dialed it, jotting it down on his telephone book.

"U.S. Customs, agent Cliffs."

"Yeah, hi. Could you tell me how to go about locating a specific agent working for the DEA or Customs?"

"What's this regarding?"

"It's just personal, I went to school with this good friend of mine and I haven't seen him for years and a mutual friend told me he's working for you guys in New York so I'm trying to locate him, that's all."

"What's his name?"

"Olaffson, Gus Olaffson."

"Just a minute."

Paul Morris sat on his bed and waited. He had to verify the identity of this federal agent in order to clear Valerie's copilot of any suspicion. If this guy Gus was a ghost, he'd pull Valerie out of Berlin as soon as possible.

"Hello?"

"Still here."

"Did you say 'Olaffson?'"

"Yeah, two effs."

"No, we don't have anyone here under that name."

"What about the rest of the system, you guys have lists of everyone working out of New York?"

"No, we don't have anything like that, what is your name?"

Paul Morris hung up. It was going to be a long day, unless he could get creative. He reached for the number Valerie had given him and dialed it.

"Criminal investigations, sergeant Martinez."

This sounded more like it, but what happened to the direct line to Olaffson?

"Hi, ah–yeah, I need to speak with Gus Olaffson, please."

"May I ask who's calling?"

"This is John, with Citicorp Visa. He applied for a Visa card but didn't sign the application and we'd like him to mail in another form so we can process it."

There was a momentary pause while Ramirez's brain assimilated the unlikely story. "Hang on."

Paul Morris knew his story would not hold water but he wasn't going to identify himself just yet.

"Hello?" the voice at the other end was deep and loud–good voice for a New York City cop.

"Yeah, am I speaking with Gus Olaffson?" Paul Morris tried to make his voice a pitch higher.

"Speaking–who are you?"

Bingo. Paul Morris replaced the receiver on the cradle and waited a few seconds, then he dialed the AT&T operator again. "Operator, could you please get me New York directory information?"

"I can help, sir. What number is it that you're trying to reach?"

"I need a listing for a Gus Olaffson and another one for the DEA criminal investigation division."

"Just a moment," her voice didn't seem perturbed at all by the office he was trying to reach.

"Nothing under Olaffson, Gus. Here's the other number–would you like me to connect you?"

"Please." Paul Morris heard the switching noises as his call connected over thousands of miles of Atlantic Ocean.

"Criminal investigations, sergeant Martinez."

Bull's eye!

"May I speak with agent Gus Olaffson, please."

"Who is calling?"

"Just tell him I'm calling for Captain Wall of TGA."

"Just a minute."

This time the wait was not as long. "Hello? Olaffson here. Who's this?"

"Gus, my name is irrelevant, but I'm calling on behalf of Valerie Wall."

Olaffson paused, "did she send you?"

"Yes, and please don't attempt to track me down because I'm going to hang up in less than one minute."

Olaffson rapidly waved to the two men standing nearby, signaling for them to listen in. "What can I do for you, Mr. No-name?"

"At the moment, nothing. Valerie wanted to check you out, make sure you existed. Since it appears that you do indeed exist, I will relay the news to her and we'll be in touch."

"Wait! What–?"

Paul Morris hung up. Good, this proved that Charlie Smith was clean. Nobody could list themselves in the New York phonebook under DEA unless they were DEA. Good, since Charlie was straight, their little team had an additional player on the side of the good guys.

He dressed and went out to catch some lunch. He had already located a jet charter outfit out of *Tempelhoff* airport and was going to drop in and check it out. Valerie's idea to line up emergency transportation was not totally out of line.

VALERIE HAD THE TAXI drop her off a few blocks from the hotel where Paul Morris was staying and walked the rest of the way there, sneaking in and out of buildings trying to find out if she was being followed. It seemed that she didn't have anyone watching her so she went to the hotel and found his room. Since she got no answer knocking at his door she went downstairs to the front desk and requested the room key. The desk clerk gave it to her without question, confident that she must belong in that room, in view of her good looks and elegance.

Valerie returned to Paul's room and sat down to wait.

THE ALARM RANG AT five-thirty a.m., bringing her out of a deliciously relaxing deep sleep. She didn't have to get up for another seventy-five minutes, but it was her habit to set up the alarm early so that she could have a few minutes to wake up while still laying in bed. She hated opening her eyes and having to jump in the shower without first having had a chance to become fully awake.

Valerie analyzed the plan for the day for the fiftieth time. She was going to tell Charlie about Paul Morris, which they had already decided, and Charlie had the right to know, after all he was going to be joining the gang and producing them one hundred thousand dollars. She was convinced that her idea of signing him up as her first recruit was outstanding. She would implement it as soon as they returned from this trip. The main reason for her wanting to include Charlie in the deal with Elaine was to augment her ranks. Elaine might be a little less quick ordering Valerie killed if she knew Charlie was in on the plan. They would have to arrange for Charlie to be killed as well, and that would take a little more effort.

She wondered how many people were now aware of what was going on here. Interpol was a big organization and it made her nervous because too many people involved could lead to a fuck up. Wars had been started this way, but she guessed that as long as they checked the package waiting for her at Tegel airport and cleared it of any explosives, they were welcome to the party. She had not changed her mind about opening the package, and she would tell Elaine that she'd opened it as soon as they returned to Frankfurt for the night.

Valerie got out of bed, going in the bathroom. She looked like shit. She had one hour to change into a professional-looking clean-cut all-American airline captain.

Paul Morris had found her in his room after his visit to a place where they could charter a jet and told her about his conversation with the federal agent in New York. Now they had to let Charlie know what was going on or he would freak on his next conversation with the feds. They had to tell the feds that the call to agent Olaffson was kosher or the feds would be climbing all over each other, thinking that the Organization had been tipped off about what was going on.

Valerie showered, then dried herself with a huge bath towel. She wondered what the odds were of being brought into an international conspiracy like this and decided that she should start buying lottery as soon as she got home. She went to the dresser, removing a professionally cleaned white uniform shirt, starched and folded inside a plastic bag. She believed that she must portray the airline captain to the hilt. Neatness and discipline were two qualities people associated with airline captains, so she carried with her a supply of these shirts. Her navy blue uniform hung from the open closet, and the four gold stripes on the sleeves of the coat made her feel proud. Proud of being a woman pilot and proud of the responsibility endowed to her.

She dressed, poured herself some orange juice from the small room fridge and went downstairs. She carried her flight bag, the overnight bag with the laptop computer in it and a change of clothes. She was not enjoying this, which made her angry at Elaine Griffin and her gang of murderers. Valerie loved her job more than anything in the world, yet now she was not feeling the familiar elation at taking out a trip but instead she had a knot in her throat.

How would they know if Interpol had checked out the package? Unless someone contacted her or left a note, she would have no way of knowing. This meant that the damned thing could go off when she opened it–beautiful.

"Good morning, Captain."

She loved the sound of those words.

The four flight attendants on her flight were already in the lobby, holding steaming hot cups of coffee. All four looked older than Valerie, which made her feel slightly uncomfortable. "Good morning, Ladies." She offered her handshake. "The name's Valerie."

"Morning, Valerie." Charlie Smith was right behind her.

"Hi, Charlie. How about some coffee?"

"Sounds great. Did you get some rest?"

"Yes, thanks Charlie. Let's get us some coffee." She noticed Brad Thomas, her flight engineer was not around yet. Figures.

"Charlie, we gotta talk." She glanced behind them, making sure none of the flight attendants could hear her.

He became serious. "What's up?"

"Paul Morris is here in Berlin."

"Paul Morris? Your boyfriend?"

"Yes."

Charlie Smith looked at her bewildered.

"He's staying at a hotel by the airport. I figured we needed reinforcements and he's already doing things to help us."

Charlie recovered from his momentary perplexity. "We're bringing an awful lot of people into this."

"I know, Charlie, but I had to tell him. Union makes strength, remember?"

"I guess so, Valerie. Does he know everything that's going on?"

"Yes. He's computer systems engineer and he's already checked out the laptop computer and it's clean.

He wasn't able to find anything in it that we could use just yet."

Charlie whistled. "You've been busy."

"I hate to tell you this, Charlie, but he insisted on checking you out too."

"What do you mean?"

"He cross-checked with the agents in New York to make sure you were straight with me."

Charlie's face remained impassive. "I see. And am I clean?"

"As a whistle. His idea, Charlie, not mine."

"That's all right. I would have done the same if my girl was involved in something like this. Hell, in the Navy they check you out every step of the way. So, we're going ahead with the project?"

"Yes."

"And you trust the Interpol guys and our friend in New York to come through for us?"

"Yes."

"In that case, let's play ball."

THE CREW WAS DROPPED off in front of Operations and Valerie dropped off her bags, heading for the stairs.

"I'll take care of the paperwork, Valerie," Charlie pointed out.

On the second floor she went directly to her airline's counter. The customer service agent was a woman.

"Good morning!" Valerie smiled.

"Ah! Good morning, *Kaptain*," the agent brightened. "You've come for your package."

Valerie nodded, marveling at the efficiency of Elaine's operation. Her heart was beating fast enough to become noticeable to her.

"And there you go," the agent placed a white box on the counter, not much larger than an egg carton.

Valerie picked it up "Thank you, did you receive this yourself?" smiling at the woman.

"No, that package was already here when I arrived."

"So you don't know who dropped it off?"

"No, *Kaptain*. I don't know who dropped it off, but I can ask."

"No, that won't be necessary, thank you very much."

"Have a nice flight, *Kaptain!*"

The box weighed about five pounds, and there was no writing on it nor any kind of message. Great, just great. She went through the complex security gate and exited the terminal, walking out on the ramp. The package was heavier than she had expected, and she had no way of knowing whether the bomb experts had checked it out, which left her with but one option. She walked away from the terminal building, around a parked 727 and found a spot removed from any buildings.

This was going to be no fun, but her responsibility towards her passengers and crew forced her to it. She produced her Swiss Army knife from her uniform pants pocket and inserted it into the clear Scotch tape sealing the edges of the box. She took a deep breath and cut the lid open, separating it with a decisive movement.

No explosion.

She opened the box and stared into several smaller plastic bags containing what looked like talcum powder.

Drugs.

She quickly looked around, finding herself in possession of something just as dangerous as any bomb. The area around her was deserted. She closed the box and headed back to the Operations room.

"Everything all right?" Charlie was going through the flight paperwork. Valerie looked very pale, with a box under her arm.

"Yeah," she responded, a little too quickly. "How's it look?"

Charlie studied her face searching for any anomaly. "Fine, the weather's clear all the way to London and they routed us for an arrival from the east. Fuel looks good. Check it out." He extended the Dispatch Release to her.

Valerie took the piece or paper and looked at it, not really seeing it. The enormity of the risk she had just taken was finally hitting her, and her knees were becoming slightly woozy. What if it had been a bomb? Right now she would be talking to St. Peter, or whoever. She forced herself to concentrate on the business at hand. "Ah, yeah, this fuel looks good. Full load of passengers?"

"No, we got eighty-eight I think." Charlie was obviously dying to ask her what gives but he'd have to wait until they were in the privacy of their cockpit.

"Good. Well, I guess we better head out to the airplane. Brad out there?"

"Yes, he's been out there for a while."

"Any write-ups on the airplane?" she was starting to calm down and metamorphose into the airline captain that she was.

"No write-ups, clean airplane. At least on paper."

"Sounds good." She signed the Release, dropping it on the counter so the agent could keep it with the flight documents. "Let's go then."

He waited while she stored the white cardboard box in her flight bag, then followed her out to the airplane. They climbed the ladder along the jetway and entered the 727. The flight attendants were already there, readying the airplane for passengers. Brad Thomas was not in the cockpit.

"Everything okay, Valerie?" Charlie asked, removing his uniform coat.

"Yes. I got the package and checked it out and it's clean. I mean, it doesn't have a bomb."

Charlie climbed into his seat in the right side of the flight deck. "How do you know it's clean, our friends leave you a message?"

"No, not precisely. There was no note or anything so I went outside on the other side of the ramp and opened it."

"You did what?"

"I opened the package, Charlie. I had to make sure the damn thing wasn't going to blow us all to pieces. I had to do it for our passengers. Anyway, there isn't a bomb in there. What there is, is a ton of some white powder strongly resembling cocaine or some shit like that."

"White powder."

"Yes"

"Have you lost your frigging marbles? Valerie, that was a fucking stupid thing you did!"

"Well, it's done, and that's that. I'm no expert, so it could be *Shower to Shower* talcum, but don't bet on it."

Charlie began his cockpit check, touching every switch and dial within his reach as he went along. "You're nuts, Valerie, did you know that? Taking that kind of risk was not the responsible thing to do."

She nodded, not saying anything because Brad Thomas entered the cockpit.

"Everything looks good out there and we have our fuel, Valerie." Thomas sat at his work station directly behind Charlie Smith. His panel had the most switches and dials of any of the three crew member stations in the airplane.

"Thanks, Brad," Valerie began her cockpit check and wished she had never bid Berlin.

"Valerie?" The head flight attendant was at the cockpit door. "They're ready to board."

"Go ahead. We may have an ontime departure yet."

"You guys want coffee or some orange juice?"

Valerie looked back. A double Scotch was what she needed. "Some coffee would be great, Bertha, if you have a minute." Valerie went out of her way to ensure she didn't provide additional work for the flight attendants if she could help it. They had enough to do without having to cater to the whims of a demanding flight crew.

Charlie got their clearance to Frankfurt and they read the Before Starting Engines checklist, readying the seventy-ton airplane for flight.

"Hey, guys, I got a real good tip on a bar in London that we can go to." Thomas had completed his panel checks and was facing forward between the two pilots.

"Forget it, buster," Valerie still had fresh memories of their trip across the Bosporus.

"Sounds good, Brad, only this time you're buying all the drinks," Charlie pointed out. He was still sore about his wine bill in Istanbul.

Brad Thomas recoiled from this rebuff. "Okay, okay. I was just sharing with you guys a tip I got from one of our flight attendants. If you don't want to go, you don't have to."

Valerie laughed. "I think I'll stick to old, well-trodden ground, if it's okay with you, Brad. Your last suggestion was rather expensive, not to mention we only got about two hours of sleep after the trip in the Queen Mary across the Bosporus."

"All right, all right, so I was given some bum information. You can't hang a guy for that."

"No, of course not, Brad," Charlie put in, "but we're just not gonna use you on the dining committee any more, that's all."

They heard the front cabin door closing, signaling that all passengers were aboard and ready to go.

"Everyone's seated and we're ready to go," Bertha announced from the cockpit door.

Valerie thanked her and reached for the PA handset. "Folks, ah, good morning, this is your captain speaking. We'd like to welcome you aboard today. Our flight to Frankfurt should take us a little under one hour and the weather is perfectly clear all the way there. Please remain seated until we have turned off the fasten seat belt sign

after takeoff and keep your seat belt fastened while
seated. Thank you for flying with us today, relax and
enjoy the flight." She knew her speech always raised a
few eyebrows in the passenger cabin, when her
passengers realized that John Wayne was not flying their
airplane.

"Captain," the mechanic's voice came in through her
headset, "we're ready down here if you get clearance to
push."

"Charlie?" she clued him.

"Good morning, Tegel ground, TGA 745 ready to
push, gate two," Charlie spoke into his boom mike half an
inch from his lips.

"*Goot* morning TGA 745, you're clear for pushback."

Valerie activated her mike and spoke to the mechanic
plugged into the airplane next to the nosewheel, directing
the tow truck. "We're clear to push."

"Release the brakes," the mechanic transmitted. He
had a British accent, probably on loan from one of the
British carriers.

"Brakes released," Valerie acknowledged, pulling the
small lever on the radio control panel that released the
potent main gear brakes.

The powerful tug revved up its diesel engine with a
cloud of putrid black smoke and started pushing the
airplane back.

"Clear to start all engines," the mechanic barked.

"Starting number one," Valerie informed him. "Let's
crank one up," Valerie ordered. Charlie reached up,
holding down the starter switch for the number one
engine on the overhead panel. Engines in airplanes are
numbered for convenience of identification, with the
number one engine being the one farthest left when
sitting in the cockpit facing forward.

"Starting *einz!*" Charlie responded. It was company
operating procedure to acknowledge all communications
between pilots by repeating all commands. They

monitored the engine start which was mostly automatic, just in case there was a malfunction. Anything out of the ordinary could very easily damage an engine costing over a million dollars so the crew was understandably careful during this stage.

"We have three good starts, you're cleared to disconnect, we're going to hand signals," Valerie instructed the mechanic ten feet below.

"Roger that, thank you captain, you have a good flight."

She waited for the man to be in sight ahead and to the left of the airplane before she asked Charlie to get them a taxi clearance. She knew of a couple of mechanics who had been killed by nosewheels in Arizona because the crews taxied out forgetting that they still had a man connected to the airplane outside. That was not going to happen to her.

The mechanic was now in full view fifty feet ahead and to the left of them. "Charlie, would you please get us taxi clearance?"

"Ground, TGA 745, ready to taxi."

The ground controller cleared them to the runway and Valerie flashed her landing lights at the mechanic, signaling that they had taxi clearance and that they were ready to move if all was clear.

The mechanic gave her a military salute indicating that all equipment was clear of the airplane and Valerie looked to the left as far as she could. "Clear right?" she asked Charlie, because she had no way to view the right side of the airplane.

"Right's clear," Charlie confirmed.

She advanced two of the three throttles, hearing the whine of the Pratt & Whitney JT8D-15 engines and feeling the power impelling them forward ever so slow at first, then beginning to gather momentum. The big jet initially required considerable power to break static friction with the ground, but once it got rolling idle thrust from the engines was sufficient to keep it moving at a brisk pace. She reduced the power to almost idle, allowing the big airplane to turn with the residual jet thrust available from the engines.

"Flaps fifteen," she called out, instructing Charlie to lower the trailing edge flaps which would allow them to take off in the short runway. That was one of the killer items which if overlooked could kill you. She was well aware of the Detroit MD-80 that crashed because the crew took off without flaps, as well as the 727 in Dallas that did the same exact thing, so she made absolutely sure that she checked the flaps several times during taxi out. She loved the location of Tegel airport and it amazed her that it was in the heart of Berlin, because it was surrounded by lovely green woods with nicely kept lawns all around. What a difference from some of the airports back home, she contemplated, like Midway airport in Chicago which was totally surrounded by buildings and it had a Target store smack at the end of one of the runways–how ironic having a target to hit in case something went wrong.

They ran through the taxi checklist and called the tower, letting them know they were ready as they approached the beginning of the runway.

"TGA 745, after landing traffic line up and wait."

Valerie timed it so they arrived at the end of the runway just as a British Airways turboprop came over the numbers, landing long. She moved the airplane into position on the centerline of the runway and set the parking brakes. "Before take-off checklist, please." She reached up, turning on the ignition on the engines, the landing lights and the transponder which identified them to air traffic control and observed the British Airways turboprop clearing the runway a mile downfield.

"Before take-off checklist is complete," Brad Thomas informed her from the back.

"TGA 745, fly runway heading, clear for takeoff."

Valerie advanced the throttles slowly about an inch to get the engines stabilized. One did not put the pedal to the metal in big jets because not all engines revved up simultaneously at first. Shoving all the throttles forward could generate maximum takeoff power on one engine ahead of the others, which could easily take the airplane into some real estate not meant for airplanes. By allowing all three engines to slowly rev up, Valerie made sure that she had all three engines developing equal power as she increased it to that necessary required for takeoff.

As is customary in most airline operations, the captain of a flight flies the first leg of a trip while the copilot tends the radio. After that, they alternate legs the rest of the trip, which allows both pilots equal time at the controls.

The airliner began gathering speed down the runway, bouncing on bumps in the concrete. Valerie's attention was totally focused on keeping the airplane on centerline and looking at her airspeed indicator. At one hundred knots each bump on the runway felt like a mountain, and she said a silent prayer for everything to work out smooth.

"Vee one!" Charlie called out, indicating to all on the flight deck that Decision Speed had been reached and that they were now committed to fly because there was no longer enough runway left ahead of them to stop the airplane if they decided to abort the takeoff from this point on, even though they were still on the ground.

"Rotate!"

Valerie slowly pulled on the control yoke, feeling the nose getting lighter at first and then the bumps stopped as the mains lifted off the concrete and the airplane left the ground and gradually began to fly. She kept pulling back until the nose of the airplane was fifteen degrees above the horizon then called for gear up.

"Gear up!" Charlie repeated, yanking up the large gear lever sticking out of the panel. They all felt the powerful hydraulics lifting the wheels into the wells and clucking as they locked in place.

"TGA 745, contact departure, goodday."

Charlie changed frequencies and checked in with the new controller who would direct them for the next twenty minutes.

Sterile cockpit rules dictated that no idle conversation could take place in the cockpit until the airplane was above 10,000 feet in order to avoid distracting the crew, since idle conversation in the past had caused tragic accidents. As they climbed past 10,000 feet Valerie turned off the landing lights which she'd had on for traffic avoidance and asked Brad to pass her a cup of coffee. The skies above Germany that morning were clear and blue and she could see for over a hundred miles in any direction. This was the view that few people ever saw, the view from the flight deck, the view that she loved.

"Looks like we're gonna have a smooth ride today," Charlie remarked. The flight to Frankfurt brought memories of bumpy rides in the past because, before the Berlin Wall had come down, they'd had to fly through designated air corridors at specific low altitudes which invariably translated into very bumpy rides.

"Yep, seems that way." Valerie drank some coffee, reaching her assigned cruising altitude and setting the airplane on autopilot.

"Valerie, are we going to hit the buffet dinner tonight?" Thomas loved to eat, and he loved it even more if he wasn't paying for it. This particular flight had a five-hour layover in London, and the union had presented the company with a choice: either procure hotel rooms for the crew for those five hours or spring for dinner. TGA had opted for the latter, and each pilot was issued a pass for thirty-five dollars which could only be used to buy food at any of the restaurants at Heathrow. It was less expensive than securing hotel rooms for the pilots, and the company preferred it. The flight attendants were not included in the deal because it was the Airline Pilots Association that had worked it out, so the cabin crew had to find a way to kill five hours on their own. The British Empire was certainly not built on its culinary abilities, but the airport restaurant at Heathrow featuring the buffet was definitely exceptional, and the crews loved it.

"Yes, Brad, that's the plan." All three pilots had to stick together because the captain was issued a chit at Operations for the entire amount due to the pilots, and they could not separate to eat.

"That's great! I sure hope they have the same roast beef they had last week. It was sinful."

"Brad, can't you ever think of anything other than your stomach?" Charlie Smith asked.

"Hell, yeah. Lots of things, but food is one of my favorites. Like wine is yours."

Valerie grinned. He got you there, Charlie.

Charlie turned in his seat to look at the flight engineer, no easy feat on the 727 because the flight engineer's seat was directly behind his. "Boy, I was drinking wine when you were still at home jerking off to the lingerie section of the Sears catalog, so don't push your luck!"

Valerie roared with laughter. That silenced Thomas, all right.

"Okay, I know when I'm not wanted," Thomas complained, standing. "I'm going to the john–if it's all right with you captain. My back molars are afloat."

"Go, go, we certainly don't want you suffering here!" Valerie yelled.

The flight engineer left the flight deck and Charlie turned to her. "Nervous about this?"

"What do you think? Of course I'm nervous. You realize this could be the last flight of my career if the Brits catch me smuggling this shit into their country?"

Charlie nodded. "I don't think that's going to happen, Valerie, unless somebody tipped them off, and even then, we have the support of the DEA behind us. They won't let us fry for something they asked us to do. Also, it's possible Interpol is aware that this operation is in progress and that they've already oiled all the right spots so we don't get in trouble."

"That's a lot of ifs. I sure hope you're right." She could see Charlie had a point. "Make sure Wonder Boy back there doesn't mess it up for us after we finish eating and leave the package on the chair. All we need is for him to do us a favor and point out that we are forgetting something."

"I'll take care of that, Valerie. He so much as burps in the direction of that box and I'll break his arm."

Valerie sat back to enjoy the view from twenty-five thousand feet. The skies over Europe were crystal clear, not a cloud in sight. She was in control of this spaceship, and she liked the feeling. Many people watched *Star Trek*, yet terribly few ever actually got to be Captain Kirk. Brad returned from his trip to the blue room with some oranges.

"Just heard a good one," he started.

"Awright, let's hear it, Thomas." Charlie loved jokes, as Valerie had discovered. Most airline pilots did because there weren't too many things one could talk about day in and day out with the same crew, and jokes broke the monotony.

"Three rats are sitting around," Brad started, "discussing which one of them is the toughest. The first rat brags, 'I am so tough, I grab the cheese from the mousetrap before the bar hits me, then I kick the trap into a corner as I walk away eating the cheese.'

The second rat laughs. 'That's it? I *grab* the mousetrap bar before it hits me, dust away the arsenic poison from the cheese, and then I kick the trap into a corner as I walk away eating the cheese'

The third rat stands up, disgusted, 'while you two gents sit here deciding who's toughest, I'm gonna go fuck the cat!'"

Charlie laughed like mad and Valerie joined in. She had a wide range of tolerance for cockpit jokes and was willing to accept just about any as long as they weren't extremely crude or denigrating to women.

"Where did you hear that?" Charlie questioned.

"One of the flight attendants just told me it. Good, isn't it?"

"Not bad, Thomas. I guess we might still let you join us for dinner tonight after all."

"Very generous of you, chief. If I tell you another joke, will you buy me a bottle of wine?"

"Don't push your luck, boy. You could still end up sitting in this here airplane for five hours eating cocktail peanuts and stale bread rolls."

"I beg your forgiveness, oh, great chief. I'll zip my mouth and pray that the gods grant you health, a long life and many women."

CHARLIE GLANCED SIDEWAYS AT Valerie, who appeared amused. She had guts, opening that box back at Tegel. Had that been a bomb, it would most likely have gone off with an anti-tampering device. He wondered if he'd had the guts to do the same thing and decided that was a tough question to answer. Anyway one looked at it, the lady had courage, no question about it.

He had blind faith in the system and knew in his heart that the DEA would not let them down no matter what, so he wasn't too concerned about carrying the drugs across customs at Heathrow. It was all probably rigged so that they wouldn't be challenged. The Interpol must be in on it by now and they would know that the cocaine or whatever it was, was onboard. The bomb deal had worried him, but now that they were past that stage he was confident that the operation would go smoothly.

The TGA crew were given instructions to begin their descent into the Frankfurt area and initiate their approach into Frankfurt-Main International airport.

They landed in Frankfurt and taxied to the gate. Operations sent a VW van to pick up the crew because their gate was too far from TGA ops to walk. Valerie and Charlie boarded the van to Operations. Valerie left the package inside her flight case on board the 727 but she was confident that it would not be disturbed because the cockpit was off-limits to everyone except mechanics and flight attendants, and she knew they would not go snooping in her bag. They drove among the dozens of Boeing 747s, DC-10s, L-1011s and Airbus parked on the ramps and were dropped off in front of their Operations office. "One down, one to go," pontificated Charlie.

"Yeah, but this was the easy one." They entered Ops and greeted the dispatchers. Valerie knew that she would not be this calm at Heathrow, but she had to control her fear. Being afraid was human, but pilots were trained to control their fear and perform under stress, and she kept reminding herself of this.

"*Gutten morgen*, captain," the tall dispatcher offered.

"Good morning, Heinz. How you all doing today?"

"Fine, fine. Your paperwork is right there. Airplane is good? Your engineer has not called in yet." Normally the engineer called in to Ops the fuel remaining on board at the gate and any mechanical write-ups, but apparently good old Brad Thomas was falling asleep on the job."

"Ah, yes, we have a good ship and my engineer will probably be calling you any minute. Everything look okay to London?"

"*Ja*, the weather is excellent, same as here, and you have a full airplane."

"Thanks." Valerie examined the paperwork prepared for her flight and signed the Dispatch Release, indicating with her agreement with the figures set for fuel, weight and balance and weather. Although she shared planning responsibility for the flight with the dispatcher, she was the one ultimately liable for the airplane and its contents after it left the gate. Final authority carried with it final responsibility.

They gathered their paperwork and left the office, catching the van back to the airplane. Now came the fun part.

"Let the games begin," Charlie stated.

They went up the jetway stairs into the waiting 727. Brad Thomas was at his panel, checking the refueling.

"Brad, Ops was pissed at you 'cause they hadn't heard from you. Did you give them the arrival fuel?" Valerie was bugged by Brad. Efficiency was the name of the game in the airlines, and her engineer was fucking up a little too often.

"Yes, I sent it in. They weren't answering when we first pulled up here and I had to hit the Duty Free. Promised Linda I'd get her a bottle of perfume she wants."

Valerie was not amused. Personal affairs had no priority in the operation of her airplane. She climbed into her seat, inserting her earpiece and boom mike in place. "Let's get this babe ready."

The passengers entered the airplane and Valerie called for a clearance to London.

"TGA 745, Frankfurt, we're not able to issue you clearance at this time," came back the voice of the German controller.

Now what? "Say again?"

"TGA 745, I say, we are not able to issue you a clearance at this time. No TGA flight can be issued a clearance anywhere in Germany. Call your company."

Valerie thanked him and dialed the company frequency on her radio. No TGA flight was being issued a clearance? What the hell was going on? "Frankfurt, TGA 745."

"TGA 745, Frankfurt, go ahead."

"Yeah, we're trying to get our clearance to London here, and we're being told that no TGA flight is allowed to depart anywhere. Care to find out what the hell is going on?"

"*Ja*, captain, we are aware of the situation and the chief pilot in Paris is trying to take care of it right now."

"What's going on?"

"Captain, a Middle Eastern passenger originating here in Frankfurt flew to New York on one of our flights yesterday and was denied admission into the United States. The authorities in the United States put him on our morning flight back to Frankfurt and he just arrived here this morning but the German authorities don't want to give him access and are demanding that we should put him on your plane and fly him to London so he can catch our evening flight back to New York."

"What the...!?" Charlie was furious. "I have very little patience for this kind of international Ping-Pong. The Germans don't want this raghead back in their country? When he originated in Frankfurt? Absurd!"

Valerie was also becoming irritated. She had enough to worry about without having to consider international incidents. "Why was this individual denied entry to the United States?"

"I do not know this, captain. All I know is that he was sent back to us in handcuffs with a federal air Marshall and now the Germans have grounded all our flights unless we accept to take him back to New York."

"This is bullshit!" Charlie glowered. "Pure blackmail."

"The director of flying in Paris is talking to the German authorities at this moment to clear the situation," the dispatcher continued, "but we don't know how long it's going to be."

Oh, crap. Valerie realized she had five hours in London to make the drop, but if they were delayed here in Frankfurt those five hours might shrink to the point where she may be unable to make the drop.

"That's all we need," Charlie noted. "Another Arab messing with the civilized world."

Valerie did not like general statements like that one. "Charlie, don't blame all the Arabs for just this one idiot."

"Why not? They're all the same. It if wasn't for the oil they would be no different than the aborigines in Australia, walking around in loincloths fucking camels."

"Charlie, I don't appreciate that kind of talk. This is an individual incident and we'll deal with it as such." She was pissed at Charlie. He was a good guy, but his racist remarks made her see red. That was one part of him she did not like.

"Sorry, sorry. Didn't mean to piss you off, commander. You haven't been exposed to the joys of the Middle East as I have, that's all. No offense intended. It's just that in order for you to appreciate Arabs you'd have to have the opportunity to live in an Arab country and feel the bite of the culture on your own skin. And those sweethearts are real fond of biting off a big chunk off of a woman's ass, if given half a chance."

"What do we tell the people?" Brad interjected, trying to cool off the air between the captain and the first officer.

"I'll talk to them," Valerie grabbed a hold of the PA. "Ladies and gentlemen, this is your captain speaking. We've just been informed of a delay in our departure. We've not been told the extent of this delay but we'll let you know immediately the moment we get additional information. Thank you for your patience and please bear with us."

"That, captain," Charlie remarked, "was a magnificent example of typical airlinese, where you said something to the people back there, but you really didn't say anything."

The head flight attendant came flying in the cockpit.

"What's going on?"

Valerie told her.

"Oh, shit! This means we might be spending the night here without seeing London?"

"We don't know, Bertha. It could be, but then again we could blast out of here in the next few minutes. We'll just have to wait and see."

"Do you want me to serve drinks?" Complimentary liquor was one way to placate angry passengers.

"No, don't do that just yet," memories of her recent experience with green eggs in Istanbul came to mind. "We'll wait awhile longer before we do anything."

"Okay, Valerie."

Twenty minutes later Ops called them to say that clearances were now being issued.

"What happened to the Arab?" Valerie inquired.

"He's on your flight, Captain."

Oh, great! "You mean we're taking him back to the States?"

"Aah, that's the official version, yes."

"What do you mean the official version? What's the unofficial one?"

"You will take him as far as London, and there our friendly Scotland Yard boys will take him off your hands."

"So he's not going back to New York on our company's flight?"

"Far as the German authorities are concerned, yes, but the British authorities have proven a bit more cooperative than the Germans and will detain the gentleman until such time when the United States decide to accept him."

Charlie laughed out loud. "God bless the Queen! That'll be a cold day in hell before the INS decides to accept him back in the States. I swear, the Brits are the only people in this continent with any common sense!"

"We're outta here," Valerie reached for the flight attendant call button, activating it.

Bertha showed her face at the cockpit door.

"Bertha, they just gave us clearance, we're leaving."

"Valerie, you are aware of the armed passenger?"

"What armed passenger?" What was this, the never ending story?

"They have a man in handcuffs with an armed cop. I put them all the way in back but I didn't like doing it. Passengers don't like seeing a man in handcuffs marching down the aisle of their airplane."

Federal Aviation Regulations and company rules mandated that when a prisoner was carried onboard a commercial airliner, the captain must be notified in writing, and if the prisoner had an armed escort with him, a special form had to be presented to the captain for his approval, because the airplane was his final responsibility, and it was up to the captain to decide whether he wanted Wyatt Earp on the flight or not.

"Nobody gave me a form about an armed guard. Please call the gate agent."

The flight attendant left the cockpit.

"I can't believe this," Valerie was exasperated. "These people know damned well that I need to authorize a prisoner with an armed escort before they even come aboard my airplane."

"Hell, they're in such a hurry to get rid of him that they forgot protocol." Charlie popped a can of Coke, placing it on the glareshield, below the windshield.

"Well, *I* didn't forget protocol, and we're not moving this airplane until all the proper boxes have been checked off."

The German gate agent entered the cockpit with a look of concern on his face. He was carrying the pink forms Valerie should have signed before the prisoner came onboard.

"Captain, I'm sorry, here's the paperwork for the armed individual. I was just going to bring it to you but things got real busy out there."

"What is your name?" Valerie believed that the only way to run a railroad was to follow the rules, but she understood how the man could have been swamped because of the irregularity of the operation.

"Karl, captain–my name is Karl Muller."

"Very well, Karl, for this time I won't report it, but in the future, always present the captain with the paperwork *before* allowing any armed individual to come aboard. Is that clear?"

"Yes, captain, I'm very sorry, I should have done so."

"Good," Valerie took the form from the agent, read it and placed her initials on the dotted line. "Here, now let's close it up so we can get out of here. We're late as hell already."

The agent recovered the form, leaving the cockpit. Valerie thought she heard him say to another German agent by the door something that sounded like 'glad to be out of there and away from that bitch. What are things coming to, female captains? *Mein Gott!*'

She would let that one ride. The pilots read the checklists and got clearance to push back from the gate. The engines were stared one by one and the ground controller gave them clearance to taxi out behind a TGA 747.

"That's our Boston flight," Charlie observed, sipping his Coke.

Valerie was not in a very good mood. The drugs she had in her flightcase irritated her very much, and the multiple obstacles they had encountered in Frankfurt did nothing to alleviate the pain.

"Hey, what the hell is that?" Charlie exclaimed.

"What're you looking at?" Valerie wasn't sure what Charlie was referring to, but his tone of voice alarmed her.

"The fuel! Look at the wingtip of that 747, there's fuel spilling out of that left wing tip!"

Valerie saw it and understood the danger. Fuel was pouring out of the left wingtip of the moving 747 with the force of a fireman's hose, splattering on the taxiway.

She reached for her push-to-talk button, speaking into her boom mike. "Ground, TGA 745!"

The Frankfurt ground controller was not extra friendly. "TGA 745, Frankfurt Ground. I believe I already gave you your taxi instructions, what now?"

"Ground, we have an emergency. The TGA Boeing 747 ahead of us is jettisoning fuel from its left wing tip onto the taxiway!"

"He's what?"

Valerie made it a point to speak slower. "The TGA 747 ahead of us taxiing to the runway is dumping fuel out of its left wing!"

Suddenly the big Jumbo came to a complete stop in the middle of the taxiway, a huge pool of jet propellant fuel beginning to form under its wing. Its captain had obviously been monitoring the frequency and heard Valerie's last transmission.

"Ground, TGA 577 Heavy, we're shutting down all engines. Please send out the emergency equipment." The voice of the old dog in command of the Boeing 747 came through loud and clear over the frequency. He'd heard Valerie's transmission and acted at once. If they had jet fuel underneath them, he didn't want his engines igniting it, so he opted to shut down all four on the spot. "Thanks, 745!"

Valerie didn't answer but instead clicked her mike transmit button twice, acknowledging.

"TGA 577 Heavy, ground, the equipment is on its way, say your intentions."

"Ah, we're just gonna sit here and wait for a tow. We have a faulty fuel jettison valve and it's dumping our fuel out of the left wing."

"Are you going to evacuate your passengers?"

"Negative. We'll stay put. A mechanic is on his way to shut off the valve and stop the fuel flow."

"TGA 577 Heavy, you are dumping fuel all over the taxiway and the ramp!" the controller redundantly pointed out.

"No shit, Sherlock," Charlie chuckled. "The Germans just can't stand it that the 747 out there is messing up their immaculate ramp."

Valerie agreed with Charlie on that. She wasn't sure which concerned the German controller the most, the danger to the passengers and the airplane or the spilled fuel messing up the ramp. The airport's emergency vehicles entered the scene, with screaming sirens and flashing lights. They surrounded the behemoth while fuel continued to pour out of the left wing at a prodigious rate.

"Looks like their left fuel dump valve got stuck in the open position," Charlie observed. Fuel jettison valves were used in big jets to dump fuel in case of an emergency, and were normally shut tight. Most jets can takeoff with considerable more weight than they can land, which is a serious problem if a landing becomes suddenly necessary after takeoff. In order to reduce the airplane's weight to meet its maximum allowable landing weight, fuel is jettisoned from two valves located at each wingtip, away from the engines.

"Looks like we're going to be here for a while too." Valerie couldn't believe her luck. One thing after another.

The fire equipment surrounded the TGA jet and dozens of men jumped out and began shoveling sand onto the spilled fuel. A tow truck approached the jet from the front, aligning with the nosewheel.

"They obviously can't shut the valve from the cockpit or they would've already done so," Charlie remarked. "They're gonna have to get a mechanic up on that wing and shut it off manually."

"How fast do you think they're dumping it?" Valerie had flown the Lockheed L-1011 and on that airplane they could dump about 670 gallons per minute, or enough to fill a good-sized swimming pool in twenty minutes.

"Heck, I don't know, Val. I was never on the Seven-Four." Charlie realized they were stuck. There was no way to get around the 747, and no way to back up. Even if they moved the Jumbo, how could they pass over all that spilled fuel with their engines running? Unthinkable. "I think we're screwed. We're gonna have wait here until they can clean up this mess."

Valerie thought about this. "Brad, call Operations and ask them to send another tow truck for us. What we're gonna do is have the tow truck back us up to the intersection we just passed."

"What if there's traffic behind us?"

"There won't be any. Whoever's behind us can make a sharp turn now and proceed on the parallel taxiway."

Brad called company operations, relaying the request.

The crew attaching the tow truck to the 747 was successful and signaled to the emergency vehicles that they were going to start moving the monster so that the crewmen could walk alongside and continue shoveling sand on the spilling fuel.

A cloud of diesel fumes from the exhaust of the tow truck signaled that the driver was ready to go. The 747 began to inch its way forward, slowly accelerating away from the immense spill.

"The Germans are going to have a fit over this," Charlie voiced.

"Yeah, and they'll probably send us the bill for the cleanup."

"Friendly chaps, aren't they?"

"Valerie, the tow truck's on its way here," Brad informed them.

"Good. I'm gonna shut them all down. Make sure you're on auxiliary power."

Brad switched the airplane's electrical system over to the APU–the auxiliary power unit–a small jet engine located between the main wheels in the lower fuselage, whose generator would supply the airplane with electricity and air conditioning after they shut down the engines.

Valerie picked up the PA handset. "Folks, this is your captain speaking. We have a small delay due to a broken down airplane ahead of us. We're going to shut down our engines and we're going to be towed to another taxiway so we can bypass the stalled airplane. This should not take long at all. We'll keep you informed. These people must be getting tired of hearing my voice," Valerie added.

The TGA tow truck arrived by the 727 and the mechanic plugged into the intercom, receiving instructions from the captain to hook up and back up the airplane so that it could taxi out on the previous intersection. Minutes later they restarted their engines and taxied past the 747 that finally had stopped leaking fuel

Twenty-five minutes later they were on their way, climbing out towards the North Sea.

"That was fun," Charlie joked, "remind me to stay away from Frankfurt."

"We're only forty minutes late," Valerie observed. They had plenty of time to carry out her assignment.

"Not bad for a clear day, Frankfurt's not one of my favorites." Charlie was flying the airplane and Valerie was on the radio.

"Frankfurt's getting real busy. It's becoming one of the crossroads of the world. You can see all the wide-bodied aircraft parked there."

Charlie laughed. "Yeah, you can see it in the runways too. Those runways are so bumpy it feels like you're landing on cobblestones. Sure wish the Germans would spend a little money fixing the touchdown area of both runways instead of having immaculately clean taxiways."

"It's all those Jumbos landing there. They're bound to destroy the runway," Valerie commented. "It's incredible, isn't it? How we can fly from Frankfurt to London in a little over one hour. Think of all those boys flying bombers during WWII, how long it must have taken them to do the same. Probably four or five hours each way, under heavy fire."

"Yeah, the world sure has changed, Valerie. Now the Germans and the Japanese are our allies. I think of that every time I turn on my Japanese-made VCR and wonder if all those WWII soldiers who died in the war are rolling over in their graves."

"Hey, you can't hold a grudge forever."

"And I'm not, I'm just saying it's ironic that things have worked out this way. Einstein was a great genius, I'll tell you that. The man was able to transform uranium 235 into VCRs."

THEY CLIMBED OUT OVER Holland and approached London from the northeast. The weather there was as advertised and Charlie flew them down with a smooth approach terminating in a graceful landing at Heathrow. Valerie taxied the airplane to the gate and shut down the engines, her anxiety on the rise.

"We're here!" Charlie exclaimed, "cheated death one more time!"

Brad stood up, stowing his seat out of the way so the two pilots could exit. "Science and technology once again overcame fear and superstition."

Valerie laughed. "Where do you guys get all these clichés, in a book or something?"

"No, Ma'am, one hundred percent original."

Valerie packed her flight bag, pulling it out of its space next to her seat. "We might as well go have dinner. The bus must be waiting."

The three pilots descended to the ramp using the stairs alongside the jetway. A large tour bus was parked next to the airplane, waiting for them. The flight attendants were all already in the bus, waiting for the pilots. Valerie knew there was still time to back out of this, to dump the package and run. Maybe she should do this. She looked back at the 727 they had just flown in, wondering if she would ever fly one again. She was brought out of her concentration by a TGA agent handing her the dinner voucher the airline provided for the crew.

The bus sped off towards one of the ramp exits, avoiding all kinds of fast-moving ramp traffic. The ramp area was strictly off limits to any person not directly related to the operation of the airport and there was even a standing order that no person could walk across the ramp at any point because they would automatically be treated like terrorists. Even pilots had to walk around the long way, remaining close to buildings. The British were not going to take any chances.

The bus arrived at a checkpoint and stopped. The head flight attendant got out, taking with her the crew declaration to be filed with Her Majesty's Customs office. Valerie's heart was coming out of her chest.

A Customs inspector came out of the building with the head flight attendant, boarding the bus.

"Good afternoon, Gents!" The inspector was an older gentleman in his sixties and he smiled as he walked up the aisle, approaching Valerie, looking left and right between the seats. She felt cold sweat dripping from her armpits and running down the sides of her chest. Should she look at the guy? Ignore him?

The customs agent reached her, smiled and kept going. He reached the end of the bus and backtracked towards the front, tipping his hat and wishing them all a good stay, he then exited the bus. Valerie was breathing hard. The driver shut the door and engaged the clutch, propelling them forward, out of the restricted area.

Charlie winked at her, lighting up his pipe. Valerie felt weak. This was bullshit. Why did she have to be doing this? Those bastards Elaine and her group deserved to be in jail! The bus stopped in front of one of the terminals and the pilots descended. The flight attendants remained on the bus because they had their own plans which included a visit to the magnificent Duty Free.

Brad was oblivious to the events developing under his nose and followed his captain and first officer up the escalator to the airport restaurant where they were going to spend the next few hours eating.

Valerie never ceased to be impressed by the number of foreigners found at Heathrow. Everywhere she looked there were Middle Easterners and Hindu, and the place teemed with activity.

The restaurant was among the most elegant at Heathrow, and the pilots knew it well, for they had been flying this route all month. Valerie wondered which table they should pick, and whether it made a difference where they sat for the safe delivery of her package. Charlie solved that by selecting a table for them. They removed their coats and she excused herself.

She had to pee so bad she didn't know how she had held it back at the Customs crossing. Afterwards she washed her hands, wondering who was going to connect with her to receive the package. She didn't really want to talk to anyone about this, and she would prefer if whoever was picking up the package waited until she was gone to retrieve it.

Charlie and Brad were helping themselves to the exquisite variety of dishes available at the buffet, and she joined them.

"Aah, good afternoon, captain!" Spiros, the man in charge of slicing off the roast beef was a huge Greek whom they all had come to know. He had given them his life history on previous visits, explaining how he had come to London hidden in a freighter and how he loved Queen Elizabeth and how this country had been *so* good to him. Valerie thought he looked like something out of Ali Baba and the Forty Thieves, but the man was so damn polite that she had to put up with him and listen to his yapping while he cut her a couple of very generous slices of roasted beef. She filled her plate to the brim and joined her crew at their table.

"I told Linda she should've come with us on this trip," Brad observed, between mouthfuls of mashed potatoes and bread. "I told her this buffet was incredible and that she shouldn't miss it, but she turned me down."

"Smart woman," Charlie said. "Who knows? Maybe this time you would've broken her leg!"

Valerie choked on a piece of broccoli, laughing.

"Hey! That was an accident. She would've enjoyed coming here tonight."

"I don't know, Brad, I think she's probably enjoying her room back in Berlin without having you around to suggest all kinds of wild activities."

"Wild activities? What wild activities?"

"Well, like going to Istanbul with your wife when all the flights are full. She was going to have a real good time staying in Turkey by herself for a few days."

Brad chuckled. "Boy, that time she was ready to cry. She didn't want to stay in Istanbul at all. What with her broken thumb and all, she wanted no part of it. I shoulda listened to you guys."

"Yeah, that you should've." Charlie loved giving Thomas a hard time after the horrendous wine bill he'd had to pay in Istanbul.

The waiter came and took drink orders. His name was Felipe and he, too was a regular, a man from Tenerife, in the Canary Islands, a very friendly individual all the crews liked. Valerie wondered if he was the one. Hard to tell with all these foreigners. She had to laugh at herself– so far they had not dealt with a native Londoner yet!

Felipe brought them soft drinks and ice tea.

"So, Felipe," Charlie enjoyed making conversation with people from other countries, "When are you going to fly back home for a visit?"

"Oh, not fly, *capitán*, not fly–too expensive. I take ship to Tenerife but not until Christmas."

"You're going home for Christmas?"

"Yes, I always go home for Christmas. Christmas here not good. Too many Muslims and other people from East and Far East. London is more foreign than English now. I do not understand why they do not go home."

Valerie gagged on some water. That was really funny, a foreigner bitching about the number of foreigners in London!

"Why do all these foreigners come to London, Felipe?"

"Ah, *capitán* but that is easy. They come here because they can get free money from government and free medical care and many other free things. They live better here without working than they would back where they came from. The U.K. is one generous state, and all these foreigners take advantage of system."

"And you don't think it's good, taking advantage of the system?" Charlie devoured his pudding and gravy.

"No! No, it's not good taking advantage of system! I work hard, every day and I never take any advantage of system. I have six children in Tenerife and I work hard to get money for them. Why can't other foreigners do the same? Because they are terrible people!"

Brad got up to go refill his plate.

"Felipe, why did you come to London, isn't there any work in the Canary Islands?" Valerie had finally managed to relax a little.

"No, *capitán*, there is no work there. London, Germany, there is work here, but not in Tenerife."

"And you can't find something more profitable than this?" Valerie wondered if she was face-to-face with her contact.

"Profitable? I do not understand, please..."

"Some other job, where you could make more money?" Valerie watched him carefully, searching for any sign that might give him away.

"No, this is the job I do," he seemed perturbed.

Valerie wanted to believe him, to believe that he was a proud hard-working man with enough guts to move to another country by himself in order to provide for his family back home, but she wasn't sure if this was indeed the case. It could all be a nice cover-up too. Shit–she had been involved with crooks for one week and already she had become a cynic.

Brad returned to the table with a plate so full it threatened to spill on all sides. He carefully set it down and began to pick at it.

"Brad, that's disgusting," Valerie couldn't help herself, "what's the matter, didn't your mom ever teach you not to fill up a plate like that?"

"Yeah, Thomas, where's your manners? Don't you know that it's better to serve yourself ten times than to show up at the table with a plate like that?" Charlie willingly contributed to the flogging of Private Thomas.

"Hey! I'm hungry, guys." Thomas filled his mouth with roast beef–medium rare–and smiled sheepishly.

"Valerie, remind me to notify the Professional Standards Committee to screen table manners of future newhires to avoid this sort of embarrassment."

"I will do that, Charlie." She enjoyed ribbing her engineer for the ineptitude he had demonstrated as a tour guide in Istanbul.

Time was passing and she had managed to forget about the package for awhile. From here they would fly back to Frankfurt and spend the night at the Mainz Hilton, where she would transmit to Elaine. She wondered what Her Majesty's Customs would think if they searched her copilot and found fifty thousand dollars in cash strapped to his waist. She was developing a liking for these fifty-thousand dollar bonuses but she reminded herself that it was dirty money, probably produced by selling drugs to children. Those bastards! And they had actually bombed an airplane full of innocent people. What kind of animals would do something like that? She finished her dinner, passing on the desert cart. Brad helped himself to three different desserts.

"What do you thing happened to the 747 at Frankfurt that was jettisoning fuel?" Brad asked, between strawberries and custard.

Charlie lit up his pipe and waited for Valerie to answer. She was the captain, and he was fully versed in the art of copiloting, giving the captain the courtesy of first option on the reply.

"I think they just shut off the valve, took on some more fuel and blasted off to Boston."

"You don't think the valve will leak again?"

"No, once they manually shut it off, it'll stay that way. All it caused was a delay and a dry-cleaning bill from the airport management."

"The Germans got pretty pissed that their precious taxiway got dirty, eh?" Brad finished up the last of his three deserts.

"They like to keep a clean house, nothing wrong with that."

"Sounds like a little fanaticism to me."

"Oh? Maybe you prefer the splendor of *La Garbage?*" *La Garbage* was a pseudonym the crews assigned to the airport at La Guardia, in New York City, due to its hygiene standards resembling a cesspool. "Or perhaps the cleanliness of *Sewage* airport?" *Sewage* was the affectionate name for Newark.

Brad wiped the strawberry sauce from his lips and chin on another immaculate clean white handkerchief. "No, of course not, but I think these Germans are a little fanatic, that's all."

"Brad, that's because you're a slob. If you had any discipline, you would appreciate what the Germans are trying to do," Charlie puffed on his pipe.

"Why'd you bring your flight kit?" Brad asked her.

"I had some revisions I wanted to insert in the Jepps manual." Quick thinking, Valerie. She knew it was unusual for anyone to haul the flight kit along on such a short layover, and she was not surprised at her flight engineer's curiosity.

"Valerie," Charlie interrupted, "I'm going to hit the Duty Free before we go back to the airplane. There's some books I want to look at. Do you mind if I go ahead?"

"No, go ahead, Charlie. I'll take care of the bill here." Thanks, Charlie! Leaving her alone!

"Brad, come along with me. I want to show you some of the best airplane books in Europe."

Brad stood up, grabbing his uniform coat and his hat. "Okay with you, Valerie?"

"Go for it. I'll catch up with you guys in Operations."

The two men left, leaving their captain alone at the table, savoring a cup of coffee. She looked around, trying to find out who her man was but the only two people in sight were the Greek and Felipe. It had to be one of them, but which one? She might as well get on with the game.

The waiter caught her wave and brought over the bill. No European waiter would dream of presenting his customers with an unsolicited bill, as was the custom in America. That would be the ultimate insult, insinuating to the customer that her presence was no longer welcome.

Valerie read the bill, unfolding the chit given to her by the station agent. The voucher covered their dinner comfortably and left room for a more than generous tip. She left the voucher on the table along the bill and put her jacket on. Should she wait for Felipe to come and get this? What if she left the package on the chair and Felipe saw it? On impulse she removed the box from her flight kit, leaving it on the chair next to her, then she donned her hat, grabbed a hold of her flight kit and left the restaurant.

There. She had done it.

She went down the escalator and passed through Her Majesty's Customs and Immigration with a wave from the agents, headed for the Duty Free. This day was turning out a lot more exhausting than she had prognosticated, and it was really irritating. What if the wrong person found the package on the chair? Then all hell would break loose and they would come for her. Shit, if Elaine was so bright she must have thought that one out already to ensure that all went well. Nothing she could do about it now, it was out of her hands. It did feel good, though, being rid of that damn package. At the Duty Free she looked for her First Officer and Flight Engineer but couldn't spot them. She bought herself a bottle of *Deneuve* perfume, giving the cashier her American Express card. The day had been stressful, and she needed something to cheer her up. The perfume was one of her absolute favorites, although she'd heard from a saleswoman at Dillard's back home that it was being discontinued. Maybe she should stock up on it.

Heathrow was full of interesting people, and she wondered what Muslim women must think of her, in her airline pilot's uniform and self-assured walk. Those women were at the opposite end of the female spectrum from her, as far as Valerie was concerned, in their full-length garments covering every part of their bodies up to their faces. Poor things, living such deprived lives. She quickly suppressed a pang of guilt. She had her own crosses to bear, and after all it was women like those with their submissive attitudes that had been instrumental in keeping females subservient for centuries. A little more rebelliousness in the early days of mankind might have avoided rivers of prejudice and tyranny from men.

She grabbed her purchase and headed for Operations. The concourses seemed interminable and she wondered how passengers found their way around. The concourse where TGA Operations were was deserted, which made her feel slightly uncomfortable. This side of the airport terminal had no flights arriving nor departing until later in the evening, and she had to go through there in order to reach her company's Ops. Their airplane was parked a mile or so away on the opposite side of the ramp, but she had to go pick up the paperwork for the flight. She would ask the agents then to give her a ride across the ramp back to the airplane because she did not feel like walking all the way back. This place was the perfect set up for ambush attack on some unwary individual, and she really had no intention of becoming that individual.

What would be the odds of her being left alone to continue her career with TGA now that she was involved in this drug scam? If the DEA came down on Elaine's Organization and destroyed it, they would have to do a damned good job of it, or any survivors would undoubtedly come after her. And what were the odds of the DEA doing such a good job? Slim to none. Truth was, there was no way in hell the DEA was going to convince her that they had totally annihilated the Organization. They could say whatever they felt like saying, but Valerie knew that even the DEA would have no way of knowing if any big fish escaped the net, and she was not about to bet her life and that of her future passengers on this. The fear of being bombed while on a flight was not something she could live with the rest of her life, *no, sir!*

So, what were the options? Going to another airline on her own was out of the question. The minute Elaine smelled a rat, Valerie's name would be mud everywhere, and she'd have to change her name–oh, great. Even changing her name was a complicated operation which was going to require help from agent Olaffson. She didn't really believe that he was going to get her and Charlie into another airline as captains. The poor guy was merely a government bureaucrat, totally ignorant of what he was offering. The enormity of his promise would eventually come to him and he would at that time renege on his promise to her. So, what did that leave? Move to Montana as a Jack-In-The Box manager for the rest of her life? Death was preferable to that option.

Anyway she looked at it she came to the same conclusion, her airline days were numbered. This realization filled her with immense fury. How could she have allowed the situation to come to this? She had been suckered into this situation by people she didn't have the time of day for, and now they were deciding her future.

She had to make them pay, all of them. Had she been a man she would have probably gone after them with guns, but as a woman she was more logical than that.

She would make them pay with money.

She would squeeze every last penny out of Elaine and agent Olaffson. At the rate she had been going she would have earned close to five million dollars during her remaining thirty years as an airline pilot, not counting a generous retirement of $50,000 a year.

Five million bucks. She would have to do better than that because they were forcing her to give up her beloved career with the airlines, and in addition to the money she would hurt Elaine and her group as much as she was able to do. She decided to use her position to win at this game.

She reached Ops and found Charlie at the computer, working on his monthly schedule.

"Everything all right?" he questioned, knowingly.

"Everything's going according to schedule."

He realized she did not want to talk about it here and dropped the subject, showing her instead the paperwork for the return flight to Frankfurt.

VALERIE AND CHARLIE HITCHED a ride back to the airplane on the operations van. They did not walk back because walking across the ramp was prohibited and following the pier was too long a walk. They returned to their seats and prepared the airplane for departure. Valerie's side window in the cockpit was open and two British Airways mechanics were propped up on ladders, cleaning the windshield.

"Good evening, mate," the mechanic on her side greeted, a young man with a friendly smile, wiping the thick windshield close to her.

"Good evening to you," Valerie answered him. She would wait until he was gone to discuss the operation with Charlie.

The second mechanic cleaning the windshield became irritated, and Valerie thought she heard him reprimanding the younger man, telling him that she was not any 'mate' of his, that she was 'Captain' and that he should never forget it.

She was tempted to set the old buzzard straight, but decided against it. This was England, and she was not going to change the way they did things here. The old guy was old-school, and she would gain nothing by telling him that there was no harm in a mechanic addressing a pilot as 'mate.'

The mechanics left and she slid her window shut. "I don't know which one of the two guys in the restaurant was the one, do you?"

Charlie looked behind them to make sure Thomas wasn't back yet. "No, I have no idea but it doesn't matter anyway, I'm sure Scotland Yard had us watched and they'll know who it was and eventually nail him."

She felt terrible to think that the waiter from the Canary Islands could be put in jail thanks to her and his children end up without his support, but then she remembered they were dealing with drugs here, and decided that if the man was breaking the law then he knew the risks. And besides, it could be the Greek.

"When we get to the hotel I'm going to send the message to Elaine. Do you want to come to my room when I do it?"

"Absolutely. Let's check in first and I'll come over in about a half hour. Don't want the crew starting rumors."

That's all she needed at this point, the crew spreading the rumor that she was shacking up with her first officer. A rumor like that would fly through the system in less than twenty-four hours, and it would do wonders for her reputation. "Excellent idea, Charlie. By tomorrow at this time you'll be the new recruit and we'll be a little deeper in this mess."

"Hey, don't feel too bad, remember? we're the good guys. The Interpol jokers are in on it now and I don't think they're going to let this *status quo* go on for too long."

"Yeah, I hope so. I still don't know what the hell you and I are going to do about all this when the cops come barging in. They'll find us, Charlie, Elaine's people are gonna find us, and when they do, they will be pissed–*real* pissed."

"Hey, it's late and we're tired. Let's not deal with bad news at night. We'll talk about it in the morning. In the meantime let's get back to Frankfurt."

THREE HOURS LATER VALERIE shut the door to her room at the Mainz Hilton, in the outskirts of Frankfurt. She was tired and irritated, and now she had to cap the day with an email transmission to Elaine.

She used the bathroom, kicking off her shoes. What she'd really like to do was remove her clothes and start relaxing, but Charlie was due in any minute now. She opened the laptop and typed the message for Elaine:

Delivery completed as per your instructions. Unable to take package without opening it first to verify contents. I work for you but my passengers don't and I have to look out for them. Once I verified that the contents were Kosher I proceeded to drop it off at the designated place.

Have found my first recruit. Will talk to you tomorrow when I'm back in town.

V.

She read the message again to fine-tune it and waited for Charlie. They would have to find another way to communicate with the New York agents, Charlie couldn't continue making long-distance calls from payphones if he was being followed, which they had to assume would be the case if he joined the Organization.

Charlie showed up and read the message then Valerie encoded it and sent it to the Berlin number of Elaine Griffin.

FIFTEEN
PRESENT TIME - BERLIN, GERMANY

"What do you think?"

"I think she has guts and knew she was defying me by ignoring instructions, but I suspected she might do something similar." Elaine Griffin had read Valerie Wall's message in which the captain admitted she had opened the package she was entrusted.

"Can we trust her to follow directions?"

"I think so, yes. She has a strong sense of loyalty and responsibility and I think she'll prove a very effective operator. She's not a stupid woman as she demonstrated by opening the package before putting it in the airplane with her."

Karl sipped his Brazilian coffee, looking around at the afternoon crowds walking past them. They were sitting at an outdoor café.

"You think she suspects anything about the Miami affair and that's what made her open the package?"

"Absolutely not. She's just a professional, and she was taking care of her passengers, like she says here. She's an airline captain, Karl, not a clairvoyant. Pilots are trained not to trust any packages assigned to them by strangers, they probably drill this into their heads day and night during training. She was just being careful, and don't forget that she did carry the cocaine with her across the border."

"So you don't think she's going to disobey every instruction we give her?"

"No, I think she'll double-check everything we give her but I don't think she does it to defy me, I think it's part of her professional behavior, that's all."

"What do you think about that recruit she's talking about? You know I trust no one, and have the habit of playing the devil's advocate with you."

"This is one ambitious lady we're dealing with here, Karl. I don't doubt she's already recruited us another captain, since she's looking at a hundred thousand dollars for doing it."

"And Escobar authorized it?"

"Yes, he authorized me to pay the money but only one at a time until each new recruit has had a chance to prove usefulness to us."

"Meaning what?"

"Meaning we have to run each new recruit for a while before we pay the dame another cent."

"Has Inga been following her?"

"Yes, and so far she's clean. Inga reported that she's been seen coming out of her copilot's room in the hotel, so I suspect she's probably sleeping with him, but other than that, no suspicious activities or behavior. Nothing wrong with a little sex between coworkers."

"How much cash do we have left?" Karl and Elaine Griffin operated with cash FedExed to them from somewhere in France and the two payments they had made to Valerie had reduced their reserves.

"We have around forty thousand left but I sent a message requesting more. Should be seeing it tonight or tomorrow morning."

"How much did you request?" Most of their transactions involving operatives were done with cash. Their cover was bullet-proof as long as they didn't come up with a paper trail showing large amounts of cash. Elaine and Karl were, for all practical purposes, international investment bankers representing a dozen international corporations spread over four continents. Their salaries and expense checks came out of Singapore, and they carried a half-dozen credit cards issued by banks from different countries.

'I requested two hundred thousand." More than that'd be too bulky to FedEx.

"Swell," Karl expressed.

Elaine Griffin was developing a liking for the TGA captain that perhaps she should avoid and be more objective, but being a woman she felt pride in the accomplishments of another woman, and this Valerie Wall was definitely a super-cookie. Becoming a captain with TGA was no small feat, Elaine suspected, one which took guts and determination to carry out. It was apparent that both were qualities which Valerie had in great quantities.

THE FOURTH STRIPE

Maurice Azurdia

SIXTEEN
PRESENT TIME - BERLIN, GERMANY

Valerie found a public telephone installed in a closet off one of the hallways in the hotel. She was puzzled by the installation, who would want a payphone inside a closet? But then again, she knew that different countries had different habits and let it go at that. She liked the fact that the phone was in a dark hallway and that she could observe both ends of it because that ensured her privacy when she used the phone. She did not know if the phone in her room was being monitored by Elaine and her group, but she wasn't about to take any more chances.

She picked up the payphone in the closet and dialed the number in New York.

"Criminal investigations, sergeant Martinez."

"I need to speak with Gus Olaffson, please."

"May I say who's calling?"

"Tell him it's Captain Valerie Wall."

The crack and hiss of international static filled her ears while the sergeant got his boss.

"Olaffson here."

"Gus, Valerie Wall, from Berlin."

"Valerie! How did it go? Everything all right?"

"Yes, everything went just fine. Thanks for coordinating with the Interpol." She wasn't sure if he had coordinated anything with anyone, let alone Interpol.

"Ah, yes–they're very helpful and we need all the help we can get."

"Gus, I am getting deeper and deeper into this mess, and before I go any further I want something from you."

"Tell me what it is and I'll see what I can do."

Really? "Gus, we're dealing with some very shrewd people here. I am an international airline captain and I stand to lose a lot here."

"Go on."

"I'm not going to beat around the bush with you, Gus. I want you to do whatever it takes and get me a certified letter from United Airlines, signed by their CEO in front of a notary public, guaranteeing me a job with their company as a captain effective the moment I show up at their doorstep. I don't care what you have to do or who you have to talk with to get it. I'm also going to need a name change and all the matching licenses and credit cards that go with it. I want a letter from your boss stating that these will be provided for me and Charlie Smith, and I want these letters faxed to me at my hotel within twenty-four hours and the originals sent out here by Federal Express in forty-eight hours."

There was a pause.

"Miss Wall," the agent's tone was not overly friendly, and she didn't like his switch from 'Valerie' to 'Miss Wall.'

"I agree that this is a very delicate situation that we're working on and that you need some reassurances, but I don't know that I can get all that you're asking for in the time frame that you mention."

"How long do you need then?" Valerie was not about to let him off the hook.

"I don't know. What you're requesting is highly unusual and not something that I would normally handle."

"Gus," she intentionally never used his last name or address him as 'agent,' "what I am doing for you is highly unusual and not something that I would normally handle either, but I'm doing it and I'm doing it because you asked us to do it for you. In return I expect you to keep up your side of the bargain."

"I never offered you any bargain."

She was losing her patience. "Gus, you told Charlie Smith that you wanted us to do some things for you and he explained to you that if we did them it would affect our careers and that we would want help from you getting on with another airline. We're up to our necks in alligators now and we need you to keep your side of the deal."

"I never promised to get you on with another airline, I told Smith that I would look into it, that's all I said."

"Are we playing games?" Valerie was mad.

"No, Miss Wall, I'm not playing games. You're involved with a very serious investigation and we're prepared to offer you protection under the witness protection plan, as I explained to your co-worker Smith, but we can't promise more than that."

"Are you trying to tell me that you can't get us on with another airline as pilots?"

"Yes, that's pretty much what I'm saying. The witness protection plan has an established program to help you out and that's what we can offer you."

Valerie felt trapped. This sonofabitch small-minded government bureaucrat was really irritating her. "Let me get this straight. You got us involved in this mess and now you're gonna go back on your word?"

"No, I'm not going back on my word. Like I said, I told Charlie Smith that we'd help you out and we're still willing to do it, and by the way, we didn't get you into anything, you're the one who became involved by transporting illegal substances on your aircraft, remember?"

Valerie was ready to blow a fuse. "We came to you for help."

"And we're willing to give it to you. You just have to keep working with us and we'll be able to eventually relocate you and Charlie Smith."

"Relocate us? You mean send us to Idaho or Montana as fast-food restaurant managers? Let me tell you something, Gus–I realize you don't have a clue as to the kind of environment I live in because I'm aware government jobs don't pay much and you don't even know people like me exist, but I'm making a hundred and forty thousand a year doing a job that I happen to like very much, and if you think I'm going to give up all this that I've worked so hard for in order to flip hamburgers in Idaho, you're crazy. You give me what I ask for or you can forget getting any help from me starting as of right now."

"Miss Wall," his tone was ominous, "you're not in any position to demand anything, you got me? I'm getting sick and tired of you prima donna pilots thinking you're the shit of the world. So, you're making a hundred and forty thousand dollars a year, so what? That doesn't impress me. Maybe it's about time you stop taking up some guy's job who has a family to support and go do whatever it is that women should do anyway. You may think flipping hamburgers is below you but I'll tell you, it's one hell of a lot better than being dead, which is how you could end up without our help. And you're gonna do what we tell you because you don't want charges brought up against you for drug trafficking."

"Fuck you!" Valerie slammed down the receiver. The sonofabitch! How dare he say that to her? To do *whatever women should do?* Charges for drug trafficking? The bastard! She was furious, storming down to the bar in the lobby of the hotel, ordering a vodka martini. She was so mad she couldn't think straight. Let alone the fact that his attitude stunk, the double-crossing agent was refusing to get them hired on with another carrier! He was a male-chauvinist pig and she was in deep shit. But then again, why was she surprised? She had known all along there was no way out of this one.

The bastard had never intended to give them what they wanted, that much was clear now. Valerie was very much aware that some men resented her position as an airline captain–most of them couldn't compete against her to begin with anyway, yet these men rationalized their envy of her by thinking that she was just another broad taking up a man's job. That was absurd, and it angered her. It was never her intention to be in the airlines temporarily, and the concept that she was taking up a man's job clearly implied that she was not a primary bread-winner so she should bow down and allow family men to take the career position they so justly deserved. Many of her male fellow pilots were not married and nobody ever insinuated to them that they were taking up space which should be allocated to married men. She had earned her position with TGA, fighting odds many times more difficult than any man because in addition to being a good aviator she had to also prove that she was capable of taking subtle insults and harassment without flinching. That DEA agent was an impertinent SOB and she should report him to his superiors.

She managed to smile–right! as if that would do her any good.

The witness protection plan! What a joke! That was probably a wonderful solution for a Seven-Eleven clerk who witnessed a murder and testified in court, but it was absurd to think that she or Charlie would go for it. Now what? The fucker had the nerve to say that she got involved with drugs implying that she had done so intentionally. Her airline career was in serious jeopardy, if not dead already. Tears welled up in her eyes, tears of frustration and anger against all the policemen and drug dealers in this world. Why did they have to pick her? Why did that bitch Elaine have to single her out? Because she was a woman, of course. Being a woman had made life difficult for her in her chosen path since the beginning, and now that she should be enjoying the fruits of her hard labor this had to happen.

She drank the martini, deciding that she had to cool off before taking action. The training which enabled her to fly a crippled airliner loaded with passengers down to a safe landing in a stormy night kicked in. She'd have to get together with Paul Morris and Charlie to formulate a plan of action. What could the DEA agent do now that she hung up on him? For one thing he could proceed with the threat of bringing charges against her which even if unfounded, would terminate her airline days and probably her life at the hands of Elaine's people. She had to call him back and apologize in order to gain some time. If he thought she was still in the game, he would not do anything to jeopardize her. This would buy her some time to think.

Valerie finished her drink, leaving a few Marks on the counter, returning to the telephone in the hallway closet.

"Criminal investigations, sergeant Martinez."

"I need to speak with agent Olaffson. Tell him it's Valerie Wall." She did not use 'captain.' Let the sonofabitch think she was coming down to his level after his reprimand.

"Valerie?" his voice sounded cold.

"It's me. I had time to cool off. I'm sorry I hung up on you it's just that I've had a lot of stress these past few days."

"I understand."

"I...*we'll* keep working with you, Gus. Just bear with me and be patient if I blow a fuse."

"No sweat. Just keep your cool and you'll do all right. Keep doing what you're doing and keep calling me twice a day. Anything out of the ordinary occurs call me immediately, okay?"

"Okay, Gus." She hoped he didn't suspect her sudden subservience.

"And Valerie, we're going to arrange for a swap with you. An agent of Interpol is going to contact you to trade laptop computers with you for a day or so. We're gonna have some computer experts go over it with a fine toothcomb to see if your friends left anything in there which might prove useful to us. After they check it out they'll return it to you. Charlie Smith gave us the exact model that you were given and there shouldn't be any problem for just a day or so."

"All right, but no more than one day. I don't know that I can stall Elaine Griffin if she wants me to use the computer, and if there is some hidden password on mine, it won't be in yours, which may give me away."

"I'll pass that on. Talk to you later."

She hung up and returned to the bar. She was in deep shit and there was no denying it. That DEA asshole had confirmed several items she had already suspected. In the first place, she could forget working for another airline, that much was not going to happen. She knew the airline world enough to know that transferring to another airline was something extremely difficult to do because of the seniority system, and although she believed that perhaps someone high in the government could produce such a miracle, given the right incentive, there was no evidence that this Gus Olaffson was even interested in trying, let alone succeeding at it.

The implied threat had been crystal-clear: cooperate or get charged with drug smuggling. If she cooperated and the feds fucked up, then she really wouldn't have much to worry about, would she? Elaine and her friends would see to that.

A real win-win situation.

She ordered espresso and called Charlie from the hotel courtesy phone.

"What's up, captain?" Charlie was just finishing his shower.

"Meet me downstairs in the bar ASAP."

"Got some news?"

"Yes, we'll talk down here." She then called Paul Morris at his hotel and asked him to grab a taxi and meet her there.

"When you go in the bar you'll see Charlie and me sitting in a booth. Don't talk to us but sit as close to us as you can just in case we're being watched."

"Everything okay? I have formulated two escape routes in case of trouble, one to be used if we have plenty time, the second one, our ejection seat, getting us out of Berlin balls to the wall. I found an outfit with a Learjet always available, and a car-rental agency close to my hotel, where we could pick up a fast car, a BMW or a Mercedes, and head for the border, if the need arose."

"Things are not alright but they're not that bad yet, but we'll talk when you get here."

"Are you in immediate danger? I obtained the number for the Berlin police and have it here next to my phone. In case of extreme danger, I can call the police and tell them that Elaine is a terrorist readying to blow up the hotel lobby, I'll give them her description and hope the Germans get to her before she gets to you. If you feel you're in danger, I'll do it right now..."

"No, no immediate danger. Just some planning we have to do."

"I'll be there in twenty minutes."

"I love you," Valerie saw Charlie Smith appear at the entrance to the bar.

Paul Morris had already hung up. She wondered how things would have been different if she had agreed to marrying him at any time during the past thirteen years. She had not wanted to get tied down, although she did love Paul Morris, but her airline career had been too important for her, and she'd seen too many other pilots and flight attendants fail in their marriages to non-airline spouses.

Charlie showed up and they found a booth away from the bar, ordering more coffee.

"So, hit me, what's up? Did you talk to Gus?" Charlie Smith sat with his arms on the table, leaning forward.

"Yes, and you won't like what he had to say." She briefed Smith on her conversation with the federal agent, trying to remain objective and repeat it verbatim.

When she finished Smith fumed. "That cocksucker!"

Valerie was not partial to heavy use of profanity, but this time she had to strongly agree with her copilot.

"The lying sack of shit!" Charlie Smith exclaimed, turning red.

"Not exactly," Valerie pointed out, "he didn't exactly lie to us, did he? He never came out and offered anything concise. All he said was he would look into it."

"Sleeker than a greased pig!"

"Yes, but he didn't lie. Not directly, anyway."

"Bullshit, Valerie! Where I come from a man doesn't have second and third meanings to his words. Olaffson understood damn well the terms of our agreement and he intentionally failed to commit himself so he could trap us."

"That, Charlie, is a fact."

"I am going to talk to his superiors..."

"Forget it Charlie, this ain't the Navy. You won't get anywhere with those guys. They are little people with little minds and they can't even phantom where you and I are coming from."

"So, what do you suggest we do then, roll over and play dead?"

"Hell, no. It's just that I have this nagging feeling that whatever action we take is going to have to be on our own. The DEA guys are not our allies in this, they want to use us to get to Elaine and her people, and they're not really concerned about collateral damage."

"Fuck me!" Charlie paused, accepting his coffee from the waitress, then he scanned he room, trying to make any possible tails.

"That's precisely what they'd like to do to us, Charlie–fuck us–Gus, and Elaine and the whole bunch, but all these fine people are making a terrible mistake because I like to chose my own sex partners, and I get very upset when I don't get to."

Charlie smiled at her, waiting. "Got any ideas?"

"Yes, as a matter-of-fact I do. Paul Morris is on his way here and he's going to sit behind us there so it doesn't look like he's associated with us. Here's the plan..."

SEVENTEEN
PRESENT TIME - BERLIN, GERMANY

Valerie selected a table away from the door and indicated to the waitress that she wanted that table. The restaurant she had chosen for her meeting with Elaine Griffin was on the *Kudam,* and was elegant but not exorbitantly expensive. She sat at the heavy wooden table, ordering a bottle of Chianti. The situation had reached critical mass, and now the chain-reaction of events she had planned was going to happen and nobody would be able to contain it any longer.

Elaine Griffin walked in, pausing for a moment at the door to adjust her vision to the dark interior of the restaurant while looking for the TGA captain.

Valerie waived, attracting the attention of the woman responsible for this mess she was in; Griffin saw her at once, moving towards her, approving of the choice of location, for the restaurant was quiet and discrete.

"Hi, Elaine. Thanks for coming."

"Hello, Darling," Griffin hugged the TGA captain in a way that would look to any casual observer as that of two friends getting together for a middle-of-the week lunch while their obviously well-to-do husbands were at their offices.

"Have a seat. I ordered us some Chianti."

"Wonderful." Griffin looked around at the other tables to ascertain that none of the other customers were close enough to overhear their conversation. "What's going on, Valerie?" Computer communication was the norm within the Organization, and she had been quite clear, explaining to Valerie how to use electronic mail for all conversations, unless something out of the ordinary mandated a face-to-face meeting.

The TGA captain had emailed her a message two hours earlier, requesting an urgent meeting, but had not included any hint as to the motive.

"Elaine, you know I've been straight with you, I have brought you your scarves from Istanbul and delivered the box to London, right?"

"Go on."

"Also, I've found you a first recruit, a pilot, who is *very* interested in making money and I can assure you he will be very valuable to your group. I'll give you his name and introduce you to him if that's the way you wish to do it after you pay me the one hundred thousand dollars I mentioned to you before. By the way, you did get approval for my fee, is that correct?"

Elaine Griffin removed a cigarette from her gold case, lighting it. "Yes, they did approve your fee, Valerie, but don't go getting too greedy thinking that they'll keep paying you every time you do something new, because that's not going to happen."

Valerie stared right at her contact. "Elaine, you have bigger problems than worrying about paying me a measly hundred thousand."

Griffin tightened up. "What do you mean by that?"

"Elaine, last night I got a call in my hotel room from a man who identified himself as a federal agent working for the American Drug Enforcement Administration."

That got her attention.

"This man went on to tell me that the FBI, the CIA and Interpol are aware of the existence of a group known as the Organization, a group responsible for drug smuggling operations worldwide, a group they suspect you belong to."

Elaine Griffin froze.

Valerie took note of the subtle change in Griffin's facial expression at the mention of the Organization.

Bulls eye.

"This man told me that your group is responsible for the deaths of several airline personnel belonging to different airlines all over the world and that this Organization is behind the bombing of a Miami flight not too long ago."

Elaine Griffin casually inched her hand towards her purse.

"He told me he was aware that I'd unknowingly brought some illegal merchandise from Turkey and that he wants me to cooperate with the authorities in catching the people involved."

Elaine Griffin slid her hand in her purse.

Valerie took on a conspirational tone, "I don't know how these fuckers found out all this, but I think you have to immediately get in touch with your superiors and inform them that the cops are hot on their trail. You must have a police informer somewhere in your network, maybe in the scarves shop in Istanbul, maybe the grandson of the owner of the store, or who knows, but it doesn't matter. The important thing is that the cops don't know I'm a member of the Organization and we can steer them away from us by feeding them shit. They, however, know your name and they want me to set you up."

Elaine Griffin relaxed the hold on the automatic pistol she carried in her purse, listening to the TGA captain.

"This Fed was a real dickhead, and he thought he was scaring the shit out of me telling me all this. I broke down crying, telling him I was scared to death and ready to jump on the first flight out of here back to the States. He bought it and did his damnest to reassure me that if I cooperated with him and stayed here, that there'd be no repercussions from the illegal contraband I brought into Germany from Istanbul. He told me I had to try infiltrating your Organization or at least finding out all I could about you and trying to set you up."

"You say he was with the DEA, and that he was American?"

"Yes, that's what he claimed. His name is Gus Olaffson and this is the contact number he gave me to call him. It's in New York City." She handed Griffin a piece of paper with the name and number on it.

Griffin took the paper, studying it. She removed her hand from her purse. "Valerie, you have stunned me–to say the least–with this news. Ten seconds ago I was ready to bolt because for a moment there I wasn't sure which side of the fence you were on. Obviously this is not a product of your imagination, since you know about the incidents of the other crewmembers in other countries, and about the bombing of the Miami flight, which proves beyond doubt that you did indeed speak with someone. The first order of business here then is to determine what level of urgency we're looking at. I'll contact the Organization right away and trace this number and the name of this agent you've given me, and go from there. Valerie, this is very serious. What exactly did you tell this man, Olaffson?"

"I played dumb and told him how you'd asked me to bring the scarves from Istanbul and how I had no idea what was in them. He asked me if I had a number where I could reach you and I told him that I had no such information, that you had contacted me because your sister had given you my name and number at the hotel. He told me he believes that you'll contact me again prior to my next Istanbul flight and that we must prepare a trap to catch you with the drugs in your possession after I return."

"He told you all this over an open line?"

"Yes."

"That's strange, usually those guys are a lot more careful. However, you did the right thing calling me here, and you're right, we have to pass on this information immediately so that we can prevent a disaster."

"Good. What do you want me to do?"

Elaine Griffin wondered about that. Valerie knew the woman was not going to entirely trust her until she could check out Valerie's story.

"Do nothing until I get back in touch with you."

"And when will that be?"

"I'll get to work on this immediately and call you within a couple of hours. Maybe we'll meet back here after I call you in your hotel room. Did this guy say when he was going to call you again?"

"No, he wants me to call him twice a day at that number I gave you. He said if I fail to call him he'll instruct the German authorities to step in."

"And when is he expecting your first call?

"Tonight."

"Very well, go back to your room and wait for my call."

The waitress brought a bottle of Chianti to their table, which Elaine canceled, explaining to the waitress that they would have to postpone their lunch until later, giving her a generous tip. The waitress took the bottle away, puzzled but satisfied with the money. The two women left the restaurant.

ELAINE GRIFFIN LEFT THE restaurant in a state of agitation she had not felt since the first time she'd smoked pot and worried that she was going to get caught. If what the TGA gal said was all true–and she suspected that it was–then things were not good, not good at all. If American authorities were on to her to the point of contacting Valerie, that could only mean that they were hot on her trail, which meant something must have tipped them off as to Elaine's involvement with the Organization. Her first thought had been to notify Escobar in St. Louis, but the more she thought about it, the more she leaned against doing it. She was perfectly aware of the way those Colombians dealt with problems, and this leak was a definite problem. The most likely result of her telling

Escobar about what the TGA captain had just told her would probably result in an immediate assassination order being arranged to get rid of her, Valerie and Hans. And if she failed to notify Escobar and the authorities went after the Organization and Escobar eventually found out that she had withheld this information from him, there would be hell to pay. Either way it seemed that she was caught in the proverbial frying pan, and she would have to think of something fast.

Reasoning with these South Americans was out of the question, since they shot first and asked questions later, and she had seen the way they dealt with operatives suspected of fucking up, and had no intention of ending up with her throat cut. Elaine Griffin caught a taxi to her hotel, wondering what her options were. If Valerie was being straight, her employment with the Organization was virtually terminated as of that very moment, because once the cops were aware of her existence, she was no longer an asset to the Organization. But how in the world did they make her? She had been extremely careful all these years, never leaving any open ends. Damn, damn. Things had been going so good that she must have gotten careless and given herself away somehow, but now it was too late to cry over spilled milk. No use wasting time trying to figure out how they discovered her. Now the name of the game was survival. She and Hans had to put into action their escape plan which they had in store for an event such as this. She would have to act quick, because she had no idea how much time she actually had before the shit hit the fan. If this TGA captain in Berlin knew as much as she did, there was a very good chance that the American authorities had also told others, and if it reached Escobar then the clock would run out.

The taxi dropped her off at her hotel and she headed straight for her room. Hans was in the room reading the Wall Street Journal, sipping tomato juice with lime, Tabasco sauce and salt and pepper.

"Did you meet the pilot? What was so important?" he asked, peeking over the paper he was reading. He had his shoes off, his feet crossed resting on a chair.

"Hans, we got problems, real serious problems."

Hans sat up at once, crumpling the paper, paying close attention to what Elaine had to say. "What's going on?"

Elaine told him.

"Oh, no, shit! Shit! This is definitely not good."

"We gotta bail out of here, Hans."

"Oh, crap!" Hans had worked on the emergency plan with Elaine years ago, but had never really thought they would need to make use of it. Now that Elaine dropped it on him, it was hard to accept with such short notice. Maybe they could still plug the leak. "How the hell did this happen? Do you think Escobar knows?"

"Hans," Elaine tried to impress in him the gravity of the situation, "If Escobar knew, you and I would probably be lying on slabs at the Berlin morgue. If there was a leak, and it certainly looks that way, the minute Escobar gets a whiff of this he is going to shut down the German side of this operation on the spot, and you know what that means."

He knew damn well what that meant. Escobar would have all the operatives killed and all records destroyed. The man took no chances, and he had no problem eliminating some good people just to cover his ass. *"Mein Gott!* What do we do?"

Elaine sat down at her laptop computer, typing furiously. "What we do is we follow our emergency exit plan to the letter, starting this very minute."

"You're going to transfer the money?" They had agreed that in order to get lost in the world and remove themselves from the long arm of the Organization, if it ever became necessary, they would need money–and lots of it–and the best way to get it was to tap the Organization's very own funds. Valerie regularly made transfers between bank accounts for Escobar, and she had access to many of the accounts the man had spread all over the world. She had passwords, amounts available, contacts and telephone numbers which gave her access to several hundred million dollars. The bank accounts she dealt with had personal identification numbers that had to be provided in case large amounts of money were transferred out of these accounts. She had several of these PINs, and she intended to use them right away. The transfers would not be noticed immediately, giving her and Hans time to escape. Escobar trusted her because he trusted his own power to reach for her anywhere in the world, should she dare betray him.

Elaine set up her computer for electronic funds transfer and hooked it up to the phone line in her hotel room. The program she had prepared beforehand would perform several dozen transfers between accounts in order to mud up the trail, until the last transfer which would go into her own personal accounts here in Berlin. As soon as the funds were credited to her accounts, she would cash out and her and Hans would get lost. South Africa or New Zealand held promise for two people willing to disappear.

The brief love affair she'd had with Escobar two years earlier had promoted her to a trustworthy position, and Escobar himself had seen to it that she gained authority and responsibility within the Organization. One quick night of sex had opened up immense wealth to her, and she was now going to cash in on it.

She suspected that Escobar consumed women with a ferocious appetite, just like he consumed everything else in life, but somehow she had managed to hit a spot in his heart and become memorable during her visit to Los Angeles two years ago, because after their stunt he had decided to make her a high officer of the Organization. Elaine suspected that he was probably "stashing" her away for when he took a little trip to Germany. Up until now she had never let him down, but with the feds involved, it became a different game.

Elaine connected her laptop computer to the fax belonging to a bank in Singapore, and began transmitting one of the letters she had typed months before, with the instructions on how to transfer half a million dollars to an account in Berlin by routing the funds through five different banks in different countries. She had prepared these transfer letters ahead of time and now she would be able to activate their emergency plan, collect their money and be on a plane to Australia or South Africa within forty-eight hours. This type of transaction was relatively routine with most of the banks Escobar dealt with, so she was confident that the transfers would be made without any questions asked. Even if anyone suspected foul play and tried to follow the path of the transfers, she had built-in enough transfer operations to give her some extra time before a hound could trace the funds to her accounts in Berlin.

"**DID YOU CONFIRM WHAT** room she's in?"

"Yes," Paul Morris sipped his beer at the St. George's bar. "She and that German fellow are sharing a suite in the fourth floor. She went straight there after meeting with you. I hung around the front desk of the hotel and used the house phone to call her but was unable to get in. She was on the phone for over an hour and was still talking to someone when I left to come here."

Valerie was not surprised by the reaction her dear friend Elaine had upon hearing the news, but she was puzzled about the woman being on the phone that long. "Paul, if that was her boss she was calling to report that the feds are on to them she wouldn't have used her room telephone for a voice conversation. She'd probably have typed and encoded it and sent it the same way she always does."

"You're right. But a coded transmission wouldn't have taken over an hour to transmit, and besides, she didn't have time to type it out when she arrived in her suite because she was on that phone two minutes after walking in." Paul Morris had stalked Elaine outside of the restaurant where Valerie had set up the meeting, had waited outside until the woman exited and walked back to her hotel at a fast pace. Paul Morris had followed her and obtained the room number of the suite.

"If she called her boss to tell him what I claim happened, she'd be exposing herself to detection on an open line, so I really don't think that's what she was up to."

"That's if she did call her boss at all," Paul Morris added. "If she's working for one of the drug cartels, I don't think she'd call her boss with news that the Americans are on to her. That might not be looked at with fond eyes in South America."

"What do you mean?"

"Think about it, Valerie. If you were some big drug lord in Colombia, and one of your contacts in Germany called you with this kind of news, what would you do?"

"I don't know, tell me."

"Haven't you read the papers or *Newsweek*? Those crazy bastards in the drug cartels kill off any judge who opposes them. Judges, Valerie, not just anybody. What do you think they'd do to Elaine?"

"I think you're right, Paul Morris. I think we just might have scared her enough to make her run. And if she runs, she's going to need lots of cash."

"And the woman obviously has access to tons of cash. Look how easily she came up with the money she paid you."

Valerie smiled. "I think you're right. If she was able to cough up a hundred thousand to us with such incredible ease, I suspect she'll have access to a lot more for her own purposes." Valerie paid for the beer, standing up.

"Paul, I'm going to my room to wait for her call. If she decides not run and squeal on me instead, then she'll probably receive orders to eliminate me, then she'll call up and try to set up a place."

Paul Morris did not like playing cops and robbers with Valerie's life, but he agreed to her plan because he knew Valerie would go ahead with it regardless of his objections. "I'll be right behind you. She makes one false move and I'll come down on her so hard she will never know what hit her."

Valerie was amused to hear Paul Morris talk this way. He was not a physical man, and it intrigued her to observe the metamorphosis taking place with him. She depended on him and Charlie to pull this one through, and felt confident that between the three of them they could handle most situations. "I think she has a gun in her purse. I saw her slowly going for the purse when I gave her the news about her cover being blown, but she removed her hand from the purse when I told her that I was on her side and that we should find a way to fuck the feds."

"If I see her reach for that purse I'll break her arm," Charlie interjected. "And I don't care if she was only going to fetch a Kleenex."

Valerie squeezed the big man's arm. The three of them stood up and separated before heading for their respective stations.

Valerie returned to her hotel room, stopping at the front desk to ask if she had any messages.

There were none.

She popped a beer and sat on the low bed, pondering about their next move. If the feds were not going to play ball with her and Charlie, then–by God–she was going to play ball with Elaine, milk her for all she could and then disappear before they decided that she was expendable. She was left with no other choice. It was obvious from her conversation with the feds that they were not going to give a shit whether her involvement in this affair cost her career. Those poor bastards couldn't even begin to phantom what her career meant to her, and it angered her that they had the gall to ruin her whole life without giving it much thought.

She probably made more money than any five of those G-men put together, and they probably resented the shit out of her for that. The Witness Protection Plan– yeah, my ass!

The phone rang.

"Valerie?" it was Elaine.

"Speaking. Hi."

"Valerie, I've passed on the information you gave me this afternoon and the gentlemen concerned are evaluating it and they'll take whatever action becomes necessary, should your information prove correct. While that happens, they want us to continue operating business as usual and keeping our ears open for any other bit of news."

Elaine's voice seemed more calm than during the meeting, Valerie decided. "And what do you want me to tell the Fed when I talk to him this afternoon?"

"Tell him that you're on stand-by for whatever assignment he wants to give you. We'll be able to stall any action on their part if they think you're awaiting orders."

"Okay. When do you want to meet again?"

"I will call you in a couple of days. You have another Istanbul flight coming up, no?"

Valerie wondered who'd given this woman her monthly flight schedule, probably her sister. She would have to find a way to fix her too. "Yes, I do. Did you want me to bring you any more scarves?" No way she was flying to Istanbul just now, sweetheart.

"No, no. Just fly the trip as you normally would. I think is better that we don't do anything until this little inconvenience is taken care of."

"Sounds good to me. What about the other issue?"

"What other issue?"

"The new recruit."

"Oh, that. Tell you what, Valerie, let's wait on that for a few days. I don't think it's a good idea to do anything else at this time. If what you told me turns out to be correct, then we have a leak somewhere that needs to be plugged, and it's better not to bring any more players to the party until the situation is back to normal."

"So I don't get my money until things get back to normal?"

"You're too nice to be a greedy bitch, Valerie," Elaine fumed, "but that's correct. When everything's been smoothed out, then we'll talk about your recruiter's fee."

"Okay. I'll wait for your call."

"No, don't wait for my call. Check instead for e-mail at this number I'm going to give you. Just have the computer dial in and download any messages you find there."

"Okay." Valerie took down the number for the server, said good-bye, grabbed her leather jacket, and headed for the St. George's bar.

Greedy bitch? Elaine dearest, you don't know just how greedy you've forced me to become.

PAUL MORRIS AND CHARLIE Smith listened to Valerie's account of her conversation with the Griffin woman.

"She's been to eight different banks already this morning," Charlie offered. "Each time, her husband goes in with her carrying two large briefcases, they spend about twenty minutes inside, lock the briefcases in the trunk of their Mercedes and go on to a new bank."

"Eight different banks," Paul Morris repeated, "and they go in with the same two briefcases?"

Charlie sipped his beer, wiping his lips on a paper napkin. "I don't know, I haven't been able to get close enough to peek inside the trunk, but since they're not emptying the suitcases in the trunk, I suspect they must be using different suitcases each time."

"Why would they be going to all these banks?" Valerie and the two men spoke quietly, sitting in a booth at the St. George's.

" I don't know, Valerie," Charlie continued, "but it seems damned strange to me that as soon as you blew the whistle on the feds, all of a sudden this pair suddenly decide to visit every big bank in town. If you ask me, they're are getting ready to pack up and take a vacation. Fly the coup, so to speak."

"And they're visiting all these banks to close their accounts?" Paul Morris asked.

"It doesn't take a fucking genius to figure that one out guys, of course they're cashing out. What the devil else could be going on?" Charlie was excited about the developments that morning. He had not felt such excitement in a long time. "Who knows? Perhaps. Fact is, she told Valerie to lay low and don't do anything to attract attention, and that is not exactly what those two have been doing."

Valerie had to agree with Charlie. Elaine instructed her to lay low, yet Elaine was running all over Berlin visiting banks. Something was definitely funny. "I called crew scheduling in New York and told them I am unable to take that Istanbul trip day after tomorrow. I cited female problems and they said they're going to call around the crews stationed here to see if anyone wants to take the trip for me."

"Fine. Not a good idea, going to Istanbul just now," Charlie interjected, "We're all fully aware of how easy it would be to hire someone in that city to knock you off, Valerie, if that's what's on the menu."

"I didn't think so either, Charlie."

"I'd be rather curious to see what those two are hauling around in those briefcases, though." Charlie was relieved that the Griffin woman had postponed meeting him as the new recruit.

"So you think they're cashing out and filling up those suitcases with cash?" Paul Morris asked Valerie.

"I think Charlie is right, Paul Morris. Why else would they be visiting all these banks? They must be cleaning house in preparation for a quick departure. Way I look at it, you can easily fit half a million bucks into one of those suitcases. Sixteen of them so far, makes for about eight million dollars."

"Looks to me like Valerie is right," Charlie added. "And I don't think it really matters whether they're flying out of here under orders, or on their own initiative. Money is money, and what we have to do is intercept them and take it from them."

Valerie thought about this. She'd gambled that this was going to be the course of action Elaine was going to follow, and from what they had seen so far, it appeared that she'd succeeded in scaring the bitch enough to make her cash out and bolt. If those two bolted, it would probably mean one of two things: one, that the big shots at the top of the Organization wanted to close shop in Berlin, which made Valerie expendable, or two, that Elaine was getting ready to bid farewell to her unsuspecting employers, taking a golden parachute along for incidental expenses. "Guys, we have to find out what the hell's going on. If those two are indeed moving shop elsewhere, then they don't need me anymore, and I know too much." The implications were clear.

"She's right," Paul Morris observed. "We have to find out what those two are up to. I personally believe that they're flying the coup without letting their people know. Think about it, if a big drug organization was going to transfer a lot of money, they'd probably do so electronically, using bank transfers. If we assume for a moment that this is not the case, because the drug Organization boys don't want to leave a paper trail, then they'd cash out, the way it appears Elaine is doing, but don't you think they'd have an army of goons armed to the teeth protecting all that money? Bet your ass they would."

"I agree with you, Paul Morris, I'm not happy with these bastards."

Valerie smiled at him. When she had first sprung the plan on him, he'd been reluctant to go along because it would probably mean the end of his flying career, but she'd eventually managed to convince him that their flying careers were already over anyway. The federal agents and the Organization had done that to them, and it was no use denying it. Now, it was up to them to take the initiative and try to salvage something for the future, while at the same time protecting themselves from getting killed. Charlie Smith stared into her eyes. "We have to find out if it's really money they're hauling around in those briefcases."

"And how do you propose we do that?" Valerie interjected.

"I say we go visit 'em and ask them to tell us." Paul Morris offered.

"Just like that."

"Yeah, just like that."

"Paul Morris," Charlie Smith smiled, "if we were to casually drop in on those two—as you so candidly suggest—we'd probably get shot up full of holes and they would just speed up their departure. Those two are probably armed to the teeth. And besides, we don't want to tip them off too soon, not before they have withdrawn all of our money from every account they possess!"

"Our money? I had initially just wanted to get Valerie away from this mess, but now it seems that we're all getting greedy."

"Yes—our money, Paul Morris. Those two play dirty, and they've managed to frame Valerie and myself in a real shitty way. We have no option but to make them pay us for the inconvenience."

"So you think we should just take their money?"

"Paul," Charlie Smith smiled, "that is not their money either. They made that money dealing drugs, hurting poor people God knows where. We won't be doing anything wrong by taking that cash away from them. What do you think they're gonna do? Go to the police and file a report?"

"Okay, assuming what you think is correct, and that's drug money, don't you think the mob that money belongs to is going to come after us?"

"What are you, kidding? Valerie and possibly myself are already probably on a shit list with those gentlemen in South America. We're gonna have to run anyway now. Don't you think it'd be better and easier to get lost if we had some pocket money?"

"In that case, I propose that we arm ourselves as well."

"Paul Morris," Charlie Smith smiled, "now you're talking."

Valerie did not like guns, but she had to agree with the two men. "How can we get a gun? Germans don't like selling guns to foreigners visiting Berlin, and I didn't bring a gun, did you guys?"

"No, I don't have one here either," Paul Morris became serious, "but I think I know where we can get our hands on something that will give us a definite advantage."

NEARLY TWENTY-FOUR HOURS later, Charlie Smith got off the airplane at Sky Harbor International airport in Phoenix, Arizona, and headed for the TGA counter.

The airport was packed with travelers, and he wondered how he was going to find his contact. A white Panama hat, Paul Morris had explained. The contact would be wearing a white Panama hat. Well, Charlie wasn't really sure what on earth a Panama hat looked like to begin with, so he searched the area for men wearing a white hat of any kind.

"Captain Smith?" the man was short, unshaven, about twenty-three and had fresh breath, a friendly face and long hair. He was wearing a wide-brim white hat. Must be a Panama hat.

"Pete?" Charlie offered his hand. The man shook it, gesturing to Charlie for them to move aside, away from the main flow of airport traffic.

"Paul called me and told me about the purchase you guys were interested in making." The man handed Charlie Smith a leather bag, similar to the type used to carry laptop computers. Charlie Smith accepted the bag, surprised at how much it weighed. It must be thirty pounds.

"Thank you."

"You're welcome. If that's all, I'm outta here. Good luck!" the man kept looking around, as if trying to spot someone in the crowds.

Charlie shook hands with the man again, then watched him lose himself in the crowd. He stood there a second longer, daydreaming, then he headed down to his airline's operations office in the basement area of the airport. He bypassed security by going through the airline front counter out into the ramp, then walking among the parked airliners until reaching the ramp office, where the crew lounge was located. His TGA pilot uniform and I.D. guaranteed him safe passage through the airport operations area. He was just another airline pilot going to his airplane.

He had come all the way from Berlin, traveling close to nineteen hours, and was going to get some rest in the crew lounge before catching the red-eye back to Kennedy in four hours.

Charlie Smith locked himself in the crew bathroom. Once he assured himself that no intruders would interrupt, he unzipped the black leather bag the man with the Panama hat had given him. Inside was one of the deadliest killing machines ever conceived by man. Colonel Gordon Ingram, a member of the U.S. Special Forces had created the MAC 10, in .45 caliber, to compete with the Israeli Uzi submachine gun. Colonel Ingram had considered the Uzi a good but heavy weapon, so he had fathered a new type of automatic light attack machine gun, one that commandos could easily carry, and named his creation the Ingram Mac 10. The next step in the evolution of this fantastic attack weapon had been the M12, and this was the machine-pistol that Charlie Smith gazed at, fascinated.

The MAC 12 machine-pistol was approximately nine inches in length, and it could fire 1250 rounds of 380 ACP caliber subsonic ammunition per minute. That came out to roughly about twenty rounds per second. One 380 slug could knock a man off his feet with all the grace of a sledge-hammer, and twenty rounds could clear a room in one second. Charlie had heard somewhere that the Mac 12 was affectionately known as the "room sweeper," and it was no secret why. It could easily saw a man in half with all the finesse of a chainsaw.

The particular machine that he held in his hands had an added feature that made it incredibly more lethal than its sisters. This one came with a 12-inch long noise suppressor, also known as a silencer. Twelve-hundred and fifty rounds a minute, and no louder than a little school girl clearing her throat. Charlie Smith felt the surge of power flow through his hands, moving up to his arms and filling him with a warm, quasi-sexual feeling. That was the effect this silent killing machine had in individuals who knew its potential. He briefly thought about the irony of such powerful weapon having a phallic form.

This black piece of beautifully-crafted steel gave whoever held it the power of the gods, the power of life and death, and Charlie Smith knew this. He was too tired to contemplate the risk he was taking, traveling by air between countries carrying an illegal machine-pistol prohibited in most countries on earth, but what the heck! These past few days had become a tangled absurdity anyhow.

Paul Morris had called a friend of his in Phoenix who collected arms, and offered him fifty thousand dollars for the machine-pistol. The man was a starving medical student who had paid eleven hundred dollars for the Ingram, and had jumped at the offer. Arizona was still the Wild West, and its residents were allowed to own fully automatic weapons such as the Mac 12s, and even silencers.

Each automatic weapon and its silencer had to be registered with the FBI and the Bureau of Tobacco and Firearms, and an ownership permit was issued to the owner provided he had a clean police record. The FBI had to be notified in each case of ownership transfer, because each new owner had to meet the same qualifications for ownership. Paul's friend had received a cashier's check for fifty thousand dollars by Federal Express that morning, had gone to the Bank of America to cash it and then had called the FBI and the local authorities to report his gun as having been stolen from his parked car while he was inside a supermarket.

Charlie Smith now held the gun in the bathroom of the crew lounge, having bypassed security screening and waiting for his ride back to Germany. The Mac 12 came with ten plastic clips, each holding thirty-two rounds of subsonic ammunition. At sixteen cents per round, this beauty could fire for one minute at a cost of $200. No wonder wars were expensive. Charlie would carry the pistol all the way back to Germany without detection because he was able to avoid security and customs by exiting the airplane from the jetway stairs and going directly to TGA operations in JFK, Frankfurt and Berlin.

One of the fringe benefits inherent to the airline piloting profession.

He must be out of his fucking mind.

Charlie found a comfortable Lazy Boy couch in the empty crew room, placed the black leather bag under his lower back, set his Casio calculator watch to midnight and went to sleep.

The electronic alarm woke him at midnight. He had a few seconds of not knowing where he was, then got up and headed for the restroom with the black leather bag. After washing his face, he went out in the small lobby of the ramp operations area and signed his name on the clipboard where jumpseaters had to register to ride the cockpit.

When the MD-90 arrived half an hour later, Charlie introduced himself to the crew and hung around with them for thirty minutes trading stories. When the captain finally signed the paperwork for the flight heading out to the airplane Charlie followed him and the first officer out on the ramp. They climbed the exterior jetway staircase up to the airplane and entered the First Class area of the cabin. Charlie stowed his bag in the cockpit and visited with the flight attendants while the captain and his copilot initiated their preflight checks.

Once all the passengers had boarded and there were still a few First Class seats left available, the flight service manager invited Charlie to one of them. He went back in the cockpit, retrieved his leather bag and settled himself for the six-hour flight to the Big Apple.

He thought about the ridiculous situation they were involved in. They suspected the woman Elaine had been getting money out of all those German banks she had been visiting with her briefcases, so if this was true, then by now she must have a small fortune in her hotel room. They'd have to pay a visit to the little lady in order to find out, and Charlie knew that Elaine and her husband–if that's what the dude was–were not going to just sit there and be friendly and cooperative. They were going to be real pissed at this intrusion, but Charlie was going to have the MAC 12 to kinda even up the odds a little. Neither Valerie nor Paul Morris had any formal weapons training, which left it up to him to handle the firepower. Would he fire on those two if provoked? He thought of the crew and passengers of the airliner that was taken out of the sky on approach to Miami.

Bet your ass he would.

He'd helped himself to a roll of silver duct-tape from the TGA operations office. Elaine Griffin and the German puke with her would have to wait for room service to come untape them, after he was done with them.

The McDonnell-Douglas MD-90 crossed the United States in five hours and six minutes with the help of a powerful tailwind, landing at New York's Kennedy airport a little after nine a.m.

Charlie woke up just as the wheels met the pavement, startled that he'd slept the entire way. He sat up, trying to adjust to the bright daylight, feeling the beard that was now more than just a stubble. Kennedy airport, he observed, was its usual frenzy of activity.

The MD-90 parked at the gate and Charlie thanked the crew for the ride on his way out, exiting the airplane into the main area of the terminal. He was already inside the secure area of the airport, so he wouldn't have to dodge security this time. The airline had a nice crew lounge downstairs where operations was, and he headed there. The main door had a combination lock on it which prevented unauthorized entry by non-airline individuals.

Charlie punched the combination, which was the same for every operations door lock throughout the entire country–great security, he thought sarcastically–heading for the men's room. He'd brought with him a small shaving kit, which he used to shave and freshen up in front of a mirror in the bathroom. His uniform coat, hat and leather bag sat in a corner on the floor.

Although he felt like shit warmed over due to his disrupted biorhythm, the clean face made him feel almost human again. Nothing bugged him more than being unshaven while in uniform.

He went back upstairs to the main concourse, bought a newspaper and found an empty table at a restaurant, not looking forward to nine hours of airport lounging until his flight left for Frankfurt at six that evening. He strongly suspected that automatic weapons were probably banned from the state of New York, since the good people of New York didn't even allow handgun ownership to its citizens, so sitting there at Kennedy airport with a MAC 12 in his possession, he was as hot as Chernobyl at its best.

The feds knew about him, they had his name on record, which probably meant that for the right amount of money the drug kings that were involved in this adventure would have access to his identity. He was no longer merely an observer. Now he was as deep as Valerie in this pile of shit. Once again, he was amazed at her intelligence and powers of perception. How the hell did she know that the feds were bullshitting them about getting them a job with another airline? The woman was amazing. He himself would never have doubted the word of a government agent.

Must be the Pavlov dog syndrome they drilled into him in the Navy, he mused. Obey without question. It is not for us to ask the reason why...he was fully aware that their airline would fire their butts the minute any of this came out in the open. Not that it made much difference anyhow if the drug sweethearts came after them.

A real nice situation.

By the time his flight was ready to board that evening, Charlie caught up on all his reading of *Newsweek, The Wall Street Journal, U.S. News, Flying* magazine, *Business Week, Time, Life, Playboy,* and a couple of restaurant menus. He was at the boarding gate one hour prior to boarding, waited until the last passengers had gone into the jetway and presented the gate boarding agent with his ACM–Additional Crew Member, authorization slip and his airline I.D.

"Thank you, jump right in and have a good flight, sir," the airline gate agent chirped. She was a cute brunette with a cheerful smile.

Charlie strolled into the jetway, entering the First Class cabin of the enormous Boeing 747 jumbo jet. He greeted the flight attendant at the door, climbing the stairs to the cockpit which was located above the First Class cabin. He introduced himself to the crew, swapping jokes, telling them he was based in Berlin but that had gone home "to get some." They all approved. The captain on the transoceanic flight was an old veteran with white hair and years of experience, and he instructed Charlie to hang around in the cockpit until the doors of the cabin were shut and then go back and grab himself a seat in First Class.

Charlie waited until the flight engineer confirmed by looking at his panel that indeed, all cabin doors had been shut, thanked the crew and went back into the upper deck of the big Boeing to grab a comfortable seat for the ocean crossing. The flight attendant taking care of the upstairs First Class area was also a senior employee, probably a contemporary of the captain, and she was very pleasant and offered Charlie a Coke before departure. He was not allowed any liquor while in uniform, not that it would have crossed his mind to drink while carrying this machine-pistol with him anyway. The nine-hour flight to Frankfurt was nothing more than a continuous five-star first-class meal, which Charlie had no intention of partaking. He asked the flight attendant to ignore him during her meal service because he intended to sleep the entire crossing. Somehow the airline felt that First Class passengers had to get their money's worth by feeding them the best the world had to offer during the entire flight, and although this was a noble idea, it precluded uninterrupted sleep, which he was going to need if he wanted to be fresh upon his arrival in Berlin the following morning.

He requisitioned two airline pillows and a blanket, preparing himself for a nine-hour nap. He would have to wait until the flight took off before reclining his seat for sleep, but this gave him the chance to enjoy the Coke the flight attendant had brought him. The upper First Class cabin had twenty wide seats in it, but there were only four other passengers up there with him. He placed the leather bag between the window and his lap, wedging it in tightly to assure that if anyone tried removing it while he slept that it would wake him.

Once again, Charlie woke up as the eighteen wheels of the jumbo jet touched down at Frankfurt-Main airport in Germany. The weather was clear and beautiful, and he rubbed the sleep from his eyes, contemplating his next move. He would exit the airplane with the crew directly into the ramp via the jetway stairs, since the TGA operations office was located directly below this gate and he would just hang around there and head for the Berlin flight with the crew of that airplane which was probably at operations getting its weather briefing that very moment.

After the airplane reached the gate Charlie hit the restroom, and joined the crew exiting the airplane through the jetway, bypassing customs and immigration. As planned, the crew for his flight to Berlin was in the operations office getting their paperwork. He recognized the captain standing at the counter, studying his dispatch release.

"Good morning, Sean," Charlie greeted the captain. Sean Boline was an old friend who adored being stationed in Germany and who was constantly singing praises for the German way of life. A true gentleman.

"Charlie! What the hell you doing here? Did you just come in from New York?"

"Yep. Quick trip over there to pay bills." Pilots based in Germany did not use German mail to send correspondence or monthly payments back to the States while they were based in Germany because the European mail system was notoriously slow, so instead they gave their mail to other pilots or flight attendants headed back so they could drop the mail in a U.S. mailbox.

"Going back to Berlin?"

"If I can hitch a ride with you guys."

"Absolutely," Sean Boline turned to the operations agent–a German national–"Kurt, get Charlie here an ACM form, wilya? He's going back to Berlin with us."

PRESENT TIME - ST. LOUIS, MISSOURI
UNITED STATES.

"¡La gran puta!" Esteban Escobar bellowed. He
slammed down the telephone receiver with such force
that its plastic casing shattered all over the coffee table.

Alfredo Hidalgo observed his friend flying into a rage,
cursing and yelling at everyone for five minutes. When
the man finally calmed himself, Hidalgo approached him
questioning the object of his fury.

"The bitch went over to the feds! That new TGA
captain Elaine recruited in Berlin, she went over to the
feds and now they're onto our operation in Istanbul!"

"How'd this happen?"

"How the hell should I know?! That fucking Elaine
was vague about the details because she was at a
payphone, but she told me enough. The German
operation is shot. That stupid Elaine fucked it up! I
should've known better than to give her all that
responsibility. Go trust a fucking cunt! How the hell did
she attain such a position of responsibility anyway?"

Neither Hidalgo nor Escobar touched on the subject
that Escobar's libido might've had something to do with
the level of responsibility Elaine had attained within the
Organization, or that Escobar himself had sang many
praises for his one-night lover, while promoting her to her
present position of responsibility.

"What's the situation?"

"Not good. It appears that the DEA in New York's
trying to cut a deal with the TGA bitch, and Elaine feels

it's all a setup and that the feds are on to us in more ways than one."

Hidalgo became serious. "Esteban, we must shut down Germany for a while."

"I fully agree, my friend. Shut down Germany immediately. Sooner the better. If you can do it as of yesterday, all the better for us. You take care of it."

Hidalgo was already mentally enlisting the personnel he'd be sending to Germany that afternoon. "Esteban, do you want to keep Elaine?" he would not eliminate the boss' piece of ass unless directly instructed to do so.

"Keep Elaine? What are ya, crazy? Hell, no! The bitch fucked up! Get rid of her. Get rid of the whole damn bunch. We cannot risk detection. I should've never given her my number here."

Hidalgo agreed, but wisely refrained from saying so. "I'll send a team to Germany this afternoon, Esteban. By tomorrow evening, our German division will be out of business for a while."

Escobar smiled, reaching with one arm to hug his friend in the typical Latin gesture of the *abrazo*. "Thanks, Alfredo. This is just a small inconvenience, right *amigo*? but it did irritate me so. Will you join me for some excellent artichoke hearts?"

"No, thanks, Esteban. I have to get the team organized and make sure they have all they need. Thanks a lot anyway, but I'll have to pass this time."

"Of course, how stupid of me. Go do what you have to do and we'll talk over dinner tonight, eh?"

"That sounds like an excellent invitation, Esteban, thanks. If you don't mind, I'll use the computer in your study to get things started."

"By all means, go ahead. I'll have Lucia bring you down some artichoke hearts and some bourbon, How's that?"

"That'll be a nice gesture, Esteban. Thanks."

After Esteban Escobar saw his good friend leave, he poured himself a double shot of Chivas. He had to learn to control his temper a little better, but that bitch Elaine had really pissed him off. She'd been good in the sack, but he shouldn't have given her as much information as he did. It came to him that she had access to most of his accounts, since he had put her in charge of transferring money to accounts nobody knew about, not even Alfredo Hidalgo. Dammit, he should've remembered what his father used to tell him "don't give women all the love nor all the money." He should immediately go contact his banks and lock her out of the accounts. Alfredo would take care of her shortly, but it'd make him feel better to know that he had removed her ability to enter his wallet. He walked downstairs to his study and joined his friend, sitting in front of a second Pentium computer. "I'm going to take care of some e-mail, my friend, while you take care of our business."

THE FOUR SOUTH AMERICAN men arrived at the Louisville Kentucky Executive terminal almost simultaneously, four different taxis depositing them at the curb. All four had come from different parts of the world, yet they were familiar with each other, for they formed one of Esteban Escobar's lead "cleaning" teams. They were sent to clean up the messes others created.

The four men could have been taken for pro football players as they crossed through the lobby of the fixed base operator, where they were met by a pilot in a white uniform shirt with gold epaulets.

"Mr. Zepeda?" the pilot held out his hand.

"Yes," the first of the men replied, shaking hands with the pilot.

"We're all ready for departure, if you and the other gentlemen will follow me. The flight to Berlin will take a little over eleven hours and we've set up an excellent dinner for you."

The men were ushered out to the ramp, where a gleaming spanking-new fifty-million dollar Gulfstream G-V was parked. The whine of its auxiliary power unit greeted them as they boarded the luxurious corporate jet, owned and operated by a corporation dedicated to transport critically-ill children to hospitals worldwide. Another one of Hidalgo's enterprises.

What government agency in its right mind would dare investigate such a corporation dedicated to the non-profit helping of children? The airplane taxied out and departed promptly, headed east.

The Gulfstream G-V landed at Tegel airport in Berlin after flying all night from Louisville, Kentucky. The flight took longer than a normal commercial flight would have taken because corporate jets are not allowed to fly across the Atlantic on the most direct routes. Corporate jets have to go the long way, remaining north of the heavily traveled so-called airline oceanic tracks, which added an additional ninety minutes to the crossing.

The four South Americans sat patiently in their luxurious leather seats as the crew taxied the jet to the corporate parking area, then respectfully handed their passports to the German immigration officer who went onboard to check the documents of these men who were obviously CEOs for some powerful American companies. The customs officer ran a check of the baggage, shifting his hand through expensive cotton shirts and silk ties, then gave the authorization for the airplane to unload.

After the German officials left the airplane, the South Americans quickly and efficiently removed a side panel from the rear cabin, exposing an arsenal that would have made a South American dictator weep with envy. The leader of the men took out a plastic camera case filled with plastic explosive, adding it to the baggage he and his men would be taking to their hotel.

EIGHTEEN
PRESENT TIME - BERLIN, GERMANY

Captain Adam Dee completed reading the "Before Engine Start" checklist, replacing the plastic-laminated card in its slot above the glare shield.

"Ask one of the gals if she has a minute to get us some coffee, wilya, Mike?"

The flight engineer slid his chair back on its tracks, reaching for the cockpit door handle, looking for one of the First Class flight attendants.

They were sitting at Tegel Airport in Berlin, starting on a two-day trip to Istanbul via Frankfurt.

"So you were going to go visit the Porsche factory down in Stuttgart?" Stu Jurgens was Adam Dee's copilot on this trip, a friendly man in his mid-thirties from Springfield, Missouri.

"Yeah–that's what I'd planned, until crew scheduling called me asking if I could take this trip for Valerie Wall."

Stu Jurgens had been looking forward to flying with the dame, never having flown with a woman before. He had been disappointed to find that she'd reported in sick and that they had assigned Adam Dee to his flight. He'd never flown with Dee, not an unusual occurrence among airline crews, but now he would not know what flying with Valerie would be like, because after this trip he would be done for the month and would be flying back to the States and to his wife Ruth tomorrow afternoon.

"You gonna buy a Porsche?"

"Don't know yet. Just thought I'd go down there and take a look. One of the gals who works security at the Stuttgart airport invited me to spend the day with her and visit the Porsche factory, so I thought I'd kill two birds with one stone."

Stu Jurgens smiled, eyeing his captain's left hand. The guy was married, yet he was going to have a good time spending the day with some woman in Stuttgart. Typical airline behavior, he mused. Buying Porsches in Germany and shipping them back to the States was also one of the favorite pastimes of airline captains. Stu had heard it many times, about how much money would be saved buying the sexy sports car at the factory, about how it was just good business sense, about how tons of money would be made reselling it in the States. He smiled, thinking that it was all just a smokescreen put up by some big boys to justify buying expensive, unnecessary toys.

"You ever flown with Valerie Wall, Adam?"

"No, I don't fly with women captains."

Stu Jurgens wondered if Adam was one of the types who resented women for intruding in their formerly all-male cockpits. "Is she a bitch? Do you know her?"

Adam Dee turned to stare at his first officer. "No, she's not a bitch. As a matter-of-fact, she's one of the nicest persons I know. She was in my class."

Oh, crap. "I was just asking, Adam. You said you don't like flying with women so I thought perhaps you knew something I didn't."

Adam smiled. "Relax, Stu. The reason I don't fly with women captains is because there aren't any in this airline senior to me, not because I don't like women."

"So you'd fly with a female captain? If there was one senior to you, that is?"

"Of course I would. Provided she did what I said..."

All three men laughed.

The head flight attendant brought some coffee to the cockpit, advising them that all passengers were onboard and seated and that the cabin door was being closed.

"Let's get this show on the road, gentlemen."

Fifteen minutes later the wheels of the Boeing 727 left the ground, the large jet rapidly gaining altitude over the woods at the end of the runway at Berlin's Tegel airport.

The crew handled the big jet with the apparent ease characteristic of men and women doing a job they know intimately. This apparent ease was deceiving, for each of the three crewmembers had invested thousands of hours of hard study and strenuous drilling to achieve the level of skill that allowed them to take the sixty-plus ton airliner from Berlin to Istanbul.

Twenty-five minutes later Adam Dee leveled the Boeing at its assigned cruising altitude of 25,000 feet. Almost simultaneously, a loud bang was heard in the back of the airplane, and the entire airplane shook.

"What the fuck was that?" Adam increased the pressure with which he was holding the controls, rapidly scanning the engine instruments for indications of engine failure. The bang had come from the back, and the engines were in the back.

All engine indications seemed normal.

"I don't know!" Stu Jurgens had felt the loud bang which had rattled every bone in his body. The entire fuselage had been horribly shaken. Compressor stall?

"Adam, we have a hydraulic low-pressure light!" the flight engineer informed them.

"Which system?" the Boeing 727 had two main systems and a backup.

"The A system, no wait! Now the B system too! We're losing our hydraulic fluid!"

Someone was banging on the cockpit door.

"Let them in, Mike."

The flight engineer reached back to unlock the cockpit door without removing his sight from his panel. All the warning lights in his hydraulic panel were on now, and a new warning light was lighting up in the upper panel.

"Adam, we're losing cabin pressure!"

"Everyone on oxygen!" Adam Dee shouted, reaching back for his quick-donning oxygen mask. "What the hell is going on?"

The cabin low-pressure warning horn blared, telling the pilots that the air inside the airplane had now become too thin to sustain life for more than three or four minutes. In the passenger cabin, the oxygen masks automatically dropped from their overhead storage compartments, startling the already scared passengers.

"Adam, we have a fire in cabin!" the flight attendant shouted, entering the cockpit.

ADAM DEE TOOK IN the new information, his brain rapidly trying to sort out the information overload in order of importance so that he could formulate a plan of action. Hydraulic systems failure, a loud bang, a fire in the cabin. The controls would work even without hydraulics because of the manual reversion cables running through the floor of the cabin, so they could wait on that checklist. The fire could damage them the most. "Stu, call the Center, declare an emergency, tell them we had some kind of an explosion and that we're coming back to Tegel. Mike, get the portable oxygen bottle and go back there to see what the hell's going on with the fire and report back to me at once." He turned the yoke left, to initiate a left turn, expecting to feel the airplane going into the turn but nothing happened. The controls didn't respond. The airplane kept flying straight ahead, in a slight descent. Now what the fuck!?

Adam pushed forward on the wheel, expecting the nose of the airplane to drop, but nothing happened. No response, nothing. Dead as a fucking nail. He moved the wheel right and left, back and forth but it was useless. Whatever had blown up back there had disabled his controls. "Stu, try your controls!" he felt vomit rise in his throat.

The copilot moved his wheel in all directions, with the same negative results. "We've no controls, Adam!" he kicked the rudder pedals, but they felt loose and no response came from the airplane.

Adam Dee reached for the throttle levers, jamming them back to idle, but to his horror there was no change in the pitch of the engines, nor any indication from his instruments that power was being reduced.

They were inside a sixty-ton rocket ship four miles above the earth, doing better than five hundred miles per hour.

And they were out of control.

The nose of the airplane inched its way down, toward the distant horizon, and the airspeed began to build.

Mike, the flight engineer returned to the cockpit wearing the portable oxygen mask, holding the cumbersome green oxygen tank. His voice was muffled and barely audible, as he shouted through the plastic faceguard. "Adam, there's a fire in midcabin. Looks like it's coming out from below the floor. Maybe one of the main tires blew up or something, and it's burning the carpeting and the seats. The girls fired the Halons into it and have moved all passengers forward but the cabin is filling up with smoke. The flight engineer stopped. Something was wrong in the cockpit–terribly wrong–he could feel it by looking at the faces of his two pilots.

"We got bigger problems than that, Mike," Adam Dee calmly explained, "looks like whatever blew up back there has severed the control cables and the throttle cables."

The crippled 727 slowly inched its nose below the horizon, picking up speed in the process. The extra speed in turn produced more lift on the wings, bringing the nose back up again. This process continued for a few minutes, each time increasing the airspeed, until the horizontal stabilizer could no longer take the stress induced by the high airspeed, and the metal spars separated from the airplane with a sound like that of tearing aluminum foil.

The airliner immediately nosed down into a final dive.

In the cockpit, Captain Adam Dee repeated "this cannot be..." as he watched the patchwork that was the German countryside rise to meet him at a speed faster than the speed of sound.

NINETEEN
THIRTEEN YEARS AGO - ST. LOUIS, MISSOURI
UNITED STATES

Valerie arrived in St. Louis the day before the scheduled date for her class to start. She and Paul Morris had a long five-day trip from Los Angeles driving a beat-up U-Haul truck with no air conditioning. That had been a killer when they crossed the Mojave Desert between California and Arizona in the middle of the day.

They reserved a storage space in a suburb of St. Louis and dropped off all her possessions. These would remain in storage until she had completed basic training. They checked in at the Ramada-Inn by the airport and made love in anticipation of not seeing each other for six weeks. Valerie was dead serious about her basic training and she had decided that there could be no distractions at all during the six weeks when she had to learn the DC-9.

"Are you kidding? You won't keep me away for six weeks!" Paul Morris had complained.

"Honey, please. You know how much this means to me. I cannot distract myself at all. I have to live and breathe the DC-9, and if you're here I won't be able to do that."

"Even one day per weekend?"

"Even one day per weekend. I'm sorry, but if what I've heard is at all true about basic training, I can't afford to lose one day."

Paul Morris seemed to be both amused and annoyed by her persistence, but if that's what she wanted, he'd go along–under protest.

He left on a morning flight back to L.A. and Valerie drove her Chevy Celebrity to the training center for her eight a.m. introduction into the world of the airlines.

The MidAmerica Airlines training center was an enormous concrete building with lots of glass, located on the airport grounds. She parked her car and went in, dressed in a navy blue suit, white blouse and black shoes. A herringbone gold chain adorned her slender neck. She had to breathe deeply to dispel the butterflies beginning to form in her stomach. Valerie took a deep breath and marched into the building. Once inside the glass door, the butterflies in her stomach dissipated

"Valerie? Pleased to see you again, Sugar. Name's Adam Dee. We met during the interviews, remember? Outside Robert Eackle's office? I came from the Navy?" The man was huge, six foot-six at least, red-haired and all Irish, and he had managed to piss her off with his first five words. She remembered him. "Hi, Adam. I remember you, and the name is Valerie, Adam, not Sugar. If you can't remember that much I think you'll have one hell of a time learning the DC-9."

The other two men in the room laughed and poked fun at their fallen comrade.

"Del Hope," a blonde man with a Kentucky accent offered his hand, "and don't worry, I won't call you Sugar. I came from commuters. Beech 99s."

"Anthony Taylor, People's Express, seven-twenty-sevens."

The last was a chubby individual with a mustache and Valerie distrusted him instantly. "Hi, Anthony, I'm Valerie and I was flying a Sabreliner." She didn't expand that she had been the copilot, and not the captain, but let it be. This asshole wanted to impress her with his airline background flying for People's Express, and she'd leave it at that. Not that she was impressed; People's Express was no luxury liner to work for, she had been told.

The class was called to order and the instructor began by assigning each of them a dozen manuals which made a pile four feet high on their desks.

"Gentlemen, and lady, welcome to the best airline in the United States–."

Valerie felt she could burst with pride. She couldn't believe she was actually in class, initiating her DC-9 airline pilot training. How many people out there really got to live out their dream?

"–We're going to be filling up some forms here, and then I'll send you all over to the personnel office where you'll get your pictures taken and where you'll fill up another two thousand forms necessary to legalize your marriage to MidAmerica Airlines. By the time you get home tonight your hands will be cramped from all that writing."

The newhires looked at each other, nervously. They were all wearing "business attire" as specified in the letters they all had received from the flight operations department explaining the procedures to be followed.

"The rules here are few and very simple," the instructor continued, "we'll have a quiz every day and an exam every week. Eighty percent is the minimum for passing. Any person scoring less than an eighty on anything will leave a letter of resignation on my desk by end of the day."

Valerie heard a couple of the guys gasp. Eighty percent. Oh, shit.

"Those of you completing the ground school–and I expect every one of you to do so–will continue on to two weeks of simulator training and then two weeks of initial operating experience on the airplane. You will be on probation for one year to see if we really want to keep you here for the next thirty years and for you to evaluate if you really want to marry this airline."

Valerie hung on to every word the instructor said. She took notes and every once in a while glanced at the enormous pile of manuals stacked next to her elbow, wondering how she was ever going to learn all that.

The class was dismissed and they piled in Anthony Taylor's car to drive to the other side of the airport, to the personnel office. Anthony announced that he was married, originally from St. Louis and that he was irritated because Valerie was the oldest pilot in the class, making her the senior dog. She thought he was a dipshit, expressing irritation at her because she was older, what was his problem anyway?

Del Hope was also married, and Adam Dee was single but not for long, he explained. His girlfriend Louise would be joining him after basic training as his wife. Neither one had a place to stay yet, so Valerie teamed up with them to look for a pad after class.

The rest of the day was spent cruising through the airline's administrative offices filling out forms for medical insurance, life insurance, FAA crew records, dental insurance, flight time records, parking permits, uniform allowances, employee identifications, payroll deductions, and so on. The people involved were very friendly and made her feel right at home, making it less of an ordeal. After they finished their day at the office Taylor drove them back to the training center to get their dozen manuals and their cars.

Valerie, Adam and Del found a two-bedroom suite in a shady hotel near the airport, at $800 per month with maid service, a kitchen and great air conditioning, which they discovered was an absolute necessity in the humidity and heat of summer in St. Louis.

"Gentlemen, being the only lady of this group I'm taking one of the rooms. You two dorks can fight over who gets the other one." She was not about to sleep in the living room in her underwear with these two roaming about the apartment. They may have wives and girlfriends but she wasn't going to tempt them.

"I'll sleep in the living room," Del offered. He was not a very worldly individual, more like a backwoods hillbilly, but he was all heart and Valerie instantly took a liking to him. Adam was big and friendly, but he kept irritating her by calling her Sugar. Somehow she was going to beat it into his thick Irish head that it wasn't appreciated.

She unpacked and looked through her manuals, intimidated at the staggering amount of information she was expected to assimilate in a matter of weeks. Could it be done? Others had done it at many airlines before her, so she should be capable. She looked at a bunch of schedules printed on white paper, and had no idea what she was looking at. She took the package out to Del.

"It looks like a bid package to me, Valerie."

"And just what exactly is a bid package?"

"That's what you use each month to bid for the schedule you want to fly. If you're not on reserve, that is." Del's experience flying commuters was already helping him in his new job.

That made sense, although the instructions on the cover page seemed awful long. "And what do we do with it?"

"You work your way through it and decide which lines of time–schedules–you prefer then you submit your choices to the company and they let you know what you got."

Valerie hadn't realized they got to choose their routes. "You mean you pick what you like and that's what you'll fly for the month?"

"In theory, yes, but in real life you'll end up flying reserve after we finish training until they hire enough people behind us to cover all their needs."

"I don't get it."

"The way it works is like this, there are five hundred pilots in the company, right? So they make up five hundred different schedules and hand them to us in this here bid package. Ten percent of the schedules don't have trips on them. These are known as the Reserve Lines. The people who get them, usually the most junior, don't know when they are going to be called out to fly. All they know is that they get ten or eleven days off per month when crew scheduling cannot touch them. The other pilots then select the routes they want to fly, the days off they want to get, the favorite cities for layovers and then they turn in their choices. Next, the company goes to the most senior pilot flying the line and assigns him his first choice–. "

"Or hers."

"Whatever–then the company goes to the second most senior pilot and looks at his first choice. If they haven't assigned it to the number one guy, then they give it to the number two guy, otherwise, the second most senior pilot gets his second choice, and so on."

Valerie understood and dismayed at the concept. "Del, that means that you and I could end up with our choice number five hundred!"

"Yep, that's the way the system works. Until we get some seniority we're going to be sucking hind tittie!"

"Del, I don't know how your wife can stand you!"

Del Hope guffawed. "Ah think I like you Valerie, and my wife Pat will get along just fine with you, woman pilot. You can ask her yourself how she can stand me, she'll be here the day we finish ground school."

Valerie was so excited about everything that was taking place that she almost forgot to call Paul Morris. They had agreed on talking every night, but she decided to wait until the animals were in bed to call him. Del and Adam would give her a hard time if she called now.

Everyone she had come in contact with at MidAmerica Airlines thus far had been friendly, educated and well-mannered, and she loved it. It was obvious that everyone was getting paid very well–which brought out the best in people–and most MidAmerica employees went out of their way to be considerate. What a place to work!

She laughed, disgusted at the memory of flying with Jack Cranston in the Sabreliner. Two different worlds, no doubt about it.

"Hey, Valerie," Adam Dee stuck his head in her room, "I'm gonna walk over to the terminal and take a look at some of our airplanes. I need a break. Wanna come along? Maybe we can catch an ice cream over there."

She had a million things to take care of, clothes to put away, letters to write, plus she had wanted to at least skim through most of her manuals before calling Paul Morris but the thought of going to the airport terminal now that she was officially an airline pilot thrilled her. "Yeah, I'll come. Let me get some jeans on and we'll go."

"Far out. Come out when you're ready."

She changed out of her sweats and they walked the half mile to the Lambert field international airport terminal. She breathed the hot summer air, full of the fragrance of freshly-cut grass and scented flowers, and felt alive. This was what she'd aimed for all her life, and now she had it!

The terminal was bristling with passengers and activity in anticipation of the evening rush, and Valerie followed Adam Dee to the gate area. The windows were full of green and white DC-9s occupying every single gate, loading passengers at the airline's hub.

"Looks like something is going on over there, Dee indicated.

"Let's take a look," she added.

There was a crowd surrounding the arrival area of one gate, and Valerie noticed an unusual number of pilots and flight attendants hanging around. Some of the pilots had large hand-painted signs, and there was a table set up by the gate with a huge cake.

"I think these guys are receiving a captain on his last flight," Adam guessed.

Valerie had to agree with him. This was exciting stuff, seeing a real airline captain arriving from his last flight.

She noticed many of the pilots hanging around had white hair. "I think you're right. Adam. A lot of old-timers hanging around here. Guess they came to bid farewell to one of their buddies. Eh?"

"Look, Valerie, there's Robert Eackle."

Valerie had seen the chief pilot at the same time, and their eyes met. She was slightly uncomfortable at being spotted by her boss in her jeans and T-shirt, and also she didn't want to appear like she was snooping at the gate area. There was a flurry of activity at the gate as the door opened and a senior captain emerged from the jetway.

Everyone's attention turned to this man who had reached age sixty and who had brought in a DC-9 for the last time in his life. Valerie felt tears welling in her eyes at the thought of this man who would never again command a majestic silver bird again, after having spent most of his life doing so. His wife came out behind him, obviously having joined her man on his last trip.

Adam Dee caught a glimpse of her watery eyes and smiled, saying nothing.

"Let's go get an ice cream," she ordered.

"Yessir," Dee joked. He seemed amused by how Valerie had been touched by the retiring captain scene.

"Far as I'm concerned, I see it as just another old dog dropping out of the way allowing us to move up another number."

"Adam, you heartless brute. I am strongly considering ripping out your eyes."

"Okay, okay, sorry I said anything. I didn't really mean it."

They had rum-raisin Haagen-Dazs cups and headed back out of the airport.

"What do you think? You'll be able to handle those big beasts alright?" Dee pointed to a DC-9 squatting on the ramp next to them.

"I'm gonna fly the damned thing, Adam, not carry it! Besides, if you can handle it, I can handle it."

"Easy, easy, I wasn't challenging your ability. I was just sharing my thoughts, since I'm scared shitless. Valerie, I've never flown a jet. I flew the P-3 but that's still just a turboprop, and I really don't know what to expect."

She relaxed, not being used to men opening up like that to her.

"I understand." She liked the fact that he was confiding in her because he knew that she'd already flown jets, although the situation was kind of absurd. He had flown antisubmarine aircraft for the Navy and he was asking *her* for reassurance?

"It's not that hard, Adam. Matter of fact, it's a lot easier than turboprops or piston. You just have to stay ahead of the airplane, that's all." She remembered her first few flights with Jack, how she had been absolutely convinced that she'd never be able to stay ahead of the Sabreliner, how she had seriously questioned her decision to fly and how after a few more hours in the airplane she had finally gained some confidence. "Flying jets is just like flying any other airplane, it's a matter of practice, that's all."

"You sure make it sound easy, Sugar."

"Valerie, Adam, Valerie, not sugar."

He laughed, placing his arm across her shoulders. "I just love to bug you Ma'am."

They returned to the apartment laughing, a young couple enjoying a stroll on a summer evening, not a hint that they were two future airline captains.

The first week of ground school went by horribly fast. Valerie was in class from eight to five, took one hour off for dinner and then studied until one a.m. Nonetheless, she felt she needed more time to learn all the material they were fire hosing down their throats, and complimented herself on her decision to keep Paul Morris away while she was in training because she had used just about every waking hour of her weekend to catch up. They had to memorize six checklists that had everything to do with operating the big DC-9, plus they had to commit to memory all the company and airplane specifications which amounted to dozens of pages she had to memorize. The theory was that pilots had to know this stuff second-nature because in the airplane there was no time to go grab a manual and look this up. Made sense if one had a memory like an elephant.

She had never been a coffee drinker but her first week in training with the airlines changed all that. Coffee flowed in their apartment because they had to learn more things than their minds could assimilate and one way to help this process along was to hit the caffeine.

The four newhires in her class developed a routine of going to the local pizza place for lunch every day during ground school. The pizza joint near the training center had a special offer that unless your pizza came within five minutes of ordering, it was free. Anthony Taylor had discovered that the place filled up a few minutes before noon and that the staff was incapable of serving everyone so the latecomers got to have free pizza. The group had free pizza for ten days but then the manager was fired and his replacement smartened up and cooked ahead, negating any additional free lunches.

"Guys, how are we going to survive on 900 dollars a month?" Valerie munched on her last free pizza, thinking about her bank account now that reality was beginning to set in. The airline was going to raise their salaries to $50,000 after one year, but they would have to spend their entire first year with MidAmerica surviving on thirty bucks a day.

"I heard that if they fly you a lot during your first year you can make about another five or six hundred a month with perdiem," Del offered.

"What the hell's perdiem?" Valerie interjected.

"That's money they pay you to cover personal expenses while you're on the road, like lunches, dinners, toothpaste," Del explained. "I understand these guys pay forty-two bucks for each twenty-four hours away from base."

Valerie ran some quick math in her head. "So if they fly us fifteen days a month, that's about another six hundred bucks."

"Yeah, but they won't fly you fifteen days a month, remember, the forty-two bucks are for each twenty-four-hour period away from base. If you go to work tonight and come back tomorrow at noon they won't pay you for two days. Line holders fly fifteen days a month. We'll be reserves, so we'll fly ten, if we're lucky."

Del was the less educated in the group, but Valerie liked his sense of humor.

"Shit, I'll fly as much as I can. Pat's already got a job waiting as a legal assistant at a fancy law firm, but even with her salary it's going to be a tight first year."

"No kidding," Taylor agreed, "nine hundred a month is poverty level. I bet we qualify for food stamps!"

Valerie knew that Anthony's wife Linda didn't work but stayed home taking care of their two kids, which would make it very difficult to survive on first year pay, but she suspected Anthony had stashed away some savings during his days at People's Express and that his family must be helping them along, since they were pretty well off. Anthony had not kept it a secret that his family was made up of bankers with long histories in St. Louis. He'd made it a point telling his classmates how he and his family had a place down in Mississippi where they usually spent summers. Not a very likable individual. He was also the one less physically fit of the four newhires. She wondered how his chubbiness has escaped the inspecting eye of the medical examiner.

"Did you guys hear how the probationary year works?" Del kept looking at his watch, being late for class back from lunch was definitely not something they were going to be guilty of.

"We have to take a written and an oral test with one of the captains once a month. If we fail one, we're fired. Even if we passed the first eleven and bust the twelfth, they still fire you. As if this wasn't enough, every captain we fly with the entire first year has to submit a progress report to Captain Eackle. If we piss off one of these guys we become instantly unemployed."

"I heard that if we miss one single trip while on probation they will fire you," Anthony added. "That's why they discourage commuting during the first year."

"Why's that?" Valerie had heard that many pilots and flight attendants lived in other cities and commuted to work to their base in St. Louis.

"They consider St. Louis our base. If you decide to live elsewhere and miss a trip because of it, it would be because you decided not to live here, and they will fire you."

Valerie couldn't conceive how anyone would risk missing a trip considering the tremendous effort they all put into becoming airline pilots. "I think I'm going to be walking on eggs this entire first year, that is, if I get through this ground school."

"Yeah, me too," added Adam Dee. "Oh, Lord, please look after me, and whatever you do, please don't let me fuckup!"

They were just entering the most difficult part of their ground school, where they had to learn the systems in the airplane. This was the washout phase of the program. The majority of pilot candidates who failed in basic training did so at this stage. Learning the inner workings of a large transport jet was an intense task requiring uninterrupted concentration for two weeks. The basic premise being that once the pilots entered the simulator stage of their training they wouldn't have time to re-learn the airplane. At that point they had to know their airplane as intimately as a person knows her mate because their conscious self would have to be entirely dedicated to the complex task of actually flying the airplane, and decisions would have to be made based on this intimate second-nature knowledge of the airplane systems.

Valerie was amazed that Anthony Taylor was able to keep up with the program living at home. How in the hell could he do it with a wife and kids demanding his attention when she barely managed to survive? His previous airline training must be helping him. They finished their pizzas and piled into Del's beat-up '67 Chevy Impala for the drive back to the training center. Valerie had been horrified when she had seen Del's auto but had since been exposed to a new concept she had never heard of, that of the *airporter* car.

"The way it works," Del had explained to them, "is like this. You're gonna go on trips three, maybe four times a month. This means that you're going to be driving to the airport say four times a month, right? And while you're traveling all over the country flying airplanes for MidAmerica, your car is going to sit at the employees' parking lot, right? Sitting there in the sun and rain and hail, day in and day out, depreciating while the paint gets eaten by the ultraviolet rays and the acid rain."

Valerie laughed at his dramatic presentation. "So? How can you prevent it, by buying a car cover?"

"Hell, no. You buy yourself an airporter, that's what you do. If you leave a good car at the employees' parking lot you'll have to pay insurance on it too, no? If you have an airporter that cost you five hundred or a thousand dollars, the insurance will be minimal and you don't even have to pay theft insurance because no one in their right mind would steal a piece of shit like that."

"Del, if I'm making a good income, I'm not going to be driving a piece of shit."

"Of course you're not going to be driving a piece of shit, Valerie. All you're gonna do is take it to the airport four times a month, that's it. Anything else you wanna do, you use your good car. Most airline pilots have *airporters* because they realize he stupidity involved in parking a spanking-new BMW under the sun all day while they go flying. What you want to get is an old American car with a big engine. It doesn't matter if the exterior looks like hell as long as the engine runs good, has a good heater and air conditioner and doesn't cost you too much to own."

"So that's why you drive that wreck of yours."

"Yeah, that's why I drive Matilda. I don't even have insurance on her."

Valerie saw that it made sense. "Okay, Del, you sold me on the airport car idea, it makes sense, but how do you explain all this garbage you carry in here? Is this also part of the camouflage so nobody steals it?" Valerie disgustedly kicked some blackened banana peels aside, glancing at multiple soda cans, empty Frito bags and used Kleenexes that littered the floor of Del's Impala.

Del chuckled. "Naw, that's just 'cause I'm lazy. I have crap back there it's been there since I started flying commuters six years ago. Matter-of-fact, I think there's a mouse or two living in there. Permanent residents, if you know what I mean."

Valerie felt her spine chill. Mice? "Del, you shit! I'm never riding in this car again!"

The three men laughed as they entered the parking lot of the training center.

VALERIE FELT EXHAUSTED BUT proud. She had studied her ass off, more than she ever did at any time in college, more than she ever did at any time in her life, and she felt brain-fried but, surprisingly, most of the stuff had been retained in her mind. Just how long she would retain all the information was anybody's guess, but at least it would be there tomorrow for the final exam. She had memorized the different systems on the Douglas DC-9 to the point where she could draw a schematic from memory on the layouts of the electric, hydraulic, pneumatic, and anti-ice systems. This was no easy task, considering it took engineers at McDonnell Douglas years of work to come out with these layouts, but she had hammered them into her memory because she knew it was vital knowledge.

Her and Del and Adam had just finished a four-hour session questioning each other, probing the depth of each other's knowledge, and she was satisfied that she should be able to pass that dreaded final exam tomorrow. There was nothing more to do except try to get a good night sleep, and look forward to Paul's visit on Saturday. She would be starting cockpit procedures training on Monday in preparation for simulator training and that was extremely exciting. A cockpit procedures trainer was a simulator of a cockpit, identical to the one on the real DC-9 except that none of the switches did anything. Cockpit procedure trainers were intended for crews to learn the sequence of events in a jet cockpit, from the steps involved in preflighting the cockpit to starting the engines to emergency procedures. All these procedures took time to learn and the cockpit procedures trainer was the place to learn and practice them because the full-motion simulator time was too expensive to waste teaching those procedures.

The company expected its simulator trainees to show up for their first session in the box already familiar with the layout of the cockpit, the position of every switch and lever and the exact sequence of events to follow for each procedure. Anyone not prepared would have to provide a letter of resignation on the spot.

The instructor had told them that next week they would be measured for their uniforms. The company was going to finance their first uniforms and deduct the cost from their paychecks over a one-year period. After taxes and social security, she wondered what her take-home would be. If all went well they would make it to the left seat in nine to twelve years, which was about standard for MidAmerica. As captains they would perceive around $120,000 annual salary, which would make life a lot sweeter. She couldn't even imagine what it would be like, having that much money.

In the morning she drove the gang to the training center in her Chevy Celebrity. She was not about to set foot in Del's car again. They strolled into the break room where other pilots were waiting for class. Seven or eight classes were being held simultaneously, which meant around thirty other pilots were going through the same grinder as she was. Valerie had met one other female pilot from another class, a woman named Jennifer Back, three classes behind her. All the rest were men, as she had expected.

It was tough, being a female in such an environment, but the quality of the people made it a little easier to swallow. Most of these guys were very well-mannered and if there were any rednecks or bigots in the group they had managed to keep it quiet. She was very much aware of the sexual harassment frenzy enveloping the country, but she wanted no part of it. Valerie believed that if you went hunting for tigers, you had to wade through swamps, and any woman going into a predominantly male environment had to be tough enough to put up with anything thrown at her. She would never tolerate insolent sexual behavior, but such blatant behavior was not common in the airlines, or at least she had not seen it yet.

Sex jokes and Playboy centerfolds didn't offend her as long as it wasn't overdone, and she did enjoy off color jokes as much as any of the guys. If they thought they were going to have sex with her because she enjoyed their jokes then they would be thoroughly disappointed but that was not her problem. She knew this was a man's environment and that many of them secretly resented her intrusion in it, but she had chosen this field and there was no way in hell anyone was going to dissuade her from being an airline pilot just because she was a woman and she was supposed to be sensitive and easily offended by male crudity. From what she had seen of the airlines thus far she could tell that any transgression would be dealt with swiftly and ruthlessly, so she was willing to bet that most pilots would walk a very straight line with her. These airline people didn't play games. Their jobs were probably too good to risk over nonsense.

She heard that several pilots in the classes behind her had already been asked to submit letters of resignation because of poor performance in the ground school written tests. Now, that would be a real tragedy. Any pilot fired from the airline instantly became a leper, and none of the other airlines in the country would ever again have anything to do with the unfortunate individual. They would be condemned to live in the unpleasant purgatory of corporate aviation or night freight, which was tantamount to being dead, as far as she was concerned, remembering her adventures with Jack Cranston and with Vacation Airlines in Hawaii.

The members of her class went in a classroom, sat down and were given a copy of the final exam. Four hundred multiple-choice questions.

"Lady and gentlemen," their instructor advised, "you may begin."

Valerie took a deep breath and attacked the first page.

"YOU CAN GET AN airline discount at the Ramada by the airport," Del explained.

"You mean for a room?"

"Yeah, they'll give you a room for nineteen bucks if you show them your MidAmerica ID."

Valerie and Del were enjoying a beer in their apartment. Del had already finished packing his stuff, since he was leaving them to find his own place with his wife Pat who was arriving that afternoon from Louisville. Paul Morris was arriving at about the same time from Los

Angeles, and Valerie had decided to book them a hotel room where they could catch up with each other in privacy.

"Are you serious?"

"Absolutely. Most hotels will give you a fifty percent discount with your airline ID. Most car rentals too."

That was news to Valerie. Another perk for working with the airlines. "What time's Pat coming in?"

"Four thirty. I'm gonna pick her up, bring her here to have some wild sex and then we're going to look at a couple of apartments I have lined up."

Valerie laughed. "The apartment's all yours, Del. Adam won't be back till tomorrow night and I'm going to a hotel with Paul."

"You sure you don't wanna join us for a threesome?"

Valerie smiled, shaking her head. "From what you've described, Pat is already more woman than you can handle, Del. Besides, you're a pilot and I don't date pilots."

"I didn't say anything about dating, I was merely referring to pure, raw sex. And besides, why not? You got a problem with pilots, lady?"

"Yeah, matter of fact I do."

"And what would that be?"

"They like to be on top."

"Oh, shit!"

Del and Valerie had returned to the apartment after taking the final exam. The results would be posted at the training center by Monday morning, which left them with an agonizing weekend wondering what their scores were. That would be hard, not to mention embarrassing for anyone being fired on Monday.

"So, you're so sure you passed that you're going to rent your own apartment, eh?" Valerie and Adam Dee would now be left sharing the hotel apartment, which would increase her share of the rent considerably.

"Yeah, I'm sure I passed. What do you mean? Hell, that was easy."

"You're full of shit, Del. Did you forget already last night when you told us that you were worried shitless because your whole life was riding on this job? You said even Pat would divorce you if you failed."

Del laughed. "That was yesterday, baby, this is today."

"What's the difference?"

"Today I saw the test and I knew most of it."

"You are bad."

"I know, and now, if you'll excuse me, I have to take a shower so I can pick up my wife and show her just how bad I am," he stood, "*Sayonara*, babe!"

VALERIE PICKED UP PAUL Morris at the Southwest Airlines gate and drove to the hotel near the airport, burning with desire to be alone with him. She had so much to tell him, but first she was going to engage in some heavy duty body language with him.

She parked and they approached the front desk.

"Hi, I have a reservation for two nights, the name's Wall." She liked the feeling of being in control, with Paul Morris along for the ride.

The hotel clerk greeted them and keyed away at his computer.

"And when did you make this reservation, Ma'am?"

"Just this afternoon," she looked at her watch. "A couple of hours ago. Last name Wall, airline discount?"

The clerk scanned the computer screen again, shaking his head. "I'm sorry, we don't have any reservations under that name."

Valerie became slightly irritated. God, where did they get these clowns?

"I called a couple of hours ago and made a reservation under the name Valerie Wall. I'm a pilot with MidAmerica Airlines and your reservations gal gave me the nineteen-dollar rate." It felt strange, saying in public that she already was a pilot for MidAmerica.

The clerk looked even more confused. "Aah, we don't have a nineteen-dollar rate. The airline rate is eighty dollars."

Now Valerie was really getting bugged. If these hotels paid decent wages, they wouldn't end up with one-celled amoebas running the front desk.

"When I called about two hours ago, your reservations lady told me the airline discount rate was nineteen dollars. Where do you come up with eighty dollars?"

The clerk looked flustered.

"Aah, our rate has always been eighty dollars for airline employees. Please wait a minute and I'll double-check it." He disappeared through a door behind the counter.

She sighed, holding Paul's hand. He was staying in the sidelines, letting her take care of this. "I don't know what's wrong with these people. First they give me one rate then they change it."

"Honey, eighty dollars is fine, I'll pay it, it doesn't matter."

"No way, they told me nineteen and they're not going to change it now. It's a matter of principle!"

"May I help you?" The clerk had called for reinforcements. The new guy was taller, older and better dressed, and Valerie thought he even looked like he may have a brain.

"Yes, I called two hours ago and made a reservation and your reservations agent told me specifically that your airline discount rate was nineteen dollars, and now your man there is changing it to eighty dollars."

The manager looked confused as well. "Ma'am, the airline rate has always been eighty dollars here, I don't know who told you otherwise but it was incorrect. If you want a room at this rate we can give it to you, but I can't give it to you for nineteen dollars."

Valerie became furious. "What kind of operation is this? What are you doing? Telling people nineteen dollars so they can land here and then you stick them with the higher fare?"

"No, Ma'am. It's always been eighty dollars."

"I don't believe this! This is the Ramada-Inn, right?"

"No, Ma'am, this is the Marriott. The Ramada-Inn is a mile down the road."

MONDAY MORNING THE FOUR of them reported to the training center to look at their grades from ground school and found that all four had passed. Valerie was enormously relieved.

"Gawd, Valerie! Look at that!" Taylor complained, "you got a ninety-seven on the final! That's disgusting!"

Valerie laughed. Her score was the highest of the four, which made her feel extra good. Watch out boys, the women are coming! Dee got a ninety-one, Hope an eighty-nine and Taylor a ninety-four.

"Yeah, Taylor, you should've done a lot better, what with your previous experience flying 727s and all..." she didn't like this pompous ass, and enjoyed the opportunity to rib him.

"Yeah, Taylor," Del Hope contributed, "what about all this experience flying for People's Express of yours? I thought you'd get a hundred on the final. Or at least better than the dame."

Taylor became very uncomfortable and defensive. His chubby physique did not provide him with the self-confidence needed to fight off insolent classmates, and he became flustered. "Fuck you, Hope. I don't see you getting hundreds either!"

"Yeah, but I didn't fly jets for People's Express. And you got your ass wiped by a girl!" Del Hope loved poking fun at Taylor.

"Like I said, fuck you, Hope," Anthony diplomatically offered.

"Yeah, fuck you, Hope," Valerie added, "for your information, I'm not a girl, I'm a woman, in case you hadn't noticed. But maybe you're just too dumb to tell the difference."

"Behave, children. Let's go look at the CPT schedule." Adam Dee started down the hallway to the Cockpit Procedures Training room. They all followed.

Valerie noticed that the navy blue suits evident during the first days of classes had gradually been replaced by sports coats and now not even these were being worn, but were left in the cars. Just about everyone she came across at the training center was in shirtsleeves and ties, so she assumed it was acceptable wear. Each new class that started was easily discernible because they were the ones wearing the navy blue suits and never removing their jackets.

The simulator schedule was posted on the door of the room housing the simulators. She read it and saw that she had been teamed up with Anthony Taylor. Oh, beautiful. Adam and Dee had also been paired up together. Her first session was at seven o'clock the next morning.

"Hey, Taylor," Del observed "Valerie's going to be in the simulator with you. Maybe you can show her how to fly the simulator just like you showed her how to score a hundred in ground school, eh?"

"Del, you are so dumb I really don't know how you can fly airplanes"

"Heck, at least I don't go around bragging that I'm the greatest pilot alive."

"Valerie," Adam Dee offered, "why don't you and I go inside and check out the CPTs while these two children sit out here and argue?"

"Sounds good. Let's go."

THE PHONE WAS RINGING and Valerie opened her eyes, trying to get her bearings. Where the hell was she? What time was it? Still not fully awake she reached for the phone.

"Hello?"

"Valerie? Anthony Taylor. We have simulator this morning, remember? We're here waiting for you."

Simulator? Oh, crap! She sat up in a flash. "Where are you?"

"I'm at the simulator building with Robert Roth, our instructor."

Panic time. "Anthony, I'll be there as soon as I can. I don't know what happened!"

"Make it quick." He hung up.

Valerie looked for her alarm clock. Why the hell hadn't the alarm gone off? A bed pillow completely covered the clock. Oh, shit, she must have thrown away the pillow smack onto her alarm clock, preventing her from hearing it. She ran in the bathroom, washing her face. The shower would have to wait. Her clothes on, she was out the door in six minutes flat. She was only five minutes from the simulator building and she wasn't yet fully awake when she joined Anthony Taylor and Robert Roth in the briefing room.

"Sorry about that, guys. I think one of my roommates covered my alarm with a pillow."

"No problem, we just used the time to get Anthony here acquainted with the simulator."

Robert was in his mid-forties, tall, blonde and with a genial smile, Jimmy Stewardish. His soft voice did wonders for her frayed nerves. Nothing she hated more than being late for something, especially as a newhire.

"Glad you made it here, Valerie," Robert explained, "what we're gonna do is give you each two hours at the wheel during each session, a total of four hours in the box. We're gonna have nine sessions in the simulator, one a day. The last day you'll have a proficiency check with a different airman." He gave them each a few pages outlining the curriculum for the simulator.

Valerie looked at the outline and wondered, once again, how the devil she was going to manage to memorize all that.

"Since Anthony here already started, why don't we go back in there and fly around for a while."

Valerie grabbed her flight bag and followed the men in the simulator. The simulator was enormous, bigger than the front section of the real airplane, with immense television sets surrounding the windshields and the entire monstrosity mounted on powerful hydraulic jacks fifteen feet off the ground. Several simulators lined up the bay, all immaculately clean and white, painted green letters identifying each one. The simulator building where the sims where located was four stories high, with access to the simulators being provided from the second floor. They entered one labeled:

MidAmerica Air Lines
DC-9-30 Simulator

Her heart began to pound with excitement. The inside of the sim was exactly like she imagined the real airplane would be at night, dark and cozy, with the sounds of high-speed gyros, radios and air conditioning. It smelled of hot metal and leather, and oil and sweat. It was also very cold. Anthony took the right seat and she climbed into the left, the captain's seat. Her flight bag slid between the seat and the wall, into the space specifically designed for it.

She reached for her seatbelt, wondering if she should use it, this was, after all just a simulator.

"Go right ahead and buckle up," Robert suggested. "We're gonna do everything just like in the airplane." He had positioned himself on the instructor's panel behind her, and had seen her reaching for the belt.

Valerie strapped herself in, feeling a little ridiculous. She looked outside through the windshield and was astonished at the realism of the simulator visuals. They were actually parked at a gate in St. Louis, and she could see in great detail all around. Talk about Virtual Reality, this was it!

"Start the engines using the checklist just like you would out on the line and then we'll taxi out and do some basic maneuvers."

Valerie was thrilled to death. She was actually in a simulator, starting her training in the real thing!

She spent the next two hours assisting Anthony and watching him fly the airplane. She was fully aware that he had flown 727s, and if he made it seem easy it was only because of his past experience. He eventually brought them to a final landing and they shut her down.

"What'd ya say we catch some coffee?" Robert asked them, getting up and opening the cockpit door. The simulator was connected to the building by a ten-yard ramp leading to the second floor. This ramp was normally retracted during simulator operation because hydraulic jacks provided realistic movement which was not possible if the ramp were in place. Robert lowered the ramp, going across to the small rec room where there was coffee and other vending machines.

"Not bad, Taylor. What did you think, how does it compare to the 727?" Robert inserted some coins into the hot drink machine.

"A little more squirrelly, but not too bad."

Valerie hated him and his 727 experience. Now she'd have to go in there and try not to look stupid in front of these two men, while trying to get the feel for a big jet. She wished she'd gone first, but maybe it was for the better. She had learned a couple of things by watching Anthony, which she would now apply.

Anthony helped himself to a bag of Twinkies, evidence of how he got so chubby, and parked himself on a chair.

His tie was loose and perspiration had soaked his shirt in spite of the low temperature inside the simulator, which made Valerie try to remember if she had used deodorant that morning, what with being late and all.

"The thing to remember with any jet airplane," Robert sat down with a cup of steaming coffee, "is that you have to plan ahead. You don't do anything in a hurry in a jet. If you need to do something in a hurry, it's too late."

Valerie wanted the break to end and get back in the sim because she was getting restless. Easy for these two to relax when it was her turn at bat next. She began to perspire.

"You may fly a 727 again," the instructor confided to Anthony.

"How's that?"

"You haven't heard the rumor?"

"No."

"Word has it that Trans Global Airlines is looking at us to buy us."

Valerie's heart jumped. "TGA?"

"Yeah. Everybody's merging with everybody else and TGA seems to have picked us."

"Is this a rumor or is there any proof?" Anthony was already trying to figure out how long it would take him to change over to the 727.

"Rumor, just a rumor. Remember, the airlines have more rumors than any other industry because our crews travel all over the country and the world. A rumor originated this morning in Cairo could be in Los Angeles before dinner."

"What happens to us if we end up merging with TGA?" Valerie was suddenly concerned.

"I imagine we'd all end up on their seniority list, but don't quote me 'cause this is just rumor. I wouldn't give it much thought. You guys have plenty to think about as it is."

Valerie decided a merger with TGA would not be all bad, didn't they have 747s and L-1011s? Maybe she would get a chance to fly the Jumbo jets? That would be a thrill!

"Of course, there's always the possibility that we may end up on the street, right?" Taylor had seen People's Express merge with Continental, and the marriage between the two pilot groups had not been a happy one.

"You mean, if we merge with TGA?"

"Yes. There's always a chance they'll just take the airplanes and the gates and leave us out of the party, no?"

Captain Roth switched his pipe to the other side of his mouth. "There's always a possibility things can go wrong, but we're not going to worry about that now. You guys have enough to worry about just learning the program here."

End up on the street due to a merger between MidAmerica and Trans Global? Oh, beautiful. Just what she needed. Put out all this effort just to end up pounding the pavement again looking for a job with another airline? The thought gave her the creeps.

They finished the break and piled back into the simulator, where Valerie swapped seats with Taylor.

They quick-started the engines to avoid repeating a procedure they had already practiced. With a touch of a button Robert got both engines going and got them ready for take-off.

Valerie inhaled deeply, staring down the row of lights marking the runway she was going to use.

"Anytime you guys are ready," Robert prodded, "fly runway heading, climb and maintain 10,000 feet."

Valerie slowly advanced the throttles and kept the airplane on centerline, feeling the acceleration. What she was actually feeling was her body weight pressing onto the back of her seat because the powerful hydraulic actuators holding up the simulator were tilting it straight up, at a seventy-degree angle, simulating the feeling of acceleration on her back by nearly tilting her onto the back of her seat. The visual in front of them did not tilt, which combined with the pressure on their backs added to the illusion of actually accelerating.

That first period Valerie felt all thumbs. She was unable to maintain straight and level flight and the damned airplane felt squirmy as hell. She began to sweat.

The airplane was a handful just to keep right side up, and she was expected to fly this sucker on instruments and with precision? Fat fucking chance.

She finished the period feeling grossly inadequate and terrified that all her dreams would come crashing down. How could she think that she could fly a big jet? Whatever had given her that idiotic idea? She should have listened to her mother and gone into medicine instead.

Robert told them they didn't do too bad for the first day and released them after reminding them that the following day they were due for a late night session.

Valerie went back to the apartment feeling like shit. Adam Dee was in the kitchen, fixing some Halibut with garlic.

"Hi, sugar! How'd it go on your first ride?"

She was so drained that she ignored his 'sugar.' "Terrible. I fucked up royal. Couldn't fly the damn thing at all."

Dee laughed.

"What the hell's so funny?"

"Don't worry, I went through the exact same thing and I talked to a couple of other guys in a class ahead of us and they told me they did the same thing. It took 'em about four sessions to really get the hang of it, but they all agreed that the first time they flew the DC-9 simulator they felt terrible."

"What kind of backgrounds did they have?"

"I don't know, same as the rest of us I guess."

"Well, Anthony flew that simulator like he was born in it. Made me look like shit."

"Hell, Anthony flew 727s, what did you expect? Of course he's gonna fly that puppy better than you. At first anyway."

"I am worried to death. We only have a total of eight periods and then the checkride. No way I'm going to be that proficient in eight rides."

"You will. You'll see. Now just relax and help me cook dinner. I got enough for two here."

As it turned out, Dee was right. Every time Valerie climbed back into the simulator after that first experience she felt slightly more confident, until it became a pleasure to show up for each training period.

The only item she still had trouble with was the single engine approach to land in Cat-II minimums where she had to hand-fly the airplane all the way to the ground. CAT-II minimums instrument approaches consisting of flying the airplane down to a decision height of 100 feet above the runway kept giving her trouble. With one engine out, the airplane became a touchy two-year old foal, totally unstable and temperamental, and all it took was for her to lose concentration for *three* seconds and the whole approach went to the dogs. She had to fly the 70-ton airliner with one engine inoperative all the way down to 100 feet above touchdown by looking at her instruments only, and then-at one hundred feet above touchdown, she was allowed to look up at the milky soup outside, and try to discern the runway lights and land the sucker at nearly 140 miles per hour. Easier said than done.

She tried several times but at the last moment she would lose it and would have to execute a missed-approach procedure on one engine, no easy feat in itself. She tried everything possible not to crash the airplane, yet the more she tried, the worse her approaches became, although she did not crash.

"Valerie," her instructor pointed out, "you have to calm down. You gotta be able to land the airplane out of this approach or you can't pass the checkride."

The horrible unspoken reality was that if she failed to pass the checkride she would be expected to submit her resignation at once. Fired, *Kaput*.

"Let's call it a day and we'll try it again tomorrow," Robert dictated, releasing them for the day. Anthony was no help, keeping his mouth shut and hardly helping her. She went home and had one beer.

Two more sessions and then the checkride, and she still was unable to land the fucker with one engine out in low visibility conditions. Why? What was she doing wrong?

She sat down with pen and paper and analyzed everything she was doing during the approaches. The only plausible explanation was that she was wasting too much time remembering all the steps she had to perform along the way, which in turn was distracting her from the operation of the airplane.

She placed a chair in the middle of the living room and sat there with her checklists and her notes. She slowly went through the entire procedure from beginning to end, taking forty minutes to recite out loud each single event that she had to perform, from fastening her seatbelt to moving every single switch that was required to be moved during the flight.

Forty minutes!

Not good. The entire flight simulation was taking about fifteen or twenty minutes in the simulator. If it was taking her forty minutes just to recite the steps, she was dead! She prepared a strong pot of coffee and started over, reciting out loud the steps to follow after the engine failure all the way until she was back on the ground. This time it took her thirty-two minutes. Better.

By the end of the day Valerie had it down to fourteen minutes, and she could recite each procedure from memory without mistake. Her brain was fried and she tried to get some sleep but she kept having nightmares. The prospect of flunking out was too devastating to contemplate.

The next day, however, she surprised herself, Anthony and their instructor by executing a perfect single-engine emergency landing in the simulator. That afternoon she once again placed her chair in the middle of the living room and recited by memory every one of the two-hundred seventeen items she had to do after the engine failure. By the time she went to bed she had it down to nine minutes, with no mistakes.

The day before her checkride she repeated the procedures twenty times, sitting on her chair in the middle of the living room. Adam Dee knew what she was doing, and refrained from interrupting her. At this stage in the game they had too much invested to risk failure by fucking around.

That evening Valerie took a walk in the fresh summer air and headed straight for a small church she had seen in the neighborhood. It was a very beautiful wooden church, surrounded by green luscious trees.

She didn't know what she was doing there, but since she was there, she decided to go in. There were only two other people besides herself, and she sat at a pew in the back.

"Oh, God, please don't let me blow it tomorrow. Please, be my copilot in that simulator tomorrow. Please." She left, feeling strange because she was not a religious person by any means, yet she felt calm and self-assured. She had done all she could, now it was time to perform.

There was good Karma in the air.

THE FOLLOWING MORNING VALERIE felt great. She woke up well ahead of schedule, showered, dressed and had time to prepare herself bagels with Philadelphia cream cheese and some orange juice. She had set three alarms, just to be sure she was not going to oversleep.

The weather was cloudy and stormy, but she didn't care. Typical Midwest summer. She drove herself to the simulator center and found that for the first time that week she had beaten Anthony Taylor there. Their simulator instructor arrived fifteen minutes after her, and she was delighted to meet the man. Captain James Nelson was a gentleman. His slim, strong body belied his white hair, and his infectious smile made Valerie want to hug him. He was impeccably dressed in a lightly-starched white shirt with a Parsley tie and red suspenders, and the gold watch with the chain hanging from his pants added to the image of a delightful man. He was obviously a shade or two above everything she'd met since arriving in St. Louis and it bode her well. He even mentioned that he drove a BMW, which fit the image to a "T."

Taylor arrived fifteen minutes later and she could see that, he was slightly taken back by her being there already. Good.

Captain Nelson invited them to get a cup of coffee each and follow him to the briefing room. There, he explained how he would conduct the checkride, that it would be based on everything they had already been practicing all week, and that they were to expect no surprises and help each other as much as possible, just like they would be doing out on the line. That said, he asked who would be going first and Valerie said she would. She had already talked to Anthony, who had grudgingly agreed to let her go first. She needed to tackle this checkride first thing in the morning, while she still had her full stamina.

They entered the simulator and Valerie felt no fear whatsoever, but instead felt absolutely confident and relaxed about what she had to do. They all took to their stations and Captain Nelson began the checkride.

Ninety minutes later, Valerie parked the brakes at the end of the runway, tired but feeling very good. She had just completed a near-perfect checkride.

"That's all I had for you, Valerie," Nelson stated. "Is there anything else you'd like to do? Any maneuver you'd like to practice some more?"

Valerie smiled, not believing what was coming out of her mouth. "How about another single-engine approach, James?"

Anthony Taylor about shit.

Nelson gave them instructions and they began the procedure again. Twenty minutes later Valerie managed another near-perfect single-engine landing, parking the brakes at the end of the runway.

"Time for a break," Captain Nelson announced.

"No shit," Taylor agreed, loosening his tie and following the instructor out of the simulator.

Valerie hit the bathroom first, looking at herself in the mirror with new eyes.

She had done it.

The two men were in the break room, drinking coffee when she returned.

"That was very good, Valerie," Captain Nelson complimented her. "Very good indeed."

They sipped their coffee without much conversation and returned to the simulator to give Anthony his checkride.

Outside the simulator building it was raining cats and dogs, a typical Midwestern summer storm.

Anthony whispered to her, "what the fuck were you trying to pull back there, asking for another single-engine approach?" he was worried sick that Nelson would make him do the same thing.

"I needed more practice," Valerie said simply. The jerk had not helped her as much as he should have during her checkride, not wanting to be reprimanded for coaching her, no doubt, but she was not going to act as shitty to him. She was going to act like a good first officer and help him as much as she could.

The checkride began and she was in Heaven. She had passed, she was sure, but she wasn't going to gloat or let the thought distract her from her present job. She would have ample time later to celebrate.

Anthony performed as expected throughout most of the ride, and at a certain point they heard a loud bang and the simulator went dark.

"Ignition to override! Auxiliary power!" Anthony commanded, while reaching up on the overhead panel for the engine ignition switch. He then flicked on the emergency switch but nothing happened. No emergency lights, no instrument lights. A loud impact jerked the simulator, as it settled on its mounts.

Nothing, just pitch black.

"What the fuck...?" the instructor had done something to simulate complete electrical power failure, of that he was certain, but what? He had followed the recommended steps yet nothing was restored. Taylor began to panic, this was his final simulator checkride, and some emergency had been given to him by the instructor, and he was not able to determine what it was!

"Ah, I think we have a problem," Nelson's voice came from the dark void that was the back of the simulator.

Anthony noticed that the motion had stopped. That was unusual.

"I think we have a power failure," Nelson stated.

"Yes, that's what I thought," Anthony complained in the pitch black cockpit, "but nothing seems to be working. I activated emergency power but we're still in the dark." He was getting pissed. The instructor was not supposed to give him weird-ass emergencies they hadn't practiced.

"No, Anthony, I mean, looks like the entire building's lost electrical power."

Anthony had been so engrossed in flying the airplane that he took a few seconds to understand what the instructor was talking about. After flying the simulator for a few hours, it was easy to forget that one was not in the real airplane after all.

"Can we get out of here?" Valerie asked. "Looks like the simulator has shut-off. Something's happened outside."

"Hang on," Nelson walked back to the rear bulkhead and opened the door to the outside world. A faint light entered the simulator. "Hey! What's going on out there?" he yelled to someone below.

"Everything's down!" the voice outside replied. "Lightning hit the transformer in front of the building and all the power's gone!"

"Shit! No wonder nothing worked!"

Valerie laughed. Anthony and her had thought Captain Nelson had given them a simulated complete power failure when that wasn't what had happened at all. Mother Nature had decided to give them an emergency of her own.

Valerie saw Anthony visibly relieved, probably because he must realize he hadn't made a mistake with his procedures and because this interruption provided them with a temporary break from the intense checkride. He was perspiring profusely with what must be relief.

"We're gonna have to stay in here until they can restore some power," the instructor explained, "because the ramp is electric."

Valerie thanked God it hadn't happened to her. Last thing she needed was a break in the middle of her checkride before shooting the single-engine approach.

They sat in the sim for nearly an hour before power was restored. When everything went back to normal Captain Nelson repositioned them where they were in the air before the blackout and Anthony continued his checkride.

He had no trouble with it and after he landed the airplane and parked the brakes, Captain James Nelson shook hands with each of them. "Far as I'm concerned," he stated, "you're both employees of MidAmerica Airlines."

The relief she felt was indescribable. She had passed what she considered the toughest challenge in her professional life and she had done so with great style.

That night she went out to a local hangout with Adam Dee to celebrate her achievement.

'When's your sim ride?" she sat on a stool alongside Dee.

"Friday. Sure hope it goes as smooth as yours, Val."

"Just make sure you've memorized every procedure down pat. When you're flying the simulator you don't have time to pause and think about what you need to do next, it has to be there when you need it without having to think about it."

"I'll try." Dee was understandably nervous about his coming checkride, and Valerie felt mildly guilty about asking him to join her for a beer to celebrate her own victory but what the heck, he was a big boy and he could take it. Besides, she hated drinking alone, and Dee had told her that he liked her friendliness and straightforwardness and felt that she was a definite asset as a friend.

"When do you get to fly the real airplane?"

"Monday. Anthony and I have been scheduled to do our landings at two o'clock in the morning."

"Guess that's when they have an airplane available, eh?"

"Guess so, but I don't care, I'll fly anytime. You kidding? Fly a DC-9? I've been waiting all my life to do this, Adam."

He smiled at her, "Same here. I hope I can fly that bitch. You're so much like me, Sugar, you love flying and everything associated with it. I'd never met a woman who felt this way before and what can I say, it's a different experience for me. I guess if you think I'll do alright, then I can't let you down now, can I?"

Valerie felt the irony of the situation and was amused by it. A Navy antisubmarine jock seeking reassurance from her! That was funny. "Adam, you'll do just fine. Have another beer."

"What you trying to do? Get me drunk? It won't work, Valerie, I already have a girlfriend, so your gallant attempts at seducing me won't work."

"In your dreams, Adam."

He roared. "That's what I like about you, Valerie, you are one of the guys."

"I don't know if I should take that as an insult or a compliment."

"Hey, you're not interested in my romantic advances and you're damned good with airplanes, so like it or not, you're one of the guys. How much longer you plan on living with me?"

"I'm going out apartment-hunting this weekend." Now that she had passed the simulator checkride she felt confident that she would be able to retain her job with MidAmerica, so getting an apartment was the next step. Living with Adam in the hotel apartment was fun and convenient but she wanted to get her own things out of storage and begin settling down in St. Louis. "You gonna stay at the hotel by yourself?"

"No, too damn expensive. I'm going to look for a place of my own over the weekend. I don't know what I'll be able to afford on nine hundred a month, but I'll try."

Valerie didn't like the idea of being paid $900.00 a month either when some of the flight attendants were grossing close to $40,000 a year but she understood that it was all part of the game. One year on probation and then they would taste the sweet flavor of money. Their salaries would jump to fifty grand on the second year and progressively increase to around eighty thousand over a period of five or six years, only to jump again when they made captains. The added responsibility acquired with the fourth stripe brought with it considerable remuneration, and this was what they all looked forward to. The company–Robert Eakle had told them–did not hire first officers, they hired prospective captains.

"Do you have any savings to help you make it through this first year?"

Valerie had already calculated that she needed two thousand dollars a month to sustain a decent living, so she would fly as much as possible to supplement her nine-hundred-dollar salary with per diem and make up the rest from her savings.

"Yeah, I got some. You don't go through all my years in the Navy out in ships without saving up a bundle, but I still wish we'd make a little more."

"This first year we're gonna have to watch it. I hear that some of the captains like to bust new first officers just out of spite." Stories like that one circulated among the newhires like wildfires.

"Yeah, there must be some assholes out there, but I just hope I don't get one. If you're straight, do a good job and don't step on anybody's toes, you should be alright."

Valerie was somewhat concerned about this. Her only experience flying with men had been with the delightful Jack, and she didn't know if she could take another situation similar to that one. Adam had a tremendous advantage being a man because he would blend right in, where she would immediately stand out like a sore thumb. What would she do if some captain harassed her and tried to hit on her? She hadn't had much time to give this some thought, but her first gut instinct was to take it to the chief pilot, although she suspected that, that too, would be a mistake. No, on second thought, she might be better off just riding it out and ignoring any such situation, at least during her probationary year. After that, she would have the union to protect her, and she'd heard that the Professional Standards Committee did not look fondly on sex offenders in the cockpit. "Most of the pilots I've met here have been extraordinarily nice," she explained. "Of course, what goes on in training could be completely different to what goes on out on the line."

"That's what I hear. Seems that once we get out on the line it's a lot more fun. One of the guys in a class ahead of ours who's already flying the line told me it's the most fun he's ever had with his pants on."

"Adam, I'm going to have one hell of a time getting the Navy out of you."

"Listen, Sugar, if you wanted clean, politically correct language, you should've gone into some other field, here you are surrounded by real men, and in case you haven't noticed, you're outnumbered, so learn to enjoy vulgarity."

"Adam, I think we should put you in charge of the airline's vulgarity committee."

"Is there a salary involved?"

THE FOURTH STRIPE

Maurice Azurdia

TWENTY
PRESENT TIME - BERLIN. GERMANY

Valerie opened the door of Charlie's hotel room, where she had been hiding while the pilot returned from his trip to Phoenix.

"Charlie!" he was standing in the hallway, looking tired and in need of a shave.

"Good morning, Valerie." He entered the room, accepting a hug from the woman who'd been flying as his captain. Strange situation.

"What happened?" she was relieved to see him back in one piece. "Did you get it?"

Charlie plopped his leather bag on the bed, removing his uniform coat, loosening his tie. "It's there," he added, pointing at the leather bag.

"No shit!"

"No shit."

Valerie slowly grabbed the leather bag, unzipping it. She abhorred guns, disliked them intensely because she saw no need for them in a civilized world. Her father had insisted on teaching her how to fire a revolver years before, when she was getting ready to go to college, over the objections of her mother, but she had failed to develop a taste for guns. She just didn't like thinking that there was a need for guns in her world. Much better to use one's intelligence to stay out of situations which required the use of guns. "And nobody stopped you?"

"Nobody stopped me."

"Incredible."

"Anything more happening since I left? Our birds haven't flown the coup, now, have they?" Charlie reached for the fridge, grabbing a beer. He looked tired and irritated.

Valerie peeked inside the leather bag, admiring the black metal box that was the weapon Charlie had smuggled across two countries. "No, they haven't flown the coup, and yes, a lot's been happening since you left. The dynamic duo have spent the past twenty-four hours visiting even more banks in town. Oh, yeah, and also a travel agency. We don't know what they did in there, but Paul Morris and I believe it's safe to assume the little birdies are now getting ready to fly the nest."

"Time for a vacation in the Bahamas, eh?"

"You think they were given orders to clear out?"

"Seems that way."

"How many briefcases do they have now? Have you guys been able to keep track?"

Valerie helped herself to a beer. Now that Charlie was back, she could breathe a little easier. "Paul's been following them. Get this, they have over sixty briefcases."

Charlie Smith whistled. "Thirty million dollars!"

"That's if they have half a million in each."

"Have you heard any more from Elaine?"

"Not a word since you left."

Charlie didn't like the sound of it. If Elaine and her buddy were clearing town, what about Valerie? Would they just leave and forget about Valerie? Not likely. People like that didn't usually leave loose ends behind. "I think you better stay here, Val. Your room has become a hot zone, and you better avoid it for the time being."

"I'm ahead of the game, Charlie. I cleared out of my room the moment you left," she explained, pointing to her suitcase resting on a small bag stand by the window.

"Where's Paul Morris?"

"He's at the *Steigenberger*, standing guard outside their suite. He doesn't want them to just vanish into thin air with our money. Must keep them in sight."

"Our money? I like that. You mean he's in the hallway on their floor?"

"He's on their floor but I don't know exactly where he's at. I think he's sitting by the elevators, pretending to read a newspaper."

"How long has Paul Morris been at it?"

"Since you left."

"That many hours? I think I better go take over for a while then. If nothing else develops, I wanna get together here tonight after Elaine and the other guy fall asleep. I am betting that they'll sleep and not try to sneak away under the cover of darkness. If they're gonna fly out of Berlin then my guess is that they'll do it in the morning. Not too many flights leave out of here during the evening."

"But Charlie, aren't you exhausted?"

"Naw, I've been sleeping on the planes. Talk to you in a little while."

"Okay." Valerie had remained in Charlie's room most of the past twenty-four hours. She was aware that they were playing with fire, but now Charlie had provided them with an excellent fire extinguisher.

Paul Morris returned forty minutes later.

"Any change?" she hugged him. He smelled of perspiration and needed a shave. His suit was a wrinkled mess.

"No, they're still in the room and going nowhere. Ordered room service for breakfast so they may be finished with the banks, who knows. God only knows how they're planning on transporting sixty briefcases out of Germany." He saw the black leather bag on the bed. "Is that?"

"Yep. Charlie managed to get it through. I ordered you some breakfast from room service."

"Thank you, darling."

Paul Morris walked over to the bed, unzipping the bag.

"Paul, don't mess with it until Charlie shows us how to use it."

"It's okay, I just want to see it."

Valerie wondered about this lunacy they were living. They were airline pilots, not secret agents nor cops. She must have been out of her mind to even think that the three of them could corner Elaine and Karl and hopefully, take from them the money she believed they'd been accumulating for the past thirty-six hours. Of course, there was always a chance that those briefcases didn't contain cash, but she was willing to bet her future that that wasn't the case. However, if the police in all the civilized countries of the world had been unable to nail these bastards so far, what in heaven's name gave her the idea that they would be successful at anything other than getting killed?

"It's a very impressive gun," Paul Morris observed, manipulating it, feeling its weight.

"Now we're fifty thousand dollars poorer, though," Valerie exclaimed.

Paul Morris met her eyes. "Fifty thousand dollars won't do us any good if we're dead, Valerie. This little darling will serve to ensure that we don't end up that way."

"Paul Morris, you really think we'll be able to nail these bastards?" her usual self-confidence felt in terrible need of a booster shot.

"Valerie, the way things look at the moment, we don't have a choice, we have to take action. If we do nothing and your friendly Elaine disappears from view, you'll spend the future looking behind your back, waiting for the knife that will eventually come. The feds are sitting on their ass, waiting for you to provide them with something tangible that they can use, and that's not going to help us at all if Elaine and her friend decide to get lost in the crowd. We need to go in there now and get whatever money we can so that we can get lost. We're going to have the Colombians or whatever the hell they are, the Interpol and the DEA after us, so we better get as much as we can because it's going to be a one-shot deal. Charlie wants to go in there, duct tape them and walk away with the suitcases."

"Duct tape them?"

"Yeah, your copilot is using his head. He brought some duct tape back with him from the States."

"And what if they don't have the money we think in those briefcases?" she grabbed two Coke cans, offering him one.

"Then that, would be a problem, however, I do not believe for one minute that those two are collecting anything other than hard cash at all those banks. What the hell else could they be doing? Collecting paperwork from safe deposit boxes? Fat chance, too many of them. Drugs, maybe? Not likely. Cocaine has value only if it circulates, not by sitting in some safe deposit box in some bank. What it gets down to is that you won't be able to continue flying airplanes, and that you're rapidly joining everybody's shitlist. That being the case, we may as well take the initiative. When we go in there and stir things up, the Organization of drug dealers is going to become a very pissed off swarm of African killer bees, and we don't want to be anywhere near it."

"So you still think my plan's good?"

"Darling, your plan is brilliant, and anyhow, we don't have any other alternative at the moment. Looks like Elaine and her buddy are getting ready to get lost with a bunch of cash, and that's precisely what we ought to be doing in the immediate future."

"And go where?"

Paul Morris sighed loudly. "Valerie, my best guess at this time would be to head for some remote place, like Puerto Escondido, off the Pacific coast of Mexico, or Barriloche, in Argentina. It has to be somewhere where communications are scarce or nonexistent."

"Oh, shit, and then what? Spend the rest of our lives in hiding? Maybe this wasn't such a good idea after all..."

"Valerie, like I said, your idea was brilliant, and now we have to go through with it, or we'll spend the rest of our lives looking over our shoulders and very poor. Or just plain dead. Let's not think negative thoughts, though. We're going to succeed at this. We're not stupid people, and we will succeed." He put the weapon on the bed and reached for her, hugging her. "This is fourth down and guess what? We are not going to punt, we are going to run with the fucking ball."

CHARLIE RETURNED TO HIS room at the *Sweinzerkof* near midnight. "Looks like the little birdies have gone night-night," he informed.

"Did they go out at all?" Paul Morris was up and ready to take his turn watching the suite again.

"Nope. Stayed put all day. Walked past their door a couple of times and heard the TV going. Other than that, they never went out. Ordered room service many times, though."

"I'll go watch them." Paul Morris kissed Valerie on his way out. "I'll call you every thirty minutes. You don't have to answer it, but if I don't call you after thirty-five minutes, come looking for me."

"Sounds good, Paul Morris." Charlie reached for the black bag containing the machine pistol, and began checking the ammunition in the plastic clips.

The phone rang all night, every thirty minutes, with Charlie and Valerie staying awake, trying to build up stamina for the upcoming events. They had decided to drop in on Elaine and her friend or husband or whatever the heck he was, in the morning. Enough waiting around.

At eight a.m. the phone rang. It was only five minutes after Paul Morris had checked in, so that was unusual.

Valerie picked it up. "Hello?"

"Charlie?" it was a man's voice. Valerie had forgotten that they were staying in Charlie's room. "No," she paused, cursing herself for answering the call, "You want to speak with Charlie? Hang on just a minute."

"Who's this?"

She hesitated, wondering if she should give a fake name. "This is Valerie Wall, who is this?"

"Valerie! This is Carl Steineke," he was a TGA pilot flying out of Berlin for the month, also staying at the hotel. Although Valerie had never met him, she knew the name. Damn, now he'd assume that she was shacking up with Charlie! She suddenly realized how ridiculous the thought was, they were in a life and death situation, and here she was, worrying about her reputation. "Carl, Charlie is right here, if you hang on just a second, I'll get him for you."

"No, I mean yes! Haven't you heard?"

"Heard what?"

"Flight 537 crashed. Our Istanbul flight crashed twenty minutes ago."

"What!?" Valerie felt vomit raising to her mouth.

"Yes, I just got off the phone with operations. They crashed shortly after takeoff. They had some kind of an explosion aboard and crashed while attempting to return to Berlin."

Valerie felt the room spinning. "No!"

"The Germans are all over the crash site as we speak. Operations thinks there were no survivors."

"What's going on?" Charlie Smith straightened up on one elbow. Valerie's tone obviously alarming him.

She lifted her index finger, indicating for him to wait. "Carl, this is confirmed? I mean, operations is sure it was our flight?"

"Without question, Valerie. Adam Dee was the captain. Stu Jurgens was the F/O."

Valerie sat down on her bed, suddenly feeling faint, tears of frustration welling in her eyes. "Adam? No!"

Flight 537 was *her* flight. The flight that she was supposed to have taken out this morning to Istanbul. Adam? How the hell had Adam ended up on her flight?

"Flight 537 crashed twenty minutes ago," she croaked to Charlie Smith, who was growing more alarmed by the minute.

"*What!!?*" he jumped out of bed, standing between the two beds.

"Carl Steineke just talked to operations and they told him that there was some kind of an explosion onboard and that they..." she choked, unable to continue. She handed Charlie Smith the receiver, rushing to the bathroom, where she vomited in the sink.

Charlie Smith lifted the telephone. "Carl? Charlie here. What the hell happened?"

Minutes later, Charlie set down the receiver, a very angry frown distorting his features.

Valerie came out of the bathroom, wiping her mouth with a white towel. "Charlie, Adam Dee was the captain on the flight." Charlie didn't answer her, he was sitting on one of the beds, furiously attaching the silencer to the automatic machine pistol.

"Do you think Elaine did this?" she watched, concerned, as the pilot assembled the weapon.

"No, Valerie, I don't think Elaine did this, but I'm sure she has a pretty damn good idea of who did. That was your flight. This is no coincidence, no mechanical failure."

"Adam was in my class."

"I know. They were going after you. Whoever their informant is with crew scheduling wasn't able to inform them that you had ditched the flight. I guess this pretty much ends the guesswork for us."

"What do you mean?"

"Elaine and that asshole she's staying with up in that suite have decided that you've become expendable. Along with the entire crew and passengers on flight 537. We're moving in right now."

She felt cold.

"I want you to stay here while I go to the *Steigenberger* and take care of business. If I don't get back in here or call you in twenty minutes, get the hell out of here." He was obviously very angry.

"What about Paul Morris? He's out there watching them." She wiped the final taste of vile from her lips, beginning to feel the same anger growing in her.

"I'll warn Paul Morris and get him out of the way while I drop in on those two."

"What are you gonna do?"

"I intend to pay a visit to your friend Elaine and then call the German police and the Interpol. I am going to turn them in. These people are animals, and they need to be dealt with. If I had moved sooner, perhaps this tragedy may have been prevented."

"Charlie, I thought we'd agreed that we couldn't trust the Germans...and we have a plan!"

"That was before, Valerie. This has now become my personal business, and I will gamble on the German police to help me out once I get those two."

"You're not going to shoot them, are you?"

"Only if they shoot at me first." Charlie Smith inserted a fresh ammunition clip into the pistol, standing up, stuffing the remaining clips into his pants' pockets. He grabbed a towel from the bathroom, and threw it over the pistol he now carried on his right hand. "Stay here and don't open the door for anyone. If I'm not back inside of twenty minutes, like I said, grab the fifty thousand and get lost."

"I'll come with you!"

"No. Stay here. You'll be safer and besides you don't have a firearm so you can't help me." He turned for the door, exiting the room.

Valerie was left alone, stunned by the velocity of events. Now what? Things were happening too fast even for her. This was not a comfortable feeling for someone used to being in command. Charlie was going to the *Steigenberger* to confront Elaine, and she was here in this room, waiting.

Like a helpless female.

Over her dead body!

Valerie grabbed her leather jacket, exiting the room, rushing for the street. If Charlie was going berserk and was going to get the Germans involved, she had to make sure they got some of the money out first, or all would be over for them. He was just too upset to think straight.

Charlie Smith walked the one thousand yards to the *Steigenberger* hotel at a brisk pace, fuming inside. The machine pistol covered by a white hotel towel drew some stares from passing pedestrians, but typical German courtesy kept any of them from more than wondering what the man was hiding. Charlie did not feel bound by social conventions and legal niceties any longer. He was going to find out exactly who was behind the sabotage of the TGA flight, and if he had to kick some ass in the process to obtain that information, he would enjoy that very much indeed.

He opted for the stairs instead of catching the elevator, taking them two at a time, arriving on the floor where Elaine Griffin and Karl had their suite. Paul Morris was nowhere in sight.

Good. The less people, the less chance for anything going wrong.

Charlie knew that the couple of murderers were not going to simply open their door and invite him in, so he removed the safety on the machine pistol, chambering the first round.

He arrived outside the door of the suite. The hallways were deserted in both directions. He lifted the Ingram, pointing the muzzle of the long silencer towards the door lock. He angled it down, so as to avoid hitting anyone inside standing behind the door.

His finger applied six pounds of pressure on the trigger and the machine pistol jumped, generating a cloud of white smoke and a loud crack from the splintering wood. The handle and lock were suddenly nowhere in sight. Gone.

Charlie Smith kicked open the door and barged in, the gun ready.

"What the fuck...!?" Elaine Griffin was sitting at a small desk by the window, typing away at a laptop computer. Her surprise was total.

"Freeze!" Charlie commanded, aiming the gun at her. The man was nowhere in sight. Out of the corner of his eye, he suddenly caught movement in the other room. A face made a brief appearance and then it was gone.

"Just sit there, don't move!" he barked at the woman, covering the distance to the bedroom in two long steps. He kept the muzzle of the Ingram on the woman, while going flat against the wall leading to the bedroom.

He quickly peeked inside the second room, catching a glimpse of the man in the process of aiming a small-caliber semiautomatic at him.

"Oh, shit!" Charlie jumped back into the middle of the small living room, swinging the Ingram around to face the bedroom door, just in time to point it at Karl as he came through the door.

Karl fired two very loud quick rounds, too high to hit anything. Charlie heard something shattering behind him, then he hit the coffee table, losing his balance, falling back.

Charlie squeezed the trigger as he landed on his back, steadying the long gun with his free hand. He was flat on the ground, and he prayed that he would hit something, or that asshole's next shot was going to find him, because he was immobilized on the floor.

The Ingram sounded like cloth ripping, and Karl was thrown backwards, his pistol flying out of his grip at an astonishing speed. Charlie jerked his hand from the silencer, which had become too hot to touch. God only knew how many shots he'd fired, but he'd lucked out and hit the bastard.

VALERIE REACHED THE LOS Angeles *Platz,* entered the *Steigenberger* hotel and headed for the stairwell, running up the flight of stairs, two at a time, pausing at the landing to catch her breath. She didn't want her loud breathing giving her or Charlie away. As she waited inside the staircase, she thought she heard muffled shouts and a door slamming very loud, or was it a shot? She opened the service door into the floor where Elaine's suite was and headed down the corridor to her suite.

Thunder clapped in the room then, and Charlie felt as if a mule had kicked him on his right shoulder. Once, as a kid, he'd been visiting his aunt Bev's farm in Iowa, and the local mule had planted one square in his chest, and this felt just like it.

He rolled over using the inertia imparted into his shoulder by what he knew must be a bullet, and faced the Griffin woman standing behind her desk, a smoking Walther PPK .380 caliber semiautomatic pistol in her hand, quickly trying to adjust her sight for Charlie's movement. He knew he was in deep shit. No way he was going to bring the Ingram around before she fired again, and at this range she could not miss him.

"Stop!" the voice came from the door.

Elaine Griffin looked away from Charlie for an instant, straight into the eyes of the TGA captain, Valerie Wall, standing in her doorway.

A second later, Elaine's body was violently catapulted back, splattering deep red blood on the wall and windows behind her, a look of total surprise in her eyes. She hit the corner of the window with a loud crack and collapsed into a heap. Simultaneously, the window glass shattered and the desk collapsed, splinters flying up like mad hornets.

"Shit! Oh, shit!" Charlie groaned, not releasing his grip on the trigger until the clip was empty.

Crimson orchids of blood dripped from the wall.

"Charlie!" Valerie took in the scene. "Charlie, you've been hit!" He had a red carnation growing from his right armpit, yet he seemed unperturbed.

"Dammit, these fuckers didn't gimme a chance to talk. The guy came out shooting, and then she shot me!" He was talking fast and loud, adrenaline pumping into his system. He quickly replaced a new clip in the Ingram, getting himself up on his feet, walking over to check on the fallen man.

Dude was fried, no question about it. Charlie hadn't seen too many dead bodies in his time, but this guy definitely fit the bill. The German was sprawled on the floor, blood soaking the entire front of his white shirt and the beige carpet, his dead eyes staring at something in the ceiling. No way of knowing how many times he'd been hit without removing the shirt and washing him.

He shook his head in an attempt to clear it. It was getting hard to breath. More breaths but less air coming in with each one.

VALERIE REMOVED HER BELT, hurrying by her copilot's side, wondering how she could apply a tourniquet to what looked like a chest wound.

Charlie stood still for a moment, allowing himself to catch his breath, letting Valerie look at his chest.

"The bitch put one right through my chest." He looked over at the desk. "No movement from there. The nerve of that woman, shooting at me! Valerie, we gotta get out of here. I don't see any of the briefcases in this room. Where the hell did they stash the cash?"

"Jesus Christ!" Paul Morris entered the room, taking in the situation in an instant.

"Paul, help me, Charlie's been hit!"

Paul Morris was behind Charlie in an instant, helping Valerie remove the man's shirt. Blood was now soaking Charlie's pants and shirt.

"Forget about me!" he ordered them. "Paul, you go over there and check in her purse for car keys. If she doesn't have any, check that guy's pants. The money's not here, so they must've stashed it away in a vehicle, possibly downstairs in the hotel lot."

"Charlie, we've gotta get you to a hospital!" Valerie found the bullet hole, near Charlie's right armpit, placing a towel on the wound to stem the blood flow.

"Charlie, you have two wounds. The bullet cut right through you! Hold this tight!"

"Fuck it. We can deal with that after we find out what they did with the money!"

Paul Morris walked to the desk area where Elaine Griffin rested, looking like she'd taken hits everywhere. He found the woman's purse, searching for keys.

A set of keys with a Hertz keychain sat on top of whatever else Elaine Griffin had carried in her purse.

"Bingo! I have the keys, let's get out of here!"

"Wait! Get her laptop! Valerie, get Elaine's laptop, bring it with us!"

"Go, go!" Charlie Smith shoved Valerie towards the door. "This place's gonna to be crawling with people in just a few minutes."

Everyone on that floor certainly had heard the three unmuffled shots fired by the couple, and the police were sure to be making an appearance very soon.

Charlie was having difficulty breathing.

"If the bullet hit the lung. I am dogshit," he mumbled.

Valerie knew he was right. If the bullet had pierced Charlie's lung, his lung would fill with blood and he would die, drowning in his own blood. What a way to go.

She would not let this happen, they would get him to a hospital!

The trio ran down the hallway, hitting the staircase at a full run.

They descended the stairs two at a time, reaching the garage level, crashing through the door, storming into the dark parking garage, with Charlie still fully conscious. Elaine must not have hit the lung, Valerie prayed.

"Now what?" Valerie cried.

"Look at the keychain," Charlie gasped.

Paul Morris looked at the keys he was clutching.

Valerie was breathing hard. A license plate number, please, let there be a plate number!

There was no number of any kind on the keychain.

"Fuck! There is no I.D. on this keychain!" he stared at Valerie.

She looked around at the crowded parking garage. How were they going to find the right vehicle?

"It's gotta be something big," Charlie added, holding the towel to his chest. "To put all those briefcases in one vehicle it's gotta be something big."

He was right. She surveyed the immediate area. An Opel minibus was parked across from them. She ran to it, trying to peek inside the commercial vehicle, but was unable to see anything past the two front seats.

Paul Morris tried the key in the keyhole, and suddenly all pandemonium broke loose. An anti-theft alarm went off in the Opel.

"Holly shit!" Valerie cursed. Now they'd done it. The security guys would be there in no time to investigate. This wasn't the States, and she was sure the ultra-efficient Germans would not allow a car alarm to howl unattended, as was the case back home.

She began to stress out. Wait! There! She glimpsed a yellow bumper sticker on a VW minibus parked across from the elevator. She ran to it.

Hertz.

"This has got to be it!" she yelled at her two companions. The minibus was also a commercial model, without passenger windows. Of course, Elaine would have parked it next to the elevator to facilitate loading.

Paul Morris ran past her, trying the key on the door, praying that it wouldn't set off a second alarm. Not that it would make too much difference at that point.

The key unlocked the door.

"Hot dog! Everybody get in!"

Valerie helped Charlie into the front seat, climbing between the bucket seats. She stuck her head in the back.

The back was crowded with neatly-stacked glistening aluminum briefcases.

"The briefcases are in here!" she announced to the men, holding on for dear life, Paul Morris had the engine going and was accelerating out of the parking lot like a parking garage attendant with a new Ferrari.

"Find a parking ticket! There must be a ticket somewhere!"

Valerie lowered the sun visors.

A pink card fell on Paul's lap, just as he braked to a stop at the toll booth. He showed the card to an older man with white hair dressed in a security police uniform. The man waved them by, raising the wooden boom. Paul Morris shot out into the morning traffic, heading for their hotel.

The situation was very clear to her now, they had to get Charlie to a hospital and then get the hell away from Europe to some remote area of the world and plan their next move. She momentarily thought of all the pension money she'd accumulated with her airline, money that now would not ever be hers, then felt ridiculous about it, here she was, sitting on God only knew how much cash, and she was thinking of her pension money!

How were they going to sneak this van full of cash across Europe? She was not sure if the European

Common Market had eliminated customs between European countries, and she cursed herself for not paying more attention when reading about it in *U.S. News*. No, that was a stupid idea. Driving took too long, and they'd be sitting ducks. What they had to do was fly out of here, but how? Flying out of Tegel was out of the question, since that airport would be the hottest spot in this city.

Then there was the Interpol. Soon as the news of what occurred in the hotel suite at the *Steigenberger* reached the spooks, they would be after her and Charlie along with the drug dealers.

Hell of a deal. The good guys and the bad guys joining forces to come after her ass. If they drove to Frankfurt and tried to get on an airplane back to the States as jumpseaters, they may get caught. The possibility existed that Interpol would notify operations offices at most airlines, warning them that two TGA pilots suspected of murder would be trying to jumpseat. That was way too risky. Besides, there was the small matter of a van full of briefcases, her boyfriend who couldn't jumpseat because he was not a pilot, and Charlie bleeding all over. She placed her hand on top of the one Charlie was using to hold the now red towel against his armpit.

"It's not as bad as it seems," he reassured her. "I don't think she hit the lung, or I'd be dead by now."

"We need a plan!" Paul Morris announced.

"Forget it!" Charlie yelled. "Run first, think later."

They could not even hole up in some countryside hotel somewhere in Europe and sit still until the storm blew over, because all hotels routinely gave the local police the names of their guests, and if Interpol did its job, they would get caught.

Getting caught would be a definite disaster, since no one would ever believe their side of the story, not with the Mac 12 in their possession and two dead people on record. TGA would fire them on the spot, the Germans would shove them in a dark cell for the rest of their lives and the drug people would eventually bribe their way into these cells and kill them.

Valerie considered calling the DEA man in New York, he was an American and perhaps they could find an ally there. Right! –and immediately thereafter she would be fired by TGA and the feds would confiscate the money and they'd put her and Charlie and Paul Morris in a German jail and throw away the key. That sonofabitch Olaffson was no better than the drug lords, lying and cheating to suit his own needs. Face it, girl, Charlie flew across several countries carrying an illegal weapon which he then used to kill two people, and now they were running with God knew how many millions of the mob's money. Yeah, right, call in the feds? In your dreams! Charlie was right, run first, think later.

She anxiously scanned the drive-up area of the hotel, expecting to see police vehicles waiting for them. As they approached the entrance, she also casually examined the lobby area, searching for any signs of danger. Of course, she would not know what form the danger might come as, but if she noticed anybody moving fast or looking at them for too long, she'd assume that they were it. And then they would bolt.

"We're doing this wrong. We can't just drive off without having any sort of plan."

"We have a plan, to get the hell away from here as fast as we possibly can." Charlie gasped. He was getting lightheaded again.

She looked around. They were parked along other cars on a side street, and they did not stand out abnormally. Nobody would notice them, they looked just like three friends planning their days' work. Good, she had to talk with them. "Charlie, we cannot drive anywhere. We can't even attempt border crossings with this money on us. Besides, the Interpol will eventually get their shit together and bulletin all airports and borders, and they'll nail us. And, you need immediate medical attention."

"Why are we going to our hotel?" Charlie asked.

"You guys need your documents and your uniforms," Paul Morris explained, shutting down the engine. "Stay here with Valerie, Charlie. I'll go upstairs, pack all you two need into a suitcase, and we'll go to my hotel."

"Got any ideas?" Charlie decided it was better to utter short sentences instead of long ones. Long ones made his chest hurt.

"Not yet, but I'm sure Valerie has more ideas than we need." He left the van, entering the hotel lobby.

Valerie assessed the situation. Not good. They had taken action without having looked at all the angles ahead of time, and now they had to improvise, and get it right the first time. Paul Morris had looked into that Learjet that they could charter. She wondered how that would work. Could they get all these suitcases into a small Lear? She doubted it.

"Alright, first of all, let's analyze this. Did anyone see you going into Elaine's room with the gun?"

"Nope. No one that I noticed anyhow."

She hadn't seen anybody either, so the possibility existed that when the police found the bodies of Elaine and Karl, that they wouldn't have a clue who had done it. Their confusion would not last too long, though. Soon as Interpol heard the news, they would immediately make the connection with Elaine and Charlie and seek them out.

"It doesn't matter if nobody saw me, Val, the cops are going to come looking for us the minute they put two and two together." he glanced at the Ingram, on the floor. "You've got to get rid of that. I don't think we'll need it again. Now we must use our brains to get lost."

"Don't worry, we'll take care of that gun."

"Do you think those are the suitcases with the money?" Charlie knew the dice had been cast, and for better or for worse, they'd entered a situation where they had to change their lives drastically, and to do that they needed money, and lots of it.

Valerie stepped back, reaching for one of the metal briefcases. It was very heavy. "Locked." She examined the lock. It appeared solid enough to defy a bullet. The briefcase felt heavy, the way it would feel containing three Yellow Pages directories. "I don't think I can open this, Charlie, but I believe it's probably a good guess that they contain cash. What else could they have?"

"Gimme..." Charlie reached for the briefcase, grimacing in pain.

"Forget it! You just keep your hand on the wound. Paul Morris and I'll find a way to open one of these soon as he returns. You just stay put."

Where the hell were they going to find a doctor? Bullet wounds were serious business, and any public clinic or hospital would immediately notify the police. They had to get a private doctor, one with his own private office. How was she going to find such a man in Berlin when none of them spoke a word of German?

"Valerie, Paul Morris said he'd found a Learjet that we could charter to fly us out of here. If we move quickly, we may be able to catch the plane and depart before the shit hits the fan."

"You may be right, Charlie, but we're going to take care of you first."

"I'm fine. Let's just get the hell out of here."

Paul Morris returned with her crew suitcase, throwing it in the back, on top of the briefcases. "That's all we need. Now let's get Charlie some help."

"Wait! I've an idea! Stay here while I make a call." She ran out of the van, heading for the lobby of the hotel, leaving the two men wondering what she had in mind now. She went to the front desk, choosing a woman clerk with an intelligent face.

"Good morning."

"Gutten Morgen," the woman smiled.

"I need you to do me a favor."

"Of course, what can I do for you?"

"I don't speak German, so I'd like you to please call the telephone information and find out the number for an air ambulance service out of *Tempelhoff* or Tegel airports."

"Air ambulance?"

"Yes, a jet airplane with a doctor, and a nurse. The kind they use to transport critical patients."

"One moment please." The woman picked up the phone, speaking in German. She thanked the person at the other end, writing down something on a piece of paper which she then handed to Valerie. "There are two air ambulance outfits, one at each airport, these are the numbers. Would you like me to connect you?"

Valerie took the piece of paper. "No, thanks. This is fine. Thank you very much for your help." She quickly ran upstairs to the mezzanine, where she knew there was a pay phone.

She dialed the number in Tempelhoff, and after some confusion, was transferred to a man who spoke English.

"I need to charter an air ambulance to transport a patient. Do you have any jets?"

"Yes, we have jets. Where is the patient?"

"The patient is in Berlin. He has a badly fractured femur and we'd like American surgeons to reset it."

"You want to fly patient to America?"

"Yes. Do you have any jets with the necessary range?"

"No, we don't, but call Zemke at Tegel, they have long range airplanes." He gave her a third number.

"Thank you." She dialed the new number. The woman who answered at Zemke Aviation spoke beautiful English.

"We need to charter an air ambulance to fly a patient to the United States. We need a doctor and a nurse on board. Do you have anything like that available right away?"

"Is this a private charter or for an institution?"
"Private."

"Just a moment."

Valerie thought about the events of the past half hour. She shook her head. How could things have gone so far out of control? Charlie shooting Elaine and Karl had not entirely registered yet either. She wondered if the drug people were looking for her yet, but remembered that whoever Elaine's boss was, he thought Valerie had died in the TGA crash this morning. It would take at least a few hours for the press to get the names of the crew, if at all. Maybe the Germans would not release the crew names with the same facility as they did back home.

"Miss?"

"Still here."

"How soon do you need the airplane, what's the patient's condition, and where is he?"

"The patient is...being flown to Berlin as we speak. He'll be here in less than thirty minutes. He has a fractured femur."

"What airport is he coming into?"

"It's a helicopter flight. He's going directly to one of the local hospitals. I still don't know which one. He was mountain climbing in southern Germany and broke a leg. The bone has to be set, probably with an intramedular pin, and he wants it done in the United States."

"We have a Canadair Challenger available for air ambulance. Being a private charter, you'd have to put up a major credit card with us. The cost will be approximately forty-thousand dollars. Does the patient have insurance to cover this transportation expense?"

"Yes, of course he does, but don't worry about that. Just put in on my American Express." She wondered if the American Express folks would authorize such an expenditure, seeing how her most expensive card purchase she'd ever made had been seven thousand dollars for photographic equipment. It didn't really matter; they could put up the difference in hard cash. She gave the woman her card number.

"The airplane will be ready in forty-five minutes. Do you know how to get here?"

Valerie received directions from the woman, concluding the conversation and running back out to the van outside.

"I got it!" she announced, slamming shut the door of the van.

"Where to?" Paul Morris asked.

"Tegel. Here's what we're gonna do."

"Valerie, I've been dating you long enough to know that it wouldn't be too long before you'd take charge of the situation."

Paul Morris drove through the Berlin streets, careful to observe the posted speed limits. They could not afford to be pulled over for any reason.

Valerie was amazed at how the Germans used their traffic lights, with blinking yellow after red and before green, to warn motorists to be ready to go.

The fixed base operator at Tegel airport was not located close to the airline terminal, and Valerie was grateful for that. She didn't want to go anywhere near the airlines at the moment. They drove to the front of the elegant glass terminal, parking in a handicap spot.

"Wait here," she ordered the men. "I'll go inside and take care of the paperwork and have them open the gate so you guys can drive up to the airplane. Charlie, put that jacket on your leg and cover your side with this so the blood doesn't show so much. You're supposed to have a fractured femur." She entered the lobby, admiring the aluminum, leather and wood decor. Classy combination.

"*Gooten Tag,*" the blonde receptionist smiled. He was tall and impeccably dressed.

"Hi, my name's Valerie Wall, I called a little while ago to charter your Canadair Challenger for a flight to the United States?"

The man studied her blue jeans and crumpled hair, not sure whether he was looking at an eccentric rich American woman or some white trash trying to pull a joke.

"*Ya*, we have some forms that you need to fill up, and you have credit card, yes?"

Valerie handed the man her American Express Gold, beginning to fill the form she'd been handed on a clipboard. "You have the doctor and the nurse ready?"

"*Ya*," the man smiled, "they are in the airplane. When will ambulance arrive?"

"No ambulance, the patient has already arrived, he's outside in my van. We need to drive into the ramp to park the van below the airplane."

"Yes, of course." He keyed into an intercom, issuing orders for the front gate to be opened.

"And here's your card," the man handed it back, after running it through the magnetic scanner for authorization. She realized the American Express boys had authorized what must be an enormous bill. She would've had fun with that at Sak's Fifth Avenue!

"The captain will need the destination airport to file the flight plan and order the fuel."

She needed as much fuel as possible. "Aah, Atlanta, Georgia."

"Very well," the man keyed back into the intercom, relaying the information to the mechanics outside. "If you please, sign here," the customer service man was very efficient and had all the necessary formalities completed in a manner of minutes. He stepped from behind the front counter, bidding for her to follow him to the ramp.

A white jet airplane with orange stripes squatted on the ramp, a fuel truck parked alongside, pumping gas into its wing tanks. The van was already parked at the base of the airstairs, and four men had lifted Charlie into a stretcher, very skillfully transporting him up the stairs into the cabin. She hoped nobody would point out the obvious, that the man's leg did not appear to be shattered, nor that he had blood all down the side of his shirt.

She held her breath.

Paul Morris was unloading the briefcases from the van, taking them up the steps two per trip. The four men who carried Charlie into the airplane automatically joined in to help Paul Morris with the briefcases, and they had the van unloaded in under five minutes.

No questions were asked, although Valerie could only imagine the rumors that would flow among this crew after work tonight. A woman and two men, one of them bleeding badly, sixty metal briefcases, a doctor, a nurse. Drugs? Gold? Money? Sex? Perhaps all of the above?

Tabloid heaven.

She didn't even want to think about it. They had to get away from German airspace as soon as possible.

She instructed one of the men to park the van at the executive terminal's parking lot, because she'd want it there when she returned, then joined the others in the airplane.

The interior cabin of the corporate airplane was outfitted like the cabin of a luxury yacht, fine woods and leather seats, and she was pleased to see the doctor bent over Charlie, examining him. She had to act quickly. The sound of the engines starting filled the cabin.

"Paul Morris, do whatever you have to, but open one of these briefcases for me."

Paul Morris laid the briefcase on a seat, examining it.

Valerie anxiously awaited. The briefcases were built very strong, of excellent quality, and it could take a lot more to open them than Valerie had originally thought.

Paul Morris walked over to the flight attendant, asking her if the crew had a toolbox that he could use. She nodded and went to the cockpit.

The airplane began to move.

The flight attendant returned from the flight deck carrying an orange plastic tool box the size of a laptop computer, handing it to Paul Morris.

Paul Morris opened the toolbox, removing a very stout screw-driver. He inserted it into a slit and twisted. The lock gave with a loud crack. He repeated the operation on the other lock, lifting the lid. Less challenging than they'd anticipated.

He gasped.

Inside were neat stacks of American one-hundred dollar bills. Valerie had never seen so much cash together. Two, four, six...she rapidly estimated twenty stacks by God knew how many in depth.

She reached across him, removing a stack of bills. She then walked back to where the doctor was attending Charlie. "Doctor, may I have a word with you?"

The Canadair Challenger reached cruising altitude twenty minutes out of Tegel, headed northwest bound, towards London. The route of flight to Atlanta the captain had programmed into his Inertial Reference Navigation System called for overflying London, then Scotland, then on to the St. Lawrence delta and down to Atlanta via western New York.

Heinz Knocke, the captain on the Challenger, was happy with this ambulance charter that had popped up. He always enjoyed flying to the United States, and the weather was good over most of the Atlantic. Knocke, at fifty-four, had been unable as a young man to secure a much-coveted position as a flight officer with Lufthansa, which had been his life's dream, and had ended up ten years earlier as captain with Zemke Aviation. He was not happy with his job, because he never knew where he was going next, or when he was going to be at home with his wife and three girls. The job paid well, but because the cost of living in Berlin was so high, it did not pay enough to accumulate any kind of money to start his own business. Besides, he was tired of being the pilot, dispatcher, the flight planner, the refueler, the baggage coordinator and the master of ceremonies. Often, he'd considered switching to some Asian outfit flying cargo out of the Philippines just so he didn't have to deal with all the bullshit.

The truth was, flying was not all that important to him. He wanted to be home more days to be able to enjoy the company, and the body, of his wife Erika more. He'd averaged only ten days a month at home during the past year, and it was tough on their marriage.

His copilot was a young buck eager to build flight time because he still had hopes of getting on with Lufthansa, or LTU, but Knocke himself wanted a more relaxed existence. He'd had enough flying for a lifetime, and surprisingly, found himself enjoying fly fishing a lot more than flying.

He thought about his passengers wondering what important American corporation his injured passenger worked for. The man must be extremely valuable, for them to charter the Challenger to fly him back to the United States. In his opinion, Doctors in Germany were as good as anything the Americans had, so Knocke took some offense to this attitude of flying the man back home so the "natives" wouldn't hurt him.

There was a knock on the cockpit door.

Heinz Knocke had a set protocol in his airplanes, and knocking before entering the cockpit was one of the procedures he demanded of his crew. He may not have made it to the big leagues, but he ran his operation just as if he'd made it to Lufthansa.

Krista, one of the two flight attendants, entered the cockpit reporting that the American woman passenger was requesting to talk to the captain. The woman had indicated that she understood that they were already at cruising altitude, and that if it was convenient for the captain, that she would appreciate it, if he could step back at his convenience to talk with her.

"She called me *captain*?" Knocke questioned Krista.

"Yes, whenever she referred to you she called you captain."

Heinz Knocke normally did not like leaving the cockpit of his Challenger, particularly while in the busy skies over Europe, but the request puzzled him. In the first place, how did the woman know that they were at cruising altitude? How did she even know what the term meant? In second place, she had conveyed a very polite message, addressing him with his rank of captain.

That, had some merit.

"Wolf, can you handle her for a moment while I step back?" he slid his seat back.

The copilot reached for his oxygen mask, donning it with one quick motion of his right arm. Anytime one of the pilots left the cockpit above 25,000 feet, the other one would go on oxygen, because the rarefied air at that altitude could no longer sustain life, and in the case of a loss of cabin pressure, the pilot left up front alone would already be prepared.

Heinz Knocke paused to give the situation one quick check. They were approaching Brussels, the sky was crystal-clear, the automatic navigation system had the airplane, and there was nothing much for his copilot to really do except monitor everything and talk on the radio. Once they approached Lockerbie, in Scotland, it would get real busy, because that would be the initiation of the oceanic segment, but for the moment Knocke felt confident that he could step out.

He walked back to the passenger cabin, trying to adjust his eyes to the difference in light intensity. His cockpit was as bright as a parking lot in Yuma at noon in July, while the passenger cabin was comfortably dimmed. The doctor and one of the nurses were working on the patient, and the other nurse was opening some supplies. The American couple were seated in the back of the airplane, around a small conference table. Knocke followed Krista back there, allowing her to introduce him to his two passengers.

"Captain," Valerie started, "you fly international, so your English must be good, no?"

The flight attendant left the area, pulling shut a small beige curtain separating the rest of the cabin from the small area.

"Yes, thank you. I speak English. Do you speak German?"

"Afraid not, captain. Just English."

He liked the fact that she knew enough to address him with his title. So many of these Americans had no idea how to behave in a civilized manner.

"Thank you for coming back here to talk to us."

Knocke studied the couple. The woman was not as young as she'd appeared at first sight. The crow's feet around her eyes and her mouth belied the initial impression of youth. She had an intelligent, likable face, and Knocke decided that he liked her. The man with her was in his late thirties, slim and fit, with black hair and sharp eyes. Knocke had difficulty reading the personality of the man.

"You're welcome," he made it sound as if he'd said: 'velcome.'

"It is always a pleasure, talking to my passengers. I trust the patient is doing well?" he'd been told by operations that the patient was nothing more than a broken leg.

"Yes, thank you, captain. Dr. Zontag is taking very good care of him."

"Good."

"Captain, what is the range of this aircraft with the fuel we have onboard?"

Knocke was mildly surprised at her question. Most passengers would have asked him 'how long can this airplane fly?' or some other non-technical jargon. The fact that she knew what 'range' meant puzzled him further.

"This is the newest long-range model. We can fly for almost twelve hours."

"Twelve hours," Valerie repeated.

"Think that's enough?" Paul Morris asked her.

"I don't know," she felt relieved. Twelve hours might not be enough to just keep then going nonstop to their real destination, but if they put down once to refuel, they could go anywhere in the world. "I need to check this with a map, I mean, you need to confirm for me, captain, but, could this airplane fly us to a different destination from here?"

"Oh, a different destination?" Knocke was surprised. "You do not wish to fly to Atlanta?"

She stared at him. "That is correct, captain. We do not wish to fly to Atlanta."

"And where do you wish to go?" he was not amused. Knocke did not like changes when he wasn't expecting them. He hated surprises.

Valerie told him. "For the time being, let's proceed with the Atlantic crossing as planned. Once we get over North American airspace, we want you to change our destination to this airport." She pointed to a colorful map she had found in a magazine.

You can file a new flight plan enroute and just divert from there, then we land in Kansas City to refuel and go non-stop." She noticed the German pilot was not smiling anymore, so she pushed forward towards him the metal briefcase Paul Morris had in front of him on the desk. "If you take us where we want to go, and help us with some minor administrative details, we are willing to pay you one million dollars in cash for your trouble." She pulled back the lid, exposing the neatly stacked rows of hundred dollar bills.

"Do we have a deal?"

TWENTY-ONE
PRESENT TIME - BERLIN, GERMANY

Pepe Zepeda stepped off the elevator, followed by his three traveling companions. Born and raised in Panama, Zepeda carried across his face the smallpox scars prevalent among the mulatto population of Panama. At one time, he'd enjoyed thinking that he resembled Noriega, but after the leader was dragged off in chains by the Americans in humiliating defeat, Zepeda no longer liked comparing himself to his one-time idol.

Thirty-three years old and quick as a snake, he was Alfredo Hidalgo's executive arm. Whenever action had to be carried out on the field, Pepe Zepeda was the man to do it. The Americans had so graciously trained him at their School of the Americas, in the Canal Zone, where he'd become an expert sharpshooter, an expert in explosives and adequately skilled at intelligence matters. The Panamanian *Guardia Nacional* had provided him with ten years of invaluable field experience. Panama did not have a police force nor an army in the pre-Noriega days, so the *Guardia Nacional* had taken on both roles.

Zepeda had been a very good student during his years with the murderous police force of Antonio Noriega, and through a generous fate, had evolved into a highly paid specialist.

Bribing the Lebanese baggage loader at Tegel had been child's play. The dumbfuck Arab had nearly orgasmed when Zepeda paid him twenty thousand dollars to load the suitcase on the TGA plane. Whether the suitcase contained explosives of underwear, the Lebanese employee obviously couldn't have cared less. Zepeda smiled, German security was no match for his money.

The party of four walked quietly, like panthers, approaching the room they had to clean up. Zepeda had no idea why his boss wanted this man and this woman killed, nor did he care. He got paid handsomely for his services, and was grateful for the opportunity to make what he saw as an honest, decent living. His operations paid for his home and family, so he went through extraordinary trouble to make sure everything worked out just like his boss wanted it.

All four men removed silenced weapons from holsters secured inside their jackets. One of the advantages of traveling in one's private jet was that one could bring along items such as pistols with silencers across borders without having to give too many explanations.

The door to the hotel suite was open. One of the men kicked it open with caution, holding his weapon at arm's length in front.

"*Coño, ¿pero qué pasó aquí? –Cunt, but what happened here?*" The first man took in the scene inside the suite, stepping in, rapidly inspecting every room.

"What's happened here? Looks like someone's ate our lunch! That's what's happened here!" Zepeda stated. He took in the room with the dead woman crumpled behind the desk and the dead German on his back in the bedroom. These two were as dead as if Zepeda had killed them himself, so that part of the job could be considered done.

"Those must've been the sounds we heard in the elevator," one of the men remarked to Zepeda. Zepeda agreed with his man. They'd heard loud raps while waiting for the elevator, but it did not occur to them that anyone would have been firing a gun in the hotel. The Germans were too civilized to act like Zepeda' countrymen. Besides, these two assholes hadn't been killed with just two bullets. They looked like they'd been stitched up real good with a rapid fire machine gun. A muzzled, machine gun. Nice job.

"Time to leave." The men quickly retreated, leaving the room without as much as a backward glance.

Zepeda decided to get out of the hotel before the police arrived and started asking questions and frisking people. He would touch base with Captain Hidalgo and notify him.

THE CONNECTION CROSSED THE Atlantic Ocean, yet it was as clear as the pin dropped by Candice Bergen in the Sprint commercials.

"Somebody else did your job for you? Who?"

"I don't know, *Capitán* Hidalgo, we got in and out in a hurry 'cause the place was hot and getting hotter."

"But you say they used a machine gun?"

"Yes, probably an Ingram or an Uzi. I found empty shell casings in the room. 380 caliber rounds. Seems about the right caliber. And the way those two looked was evidence that they were hit with a machine gun."

"What do you mean?"

"They were torn to shreds."

Hidalgo was sorry he'd asked. "And there was nobody else in the room with them?

"No, sir. Just the two of 'em. They were apparently taken by surprise, 'cause the door lock was shot off."

They were talking through a public line, but both Alfredo Hidalgo and Zepeda had powerful scramblers attached to their respective phones, precluding undesirable monitoring of their conversations. Zepeda was sitting in the lavish cabin of the Organization's Gulfstream jet that had flown him to Berlin. The airplane was nicely equipped for this kind of communication.

Alfredo Hidalgo was puzzled, and he did not like being puzzled. He hated being puzzled, and this was definitely a puzzle. He decided to check some more. "Well, anyway, Pepe, good job on the fireworks, looks like you rid us of a nasty bitch. Let me talk this over with the bosses and I'll let you know what else needs to get done. Call me back in one hour."

He hung up. There was something definitely amiss here. Who the hell had killed Elaine Griffin and that guy with her? Other drug traffickers? That was one possibility, but just at this moment? Too much of a coincidence. Something else must be going on.

Regardless of the mystery, the situation appeared under control in Germany, with the American pilot out of the way, and Elaine and Karl dead. They could let things cool off a little before restarting there. He picked up another secure phone, dialing Esteban Escobar. Maybe Escobar would know if any of the other boys in the business may have had a grudge against Elaine.

"What!? How much!?

"Forty-two million dollars," Escobar repeated. He was not amused. Just ten minutes before Alfredo's call, Escobar had finished his personal auditing of their multiple bank accounts, which he updated once a week, and had found huge gaps in several of those accounts. The ones that Elaine Griffin had access to.

"She took out forty-two million dollars? How the hell did she do that?"

"She used faxed instructions, Hidalgo. Transferred the dough to her accounts in Berlin and then must've simply withdrawn the money."

"Why did she have access to all those accounts? No, never mind. I know why she had access to those accounts. Esteban, normally I don't call a spade a spade, but this irritates me. If you can't keep it zipped in your pants, at least you should refrain from giving the house away to your whores."

"I gave her access to those accounts, Alfredo," Escobar grudgingly admitted, not an easy thing to do in the Latin culture. "I thought I could trust her. Damn cunt."

"You're sure that's all she took?"

"That's what it looks like so far. It'll take a few more days for all the accounts to be fully updated, but it does seem that she intended to take some of our cash for going-away money. Did your men find the money in her suite?"

"Zepeda said nothing about any money. You think she'd have it in the suite?" Hidalgo did not like this. His men would have immediately noticed large sums of cash laying around. That was not something his men would have overlooked.

"No, that bitch was too clever to keep the money in her suite. She probably transferred it to some numbered account in Switzerland. I'll call our bankers there and inquire about it. If any deposits matching our losses were made, they will reimburse us, without question. I'll also check with Elaine's bank in Berlin."

The two men had access to immense sums of money, and forty-odd million did not even amount to the monthly interest payments on their fortune, yet Hidalgo was aware that Esteban Escobar was not in the habit of allowing anyone to steal from him, dead or alive.

"Well, that's good news, then!" Captain Alfredo Hidalgo managed to relax a little, in the studio of his luxurious mansion in the El Pedregal neighborhood of Mexico City.

"Zepeda is calling me back in an hour, so I'll have him investigate the whereabouts of our money and after he finds it I'll recall him and the others and this unpleasant business will be behind us then."

Escobar poured himself a stiff Vodka. He was furious at his own stupidity. These damned women could not be trusted! The fact that he had ordered her execution before learning of her stealing his money did not even cross his mind.

He drank a swig of the clear liquor, booting his computer. The computer autodialed the number of one of his main banks in Bern, Switzerland.

"*Etendart Bank*," the female voice greeted.

"Hello. Please put me through to Mr. Meyers."

"Just one moment, please." The number dialed by the computer was the direct and extremely private line of the bank officer assigned to personally manage *very* special accounts. In that corner of the world, *very* special meant in the hundreds of millions. This bank officer never asked for names, just numbers, and he would go to extreme measures to see that any request his clients made on this special line were taken care of.

"Good afternoon," the voice had a French accent.

"Mr. Meyers, good afternoon to you."

"How can we be of help, Sir?"

"Just a small check, if you don't mind. Account number is A342RE2880857." The accounts were a combination of letters, numbers and symbols to make unauthorized computer entry even more difficult.

Mr. Meyers keyed in the account.

This was a big account. A real *big* account. "Certainly. And what can we do for you today, *Sir*?" His tone of voice had become two octas more servile.

Escobar explained the situation, asking the officer to check the other account holders in the bank to investigate whether two or more large deposits had been made matching the withdrawals Escobar had already discovered. Although the bank under no circumstances would divulge information about other accounts to anyone, including Escobar, they would follow through if several very large deposits had been made into any of their other accounts matching the amounts Escobar had, for this would be evidence of tampering.

It took the bank officer nearly a minute to computer surf through most of the bank accounts in the entire country, even those not belonging to his bank. The banks had reciprocity for this type of operation. He double-checked the readout on the color computer screen in front of him before informing his customer.

"Sorry, Sir. We do not have any matching transactions for those amounts you read to me. Our system is tied into most of the other local banks here, therefore I can assure you that no such transfers have taken place into our country so far this year."

"You're positive?"

"Yes, sir. My computer does not provide me with account balances, you understand, but it does flag any matching transactions, and nothing appears on the amounts you are referring to."

Escobar thanked the man, hanging up. He poured himself another shot of vodka. Now what? He autodialed the bank in Berlin where he used to transfer funds to Elaine.

The German assistant manager was most inquisitive about his identity, asking him multiple questions about his PIN, password, account number, etc. Finally, he convinced the teller that he was legit and she pulled up the account transaction record.

Four million dollars had been wired from a bank in Singapore day before yesterday, and Mrs. Griffin had withdrawn the entire amount in cash that very afternoon, in American dollars and German Marks. That had created a minor crisis for the bank manager, since the bank did not keep that much cash available and it had to be collected from several branches.

Escobar thanked her. Now he knew Elaine had not transferred the money anywhere else. She'd cashed it out in Berlin. How big a bulk did forty-two million dollars make? Pretty big.

He dialed Alfredo Hidalgo. These scramblers they used were magnificent. Amazingly enough, they had found them on retail at a "Spy Headquarters" shop in downtown Phoenix. Escobar had been there on a business trip, and had been extremely surprised at the hardware that was available for sale to the general public over the counter. They had night vision goggles, debugging equipment, telephone scramblers, bugging equipment. He'd been like a child in a toy store, and bought heaps of equipment through one of his legitimate companies. Aah, how true it was that America was the Land of the Free. He was free to do business with all the equipment he needed.

"Alfredo? I just got through talking with the banks. Elaine cashed out, so the money's still somewhere in Berlin."

"You mean in currency?"

"Precisely. She stashed it somewhere in that city in preparation for her escape, and your guys must find it."

Escobar, we don't know who flatlined Elaine and Karl. Did it occur to you that those same gentlemen might have helped themselves to the cash?"

"I don't care if the Charles Chaplin himself came out of the grave and did it. I want our money back and I want to find out who is behind this, because I'm going to hurt them! Pain, Alfredo, that's what I desire for those gentlemen who helped themselves to our money. Lots of pain."

"I'll see what I can do."

"Keep me informed, Alfredo." His tone changed to one of cordiality. "When do you have another flight into this area?"

"Not this month, Esteban. I have one at the end of next month."

"Good! You'll come here and we'll have some *spaghetti alle bongole* the way Soledad knows how to prepare it."

"You have a deal."

Esteban Escobar realized Alfredo Hidalgo would not stay mad at him for long. The two men had too much in common not to like each other. Hidalgo was more controlled than Escobar, perhaps due to his training as an airline captain, but other than that, they both enjoyed good drink, good food and beautiful women.

THE PHONE RANG IN Alfredo Hidalgo's private study. It was Zepeda in Berlin.

"Zepeda, I need you to stay there and find out who did in the two people you were sent to fix. The boss is not happy, there are large sums of money missing from his accounts, and it seems that the woman stashed the money somewhere in Berlin. Two things: find out who eliminated our people and find the money. You can call our contact in Berlin with the local police to see if they have any leads."

Hidalgo knew that the private jet owned by their aluminum industries had been used to fly the men to Germany, and that the Gulfstream was parked in Berlin, equipped with everything the men would need while on the field, from hundreds of thousands of dollars in different currencies, to credit cards, to camera equipment, to guns and ammunition. The airplane had been specially retrofitted at the Van Nuys airport in California to have numerous hiding places and secret cargo holds to safe keep the equipment.

Esteban Escobar opened the glass door of the wooden Spanish armoire where he kept his liquor. It was time for a drink. He poured himself a High Ball with some Johnny Walker Black, activating the TV remote control.

He inhaled the deep leathery fragrance of his private studio, feeling content. He had given orders for what needed to get done, and was confident Alfredo Hidalgo would deliver.

Escobar switched channels to CNN News. Far as he was concerned, only CNN and perhaps the movie channels were worth his time, everything else was garbage. Although sometimes he did find some good documentaries on the Discovery Channel.

The anchor woman was reading the teleprompter, telling audiences about some bomb blowing up another bus in Israel. Esteban felt sorry for the Israeli. Those poor devils not only were delegated to a desert land nobody wanted, but had to spend their entire lives fighting off a tide of mad ignorant dogs surrounding them from all sides, with no other intent in life than to annihilate the Jews just because they were Jews. Escobar could not understand why the Israeli continued putting up with the onslaught without taking some drastic action. Escobar saw two very clear solutions to the problem, push the Arabs into the Persian Gulf and watch them swim, or move the state of Israel to some other, more civilized location, like the Caribbean, or some other nice place.

Let the armies of the civilized countries guard the Holy Land and allow equal access to anyone willing to visit, as long as they behaved like civilized humans. Yeah, that would be a workable solution. Jewish people had enough clout and money to purchase an entire island the size of Puerto Rico. They could buy a place like that in the Caribbean and move there to live like civilized human beings, and let the U.N. police the Holy Land so everyone can go visit without trouble.

Those who envied and attacked the Jewish culture were ignorant scum. Escobar had read enough about the Israeli to realize how much importance they put on education, and he admired this. It was no secret why they were good at everything they did, they prepared well for it. They weren't efficient and productive and smart because God had chosen them, hell, they were that way through a lot of hard work educating themselves as much as was humanly possible. Try explaining that to the ignorant masses.

A clip came on about the crash of a TGA trijet in Germany, and how the authorities feared that the unfortunate tragedy had been caused by a bomb. The transcript of the last words spoken by the captain came on the speakers, with captions spelling out on screen for those not familiar with aviation radio talk.

Escobar sat up. The captain was a man! That could not be. He waited for thirty minutes until the news repeated, wondering if the female pilot had had a male copilot and that's who had spoken on the radio.

Thirty minutes later, when the clip was repeated, they showed images of a field with what appeared as garbage strewn across the countryside. The crash site. The anchorwoman kept referring to Captain Adam Dee, as having been in command of the flight.

Escobar rushed to his desk, picking up the phone.

THE FOURTH STRIPE

Maurice Azurdia

TWENTY-TWO
TWO MONTHS LATER - NEW YORK CITY
UNITED STATES

"What do you have for me?" Agent Olaffson demanded.

"Looks like the dame's vanished into thin air, sir."

"Don't tell me that shit, Tom, just give me the facts. Interpol wasn't able to follow their trail after they left that air ambulance jet they chartered?"

"Nossir, they interrogated everyone involved, including the captain, and their stories all appear to jive. The TGA woman chartered the jet to fly from Berlin to Atlanta, under the excuse that they were transporting a medical emergency. She put it on her American Express card."

"She put it on her American Express. Right. She put a goddamn jet on her American Express card?" He thought of his own VISA card, which he had maxed out at its modest $1,500 limit.

"Yes, that's what she did, anyway, they did have one man onboard who appeared to be bleeding profusely, but none of the attendants at the airport who helped board him can confirm that he had a broken leg or other injury. The doctor involved in the air evac, ahh, a Dr. Zontag, testified to the German police that the man had a broken femoral bone and that it looked as if it'd been incurred during a fall. According to the German authorities, this doctor is a man of proven reputation and integrity in his country."

"Yeah, I bet he is. The bleeding man must be this Charlie Smith guy we talked to here at the airport."

"It seems that way, sir. He fits the description, and neither his wife, children nor the airline have heard from him in the two months since."

"What else?"

"The stories of everyone involved seem to be aligned. They all agree on the sequence of events. The chartered jet crew dropped off the TGA woman, this Charlie Smith character and the other unidentified male Caucasian in Rio de Janeiro, spent two days there for R&R and then flew back to Berlin. Nobody on the chartered jet had ever seen any of the passengers before the flight. Brazilian authorities confirm that the airplane landed in Rio, but they are absolutely adamant that nobody except the crew and medical team were onboard."

"But the crew on the chartered jet swears that their passengers got off in Rio."

"Correct."

"What about the landing in Kansas City?"

"Customs and immigration both confirmed it, nobody got off the airplane in Kansas City. It was purely a technical stopover to get fuel."

"I believe them."

"The flight was flight-planned as a medevac flight, so air traffic control gave them priority handling all the way across the U.S."

"Doesn't that make you sick. What about the boyfriend of the TGA captain Valerie Wall?"

"Like I previously reported to you, he gave notice and quit his job. His coworkers seemed surprised at such a sudden move on his part, but they added that the man, a Paul Morris had been talking about sailing around the world alone someday. He was a computer nerd, a loner, so it's not so farfetched. No relatives that we have been able to trace thus far, no police record whatsoever. Not even a parking ticket. A real straight arrow. One of his work buddies told one of our agents that he and this Paul

Morris used to go sailing to Catalina island together quite often."

"Where the hell's Catalina island?"

"Just off the coast of Long Beach, in California."

"Did you check the maritime register for any title changes on sailboats to see if this guy bought a boat to sail around the world?"

"Yes, there were none under his name. But that doesn't mean he couldn't have bought a sailboat in another country, or under someone else's name."

"So, then it looks like he was the third clown on the airplane, eh?"

"It's possible."

"But the Brazilians swear that nobody got off that airplane other than the crew, right?"

"And the medical team."

"Right. And their fucking Brazilian mother believes them. Those bastards are so corrupt we'll never know what really happened there."

"The two bankers murdered in the hotel in Berlin were killed with an Ingram MAC 12 which ballistics confirmed was reported stolen in Phoenix the day before it happened. You've seen the coroner's report. Each victim got over ten 380-caliber slugs. The FBI questioned the former owner of the weapon, a medical student at the University of Arizona, and the man is clean. He was nowhere near Berlin during that time period. He was in Tucson, in a night class, at the time of the murders. A dozen students confirmed this. As was to be expected, his alibi is solid as a rock. He probably sold the gun and reported it stolen, but we have no way of proving it."

"How the hell do you get an Ingram from Phoenix to Berlin overnight?"

"FEDEX? Private jet maybe? e-mail?"

"Or with an airline pilot. Go on."

"The female banker killed in Berlin, Elaine Griffin, was an American, so we were able to run a background check on her. According to the FBI and Interpol, no criminal record. Although she passed as a banker, she never attended any university in this country nor in Europe, and never worked for any bank in this or any other country. We suspect she was an operator for the Organization, but haven't been able to find any concrete evidence."

"What about the male banker?"

"German national. German police confirmed that the man had indeed worked as a teller for a bank in Stuttgart years ago, but was fired under shady circumstances involving some missing funds."

"What about the dozens of briefcases loaded on the chartered jet? Anything on them?"

"Nothing. The ramp attendants who loaded the briefcases swear they loaded them but did not open any of them. The crew never saw any of their contents, either, and they were taken off the airplane in Rio, along with the TGA woman and the two men."

"So, this TGA captain had something in those suitcases that somehow is related to the death of these two bankers. I do not see the connection, although I am certain there is one somewhere. The most likely scenario is that those briefcases were probably full of hard cash. Of course, I fail to see how a female airline captain could pull off something like this. That broad did not sound so smart to me. Who knows. The other weapons found in the hotel suite in Berlin had been fired, but one of the bullets was never found. Wonder if that particular bullet traveled to Brazil inside a fractured femur?"

"Sir?"

Gus Olaffson looked up at one of the department's secretaries. "Yeah? What is it?"

"Sir, this package just came for you via certified mail. You have to sign for it."

Olaffson took the offered manila envelope, scribbling his initials on the form attached to it. He wanted to get on with the briefing he was receiving, but his eye caught the stamps on the envelope.

They did not look familiar. He examined them a little closer. Brazilian.

"What the fuck?" he cut open the envelope with a pair of scissors, and ten magnetic 3.5-inch diskettes dropped on his desktop. A white piece of paper flew down to join the diskettes.

Agent Olaffson:

Unlike you, I deliver what I promise. In the enclosed disks you will find some information which you will find highly interesting.

I lucked out and came across names and numbers, events and e-mail addresses and a very detailed diary that was kept by a certain woman banker who I am sure you are acquainted with.

How could you guys and the FBI have allowed the largest drug organization since Bayer invented aspirin, to be headquartered in St. Louis, MO? I know you guys don't get paid much, but didn't your mothers teach you that you have to put in a day's work for a day's pay?

I guess I'll read in the papers about how efficiently you all are at nabbing the heads of the Organization and all of their operatives, now that I have given you all the answers to the final exam. Sure hope you demonstrate a little more skill than you have until now.

Be careful with the disks and do not damage them, for I will not be contacting you again.

Have a nice life.

Over and out.

V. W.

P.S. - I hope someday you make it to that fast-food restaurant manager position you wanted so much for me. These disks might just land you the raise that you still need to get there.

TWENTY-THREE
ALONG THE COAST OF THE SEA OF CORTES, IN MEXICO

"Do you think we should buy some of those shrimp boats?" Valerie asked.

"It may not be a bad idea, honey. I was talking with one of the waiters in the restaurant, and he told me that those Mexican shrimp boats can gross about a hundred thousand dollars per month during the shrimping season."

Valerie lowered her sunglasses from her forehead down to her nose. The sun in Puerto Peñasco was terrific. "Should we look into it then?"

Paul Morris sipped some coconut milk mixed with gin through a straw, then smiled at his new wife. "I think we should. If nothing else, Valerie, I heard those poor sailors working the shrimp boats don't get paid much. Ramón, the waiter I talked to in the restaurant explained to me that he works on the boats eight months out of the year and then he waits tables here in the restaurant the other four months. He has no insurance of any kind, and he doesn't even make enough money to buy his own place. Get this, he is married to a shrimp boat captain's daughter, and they live with his in-laws."

"That's sad. How much do the captains make?"

"They're the only ones who make a decent living. The waiter told me his father-in-law brings in about fourteen hundred dollars per month during the season."

"That's not bad at all, for a poor Mexican fishing village anyway."

"It is when you consider that he is probably subsidizing all of his kids and their spouses."

Valerie looked out at the Sea of Cortes, admiring the deep blue color of the sea where whales from all over the world came to reproduce. Charlie Smith was barely visible in the distance, skiing behind a powerful outboard. "You never get into something unless you intend to help someone, Paul Morris, what do you have in mind?"

Paul Morris laughed. Valerie knew him well. "I'd like to buy a couple of those boats and pay the men decent wages, give them medical insurance, finance a house for them, stuff like that. They can't get a loan for a house in this town."

"Paul Morris, you have a heart of gold." She kissed him and laid down on her stomach on a colorful beach towel, loosening the top part of her bikini. The sun was delicious and she was going to work on her tan.

She felt they deserved to relax, after crossing six countries with different passports and different guides, her nerves needed a break. Those Brazilian people had been most helpful. They were really a wonderful bunch, and she loved their *Bosanova*. They were not bad at producing new identities for needy travelers either.

Rocky Point, Mexico was an ideal place to circle the wagons while they all decided on their ultimate destination as a group. Charlie had recovered nicely from the bullet wound, and his wife and children would be joining them soon, and then their lives would improve even more. Not that she had any complaints at the moment. Paul Morris and her had been married by a Catholic priest in a small church in the town of Cuernavaca, Mexico. The priest there had been extremely understanding and had married them in spite of the fact that she was, God forgive her, a Lutheran, and Paul Morris a Catholic. The poor man had taken a vow of poverty, and Valerie had been heartbroken to see the level of poverty he lived in. She'd given the priest twenty thousand dollars to do with as he saw fit. Not a bribe, just a 'thank you' for marrying them without forcing them to take the required Catholic classes.

Their money was now safely deposited in several numbered bank accounts in Panama and Nassau, and they had unlimited access to it via Gold Mastercards. Each account was untraceable by anybody snooping, and they could get cash anywhere in the world, since all banks honored VISA and Mastercard. They had all the buying power they needed, yet could travel light.

She thought of the airline life she'd left behind, which she had loved so much, but then again, who knew, perhaps she could buy herself an airplane wherever they ended up, or maybe even start a small airline?

The soft warmth of the tropical sun finally seduced her and she fell asleep.

THE END

If you liked this novel, it would be greatly appreciated if you would write a book review for it on Amazon.

Just search for the title of the book.

Thank you. Grazie. Gracias.

The author gratefully acknowledges the copyrighted or trademarked status and trademark owners of the following, mentioned in this work of fiction:

America West, American Airlines, American Express, Bank of America, Bayer Aspirin, Bic Pens, British Airways, Business Week, Captain Kirk, Chivas Regal, Citicorp, CNN, Columbo, Compaq, Cross Pens, Delta, Deneuve, Dillard's, Diners Club, Econolodge, Federal Express, Ferrari, Flying Magazine, Frito, Greyhound, Gulfstream, Haagen-Dazs, Haci Baba, Heineken, Hilton, Holiday Inn, Inspector Clouseau, Kleenex, Levi's, Life Magazine, Lincoln Continental, Michener's Caribbean, Mickey Mouse.

Manuscript line edited, copy edited and prepared for publication by Cyber Rose Design, LLC

Cover design by Cyber Rose Design, LLC

About the Author

Maurice Azurdia is a pilot instructor for a major airline and has seen his writings published in FLYING Magazine and his cartoons published in the magazine of ALPA, the Air Line Pilots Association. He is a cartoonist, artist and novelist.

Maurice flew as an international airline pilot for one of America's legendary airlines, is an aerospace engineer and has operated a fleet of shrimp boats in the Sea of Cortés, in Mexico.

He currently resides in The Great American Southwest with his wife Cheryl, where he is writing his next novel.

Other novels on Amazon by Maurice Azurdia

e – A novel

The Ebola epidemic in west Africa continues to explode, as the world watches. America is not invulnerable to the virus. As the first suspected cases of hemorrhagic fever begin to appear outside of Africa, strange events surround them. Dr. Ariel Chevalier, an emergency medicine resident at a prestigious medical center in Phoenix, Arizona, finds herself in the middle of the newly developing crisis. But Africa is not the problem. The problem is something else. Something unreal. And the creepiest part is its inherent plausibility.

Available as an eBook at Amazon and other bookstores.

Lightning Source UK Ltd.
Milton Keynes UK
UKHW022326070620
364612UK00021B/451